INQUISITION

F.D. GROSS

BOOK TWO OF THE WOLFGANG TRILOGY

Inquisition
F. D. Gross

Edited by Deborah DeNicola
Internal artwork by F. D. Gross and Diana Tucker
Maps by F. D. Gross
ISBN: 978-1-5356-1507-5

For the vampire, and those who hunt them…

Walters

The Great Carpella Road

Westings

The Devils Drain

Stella marie
Ruins

The Cordova Mountains

N
W   E
S

Decameron Forest

The Great Carpella Road

Blood Mountain Pass

Cornwalls Bluff

Delore

Widow

Egleaseon Ruins

THREE DAYS AGO...

PROLOGUE

DIANA

COLD. LATE SEPTEMBER.

It is morning as I watch the carriage turn down the stone gravel path. Black as pitch, it rattles its way along the wear of the road like some menacing beast, carrying the one thing I adore most in life. My husband. Tenor Alvadine Wolfgang, the vampire hunter.

The driveway leads across the grounds to the road's edge, which is mostly covered in turning foliage of yellows and oranges, a stark contrast to the dismal gray rocks and sky surrounding Wolfgang Manor. The carriage turns again, crushing fragile leaves as it spins its way along the road lined with conifers, darting behind the trees like a terrible shadow stalking its prey. It continues moving away from me, farther and farther, until it vanishes into the morning fog.

As I stand alone on the balcony, the wind blows against my skin from the north, sharp and crisp. It reaches the many parts of my body, finding its way into my fragile bones while seeping into the core of my soul. The winter solstice isn't far off. I can see its incipient arrival in the leaves falling from the trees. It hides in the roots at the base of the trees. Twirling wisps of debris loop in great arcs like fairies dancing along the air. It passes amongst the workers in the field as far as the eye can see. Their caps and brown uniforms bob up and down as the men turn fresh soil for the new harvest.

So beautiful is this land, this place I call home. The sights. The smells, serene and perfect. Yet despite my everyday happiness, sadness lingers over me today. Not sadness for the sake of my husband's departure, for I know his faithful servant and friend Kronklich goes with him—they will be safe, I am assured—but for another reason. Something unseen, yet I feel something, an intuition, a slight sense of anxiety. I feel it with my heart and all of my body. It lives inside me.

Passing my hand over my stomach caressingly, I rub the same spot I've rubbed for days.

A tear drips from my eye.

I was going to tell Tenor, but I couldn't. I saw his stress in his eyes before he left. They told me everything. A troubled look of foreboding or worry about something. A distant look.

A knock on the door startles me and I step off the balcony, returning to the bedroom to open the door.

"You called for me, Lady Diana?" A man dressed in a crushed velvet coat stands in the doorway. His long stringy hair hangs past his shoulders in frayed locks, black like snakes.

"Yes, Joachim," I say, wiping my face. "Dorian and I will dine in the courtyard this evening. Please make the necessary preparations."

"Yes, of course, my lady. Very good. However, isn't it a bit early for such a request?" He gives a deep, labored bow, despite the somber look on his face.

"Yes, it is, but with the list of details I must tend to today, I fear I will forget."

Joachim nods his head.

"And please make sure Dorian is wearing his coat. I don't want him catching a cold while practicing in the courtyard."

Again, Joachim bows, yet this time, he says nothing. It's as if speaking is a burden for him. He watches me like a lovesick pup and pauses a moment before leaving. His gaze is distant as if seeing a great storm on the horizon.

"Joachim. Is everything all right?" I notice the hollows under his eyes are sunken and gray.

"Yes, my lady."

I look on him with question and pity. Such a troubled past he had. Such a horrible nightmare his childhood brought him.

"Very well, then. You may go."

Joachim motions to leave but stops suddenly. "My lady—"

"Yes?"

"My lady, if I may be so bold. You still haven't told him, have you?"

It takes a moment for the question to sink in despite the thoughts I'd had just moments ago. Then the emotion washes over me like a hot fiery river. I try my best to keep myself under control, but my eyes fill with watery streams. Joachim is the only one I've ever told.

I shake my head.

"My lady, you must tell him. It isn't right. It isn't fair to him—"

All I can do is gaze at him with silent agreement.

Joachim's look of concern lingers for a moment before he retreats from the room in silence and again I am left alone in the cold to my thoughts.

Yes, I will tell him. The moment he returns.

I say it over and over to myself in the vanity mirror. My long black hair drapes the front of my shoulders like an obsidian river. I run my brush through it every time I say it, trying not to think about how long it will be before Tenor's return. The days are so much longer when he is gone. Sometimes I curse time for its unfairness, how it stretches its long hours like the vines of a rose creeping its hungry roots along the soil, searching for water, for nourishment.

I cannot blame Tenor for what he does. His family has slain vampires for centuries. It is his calling, his duty to protect, to serve. And it is my responsibility to support him in all that he does, mentally and physically. To raise a strong son—my hand passes over my belly again—possibly another.

I shiver at the thought of bringing another child into this world. A world that consumes purity and innocence with fierce hunger. Yes, we have purpose, we have roles, and the cycle of life and death never ends. But when does the strife end? When do we get to feel complete?

One sure idea fills my mind. I will protect what is mine.

A chill passes through the bedroom chamber, and I know the fire is running low. Rubbing my shoulders, I reach for the crystal pitcher next to the bedside and pour a glass of water, quenching my dry throat. My eyes fall on the leather bracelet resting on the counter. Imagining it on my wrist reminds me of Tenor, that he will come back to me no matter the cost, no matter the circumstance. These thoughts give me strength when other things cannot. Tenor has the bracelet's matching twin, and I'll never forget that day when we were nestled in the warmth of my bed and he clasped it over my skin. It was so long ago it seems. It's amazing how a simple trinket, an artifact such as this, can bring such comfort.

Snapping the buckles together, I hold the bracelet before the mirror, admiring its discoloration and imperfections, so much like my Tenor, so much like me.

It's perfect in every way.

The day warms and my enemy, time, passes on, stealing the brisk chill from the stone walls of the manor. I counter time by making my rounds, speaking with each of the lead servants of the house, ensuring they are happy and have all the necessary supplies to do their job. I like to think they are treated well, giving them holiday when the town closes its shops. With the winter solstice nearly here, I can't help but anticipate their smiling faces when the good news is delivered to them. Tonight, when Tenor returns, we will tell them together. Tell them they will have a week with their families, to rest and be merry and not be compelled to return to the manor throughout the duration.

I smile to myself, smug with anticipation of their happy faces. I smile to others as I walk through the long hall of the servants' quarters. They grin in exchange. Pleasing people is a part of me. As I turn away from the interior manor full of glowing candles and sconces, I head toward the long hall of open windows. Here, the courtyard breeze blows perfectly through the manor, even on the hottest days of summer. Dragging my fingers along the stone walls, I stop at the banister railing, allowing the overcast afternoon light to caress my skin. Glancing to my right, I search out Tenor's office, the window where he watches Dorian and me while he works. I remember him staring at me this morning and my heart flutters.

Looking down into the courtyard, I can see Dorian is there practicing like he always does, three times a day, every day of the week, without his coat. Sometimes when the sun dips below the horizon, I catch him practicing still, slaying imaginary beasts and demons just like his father taught him. With Tenor gone, Joachim now assists him, standing ever so close with tray in hand. A set of throwing knives lay across the silver tray like hors d'oeuvres served at a dinner party. Although the idea of Dorian's constant training at such a young age to fight will never truly sit well with me, I know it is necessary and could mean the difference between life and death. It is part of his heritage, and this I knew from the beginning.

The day is waning faster than I expected, and already I feel the hunger in my belly. It comes quicker these days, for life needs nourishment. After checking on the last of the servants, I make my way down to meet with Dorian, to remind him of his coat, and to remind Joachim that he disobeyed me once again.

A gust of wind showers the courtyard in a multitude of autumn colors, much like this morning and the days before. Leaves rush in torrents over the tiled roofs and the air is filled with the sound of crackling foliage. Above me, the sky is speckled with flittering leaves as I watch Dorian throw the last of his daggers into the yellow gourd at the end of the row. All the others have split in half. Entrails drip along the wall, forming small pools of sticky liquid.

"Excellent shot, sir," says Joachim in the flattest and most melancholy tone.

A slight chuckle comes from Dorian as he pulls his sword from the sheath at his side. "That's five dauntess you owe me now. At this rate, I'll have the whole of your weeks wages before you know it."

"Yes, very good, young lord." Joachim's curled lip accompanies his laugh.

Seeing they are completely oblivious of me, I clear my throat. "Eh hem—"

The two of them turn around, startled by my appearance. Joachim, after systematically brushing himself off, lowers the tray to his side, not saying a word while averting his eyes. Dorian, on the other hand, gives me the biggest smile a mother could love. He jabs his sword into the tree trunk beside him.

"Mother!" he says with surprise. "Have you been watching this whole time?"

As I raise my brow, he follows my gaze to the coat draped across the back of the chair. His demeanor instantly changes from excitement to denial.

"I told him to wear it," chimes Joachim. He looks away. "Oh, look at the time. How the day escapes us all. I'll go fetch supper."

Dorian pulls a chair out for me as Joachim exits from the courtyard.

With my stern gaze still on him, Dorian furrows his brow as he pushes in my chair. "I was wearing it, Mother, honestly. It's just—you know how hot it gets when I practice." His smile is bewitching, the same as his father's. With his golden hair falling across his dark eyes, I can't help but admire his beauty. He received the best of both worlds from his parents. Stark yellow locks. Obsidian black eyes. Every time I look at him, I'm reminded of Tenor's absence.

In a short time, Joachim returns with bergamot tea, Kronklich's favorite, and a roasted ham coupled with sliced biscuits. The day wanes quickly as we converse over food, and soon fireflies begin glowing around our heads. As I spend time with my son, for once, time seems to leave us alone, forgotten almost. Not once does Joachim come to bother us. Not once does a servant distract us with noise. Just Dorian and I supping together—until there is smoke in the air. Not that of cooking fires but of burning flesh.

Looking up, I see the fluttering leaves from before, replaced with burning embers. A look of terror steals the smile from my boy's face. Dorian shouts at me, competing with the growing screams suddenly rising from the manor. I cannot hear what he is saying. A servant crashes through a window of the second-story floor, screaming the way down to her death. I see Joachim running across the courtyard toward us.

"Joachim!" I shout. "Take Dorian! Get somewhere safe!"

Joachim immediately obeys, engulfing Dorian in his arms. But Dorian resists.

"Mother, I'm not leaving your side!" argues Dorian. "Father is gone, so I must protect you. Joachim, go with the others and barricade the doors."

Seemingly startled by screams and burning flames, Joachim stands bewildered, temporarily dazed in the haze of smoke—looking at me, then at Dorian—until Dorian screams in his face. "Go!"

Joachim takes off, gathering two of the stronger-looking male servants and convincing them to follow. Dorian moves to the tree trunk with the sword and pulls it free from the base. "Stay behind me, Mother. I'll protect you!"

There is a loud scream and a crash followed by growls and moans.

Dark sinewy creatures pour into the courtyard like ants, clawing their way forward on talon like nails. There are so many of them. What is happening? I clutch the dark fabric of Dorian's vest and bury my face in his back. The creatures surround us in a matter of seconds. Where a pair of eyes should be, only one exists. They look around spastically, searching, seeking. Sharp teeth glisten from the spreading fire as they gurgle back and forth to each other, breathing heavily, and drooling saliva from the gaps of their missing teeth.

One of them lurches forward, enough to cause Dorian to react. The menacing creature howls in response as Dorian drives his blade through the creature's face, causing it to convulse as its eye dislodges from the socket. Blood covers the ground as the monster retreats, whimpering.

Covered in gore, Dorian wipes blood away from his eyes as he readies his sword for the next assault.

But it never comes.

Voices in the distance, sounding almost playful, echo from the shadows of the awnings and burning fire. Six figures emerge in total. They are dressed in red robes and golden masks and flood into the courtyard. Long stag horns protrude from the top of the masks in waving curves. Wearing white gloves smeared with blood, one of them playfully hits one of the others, instigating a reaction. "Stop, Caesar! You're acting like a fool."

"Just having a bit of fun, Constable," says the other.

The lead figure at the head of the group carries a royal golden rod, a king's scepter, bejeweled with silver-studded tips, now covered in blood.

"Greetings, happy family!" says a muffled cheerful voice behind the golden mask with the golden scepter. The tone is male without question, yet the delivery is higher, like a tenor singer. Almost musical in nature. Long locks of golden hair fall freely from the sides of the mask adorned with the image of a tragic smile. The notion of pain comes to mind right away as I peek over Dorian's shoulder.

"Such a lovely home you have here," says the man playfully.

"Be gone, foul demon!" I shout, stepping out from behind Dorian.

"*Be gone, foul demon*," mocks the masked man back. He laughs out loud and the others laugh with him. "Demons. If only we were, then life would be much grander." The masked man bows. "However, I believe you are in no position to negotiate."

"No, Mother, what are you doing?" whispers Dorian under his breath.

The masked man raises his arm, motioning with the golden scepter. Off to the side, Joachim is thrust forward with his arms bent behind his back. He is badly bruised and bloodied. Cuts and scrapes cover his exposed skin. After taking another step forward, his knees buckle and he falls to the ground. More laughter follows, but this time I notice a different voice, an obnoxious female cackle that carries on and on before the one figure next to her tells her to shut up.

Before I can say another word, before I realize what is happening, the masked figure standing over Joachim bends down, pulling away the hair from his face, and moves its mask just enough to close in on Joachim's neck. It latches on to him like a wild animal feasting on blood and Joachim begins to shake. I cry out in empathy as the color drains from Joachim's skin; a look of horror comes over his face.

Biting into its own wrist, the figure cradles Joachim's face with its other hand, smearing blood over Joachim's pale white complexion, and forces him to drink from the gushing wound. Blood spurts over Joachim's face like a fountain, covering his lips and mouth, choking him. He gasps for air.

The grotesque sinewy creatures surrounding us seem to react to this behavior like the carnal beasts that they are, anticipating something more, a bonus for what's to come. Joachim buckles forward, landing on the floor face down, and begins gagging and vomiting. His body shakes violently.

"What did you do to him!" screams Dorian, standing helplessly by.

"Well now, the prodigy son speaks!" says the leader with golden hair, spinning the scepter around in his hand like a baton. "And here I thought you were a mute." The masked man cracks his knuckles and points the scepter at Dorian. "You are the reason we came, boy. Now, don't you feel special?"

I sense a smile underneath the man's mask as he cocks his head to the side.

Dorian responds immediately, lashing out with his sword and slicing the air before him. I see anger in his eyes as he stabs with the Wolfgang's ancient weapon, the house heirloom sword with the braided handle of red, white, and black. Passed down through the generations, the weapon has killed countless vampires and monsters alike, but his attack is deflected as the man with the golden hair, remaining calm and collective, parries each blow with precision. Over and over, Dorian tries to breakthrough his foe's defense. The man, pompous and arrogant, laughs behind the mask. "There's all that fight boiling up inside. That's what we want to see. Blood of the son."

And then, as if on purpose, the masked man drops his guard, allowing Dorian to surpass him, and the sword pierces his body. The masked man laughs, as the sword does nothing, sliding through his body, red robes and all. As Dorian's expression registers surprise, the masked man raises his scepter and brings it down on Dorian with swift response. Dorian crumples to the floor instantly. His head wavers back and forth as he tries to recover by up-righting himself.

Paralyzed with fear, I cannot move. Who are these men? Why did they come? The one man said "blood of the son." What did that mean?

As if reading my mind, the masked man now staring at me says, "It means we have come to the right place." His eyes seem to glow red from behind the mask.

Suddenly a crushing force engulfs my throat and I cannot breathe. I am lifted from the ground effortlessly by his one hand.

"Watch—boy," says the masked man to Dorian. All I can see is the tragic smile on the mask. "Remember this day as the day your mother lost her humanity."

Dorian makes a sound, but nothing coherent. I hear him scream, but the sound around me becomes muffled, as if submerged underwater.

The masked man pushes his mask aside, exposing his perfect face and gleaming pale skin underneath. Long yellow fangs protrude from ruby lips as I feel cold breath on my neck.

Then there is pain. Cold, sharp, pain. It moves from my neck and down into my body, numbing me limb to limb. It is like poison surging through my body, snuffing out every corner and shadow. It kills all traces of life. Unstoppable. Vulnerable, I can do nothing but submit.

I hear Dorian's voice calling for his mother, but I can say or do nothing, as I am rendered powerless. The masked man forces me to drink from his wrist and I am flooded with the metallic taste of blood. I choke, gasping for air, and my mind becomes blank. For one terrible second, I open my eyes to see my assailant staring back at me, enjoying every last second of my torment.

I was going to tell him.

Tell him how much I loved him. Tell him how much I missed him. Tell him about our child nestled in my belly.

But that is all forfeited now.

My energy is beginning to rise, peeling away from my body like the skin of a fruit. Higher and higher I rise, looking down on my being that once was full of life.

Tenor is there. Cradling me in his arms. He laments to God, shouting into the heavens. Screaming about something, but I can't understand him. Why can't I understand him? What is happening to me?

Smaller and smaller the image of Tenor becomes. He is holding me, but he is surrounded by blood. My blood. There is a stake in my heart.

The distance grows further between us but my determination grows in strength. It is getting very cold now, but the emptiness inside me is replaced with new energy. I know now what must be done. I know my place and the echoes of my actions. I must protect what is mine.

Curse you, Tenor. I will always love you.

DAY FOUR

WOLFGANG

CHAPTER
I

I DID EVERYTHING IN MY power to save my son.

But I failed.

There are pains in my stomach thinking about it.

The Carnalreesee. Devious servants to the late Egleaseon, lord of the vampires. They have him now, down there in that valley.

Standing at the edge of a cliff in the Cordova Mountains, I shiver from the thick snow around me, watching the glow of campfires in the Decameron Forest below. Tendrils of smoke curl between fir trees. It is a wandering caravan, and I stare at it with loathing, knowing Dorian is down there, prisoner to those dark lords, waiting out the day in those wagons.

When night comes, they will move.

Raising my arm out over the cliff, I hold before me the small relic that started it all, the cause of my woe.

The Hand of God.

How can such a small thing cause so much trouble? The size of my fist, it is made from two bars of metal, twined together with thorn wire. The artifact was used to destroy Egleaseon years ago, but in a way most would never know. Egleaseon wanted it for his own so he could be human again. Willingly, he took it from me, and I watched him change back to his human form. In an instant, he aged all the years of his immortal existence, and then was rendered to dust.

Staring at the cursed thing with hate, I bring my arm back to throw it off the edge, but something stops me. I begin to tremble. My hand goes to the staunched wound in my side where Bronin stabbed me. Drops of blood stain the snow at my feet. The cloth is caked, frozen to my skin, and every movement sends prickling pain down my side.

The biting cold. It does wonders for my scarred face and blistered hand, but I cannot say the same for my body.

With only leather plate proofing covering my chest, arms, and legs, I would give anything for a cloak to block the wind. Lowering my arm, I stare at the Hand of God, feeling weak and disgusted with myself.

"Good choice," says a voice behind me, and I am reminded again of Kronklich's company. It's hard to believe he is here sometimes. It seems forever I was down in the dark depths of the ruins alone, never seeing the sun. Now it gleams on my face, but there is no warmth. The wind is too much.

Cold like me, Kronklich has been quiet all day. The lack of food and water has taken its toll on us both, no doubt. As I turn around to face him, he is whittling new bolts for his crossbow.

"And why is that?" I ask, already guessing his answer.

"Because it saved us from an early grave," he says, lifting a piece of stick over his shoulder. His gray suit is disheveled beyond recognition with tears and rips all over. Dried blood shows through the exposed white lining underneath. "It gave us light when we had none."

I remember following a light in the darkness below the ruins of Egleaseon's castle, but not the one Kronklich speaks of. My beloved, dead wife, Diana. It was she who guided us to the Hand of God—she, now a disembodied ghost. Kronklich wouldn't believe me if I told him. She wanted me to find it. Uncover its secrets. Damn cursed thing. It is because of her I still hold on to it. Nothing more.

"And," continues Kronklich, "we need it."

I am not so sure. Kronklich doesn't understand how the relic destroyed my family. I was the one who handed it to Egleaseon. I remember the words the traitorous priest Bronin said before he died. "Blood from the one who killed Egleaseon fused with the blood of his son will make the perfect vessel for our Lord's return." The words still haunt me now. Blood of the father. Bronin, that sick bastard. Working with the Carnalreesee. Wanting to be like them. A vampire.

The whole time they were after my blood. They took my son, burned my home and turned my lovely Diana in the process. I was forced to kill her with my own hands, and the thought of driving a stake through her heart was too much for me. Again, tears escape from the corners of my eyes. I love her so much; I couldn't bear to watch her turn into the very thing I hated.

And the worst part about everything was that it was done to lure me away. Lead me to the gathering below the ruins where I found them sacrificing my son. And yet somehow my blood was the key. *My blood.* Attempting to stop them only delayed the process further, and they escaped with Dorian as their prisoner.

Tucking the cursed relic back into my belt, I still cannot make sense of what happened down there in the ruins. I look up at the Cordova Mountains, watching the shadow on the west precipice rise. "We are losing daylight. We need to be down there before the Carnalreesee wake. It is the only chance we have at killing all six of them and saving Dorian."

I remember how my Bawaka was useless against the Carnalreesee. How they simply batted away the four-bladed weapon with ease. Why, I do not know. Only that I fear the worst, that somehow the Carnalreesee have become stronger, tolerant to my weapon of destruction. My only aim now is to rely on old traditions. To kill them in their sleep. A stake through the heart.

There are no questions from Kronklich as he rises to his feet, ready to go with me.

Another gust of wind blows, forcing me to tuck my body forward. The cold is unforgiving. We will freeze if we stay on the mountainside any longer.

Setting our plan in motion, we descend the cliff in silence. The way is treacherous and unmarked, making it impossible to move quickly. Boots crunching through snow, there is no easy way to navigate. Large jagged crags jut out from white patches, and where there is no snow, the ground is black.

"Stay clear of the ice," I say to Kronklich, focusing straight ahead, slipping despite my own warning. At this rate, it will be well past dark by the time we reach the Carnalreesee.

"This is madness," says Kronklich, slipping on a patch of ice. The wind whips his hair about as I watch him gripping the edge of a crag, unable to get a firm footing on the ground. His feet continue to slide.

There has to be a sane way down, but time is of the essence. The wound in my side burns from my arms holding my body in place. Not far below, I see a mildly slanted platform on the side of the cliff, enough to hold me, possibly Kronklich. "You see that," I shout over the howling wind, "You have to time it right."

But my words are useless. Kronklich slides past me, his arms and legs kicking, trying to find an anchor. His body hits the side of a stone and there is a grunt as he tumbles through the snow. I push off from the crag I am anchored to, arcing my body along the black surface, trying to stay with Kronklich. But it is no use. Kronklich misses the rest of the crags, gaining speed toward the platform. If he doesn't slow down, he will slide off the edge.

"Kronklich!"

A glint of steel flashes in the fading sunset as Kronklich slows his descent, his sword drawn, carving into the ice like a sculptor. "No problem here, Lord Wolfgang!"

The rock supporting me suddenly breaks and I fall, hitting the icy surface with a thud, and sliding down the mountainside. Arms and legs spread, I do all I can to slow my momentum. Body leveling flat, I come to the edge of the cliff, stopping with one of my arms hanging off the ledge. Heart racing, I use the Bawaka blade at my side to ice-pick the snow, pulling myself to safety. Breathing heavily, I swallow back the dryness in my throat while staring at the broken rocks below.

"That was a close one," says Kronklich, helping me to my feet. He points to what looks like a path at the other end of the cliff side. "That is our way down, I think."

The thought of saving Dorian feeds my adrenaline as we run for the weathered path leading down, but something hidden in the snow catches my foot and I am sent face down into white powder.

Laughter fills the air as I struggle to free myself from the thick snow.

"They told me to stay behind," says a jovial voice. "But I didn't think I'd have to do anything—physical."

Coming to terms with the ground, I am on my feet, ready to throw my Bawaka blade. But as I look, nothing is there. Only the laughter of the enemy somewhere near me. My eyes dart back and forth, but there is only Kronklich and I. Crossbow aimed at nothing, Kronklich has the same idea as me.

"Show yourself," I say, focusing my attention on a rock in the snow, waiting for any sign of movement.

"I didn't think you'd actually survive," continues the voice sarcastically. "Falling down that hole was a safe bet you were dead. And to think our hopes and dreams were lost forever. How lucky we are." The voice is suddenly in my ear.

Spinning around, I slash through the crisp air with lightning speed, striking nothing but the blowing wind. The laughing voice laughs harder.

They were lucky I didn't die? What was that supposed to mean?

"There," says Kronklich, firing his crossbow at the figure crouching in the snow. The figure bats the bolt away like a fly buzzing around food as it stands upright, rising to the same height as me. Wearing a gold mask with stag horns coming out the forehead, the lower half of the face is exposed and broken. Teeth yellow like mold, it smiles at me as if entertained. I know what I face. A Carnalreesee.

Clothed in red robes, the Carnalreesee begins walking forward quickly, laughing like some deranged lunatic. "Blood of the father. Blood of the father!"

I throw my Bawaka. It spins toward him with deadly intent. The blade makes two passes, but my enemy seems to be everywhere at one time. In the air. On the ground. Such speed. Such agility. The blade never makes contact. In the blink of an eye, he is before me with weapon in hand. An extraction dagger, the same one Bronin used on me in the ruins. Over and over he thrusts with precision toward my chest, but I sidestep. He ducks suddenly, anticipating the Bawaka's return trip. He lashes out, slicing my leg on the flank. I wince and stagger.

Thrusting again, he misses as I tuck away, the dagger passing close to my neck. The blade has to penetrate my skin in order for it to work. I remember Bronin holding that tiny vial in the light, examining my precious blood. *Blood of the father.*

A wooden bolt pierces the Carnalreesee's neck suddenly and his eyes open wide; blood issues from his mouth as he staggers through the snow. A gurgling sound rumbles from his throat, but it is not the sound of someone choking on their own blood. The bastard is laughing.

Kronklich rushes to my side as the Carnalreesee stands and slowly extracts the bloody arrow from his neck. Where there should have been a gaping hole, there is nothing but solid white flesh.

"It's going to take a lot more than that," says the Carnalreesee, casting his golden mask aside. His face is purplish-white as veins spread from the back of his head to the front. Pale, iridescent eyes stare at me with loathing hate. His teeth form a smile.

The Carnalreesee comes with lightning speed and there is no time to react. Kronklich shoves me at the last moment, taking the Carnalreesee's dagger into his arm. He lets out a grunt as he clutches the vampire's arm.

The Carnalreesee lets out a growl, plucking the dagger from Kronklich and casting him aside with ease.

"Run, Lord Wolfgang!" shouts Kronklich from a pile of white and red snow. "It's your blood he wants."

I have no intention of running.

The Carnalreesee watches me with intent, circling around me like a hawk. His blue eyes run the course of my body, searching for a weak spot.

"Why my blood?" I ask.

The Carnalreesee continues grinning, never saying a word. He is getting closer.

"Answer me."

His long hair flaps in the wind. The Carnalreesee tosses its dagger from one hand to the other.

"Come on!" I shout. "If you want it, come get it!"

The Carnalreesee comes at me like before and I anticipate his move, dropping to my knees in the wet snow. I thrust up with the Bawaka. One of the four points pierces his underarm and I hear the quick draw of his breath. Blood pours from the wound, running thick over my hand, dripping off the edges of the other three blades.

The air smells of iron as the Carnalreesee laughs. "Wolfgang the persistent. Nothing has changed my friend." Blood drips between his grinning teeth. He is right. My Bawaka is useless.

Before he says another word, I thrust the Hand of God against his chest, and his laughing stops.

Brilliant white light emanates from where my hand covers his breast. His pale eyes turn brown and his fangs retract. Using the holy power to force him back, a burst of energy sends him through the air and I follow, holding on to his body and slamming him onto the ground. We slide through the powdery snow, stopping at the edge of the cliff.

"Tell me!" I demand. "Why me? Why Dorian?"

The vampire's face is wrought with fear as his head shakes back and forth. Smoke and light engulf him, causing the pale white skin of his face to crumble away. Within seconds, I find myself staring into the wrinkled face of an old man. Most of his teeth are gone and his skin is blotchy and discolored. He looks so frail. I could snap his neck if I wanted to. I press the Hand of God against his chest further, anger channeling through me. I feel I could push it all the way through him but realize he is holding on to me. His body hangs off the cliff in midair, and I can do nothing, as the weight of his body holds me down.

His terrible dull eyes stare into mine and I see him smiling under those cracked lips.

"Tell me. Tell me now! What do you plan to do with my son?" I ask desperately.

"Wouldn't you like to know."

The Carnalreesee lets go of my hands and disappears from the edge of the cliff.

"No!" I scream, but it is done. His body falls through the icy wind of the mountain, bouncing along the rocks below, cracking with each hit until there is no sound.

CHAPTER
II

BREATHING HEAVILY, THE COLD AIR hurts my lungs. I am reminded again of the wound in my side, its crippling effects.

Lying flat in the snow, I hold the Hand of God before me, bewildered by its demonstration. It's the second time now I've seen it used—its ability to render vampire to human.

I catch my breath. Everything in my body hurts. The coolness of the snow provides comfort. I feel I could stay here an eternity, lying face up, watching the stars pass by, the thin clouds snaking along their pointless course.

I hold up the Bawaka blade, comparing it next to the simplicity of the Hand of God. How similar in shape they are, yet what was I not getting? How did the Bawaka, the same weapon I've used to destroy countless vampires, fail me again?

Looking beyond the instruments of destruction, the sight of Kronklich comes into view. He holds his hand out to me and I am inclined to take it.

"There is no time," says Kronklich, brushing the snow from my proofing. "We've lost too much already. We need to go now."

This I know. The sun sank well past the western mountains minutes ago and so we take off once more, jumping and rolling, treading through thick groves of powdery snow, spending no time to check our footing, no time to see if the ledge ends in places. With so much time lost from the fight with the Carnalreesee, there's no telling whether the caravan is still in its place. From our vantage point, it is too dark to see and the trees block our view. I hear Kronklich's breathing over my own as we struggle through the never-ending white blur. We pass green branches jutting out from thick snow while some of them scrape against my face, cold and dry. We are losing light; the purple hue is rapidly fading to blackness.

Relentlessly, we surge on. While I use my Bawaka to hack away huge chunks of stuck snow, Kronklich uses his crossbow, its wide surface area proving more efficient. My feet stumble on knotted roots hidden under the snow and soon the ground levels out. With the light all but gone, I notice the orange glow of campfires in the distance. The general area thins into a scattered open wood where dead branches poke from the white ground under the foliage of the canopy.

In the distance I see the silhouettes of the caravan wagons, drawn close around campfires—if they can be called campfires. The flames are nearly died out, yet one continues to burn brightly, a mighty flame within the heart of darkness. I signal Kronklich behind me and he moves to the right. There is no need to review plans with him. He has done this many times before. Moving in the shadows. Stealth. As I approach straight, my pace slows in attempt to soften the crunching snow. Looking above me, there are no birds in the trees, no squirrels chattering about the branches. In fact, there are no sounds at all.

I hear my teeth chattering and use my hand to keep them still. I am freezing and the fire looks inviting. Its warmth could save my life, but I can't stop. Dorian is here, somewhere. The lack of movement all around me couples the eerie silence of the camp. Looking to my right, Kronklich is no longer in sight. Good.

As I approach one of the caravans from the back, I make sure to stay within its shadow. I creep onto the frozen wooden deck of the tiny house—the outside looks more like a shack on wheels. I peer through one of the windows and can hardly see anything inside. Small beams of light pass through the cracks between the shiplap. Angling it just right, I make out an inanimate figure lying on the floor. Is it a human? A vampire? The darkness inside prevents such details.

Testing the window, I find it open and move over the threshold within seconds and begin exploring the inside of the dirty, musky interior of the caravan. Bawaka blade at the ready, I crawl to the figure lying face down, examining it ever so closely. Laying a hand on its shoulder, I turn it over, revealing a contorted face of a man, his eyes and mouth open as if screaming in his last moments. Frozen red splotches catch my eyes in the light and immediately my hand goes to his neck.

There are two large gaping holes.

Kicking open the door, I am bathed in orange light as the cold outside air greets me. Immediately, I am repulsed by what I see. The campfires, which should bring warmth to my heart and bones, bring only the chill of death. Mothers and children lie huddled next to one another, still in their positions of forever sleep. The heat of the fires keeps the snowflakes from collecting on their bodies. They glisten in the firelight. A dead man's body lies across a log, split open at the belly, his entrails frozen in the red snow, his neck filleted like a fish. Maybe wolves were here.

Maybe.

It is impossible to tell with the fresh snowfall, but as I examine more of the bodies, I realize something…else. Most of the bodies, if not all, have been decimated. Their backs ripped open. Their spines removed. No, it wasn't wolves.

I look around. Why would the Carnalreesee do such a thing? Walking around the center campfire, everything is still as it was. Sticks for building a fire. Dolls for the children. The air is thick with the scent of blood and—food? Perplexed by this strange find, I raise my hands to the fire for warmth. But as the tingling sensation returns to my numb fingers, despite the magnificent comfort it gives me, my blood runs thinner yet. Smoldering in the fire, an ashen heap of bodies fuels the flames. Suddenly, I am cold again. Closing my eyes, I shudder.

Loud banging comes from across the camp, and immediately, I open my eyes to see Kronklich kicking in every door of the remaining caravans. He emerges with the same results from each of them: a loaded crossbow and a shake of his head.

I sink to my knees in the snow, slumping my shoulders. How much of a head start did the Carnalreesee have? I feel light headed at the moment. I cannot remember the last time I ate.

I watch Kronklich circle the outskirts of the camp, crouching, testing the snow. Before I know it, he is at my side again, reporting his findings. The man never stops.

"It's impossible," says Kronklich. "The snow covers everything. I can't tell how long they've been gone. Judging by what's left, they are traveling light and fast. One wagon, maybe two." He pauses a moment. "To tell you the truth, I don't think they took anything. Weapons. Supplies. People." He looks at me warily. "Everything is covered in frost."

"Make no mistake. They took something all right," I say sarcastically, remembering the spines ripped from the gypsies' backs.

The neighing of horses draws my attention away to the darkness beyond the campfires. *Horses?*

Seems not all is lost after all. "We must hurry. We can still catch them." I notice the remaining wagons with their breeching and straps hanging loosely over the pulling shafts. We could tie off two of the horses, double up if there's more. I envision us riding hard, a team of four, wagon blazing through the forest, mud and leaves kicking up from the torrent of the wheels. We will have the upper hand, and then we could save Dorian.

The horses are close by; I can smell them. I begin to move toward the edge of the camp to free our transportation, yet a firm hand suddenly grips my shoulder.

"No, Tenor," says Kronklich in a stern voice, hair falling about his face in wisps. His gray eyes stare into mine. "We have to survive. We have to live—don't you agree?" It is the first time Kronklich has used my name since we left the manor. "Can't forget we're human, can we? You have to remember. If we die, Dorian dies."

Die? What the hell was he talking about? "We don't have time for this," I say, but the moment the words leave me, the point hits home, as suddenly I am overwhelmed with exhaustion. I stagger some, losing my footing on a patch of black ice hidden beneath the snow.

"Well then, you see? Can't have you riding off through that scary-looking forest over there without putting something in your belly." Kronklich tugs at the seams of his coat, straightening his hopeless attire. Seams frayed and torn, it's a wonder the clothing stays on him. "But first," he says, reaching down and picking up the Bawaka blade from the snow, "we must purge these grounds." He hands it to me. The handle is colder than my already numb hands. Is it time already? We both know it must be done.

Walking to a nearby corpse, I spin the Bawaka in hand and draw the silver stake tucked in my belt. In two motions, I pierce its heart and sever its head. The body topples over into the snow like a frozen log. I move on to the next. Over and over I follow this procedure, hacking at the stock of bodies until all of the dead are dead again. I know it takes one day for victims to rise as vampires, but I act upon it more in anger than in necessity, channeling my frustration and agitation with each head removed from a neck. Slicing the head off a child, I notice Kronklich looking at me. Is he thinking disgust? Abhorrence? No, of course not. He knows me better. He's been with me for so long. It's the look of concern he gives when he isn't being facetious. I say nothing as I breathe in the thin air, the scent of blood nearly frozen away.

Instead, the aroma of food lingers in the air. There is a steaming pot over one of the other fires not fueled by dead-body compositions. I move toward it and remove the lid, finding its contents inviting. Using one of the many ladles resting inside, I stir, watching mushrooms and meat rise to the surface. The aroma is rich and I notice pieces of garlic floating. My mouth waters as I stumble around, pushing snow away, looking for something to hold the stew. Ice, wet leaves, small rocks, red-stained snow. Surely there is something here. I push bodies aside, their stiff forms like ice sculptures sliding across the ground.

Kronklich watches me as he rubs his hands together. "I'll check the wagons."

But as I move another body, I notice the thing I am looking for. I wipe down a filthy wooden bowl, caked with mud and snow.

"No need," I say, seeing there is a second one, and tossing it to Kronklich. My stomach aches. I splash the clear brown stew into my dish. The steam whips about my face as I burn my tongue, but I don't care. I'm starving. As the liquid goes down, I feel the heat spreading through my body. I watch Kronklich sift through the pot with the giant spoon, pulling out large chunks of what looks like deer meat. With the heat of the soup rising to my face, my skin tingles and the scars on my face burn. I recall the hellish bogart tearing open my face just below my right eye. It is a haunting memory that will never leave my thoughts. A few more inches above and I would have been blinded. I cringe at the thought of losing my eye.

Biting into a piece of meat, I sense someone or something looking at me. I glance up from my food and see a boy's face staring at me from outside the circle of the campfire. One of the heads I severed. Mouth open, his eyes stare at me, dull and brown in a sea of white. I sigh to myself. Soon his head will vanish under the snow like the rest. No one will ever come looking for him. He will be forgotten like all the rest. Everything vanishes in time.

I refocus on Kronklich, who is still examining the contents of the soup. Seems his enthusiasm is curved by the concoction. "If there was anything wrong with it, I would be dead by now."

Kronklich frowns and shoves the first bite into his mouth, chewing the meat with caution. After a second bite, he clears his throat. "Don't you think it's strange?" He examines his oversized spoon.

"What? The soup?"

"No. The situation."

I pause a moment, staring beyond the pile of snow covering the bodies. "Nothing is strange to me anymore."

"I mean, look all around us. This camp. The gypsies were serving the Carnalreesee. Men, women, even their children for God's sake!"

The word God triggers a thought in my head and I recall the time I stood at the bank of the Faust River, holding the cross in my hand, ready to toss it away. Ready to toss *God* away.

"All for what?" Kronklich continues, "For them to be slaughtered like cattle? Leave their bodies in the snow to rot away?" Kronklich takes a long swig from his bowl and chews another piece of meat with determination. "They could have taken them as servants or slaves at the very least."

"They took what they wanted," I say, remembering the spines missing from each of the carcasses. Suddenly, I am no longer hungry and cast the rest of my stew into the fire. It hisses in response. I stand up and attempt to get my blood flowing into my legs, standing closer to the smoldering coals. It won't be long till all the warmth is gone from the camp.

"Did you find supplies?" I ask, turning on the spot to warm my backside.

"Indeed," says Kronklich with a hint of excitement. He seems grateful for the change of subject. "Right over there."

I follow Kronklich through the snowfall, making sure not to slip on the black ice again. I push open the door to one particular caravan and find myself staring at a stockade of supplies, ranging from pelts and coats to barrels and jars full of unidentified liquids. Cured meats hang from the ceiling along the sides of the shack and there is a box full of oiled torches. Out of the stock of supplies, something draws my attention more than the rest. A set of black masks, equipped with goggles and fastenings at the edges. Immediately they remind me of the golden masks the Carnalreesee wear, although they actually look dissimilar in nature. These masks are somewhat novelty items, pieces of clothing not very common to other parts of Ashton. Seems an age ago the last time I wore such attire. Moving to one of the barrels, I pry the lid off and am greeted with the aroma of sap and oil. I smile to myself. Vitrol. There are three full barrels of the liquid.

I turn to inform Kronklich of our fortunate find but find him engrossed in another matter, holding a fine leather coat up with both hands. Kronklich turns the dark brown tail jacket, measuring it up against his body, mocking a sure fit. Slipping it on, he seems to pay no mind as dust kicks off of it. He is like a child who's discovered a new toy. I watch him bend down and reach into the chest beside him, removing a short flat hat with the brim extending in a wide circle. Patting the inside with his fist, he attempts to remove the creases, and then methodically places the antique hat on his head.

"Not like my top hat, but this flat regent will do." His eyes turn to me. "Ah!" He reaches down again and extracts a similar leather coat and tosses it to me. "We are of the same build, I think."

I shake out the unused jacket and slip it over my proofing. Immediately, warmth takes its effect over me. It is somewhat tight at the shoulders, restrictive for me to raise my arms due to the proofing, but I can adjust. I welcome its leathery scent. For once, I feel normal again.

"'Tis a shame there's not another hat," says Kronklich, examining himself in a mirror bolted to the wall. The coats themselves are of no ordinary design. They are sewn thick with a fabric interior, dense enough to keep the elements out, fashioned with brass buckles along their fronts. Fastening all the bindings would encompass the wearer like a sheath to a blade.

Still shaking from the cold, I begin fastening the first of the buckles. Halfway through, pulling the sixth strap through its binding, I notice a case tucked away between two of the barrels.

No locks. I undo the latches, revealing a marvelously crafted set of hunting knifes, different shapes and sizes, some curved, some straight. There is one particularly shaped like my silver stake, and so I add it to my other side. The smallest of the blades I tuck in my boot. I toss a large curved cutlass to Kronklich and I stow the rest of the arsenal along the back of my belt. One can never have enough knives.

Satisfied with my findings, I step back out into the freezing night, my breath spreading before me in feathery wisps. I am unable to tell how long it has been since nightfall. The snow is falling again in strong drafts.

"If we don't get moving, we won't be going anywhere with this wagon," I say to Kronklich as he descends the steps of the caravan.

He seems extremely satisfied with himself, adjusting the hat on his head and testing the tension of his bowstring. "It's a shame really. Not an ounce of tea anywhere."

I set to arranging the horse bindings as Kronklich moves around to the dark edge of the forest. I hear the horses neighing their unhappiness. My hopes dwell on their capability to run through the night. Working through the numbness of my hands, I slide the strap through each ring, one at a time, until the left side of the shaft is ready for harnessing. Stiffly, I move around to the other side, allowing the blood to circulate through my legs, and then I hear the dreadful sound of elements in the distance. Not that of the howling wind on the mountain, or the creaking moans of the timber wood, but that of a distant rumble. A thunderous roar echoes over the previous one, until I feel the very ground shake, and the icicles fall from the awning of the wagons. My hair whips about my shoulders in a frenzy and I am reminded how grateful I am for my newfound coat. Storm clouds are coming and with it, the dread rain. Quickly, I move about the wagon, tracing a finger along the exterior, hoping it has been properly coated, but my finger scrapes dried splintered wood. The vitrol was not applied. Not good. Not good at all.

"Kronklich! Quick! The barrels!"

Kronklich appears from the shadowy outskirts with four horses trailing behind him. As fast as we can, we tie off the quad of black stallions and storm the interior of the caravan, shoving crates to the side and knocking over long brushes.

Frantically we shift one of the large barrels full of vitrol out into the open, spilling some of its contents. Its rancid aroma of fermented wood and tar is strong, causing me to gag. I hold my breath as we begin dipping long poles with scrub brushes into its dark complexion, mixing it about, creating whirlpools of vile liquid.

"Right then," says Kronklich, pulling the brush from the barrel. Beads of sweat drip from his forehead.

"You start with the wagon and I'll get the horses," I say, pulling my own brush from the barrel, careful not to get any on my skin. The transparent black liquid drips from the end like ooze as I pass it over the ground and onto the back of the first horse. The animal stamps its hooves in disapproval as I coat its mane with the foul liquid, covering all parts of its body, even the straps and guide shaft. I make sure a thick layer is applied before I move on to the next. I see Kronklich has already applied the goggles over their eyes. I cover those too. The process is over within minutes and I check once more that no spots have been missed. Slightly timid, the horses stay their ground, obedient as ever. They are used to the ritual.

Focusing on the wagon, I see Kronklich has made quick work of the tiny shack on wheels. All of the wood is now black.

Kronklich pops his head up from the roof. "There. That should do it." With a quick vault, he is on the ground, checking for any spots he might have missed.

More thunder sounds in the distance and the wind increases. With the dread rain coming, and my son abducted long ago from this camp, my anxiety has reached its peak.

"We can't linger any longer. We need to go. Now!" As I make to climb up onto the perch of the wagon, my head fills with a haze, and I nearly fall off the step. Kronklich is there to catch me.

"Yes, yes. We will go," assures Kronklich, shouldering my arm and hoisting me up onto the wagon. "We will go, but you will rest now my friend." He kicks the shack door open and we stumble into the musty interior.

"No time to rest," I say feebly. I wasn't feeling like this moments ago. Seems my body has finally rebelled against me. Kronklich was right. If we don't stop to rest, what use will I be to my son? I imagine my stubborn self riding through the woods on a black stallion, falling from my saddle with exhaustion, unconscious and alone. I remember the boy's head in the snow from earlier. No one would come looking for me. I would be forgotten like all the rest. All things go away in time.

"Here you are..." It's Kronklich's gentle voice.

I am grateful for Kronklich's services, but I am unable to express anything. I fade in and out of consciousness feeling around with my hands, the straw beneath me, and warmth above me. I hear the striking of flint and a bright glow illuminates my face.

"We have to—my son," I stutter, but my body denies me any movement and my mind deserts me.

"Don't worry," says Kronklich's voice over the thunder. "I'll get us where we need to go."

DAY FIVE

CHAPTER III

A MUSTY SMELL RISES AS I awaken. An odor like that of a barn where the floorboards have molded through from years of water penetrating the foundation, where soft straw from the horses' hay barrels blends with the scent of oats and light from the swaying lanterns leaking oil from cracked bases. *Drip. Drip.*

I stare beyond the moving shadows as I try to recall where I am. The pungent smell from the barrels surrounding me creeps its way into my nostrils, increasing my discomfort. A sudden jolt from the floor wakes me further from my drowsiness, confirming I am in transit of some sort. But as a passenger or prisoner, I cannot say. My weapons are present, and Kronklich—where is Kronklich? I scan the immediate interior and he is nowhere to be found, even though I know he was with me last night.

Rolling over to my side, there is another jolt from the floorboards and I land on my hip. I grit my teeth. A lantern in the corner sways violently again as the wheels of the wagon grind over rock and root.

Daylight shines through filthy windows covering the interior of the room in a grayish film. I hear the pelting of water drops along the roof above accompanied by an undeniable hissing sound. I grab on to a barrel to balance my unstable body and look out the window, using my hand to wipe the grime and oil smoke away.

Trees pass by through a swirling mist of low cloud cover. It is a thick fog I have not seen for some time. This caravan or wagon is moving incredibly fast for its shabby construction and I'm surprised it still holds together. Rain spatters the pane while dry-rotted branches snap against the outside wood panels. I have difficulty discerning anything outside the window. The visibility congeals itself into one large blur.

The shaking makes me dizzy.

I reach for the side panels and settle myself back onto the straw where I slept—how long have I been sleeping? The storm moved in last night and now the dread rain is melting the day. My stomach makes a loud noise and I find myself searching the area of the carriage for food. Checking the stores, I see a few baskets filled with raw carrots, potatoes, turnips, and what looks like—ebon root. I hold one of them up, examining its thick coarse exterior. Black. Rough. Most would consider this natural growth an outlawed substance, a drug if you will, and many would pay a high price for it. As I wonder what other endeavors the caravan people may have dabbled in, I feel the wagon slow down. The hissing outside subsides. Immediately, my instincts take over, my hunger—forgotten. I move to the window, yet see nothing except water from the branches. Puffs of smoke rise from each droplet hitting the ground. Checking my weapons, I find everything is secure. My hand goes to the Bawaka.

The caravan comes to a stop and my blood rushes to my hands and face. The claw marks on my face tingle. The horses outside are in an agitated state. I hear no voice as heavy footfalls thump up the stairs just outside the door. The handle rattles. Once. Twice. The third time it bursts open, slamming against the wall and shaking the room. A draft of acrid stench fills the small cavity of the shack with a gust of wind. A figure wrapped in black stands before me, masked and hooded. Goggles cover where the eyes should be. It looks like some strange creature having stumbled out of the Decameron Forest. Decayed. Wretched. A slimy film drips from its leather coat. Through the mask, the creature's breathing is filtered at the mouth and nose, creating a ghastly sigh in and out. The figure takes a few steps in, sweeping its head side to side, looking for something. Looking for me.

"Tenor?" asks the hollow voice. It cocks its head to the side once again. "Ah! Good! You're awake." After unfastening the clasps that bind the mask to the hood, the figure tears away the contraption, breathing in deep and wrinkling his face at the same time. "Good God, man, if I knew it were this horrible, I would have left the bloody thing on!" Kronklich says with an exasperated breath.

It was silly of me to think the worst, knowing I was in the care of Kronklich. But I'm afraid my current state has left me in the worst kind of thought process. Despair plagues me. I remember the nightmares spawned within the bowels of Egleaseon's ruins. Bogarts. Lechers. Caretakers. Daver hounds. Things from the pit of hell, along with a great many other atrocities, but my head hurts, and the acid smell coming from outside burns my nostrils.

Thinking more clearly now, I ask, "What's the matter? Why have we stopped?" I peer out of the caravan at the foggy morning. Pewter streaks cover whatever light the sun emits into the atmosphere.

"The rain," says Kronklich through teeth clenched on a piece of ebon root. "It has temporarily subsided." His pupils are dilated, his eyes wide and alert.

"How much of that have you had?"

He smiles at me. "Enough to get us through the night. C'mon, then. There's not much time. We have to coat the wagon and horses again or we will become new additions to the forest." He pulls the mask back over his face and steps back out of the grimy shack interior. After grabbing a cloak and mask for myself, I step out into the bright gloom of the morning.

Like stepping into an abstract painting—I am immediately surrounded by swirling mist and gray dismal light. Though I know there is a canopy of tree branches above me, I only see the occasional drip from the branches high up. With the road ahead of the horses and vast forest on either side of us, I know well enough lingering in such a place for too long will bring misfortune. The dread rain kills all things. Well, most things. It strips the flesh from those who wish to live: animals, plants, people.

Walking a few paces, my boots sink deep in the slop, muddied darker than brown. Saturated from the rain, I wonder if it was wise to stop here in such a place where one may become stuck. Still holding my mask in hand, I move to the side of the wagon, where Kronklich has already removed the top of one of the barrels.

"You might want to put that on," says Kronklich. "No telling when the rain will start again."

I glance at the sky above us, catching a glimpse of how far the tree line stretches. I cannot fathom how long this forest has endured the phantom rain. I look to my shoulder as something sizzles in my ear. A water droplet trickles down my cloak. Dread rain. Acid rain that can rot anything it touches unless it's coated in the known concoction of vitrol, a mixture of tree sap and black oil, boiled and then cooled with water. It's the infallible curse known to the Decameron Forest. But the concoction to treat it is vile and would send someone to an early grave if ingested.

The poisoned rain is yet another effect and proof of the evil that resides in this land, stemming from the cursed ruins of Egleaseon. Looking to the edge of the forest again, I cannot help but notice the extent of the decay. Wagons abandoned, melting away to mere planks of blackened wood. Animal carcasses twice removed of fur and flesh, now skeletal frames of brittle pieces and ash. Deep long gashes reside along the bark of the trees. They ooze trails of black decay, no longer providing their protective covering due to the damage of passing vehicles and rabid animals searching for prey.

I hear the hissing increasing again high above us and I am quick to don the mask, pulling each strap tight and fastening the buckles. My world becomes darker with the goggles over my eyes. The cloak and mask, even the gloves I slip on, are layered with the thick vitrol.

Speaking through the mask delivers a nasal resonance to my words. "This mask smells of death," I say, grabbing one of the brushes and dipping it into the vitrol.

Kronklich has already begun on half of the wagon. "Can't be all that bad. You don't want to know what mine smells like."

We make quick work of coating all of the wood and horses with vitrol, and in some spots, add a double layer. The effect of the rain has damaged some of the vulnerable areas of the wheel wells and joints where the shack meets the wagon platform. The wood, damp with corrosive acid, is warping. Any more damage and the whole of the wagon will break to pieces. With the dismal light of the day about us, I realize it was much harder applying the vitrol at night, coating a vehicle with a black liquid in the black night. Still, the sky is dull enough to blend into the endless vapor.

With the hissing rain increasing, our temporary reprieve ends. I help Kronklich load the barrel back onto the wagon while I hear the faintest of sounds coming from a far off distance in the forest. The noise is weak and pathetic at first—a light screeching moving closer. Maybe a baby bird has been plucked from its nest and awaits its demise. I heave the barrel onto the lip of the wagon.

Again it comes.

Kronklich doesn't seem to notice.

"Do you hear it?" I ask.

"Hear what?" Kronklich disappears inside the shack with the barrel.

The drops of rain falling around my shoulders increase, yet the noise in the forest doesn't go away. In fact, it becomes louder. Taking a few steps closer to the edge of the woods, I stop dead in my tracks at the sight of a small dark-colored animal foraging along the mud-stained ground, splashing through acid puddles, not a care in the world. Steam rises all around it from the soil it touches. It is not affected by the dread rain in the least. I have seen the animal before. An atter. Bottom dwellers of the forest, searching for decayed remains of the dead. Another appears by its side. Then another.

I step back, realizing what's happening. "Kronklich—"

The door swings open with a bang and out comes Kronklich. It's impossible to read his expression with the mask on his face. "I really wish there was some tea. What sort of caravan doesn't carry tea?"

"Kronklich," I say again, hopping onto the side of the wagon. "We need to leave. Now."

Kronklich looks to the sky and raises a hand. "Time already? It's not that bad." He situates himself down onto the perch— "Very well"—and cracks the reins—"Hya!"

The horses snap alive, sending the wagon into a jolt. Leather creaking, horses braying, the wagon rocks forward, then back.

"Hya! Hya!" More cracks from the reins. The horses neigh in frustration, trying to move forward, but their burden holds them fast. The wagon rocks back and forth again like a boat on a lake.

"Stuck! Can you believe it?" Kronklich turns to face me. His tone hints of surprise. "Dear God!" he blurts out suddenly. "Look at them all!"

I do not have to look back to know what is happening, but I do so anyway. Dozens of atters pass between trees and roots at the edge of the forest, making their way onto the road, which is now simply mud soup. Teeth chattering like chipmunks, their fast, responsive maneuvers are similar to that of the common squirrel. Sporadic. Unpredictable.

At the moment, I cannot believe how many there are. They move down the trunks of trees like an ant infestation. The afternoon hasn't brought any more light to the sky and the atters are in and out of shadow, at times massing together like a dark cape thrown over the ground.

Again, Kronklich is at it with the reins. The wagon rocks forward, then back. I know it wants to move, I can feel it nearly there, caught on some root or rut under the mud. It needs a push.

My boots splatter mud as I jump off the side. I run to the back of the wagon and brace the lowest plank of wood with my back. "Keep at it!" I yell through my mask, over the downpour of rain drowning out my voice. Pushing with my thighs, I use all the strength I can afford to clear the wagon over the cusp. In front of me, the atters are making quick work of the ground, running as fast as their little legs can carry them. Some of them are still screeching—the noise, sharp and sinister. Their eyes, covered in a white film, taunt me as I push again with my body, knowing that if the wagon doesn't move on this try, I will be dinner for these vile creatures.

The wagon teeters and rolls out of the rut, causing me to fall without warning. I splash down into the black mud, scrambling to get up before the liquid has a chance to seep into my clothes. Grabbing the sideboard of the wagon, I pull myself to safety as it rolls forward. With upper-body strength, I shimmy onto the flat of the wagon. Atters cling to my cloak like spurs, chattering and grinding their teeth together, enough to make me cringe. I shake my cloak violently, trying to knock them free, but their large pointy teeth rip through the fabric, lingering ever still.

A sudden jerk of the caravan and I am sent to the floorboards of the wagon, rolling around with three atters together. Their screeches, now closer than before, set my mind in terror as they scamper around my body. Agile. Ferocious. Fast. They bite me at multiple locations. Arm. Leg. Shoulder. But they are animals of instinct, not intelligence. The proofing under my cloak keeps their razor teeth from penetrating my skin. With the Bawaka trapped underneath me, I free one of the daggers and shove the blade into the belly of an atter. Instantly, it releases my leg, blood gushing from its wound. I raise the back of my clenched fist and smack the one off my shoulder. It tumbles along the floor and I lose sight of it. I swipe at the one attempting to chew through my arm. The blade cuts through its black skin, yet it holds on, bleeding, catching the edge of my glove. It bites down again, and its teeth sink through the thin leather and into my skin. I wince at the pain, but push through it, grabbing the atter by its body with my other hand. As I pull the bastard off, the glove goes with it, exposing my hand to the dread rain, the same hand that was burned in the painting at the ruins.

I scream as the acid rains turn my pink flesh black. The smell of corroding skin seeps through my mask.

I roll over, covering my hand from the exposure, grinding my teeth, wishing for the pain to stop. My eyes dart back and forth, searching for the atter I didn't kill. Rising up, the wagon hits another bump, but this time I've regained my sense of stability. Holding on to the panels for support, I gaze out into to the rushing roadway behind the wagon. Hundreds of white eyes gain on us.

"Kronklich! Can't we go any faster?"

"I'm trying, Tenor! Bloody road's gone soft!"

I hear Kronklich cracking the reins over and over. The sound is atrocious as he beats the horses senseless. What choice is there?

I still see no sign of the atter as I look away from the impending doom following us. These creatures. Cursed beasts, tiny in nature, deadly in numbers. Their desperation to follow after us is proof of the hunger in this forest. I hear the screech of an atter and see it pressed flat against the wall, just under the awning. Staring at me as if I were a tasty morsel, it grinds its teeth, yet turns about suddenly and scampers up the roof, heading for Kronklich. With no time to waste, I follow, leaping onto the side of the awning and scrambling up the back, boots fighting for traction against the vitrol.

Scuttling along, the atter gets within leaping distance, and before it has its chance, I spring first, throwing the whole of my body forward, arms extended. The atter screeches as I pierce its hindquarters; my body slams against the roof. My head rattles from the impact, dazing me a moment as the atter twitches about, clawing at the blade, biting at my hand, trying to free itself while trying to attack me all at the same time. I see Kronklich staring at me as my vision refocuses. A black mask, faceless, expressionless. With a powerful sweep of his crossbow, he brings the stock of the weapon down on the trapped atter and splatters its entrails all over my mask.

"Thank you," says Kronklich, standing up from the wagon perch and swinging his crossbow over his shoulder. "Here—you drive," he says, throwing me the reins.

I wipe the guts away, and scramble to control the horses while standing and bending at the knees, constantly turning around to see what he is doing. Moving to the roof, Kronklich plants both feet in a shoulder stance to keep his balance, cloak flapping in the driving wind and rain. Suddenly producing a glass flask, he arcs his arm at an angle and lobs the bottle off the back of the wagon. The ground explodes in a hellish fire before the rushing mob, spreading liquid flame all over, consuming them and everything around them. Having taken out more than half the mass of atters, Kronklich watches the few still giving chase give up within moments, realizing their numbers have depleted.

Kronklich's mask turns to face me and his shoulders shrug. "Compliments of Bronin."

I turn my attention back to the road before me, but the driving rain blurs my vision. I know the horses will stay the course, bound by the judgment of reins, as expected from any trained horse. Another slam from the ground and I know we've hit another rut. The wagon bounces and impacts the ground hard. I know I will feel that one later on. Keeping my bare hand tucked inside my cloak with the reins, I run my gloved hand over my goggles, trying to better my vision. The road is clear; the ground ahead is all one color—brown.

Suddenly, Kronklich's hands are over mine. "Whoaaaa!" he shouts as he pulls hard on the reins. I feel the strain of the leather tongues straining the rings attached to the harnesses, forcing the leather straps to dig deeply into the horses' flesh. They neigh and wail in disappointment, but the caravan's momentum doesn't slow. It continues moving forward, wheels and hooves sliding through the slick muddy ground with zero resistance. The path ahead has vanished, for the road and mud mix together like a great brown soup. Yet nothing prepares me for what happens next as the caravan stops suddenly but my body does not.

CHAPTER
IV

I LIFT FROM MY SEAT and am nearly thrown from the riding perch. Kronklich braces me with an arm. The impact is like hitting a solid wall, snapping our heads forward, then back. The whiplash is painful, but the sound coming from the horses is sheer terror. As I gaze over the team of four stallions, I realize the two upfront have sunken down into a mud pit, which covers the expanse of the entire road. They thrash about frantically, unable to escape their watery prison, sinking deeper into the mud with each movement. The rear horses panic, unable to retrace their steps. Their hooves slip along the slick gravel.

"Quick!" I shout through the acid rain. I slip off the side and move to the center of the lead shaft, boots halfway submerged in the mud, pulling at the bridles and bindings. Steam rises from the horses' legs, submerged in the muck. I see the black trails of vitrol washing away with each passing second. The horses whinny in agony. I can only imagine how they feel. Animals suffering. Acid stripping away the flesh.

"Push!" I shout over the pelting rain.

I am doing all I can, but my boots keep sliding through the mud.

"Push! Push!" I say, again and again, not giving up. We need the horses.

"Yaaaah!" Kronklich retorts back. I see him on the other side, struggling along with me, but it's no use. Our luck has run its course.

"Again!" I scream, back aching, muscles burning. I will not give in so easily.

I hear Kronklich shouting over the horses and rain. "Tenor!" There is more, but his voice is drowned out.

"What is it—?" I can only see a few inches in front of me.

The horses jerk forward suddenly, nearly tossing me into the sinkhole of churning brown liquid. Hands explode from the mud, clawing at the horses with bony fingers, pulling at their skin, latching on to their legs. The horses toss their heads to and fro, trying to break free of the enslaving mud and groping hands. A hand grabs my leg and I kick it away. Throughout the mud pit, lechers rise to meet the air, mouths open wide, steam rising from the bubbling acid pouring from their eyes and ears. Watery moans escape their gurgling jaws as the horses flail about in terror. Some of the dead clasp on to their manes, pulling them farther down, closer to the mud, their eyes meeting the surface, closer to what lies beneath. Fingers creep into the edges of their mouths, breaking teeth. I am close enough to see a horse's eye gouged from the socket as one of the living corpses slurps it into its mouth.

"We have to cut them loose!" I shout to Kronklich. He is still trying to pull the leading shaft out of the mud. It is a hopeless situation with the stallions trapped and buried. Extracting one of the curved blades found at the caravan camp, I begin hacking away at the wood, chopping bits into the mud. Each stroke brings me closer to freeing the rear horses. Kronklich follows suit. I notice a lecher rise behind him.

"Kronklich!"

Kronklich leans to the side while bringing up his curved blade straight into the lecher's face. There is a slurp and the figure wavers momentarily, dagger lodged in its brain. Kronklich struggles to extract it, but the lecher falls forward, blade and all. Another lecher sledges through the mud, taking the place of the last. Kronklich steps back, bringing his crossbow to meet the lechers face point-blank and releases a headshot through the frontal lobe. Kronklich moves away from his vantage point. "There are too many!" he shouts. More rise from the bubbling acid with arms extended.

I keep hacking away at the shaft; sweat drips inside my mask. *So close.* Two hands grab at my arm tucked underneath my cloak and pull, exposing my already burnt hand. Rain sears my hand, bubbling on the already existing burnt scars. The corpse bites down on my arm, sinking its rotten teeth into my proofing. Down goes my blade into its skull, over and over again until there's nothing left except pieces of mashed skull and brain. Dark matter drips the length of my arm as I frantically continue chipping away at the wood.

I hear a groan and a crack. I glance at the horses in the front. Nearly all of their skin is stripped away, leaving muscle mass and exposed bone for the lechers to chew on. The horses no longer make sounds. Their muscle impulses twitch.

I keep slicing into the wood as fast as I can, focusing on saving the remaining horses. If we lose our mobility through the forest, the dread rain will claim our lives.

Dorian is counting on me.

The beam buckles, breaking at the center with a loud snap. The horses suddenly lurch back away from the muck, forcing the wagon back with them. I watch what's left of the doomed horses sink deep into the muck, the lechers swarming over them like buzzards, moaning louder for more meat. I back away in disgust, wondering if it was luck or fate that saved us. What's left of the sun—now somewhere closer to the tree line—has made the lighting of Decameron Forest even more dismal and stony, darker than the mid-morning from earlier.

Tucking my hand in my cloak, I hold it close to my body, ensuring its protection from the rain. I notice a trail of bodies leading up to Kronklich, where he is assessing the damage of the broken tug stop. Splintered and frayed, there was no time for a clean cut. Walking over to him, I feel multiple aches in my body and the strain in my back where I tried to push the wagon away from the mud. My hand brushes over the Bawaka blade, safely fastened underneath my cloak. I scan our surroundings for approaching enemies, despite the moaning coming from the sinkhole in front of us. Once the horses are consumed, the lechers will come back this way. Mist rises from the corrosive ground with a hiss. It reminds me of steam rising from freshly baked bread. Already my stomach is responding with hunger again, despite my throbbing hand.

"Everything seems to be in order," comes Kronklich's nasally voice from under the mask. As he runs his hand along the straps of the surviving horses, he stops and glances back at me. "What happened to you?"

I assume he is staring at my tucked-away hand. "One of those bastard atters took my glove. It won't stop burning."

Hopping onto the wagon, Kronklich offers his own hand. "C'mon, then. There's bound to be somewhere someone can help. Another camp. A town close by?"

I gladly take his offer as he helps me onto the wagon. Glancing inside the caravan's interior, everything has overturned from the frantic ride.

"There is a place. Widow," I say reluctantly. I know well if we are to find anything there, it will be nothing short of a desolate, diseased hovel of wayward travelers and peddlers hiding from the dread rain.

"Widow? Bloody place sounds awful."

"It is," I say with a tone of unpleasantness. Kronklich snaps the reins and the wagon lurches into motion.

"Seems we'll have a bit of a hard time catching up to them now, what with two of our horses eaten," says Kronklich, pointing at the enormous sinkhole I failed to see earlier before we plunged into it.

As we pass the remains of the horses that once were and are now gone, the dead have begun to venture away from the mud hole, rain hissing and spattering against their rotting flesh. They moan and drag their feet about, attention drawn by the sound of our passing wagon. They are slow and weak, but in numbers they are deadly. As I watch them shrink away in the distance, I wonder about the evil plaguing this forest and everything in it. How do people survive in this environment, tormented day in and day out? The caravan people seemed to have managed, for the most part, running their vitrol covered wagons back and forth, but as for the people of Widow, I cannot say the same. They are a different lot.

The frequency of bumps lessens as the wagon spins along. I am grateful for it, despite the urgency to find my son. My body is wrecked. Sore. Tired.

My mind dwells on Widow.

I cannot recall the last time I was there. Such a little shit of a town. A town of few men and many women. The women outnumber the men two to one. A dreadful outlook, perhaps? Our plans have changed so much already, so I try not to think much on it. I imagine arriving before nightfall, hoping for the best. But then again, things never work out the way they are meant to.

CHAPTER
V

IT FEELS GOOD TO BREATHE without restriction, despite the awful rancid smell of acid lingering along the road. It's the first time I've had my mask off since this morning. Fortune favors us, however small a reprieve it is, as we continue our journey through this cursed forest. And although the dread rain has stopped, we still face all mannerisms of insects. Particularly flies. With no choice but to leave the goggles on, the bugs splatter against our faces as the caravan passes through swarms hovering over decomposing carcasses. I find myself wiping away slime from my forehead and cheeks.

With the sun finally fallen, the light of the forest fades into an opaque onyx. The light seeping through branches barely escapes to the ground, black rain still shining on the rims of trees. I catch the occasional atter passing along branches as we rumble along. Remembering the pack chasing us earlier, I decide they are by no means threatening in small numbers. They screech and grind their teeth at us from the distance in disapproval, clinging to branches, staring at us with those white eyes. Maybe I am the only one disturbed by it, for Kronklich stares ahead, never breaking his gaze off the road, determined to get us to Widow before nightfall. I stare at him, amazed how the man never sleeps. With his flat regent hat tilted down, reins balancing loosely in hands, he chews a piece of ebon root between his teeth. Eyes wide and dilated, I know he is under its influence. It has the capability to sustain the hungriest of men. Even now, I hear his stomach rumbling louder than the turning wheels of the wagon and the grumbling of my own gut. But he presses on, not affected in the least.

Passing under the burning drops of after rain, the road begins to rise in elevation, putting more strain on the stallions, slowing the wagon. With the monotonous turning squeak of the wheels, we settle in for an incline out of the lowest point of the forest. Uncovering my hand, I examine the festering blackness spreading across the top. This hand is unlucky. Twice it's been burned in different ways. What is worse, without treatment, it will spread. I've seen men consumed by the black scars of the dread rain before. Bodies racked with pain. Suffering. The wish for someone to kill them. My hand burns horribly. I have rinsed it twice with melted snow, which only helps for a few minutes. As soon as the numbing cold dissipates, the pain comes right back.

I wrap my hand back up and try to think of something else. Tired from the pain and hunger, my mind slowly drifts off into nothingness as my head bobs about the caravan. After a time, my thoughts move to Diana and Dorian. The day I returned to Roland after the hunt and saw everything on fire. Fields. Markets. Homes. Wolfgang Manor, my home. It's been days since I've lost everything that mattered to me. Seems the less

I think about the past, the more clouded it becomes. But for now, it lingers. I curse my memories. I love my wife and son so much. I can see the courtyard view from my office window where I watched them speak together, Diana watching Dorian, Dorian swinging his sword. My dreams used to be so vivid, but not anymore. Joachim. Nester. They are among the others I recall. Meeting Nester at the gate of Albestan Church, asking questions while hungry bogarts lurked about. I laugh to myself but Kronklich continues staring ahead. How silly the clergy boy was in the presence of danger. He is dead now, of course, eaten by those horrible creatures. And why not? It is fitting. God has left us all. Left us here to rot amongst the damned. Some God. If he was here, how could he let Nester and the others die?

I soon find myself becoming intensely vexed at everything. Bronin. That bastard. He was a holy priest of the church and yet he was anything but holy. A betraying, backstabbing fuck. That's what he was. It was a relief when I found him in those godforsaken ruins, impaled on a spike, choking on his blood, drowning in vermillion soup.

A sudden jerk of the wagon stirs me from nostalgia. One after another, trees pass by, row after row. The sun is gone now. The last rays of its light tickled my face as the wagon charged on, yet my thoughts linger still. Manson. I failed him too. I remember the promise I made to the little boy after taking him from his mother. The mother I executed after she was bitten by a bogart. *I will keep you safe*, I whispered in the boy's tiny ear. But I didn't. Instead, my carriage crashed into a tree and I was flung off a ledge, down into the icy depths of the Faust River. I failed on all fronts. Having lost my own son is proof of that.

I look up at Kronklich. "You never told me what happened the day I plunged off the cliff. What became of Manson?"

Kronklich's stare never strays from the road. "We were overrun by the willdermen. Thirteen of them to be exact. After the carriage's right wheel caught a stump, time accelerated." Kronklich finally turns his head toward me. "I watched your limp body expel from the carriage as it overturned in a spiraling pitch. Before I could say your name, my mind went black." A bump causes his head to sway back and forth and he looks ahead again. "Funny, isn't it, how delicate the brain is? When I came to, some time had passed. It was nightfall and all manner of creatures were out. I searched through the wreckage, turning over splinters of wood and torn cushions. There was nothing. No sign of anything."

Kronklich wipes his fingers over his goggles, removing bug fluid from the lenses. "At first, I thought Bronin and Manson had fallen from the cliff too, but as I scoured the grounds, I knew better. There were tracks leading in all directions, some made by boots, some by paws. I knew I couldn't linger and had to act. So I did the only thing I could. I hunted." Kronklich pauses a moment, as if reliving the moment in his head. Mind focused, he continues staring at the road. "Tree after tree, I searched, looking within the dark grooves of the trunks, traversing deeper into the thickness of Cordova Woods, losing myself and my sense of direction. A broken twig, and I thought I was onto something. Trampled leaves, and I knew I was close. There was a point I thought I heard Manson crying in the dark and I followed his voice. Followed it until the voice turned to growls and the crying no longer whined through the woods." Kronklich raises his right hand with the reins, guiding the horses along a bend in the road. "Then the willdermen surrounded me. Maybe five or six to my one. Decent odds, wouldn't you say? I could only see the whites of their teeth gleaming in the moonlight passing through the branches. One by one, they came after me, and one by one, they lost their heads. I put a bolt through one skull. Broke the bones of another. Yet one of the bastards got up and ran away yelping, waking all manner of evil within the woods."

Kronklich takes a deep breath and continues, "I knew then I had to leave, get away before something really nasty came looking for me. After that, I pursued the only thing I knew I had to do. Carry on to Egleaseon's ruins and find Dorian." Still staring ahead, he glances at me again. Suddenly, a solemn look comes into his eyes. "I'm sorry, Tenor. I did all that I could."

Thunder rakes across the sky as darkness settles slowly over us. A gust of wind blows from the west and I know it will rain again.

Hunched over like two beggars, we drive on through torrential downpour, hoods drawn tight, masks shielding our faces. I think to myself we should have vitroled the horses when we had the chance, but stopping would delay us further. My son is out there, somewhere, tormented by vampires, held as their captive, drained of blood to keep him from retaliating, from resisting. I've got to save him. I've made a promise. I swore to her. My Diana. *I promised to save our son.*

I feel a tap on my shoulder and see Kronklich raise a gloved hand, pointing at the faint glow of orange light through the misty rain. He shouts over the deafening roar of the elements. "If I were a gambling man, which I'm not, I'd say that is probably Widow?"

Time seems to take forever, watching the faint glowing lights come closer, hovering in midair through the dark perpetual rain. The road snakes drastically back and forth as we approach. Gnarled tree after twisted roots passes us. Staring through the rain is disorienting. It isn't until we get just before the divided entrance to Widow's main gate that we realize just how far we've come. The echoing pang of the rain rings on the awning above us. It is deafening as we pull the wagon to a halt before a skinny man with his hand out stretched to grab the horse's bridle—a lantern glows dimly in the other. Falling loosely around his shoulders, most of his wiry hair is covered by the soiled black hood, which conceals half of his face. The other half, from what I can tell, is pockmarked and burnt black. The dread rain does wonders to the folk around here.

"It'll cost you a dauntess ta feed and drink the horses and give 'em a proper rub, aye?" says the wretched man leering at me from the ground. Most of his teeth are missing, rotted away from God knows what. Rainwater drips off the slick blackness of his coat, pooling at his feet with a resounding hiss. The horses stamp the muddy ground in discontent, snorting through their nostrils and chewing at their bits. "'Ere, 'ere, now, beasties. I'm more friendly 'an most folk in 'ese 'ere parts. 'Ink I'd eat cha? Bwhaha!" the man chortle's at his own joke.

Hardly amused, I rise from the riding basket and step down, my boots sinking into the saturated ground. Removing my mask, I stare the man in the face. "Medicine. I need medicine."

The man freezes, struck with fear or awe; I'm not sure. "M'lord—Wolfgang! So sorry—didn't know."

"Where!" I say in agitation. I don't have time for this. My hand is rotting away.

The man points feebly and I turn on the spot.

"Don't know any'ing about medicine, but don't worry, sir. I'll take care of your horses. No'ing to worry about 'ere. No, sir," says the man as I head north into the market area of Widow, Kronklich following close behind.

There was only one time I came to this ruined town, long ago on a desperate hunt to find one of my marks, a vampire known as Creed. He was a flighty bastard I chased through the south residential awnings made of wood and copper. He burst through people's homes, snatching innocent family members along the way to leverage trade for his freedom. Back then, I wasn't so formidable. I was weak to the vampire's influence, agreeing to let him go if he set his captives free. But I was wrong and more people died. Creed vanished for a time, forgotten for a spell. Waiting for a week in Widow and speaking to the locals, I almost believed Creed moved on. But then, like always, the vampire returned. He came back because of the hunger, which causes vampires to be careless. And so my second chance was upon me. I found Creed in an alleyway, feeding on a homeless man. Timing it right, I drove my stake through his heart and severed his head. In the end, after placing his head on a stake in the middle of town, I realized the brutality and *potential* of these devilish creatures. Creed had killed more than ten families in the town of Widow. There is no compromise with vampires. I learned the hard way. Always did.

Splashing through tiny rivers of dread rain seeping underneath the long covered path, I walk cautiously with each step, scanning over every unfortunate soul who calls this place home. Women sheltering their children pass by in rags that are just enough to keep the dread rain off of them properly. A man bent over a crate hardly notices me as he concentrates on its contents, an atter furiously screeching its frustration at the sharp stick prodding into its hide. Beyond the man, a wall covered in dark filleted meat stretches across with steel pins sticking out of it. A bucket of wet black skin rests at the edge of the man's area, setting the boundaries of his makeshift market.

I look out into the center of Widow. The rain pelts its patrons as they run across the giant opening, some of them walking, enduring its relentless torment. How anyone chooses to live here is beyond me. The south end consists of residential homes, if they can be called "residential." They are more like squares of wooden planks and tar-thatched roofs. The smell coming from that direction is horrible, a mixture of feces and urine diluted with the acid rain. The north half, faring not much better, is similar in state, riddled with leaking roofs and raw animal skins. The only difference is that the smell is not so revolting.

I pass under a connecting awning where most of the roof has dissolved, a weak point neglected from the application of vitrol, and pass through the threshold of a building. My scenery changes from cold wet rain to stuffy warm interior. Hundreds of candles line the way, dripping wax onto market booth tables lined with bottles and forest herbs. There are so many items to see in the tightly packed space. Everything from potions and elixirs to pastes and oils. My head begins to spin. The air is thick with smoke. Incense. Candles. Old women with pipes hanging from their lips. I am inclined to put my mask back on but a voice off to my left calls out, distracting me from the tickle in my throat.

"Beautiful necklace for your dead wife, my lord?" asks a middle-aged woman. She wears a brown-stained cloth wrapped over her head. It might have been yellow at one point.

"What did you just say?" I ask, unable to move from the spot. Shock has taken me.

"A beautiful necklace. Turquoise onyx for her. She has moved on."

Startled by her words, I make my way through the crowd, gently pushing peddlers aside, and lean onto her fabric-covered table, dark red with gold trim.

"How do you know that?" I ask in half anger and disbelief. Was she some gypsy witch?

The woman, seemingly unfazed, raises a hand and draws the sides of her hood closer to her jaw as if subconsciously hiding her face—definitely hiding something.

"Everyone knows this, my lord, all of the wretched know it. Same as Delore. Same as anywhere. Who doesn't know? News of the destruction of Roland travels fast. The evil. It spreads." Casting her hands before her, she emphasizes her words. Her accent is thick and she gazes at me with a contemptuous look. A look that says I am the one responsible for the curse befallen Decameron Forest.

Wretched woman indeed.

I look back at Kronklich, who is at another table, lifting teas from tins, sniffing at them and placing them back. I turn to face the woman again, and she is staring at me. Her eyes are bloodshot. Strands of hair hang loosely around her dirty face. She seems interested in me. Too interested. I am, after all, a lord, and why would I come to visit her here in this rotten hovel of Widow of all places? What is she hiding?

"Medicine. That is why I am here," I say, unwrapping my pus-covered hand from the soiled cloth Kronklich gave me. Bits of black skin come off and the pain is agitating. Some of the fleshy pink has begun to show.

"It is bad, no?" says the woman. "The dread has settled. In days to come, your hand will rot away. Lost forever."

"Yes, yes, I know," I say impatiently.

Again she gives me a contemptuous look. "I can help." She turns around to another table behind her. Jars of yellow and green liquids align across the front of it, while a tray raised on metal stilts holds little canisters stacked on one another. Taking one, she clicks the contraption with two fingers and raises its contents to her nose, taking a deep breath and releasing a sigh.

She smiles. "This is what you need." She hands it to me and already I can smell its overbearing aroma. It is pungent. Very pungent. I wrinkle my brow in protest. "It is horse urine."

Of course it is.

"This won't cure you. Only stop the corruption." She drops her hood down, revealing her face. I take a step back. "Nothing takes away the black scars."

Deep lines run the length of her face, spreading from her forehead down to her chin. One of her eyes is awash in white. A faint semblance of beauty lingers behind her skin, more in her bone structure, but what it once was is now gone.

"You need. Take it," she says. "No charge."

"I can pay for it," I say, reaching to my belt with my other hand, realizing I have no dauntess to pay with.

"No, my lord. It is on Madame Celeste. I have plenty horse-urine paste."

I do not argue with the woman as I nod my head and fade into the fog of the longhouse. She goes back to lighting incense as another woman, much older, appears from behind a curtain in the back and begins yelling at Madame Celeste. I walk away, scooping the paste from the canister, generously applying the urine paste to my dissolving hand. It is soothing and cool on contact, and for once, I sense a feeling of comfort. The smell allows me to blend in with the rest of the withering, scared locals.

I begin searching for Kronklich. He was by the teas but wandered off. Walking the only center aisle of the withering longhouse, I pass many booths, taking notice of the different wares for sale by women. Strange, there are only women and no men. Occasionally, a child skitters in front of me, paying no regard to my existence, but I press on. Among a plethora of holistic remedies and food purifiers, I find faceted crystals hanging from one merchant's table, an artist it seems. I admire the work as I pass, understanding that beauty is still to be had in some of the worst places in the world. I nod to the artist, as she sees me staring, and I hold out my bandaged hand, ensuring her I am not interested. Now is not the time to be leisurely browsing. *Kronklich.* I see him in the distance, handing a merchant woman undoubtedly dauntess coins and receiving a bundled-up cloth in exchange.

"This is not the time for window shopping," I say to Kronklich as I come near him, holding my hand before him to confirm the medicine was found.

"Window shopping, hardly. Here, this is for you." Kronklich extends the wrapped bundle to me. As I unwrap its contents, Kronklich continues, "Can you believe it? Of all those teas over there, not one of them was bergamot. Damn wretched woman. How do they expect to improve business in a place like this without bergamot?"

I toss Kronklich a look of irrelevance for his obsession with tea and then examine the purchased item.

"A new glove," says Kronklich, staring at me, waiting for a reaction. "I got these as well to help with lining the interior." He hands me a few pieces of white cloth, fresh and clean. I cannot help but wonder how he found sterile bandages in a place like this.

"Thank you," I say gratefully, wrapping my hand with a fresh dressing and sliding the new glove on. It will need a proper coating of vitrol before we leave Widow.

Moving out of the hot musty interior of the longhouse marketplace, we exit through the back, where the outside air pushes against our faces. The rain beats furiously against rickety awnings high above as we explore a makeshift workshop. Various projects lie in dormant repair, carriages waiting with broken steering shafts, cracked axels, and one of the most common sights, rotten wheels. They are usually the first to go when driving through the dread rain. Since it is late, it's no surprise all of the workers have gone home. Chisels hang from walls, hammers rest on anvils. Walking past a wooden bucket, I see the bottom is full of bent nails and splintered wood.

Unable to find an exterior path to avoid going back into the longhouse, we have no choice but to backtrack. I go to pass through the entrance threshold but suddenly stop. Kronklich is standing beside a particular carriage—not a carriage exactly—but a caravan wagon with wood panels painted red and black. For a moment, I am confused. What does he see? I follow him, walking around the wagon as if thoroughly inspecting damages like a worker. Within seconds, Kronklich's crossbow is out and poised at the caravan. That's when I notice what I did not see before, red diamonds painted inside a solid black rectangle, the same markings of our caravan. The same caravan used by—

"The Carnalreesee," says Kronklich suddenly. "They are here."

Reaching into my coat, I withdraw the four-bladed Bawaka from my belt, and turn it in my hands, acclimating the feel to my new glove. "Dorian!" I shout as I charge up the steps of the wagon. "Dorian!" I thrust a boot, splitting the wood at the frame of the door, and charge in, not caring who is there or what I will find. Falling over a large object, I spin around, frantically searching the small interior for any sign of Dorian or the enemy. Panting heavily, I raise the Bawaka above my head and listen. Nothing. Slowly, I investigate my surroundings, realizing I am alone. Kronklich stands in the decimated doorway, crossbow angled up, his hand running the course of the wooden panels. I had stumbled over a large wooden coffin resting in the center of the floor. Pulling a silver stake from my side, I motion to Kronklich. With a quick shove of the boot, the lid topples over, clattering to the floor, and I move in for the kill.

But the coffin is empty, and nightfall arrived hours ago. Lifting a golden mask with stag horns, I uncover a red robe as well, lying at the bottom. I remember all too well the horrors my son went through.

"Dammit!" I say, spitting a foul taste from my mouth. I rush from the wagon and navigate my way through the workshop. I hear Kronklich calling after me, but there is no time to wait. There might be a lead, someone who might know. Madame Celeste.

I enter back into the humid interior of the longhouse, the air no longer as thick as it had been with incense. With most of the people cleared from the aisle, passing through is easier. I can almost run. Tucking the Bawaka close to my chest, I keep it out. Just in case.

"Madame Celeste," I call out as I reach the table where her oils and pastes were laid out. "Madame?" A strange feeling comes over me as I stand before an empty table. Everything is gone. The oils, the pastes, even the red cloth with gold trimming. A woman nearby, much older than average, watches me in confusion. I turn, approaching her aggressively. Instantly her hands go up in defense.

"You. Did you see a woman here? Black lines on her face? Hood?"

The woman steps away from me, shaking her hands in distress, blurting out something in a language I cannot understand. A sickening sensation lands in the pit of my stomach.

Kronklich catches up to me with a worried look on his face. "What is it?"

Gripping the edges of the empty table, I bow my head in frustration, all the while enduring the lingering aroma of horse urine. "The woman."

Kronklich leans in close, keeping his questions secret with me. "Woman? What woman?"

I stare at the spot on the wooden table stained with residue. "Madam Celeste. She is gone."

CHAPTER VI

KRONKLICH DOESN'T SEEM TO UNDERSTAND what I'm talking about. "A woman you say? What did she look like?"

I look up from the table and scan the flow of women moving about. Some of them gather to look at me, the famous Lord Wolfgang. I stare back at them, confirming just how few men there are in this broken town.

Moving into the center aisle, I look back and forth, hoping to spot the gypsy woman known as Madame Celeste. I hold my hands out. "She looked like all of them," I say, pointing at each of the women as they pass by. I become desperate. "You there, excuse me, have you seen a man with a boy?" The woman keeps walking, pulling her hood tighter around her face. I try another. "Madame, excuse me—" No luck. They are intimidated by my presence. I'm running out of patience. I start calling out questions. "Anyone. Have you seen a man with a boy? Please." I try again and again. The candles on the walls seem to respond to my desperation, flickering violently from the air currents coming from outside. "Please! Anyone! A man—"

"I have seen a man," says a shaky voice.

I turn on the spot and see a decrepit woman. It is not Celeste, but a woman similar in appearance.

"Yes, I have seen a man," she says again with more confidence. Her accent is thick and she smells like burnt ash.

I want to shake her, force what she knows from her, but restrain myself. Looking down, Kronklich places a hand on me.

"And a boy? Have you seen a boy?" I ask in a calmer tone.

"No boy. Only a man," she says, struggling to find the words. "He came in carriage. Dress nice," she manages to add. "A foreigner, yes?"

"Where did you see him? Where did he go?"

She points in the direction of the southern residential port.

My hopes begin to rise. Even if Dorian isn't here, I could still catch one of the Carnalreesee. Interrogate him. Make him bleed.

"Thank you," I say to the peddling woman and dash from the marketplace, back to the gate where we arrived with the horses. Kronklich is desperate to keep up with me. Given the late hour, we pass the empty gate with no guard standing watch. Moving into the southern part of town, we run down long stretches of maze-like awnings. We run like demons with the storm raging along the edges of the roofs above us, water spraying at the hem of our coats, splashing through puddles collected in muddy ruts. People dash from our path, wondering at our sudden flight and desperation in the dead of night. While the wind howls, Kronklich follows my lead, and the two of us begin the long search. We pass rows of housing, mostly deserted with few residential women lingering about the columns of wood-planked apartments. The homes resemble cubes, small in nature, yet full of depth. I peer through residents' windows, glance down makeshift alleyways, and search rotted walls of abandoned homes. Distraught families sleep in their beds as we maneuver through the night. Kronklich has just as much luck as me, popping his head in out of doorways and standing at awning crossroads, pointing his crossbow discreetly.

I did not realize how much Widow has grown. Now almost double in size, its perplexity is beyond comprehension. So many turns. So many avenues. At one point, Kronklich and I nearly collide into one another, mistaking one another for the villain—his crossbow trained on me, my Bawaka ready to slit his throat. We both smirk.

I'm not sure how much time has passed. It feels like an eternity. The cold of the rain rises from the ground, forming an acid mist, a choking fog cooking the earth.

"Any luck?" I ask. My hood is pulled over my head, but the mask rests at my side.

"None," says Kronklich, still searching with his eyes. Urban or wilderness, he is the best tracker between the two of us. But even now, the hopes of finding a well-dressed man in this slum of a town seem unlikely. Impossible really.

I watch our breath escape from our mouths. Little clouds of mist exhale from our lips. Sweat drips down the groove of my spine. Curse all to hell. With each second that passes, the Carnalreesee is fading into darkness. Where is he? If only I had thought about it sooner. But the thought of the Carnalreesee coming here to Widow is a mystery to me. Why a town of miserable wretches? It doesn't make sense, and as I'm about to unfold my doubts to Kronklich, there is a terrible scream in the distance.

We have no need for words. We dash from the spot, watching ahead of us, preparing for the worst.

The screaming ensues as we get closer, passing under more awnings, more streets. I feel for the Hand of God at my waist as I ensure its security. I have the sinking feeling that I will need it again. I'm almost certain.

We reach the outside of one of the apartments, which is the same as all the rest. Only the perpetual screaming from inside allows us to detect which hovel is the correct one. There is a woman inside, crying hysterically as we crouch next to the door. I listen for other things. Movement. Scuffling. Anything to indicate the woman is not alone. But I hear nothing over her hysterical crying. Nodding to Kronklich, I kick the door open and enter as he follows right behind me, covering my back.

The woman howls at the sight of us, strange men barreling into her apartment, frightening her, no doubt. We head straight through the small apartment, passing upturned tables, broken chairs, and shattered glass. She is hysterical, calling out to us as if we should understand her intent.

"My boys! My boys!"

Each subsequent shout of hers gets louder. I try to calm her, motioning with my hands, but it's useless. On the floor, back against the wall, she thrashes her head back and forth like an asylum patient. One of her arms is twisted and broken at the center in such an unnatural way and her other arm cradles a man's head in her lap. The woman attempts to place fragments of the man's brain and skull back into the open crevice. Blood covers every part of her body. Hair. Face. Hands. She is delirious and unresponsive as I grip her face in my hands, looking into her eyes. She is in shock.

"My boys! He took my boys!" she says again, lifting her shattered arm in the direction of an open doorway. Sheer terror has taken her.

Inhaling a deep breath, I stand, staring at the depressing scene before me.

"Tenor, wait—" warns Kronklich, but it is too late. Already, I am moving from the room and into the next, following the woman's request.

Surrounded by a circle of unevenly stacked stones, a single fire across the room serves as the only visible light. The glow of red and orange embers causes dark shadows to dance along the walls and floor. Immense shades extend from every area not facing the light, particularly from four wooden beams extending up from the floorboards. From what I can tell, it's a simple room, possessing little furniture, except for two beds, one in each corner. I move into the room with the Bawaka raised before me, one hand on two of the handles, ready to lash out at any movement in a moment's decision.

"It was so simple," comes a voice looming out of the shadows. "Give me one and I'll be on my way. But no. They had to be difficult."

The voice seems to come from everywhere.

Positioning my steps with caution, I stealthily traverse the room in a circle, looking up into the dark crevices of the rafters in the ceiling.

"One son is better than no sons, I say. But she wouldn't listen. Oh well, doesn't matter."

From the corner of my eye, I notice the light from the other room blotted out for a moment. Kronklich has entered.

"It's so difficult to come across good blood these days," says the voice casually.

There is a sickening crunch from high above. Vision limited, I search the room frantically, but cannot find the source of the voice. Kronklich aims his crossbow back and forth, flipping it about in different directions, trying to get a shot, but at what?

"So impure is the blood of whoring mothers. Man's blood is sour." There is a moment of silence and I hear the rattling of liquid in the speaker's throat. "Now, children's blood," says the voice in my ear, "is the sweetest blood."

I spin around, swinging the Bawaka blade hard into a wooden support beam next to me, nearly severing it in half. Laughter mocks me from every facet of the room. I feel something warm and wet tapping on my shoulder. Daring to look up, I see two sets of eyes staring down at me, unblinking, swaying in the dim glow of the embers, arms and hands extending as if requesting my help. Stepping away, I see they are two boys hanging from their feet. Their backsides have been torn open, spines removed like the ones from the caravan camp. Blood drains from their lifeless forms.

"What are you doing here?" I shout in anger, desperately searching the rafters for any sign of movement.

"What am I doing here?" the voice counters with sarcastic rhetoric. "You mean, what am I doing here in this shithole. Well, for starters, I wouldn't be here if it weren't for the wheel breaking on the wagon. Thought I'd grab a little snack before moving on. One does get terribly hungry." The voice speaks sincerely as if justifying the murder of two innocent boys.

Trying to distract him, I keep asking questions. "Where are the rest of your kin? Where are they headed?"

The voice laughs. "My kin? You are so archaic, *vampire hunter*. What is this, ancient times?" The voice laughs again. "You must be referring to we, the Carnalreesee. It just so happens we are headed to Sunstone."

The destination doesn't make sense. Sunstone is the holy city. "Why there? What do you intend to do with my son? Answer me!" But as the words leave my lips, I realize what the Carnalreesee is saying. Remembering Bronin, remembering the holy order's corruption. All of Sunstone could be under some influence. *But who? What sect? The clergy? The Archbishop? Certainly not his Holy Grace!*

"Oh, Wolfgang, always so demanding. So many questions!"

I signal to Kronklich to take a shot, but he signals back that he can't.

"I see you brought the Hand of God with you. That's unfortunate. Things wouldn't be the way they are if it weren't for that fucking thing." There is a pause in the blowing of wind. "So the rumor is true, then. You killed Caesar with it. He was a damn fool. I would have loved to see the look on his face when he turned back into a human."

"I can arrange the same for you," I say calmly. Hearing the creaking of wood, I see the Carnalreesee moving, the reaction I intended.

"Can't say that I'd like that," says the voice. "You see, I like killing very much, and being immortal, well, has its perks. To taste all the bloods of the world," says the figure with an air of satisfaction, "eternally…that is something worth being dead for."

Somewhere in the dark, I know the Carnalreesee is smiling. I need to draw it out. "You hide in the shadows like a coward. Come face me, demon spawn."

The rafters above groan in response. Dust trickles down around me. The rafters bend at the same time, indicating how fast the monster's movement is. Then the figure seems to float down from the ceiling to the floor, landing next to the fire pit. Red and orange light highlights its features. What appears to be standing before us is a man dressed in elegant clothing. Top hat. Black vest. Black slacks to go with black polished shoes. A frock coat embroidered with blue to cover his chest. Long blond hair flows down around his shoulders. He pushes some of it to the side with a blood-stained glove and in the other hand, a long golden scepter extends to the floor, a gold-colored ball at its top. An immaculate white face smiles back at us with perfect teeth. The hat, tipped forward, hides the Carnalreesee's eyes.

"Demon spawn?" asks the man as if offended. "How unoriginal." His bloody hand drops to his side, running the course of two freshly eviscerated spines hanging from the side of his belt. "I am going to give you the honor of knowing that it was Scepter who killed you. Not just yet, however," he says smiling. He pulls a strange-looking dagger from his belt, similar to the one Caesar tried to use on me at the cliff side. "First, I will need your blood."

Kronklich fires. The bolt thumps into a wooden beam as it passes straight through Scepter's body with ease. Was it a trick of the eye? Scepter's appearance next to me confirms my assumption. He brings his golden rod to meet my face but I duck in time. The wooden beam behind me explodes from the impact. Scepter follows through with another swing, seemingly to intimidate rather than kill, as I jump back. The smile on his face lingers as he steps forward elegantly, like a dancer in a play, twirling his scepter like a baton in the dim light.

"Do you know how I got the name Scepter?" he asks. "I love to bludgeon the heads of men. Their fragile heads explode like confetti."

As I back away trying to think of a way to get to Scepter, Kronklich fires another shot to draw his attention.

Scepter catches the bolt in midair and snaps the shaft like a twig. "Please excuse my obsession for killing. It is something I'm rather good at, you see?"

Kronklich charges forward, drawing the blade from his cane. Lashing out in a frenzy, Scepter deflects every sword technique by Kronklich, countering every lunge, remise, and beat. With his golden mace, Scepter uses a riposte, smacking Kronklich just underneath the elbow. The counter move sends Kronklich's blade sliding across the wooden floor. Kronklich staggers back, shaking out his arm, a surprised look on his face. Scepter presses, spinning his golden stick in a whirl of gleaming metal. "This is Malice, and he craves blood as much as I do."

I raise the Bawaka and throw it just as Kronklich sidesteps two of Scepter's crushing blows. One of the blades explodes through Scepter's chest, paralyzing him momentarily. With the sudden opportunity, Kronklich lunges forward, using the crossbow to swipe Scepter's immaculate face. Blood spurts from Scepter's mouth as the vampire tumbles to the floor, gripping his chest and rolling, stopping just at the base of the fire pit.

Scepter's lips quiver. "It's been a while since I've had a real fight—I'll give you that." With one hand, he reaches behind his back and pulls the Bawaka free, sliding the blade from his chest and dropping it to the floor as if it were a toy. He staggers forward, clutching his chest. The Bawaka pierced his torso and severed his heart. He should be dead. It's not possible he's still breathing. I pull the Hand of God from my belt and squeeze it tightly in the palm of my hand. This is the only way.

I emerge from the shadows of the room, charging forward to bring down the Hand of God to meet Scepter's bleeding face. But the vampire is aware. He is powerful. The Bawaka merely suspended him, a temporary paralysis. Scepter catches my hand and twists, avoiding the holy relic. Sharp pain shoots up my arm, forcing me to release the artifact, my only chance of killing him. It clatters against the floor as Scepter backhands the side of my head, sending flashes of light through my vision. It is like an explosion inside my head, a numbing freeze that shocks my brain. My vision wavers as I crash to the floor. I see the Hand of

God disappear into the embers of the fire pit. Small flames ignite over it in response like a chemical reaction. *No!* My head screams but my body cannot move.

Arm outstretched, I stare at my open palm, trying to move my hand, and some of my fingers move. But Scepter seizes his opportunity. With his golden scepter braced against my throat, he brings forth the dagger, never breaking his smile, never hesitating. But as I feel his body tense to plunge the extraction dagger into my stomach, he is seized from behind. A pair of arms, weaponless, embraces Scepter.

I struggle to get feeling back into my body, rocking myself, squeezing my hand, pumping blood back into my arm. Scepter stands, swaying his body back and forth to throw Kronklich from his back. "You are like a damn monkey," says Scepter with agitation in his voice. I hear Kronklich yelling over his words, but there is the smashing of wood and a cry of pain from Kronklich, and I know he is in trouble.

The feeling in my legs starts to return and I begin inching my way across the ground. The Hand of God. I have to get it out of the fire. My fingers claw along the planked floor, pulling at the warped notches.

"Really. This is how it's to be, then? You two are pathetic."

My hand clasps around a warm piece of wood. I feel Scepter grab the back of my coat.

"Enough! Time to collect!"

As Scepter raises me from the ground, I pull the wood from the fire. Lashing out at him, the flame on the other end catches fire to his pants, and the whole of his leg ignites in a flash.

Scepter screams.

Assaulting his legs with his own hands, he tries to extinguish the flames. His efforts are useless, for fire clings to vampires like glue. Using another piece of wood, I frantically dig into the fire pit while Scepter flaps about the room, setting the walls, the floors, and the beds on fire. The Hand of God is buried. I must save it from utter destruction. It is my only chance against the Carnalreesee. Through scattered ash and dying embers, I find nothing. For a moment, I contemplate jamming my hand into the ash, but I stop. Too many times I have been burned. Too many times I have suffered in the name of God. Staring into the rising flames, I see the edges of metal exposed in the bright light. Using the plank of wood, I fish the cursed relic from the heat, sending it skidding into the shadows.

Scepter dances about the children's room as the flames spread from his legs to his arms. He howls and screams, trying to find an exit, and suddenly breaks through the wall of the room, exposing a new path to the pouring rain outside.

CHAPTER
VII

THERE IS NO TIME. I have to stop Scepter.

"Kronklich, get the wagon!" I shout as I douse the Hand of God with a bucket of water sitting next to the fire pit. It hisses in response, steam rising from its surface. The room begins to catch fire and soon it will be entirely engulfed. I grab the Hand of God with my new glove and realize it protects not only against the cold, but the heat as well.

Donning my mask, I flee from the burning apartment through the new passage Scepter left. It is not hard to follow his trail, for carnage lies in his wake. Broken walls. Shattered beams. Women and children scream as Scepter bursts through one partition after another. Torrents of dread rain berate the innocent families inside. The wail of suffering drowns away in my ears as I focus ahead, never losing sight of my target.

It is hard to see through my mask as I leap over dinner tables and storage chests, pushing off of doorways and shoving people aside. In some cases, I jump over little children, never slowing my pursuit, running faster with revitalized adrenaline. I am ready to strike in an instant, despite my surroundings and distractions. Scepter is just ahead of me. Looking to my right where the open courtyard separates North Widow from South Widow, I see people fleeing in horror with no consideration of the rain; confusion begets them all. Uncertainty and fear runs rampant. Through the pouring rain, I see Kronklich driving the horses from atop our caravan wagon. Steam puffs from their nostrils like hot geysers. Kronklich stays parallel with me in the distance as I chase after Scepter.

Each time Scepter breaks through a wall, the sound is like an explosion. Splintered wood bursts from every direction as Scepter tosses obstacles into my path. I head him off from one of the apartments—passing along a side path, leaping between the connecting points of two awnings, and landing myself directly in his way.

Scepter breaks through another wall and does not see me. Crouching low, I grab his arm and pull hard, forcing him to collide with the ground. But his power is extraordinary, and he recovers instantaneously, breaking free of my grasp and rolling his body along the ground. With movement smoother than water, he brings about his golden scepter, Malice, and smashes out an awning support beam, only to follow through with another. This time, the blow hits me dead center in the torso. Feeling the impact through my proofing, the pain is gut-wrenching. The wind in my lungs is gone in an instant. I drop to the floor, gasping for air, arm and hand extended out to him to shout, but no words come and he never stops. I watch him disappear behind a bend, and then nothing.

He is gone.

Writhing on the floor like some pathetic worm, I bend at the waist, trying to subdue the rising pain in my abdomen. I hear the approach of splashing wheels and feel the horses' breath behind me.

"Tenor! Are you all right?" comes Kronklich's nasally voice. In moments I feel his hands on me and turns me over. He stares at me with his mask but I cannot see his eyes.

"Which way?" he asks while lifting me by the trim of my coat. I find it hard to speak. "Which way?" he asks again.

I manage to point as he assists getting me onto the wagon.

"Good! That's very good! C'mon, then. We almost have him now."

I want to laugh at the absurdity of his words but it hurts too much. Easing myself into the riding basket, I barely have my leg all the way in before Kronklich sends the horses into a bucking start.

"I think I have a good idea what the bastard is trying to do," says Kronklich, forcing the horses to veer hard to the right suddenly. Crashing through walkways and popping awnings from their bindings, Kronklich guides us down a destructive path of alleyways and rutted grounds. The suspension of the wagon groans under the stress of each bump, and the sides of the wagon scrape along apartment walls. We pass windows with glowing orange lights. Shutters snap from foundations as the wagon plows through the braces. Townsfolk lean their heads out in discontent, cursing the rain and us.

"Kronklich! Are you trying to kill us?" I shout over the carnage as the wagon nearly cleaves the head off an innocent bystander.

"Absolutely not!" says Kronklich, dodging a shutter from smashing his head. "We are onto him!"

Something inside me doubts his statement when, suddenly, I hear the "Whoa!" of Kronklich's voice and the wagon slides across the muddy ground. In a matter of seconds, we come to a halt. The horses stamp and mud splatters our masks. People in their homes emerge from their porches to stare at us, some of them shouting obscene words in frustration. The rain roars around us as I climb next to Kronklich, sharing the driving seat with him. Kronklich is dead still. He grips the reins in his hands as if anticipating the start of a race. I look around, searching for some sign of Scepter. All I see is a destroyed wall, a shattered awning, and the bells of some nearby goats. But I find nothing in our immediate vicinity.

I question Kronklich through the mask. "What is it?" From all the breathing and rapid movement, the familiar acrid smell of Widow returns through the breathing apparatus.

"Wait for it." Kronklich pauses. "Wait for it," he says again.

Has Kronklich gone mad?

"Wait for it."

"Wait for what?" I ask.

"The sound, of course."

There is only the noise of rain pinging off the awning sheets of metal and the gushing of small rivers running at the hooves of the horses. Those who were on their porches have gone back inside, their interest fading with the pale light of morning.

"What is there to hear?" I ask, staring about us, eyeing all the places a vampire could hide. But there is nothing. Only rows of apartments in disheveled states. "I hear nothing."

"Precisely!" says Kronklich in an aggressive whisper. It is an odd sight, watching Kronklich turn to me, a man in a mask with a flat hat. "He has to think we are gone."

"You mean trick him?" I ask, perturbed by his spontaneous mode of action. "What makes you think Scepter will fall for it?"

Kronklich raises a gloved finger to his mask. "Do you hear it?"

"No, I don—"

Off in the distance—there is no mistake, I hear the whinnying horses over the incessant rain. Before I have the chance to confirm with Kronklich, a scream of sheer terror pierces the air.

"There!" shouts Kronklich, cracking the reins, sending the wagon into a sudden lurch. At the same moment, another carriage pulled by a team of two horses explodes from the side of a large building nearby. Pieces of wood tumble out into the mud-soaked ground. Chickens scatter in all directions from the barn as a figure wrapped in a black cloak and top hat drives off with supreme skill. Lanterns sway along its backside with each bump, making it easy to spot through the hazy rain.

Crack! Kronklich whips the horses furiously. *Crack!* If he whips them any harder some of the vitrol might come off. But as he whips them again, and the horses move even faster, he turns to me reassuringly. "Not to worry, my dear boy! These beasts have seen worse days!" Kronklich stands with crouched legs as our speed gains. The gusts grow stronger with each swell and beating of the wind. We are nearly sideways, as the storm has intensified. I finger the Hand of God at my side, reassuring its proximity to me, reassuring myself that I still have a chance at destroying this Carnalreesee. This *Scepter.*

Scepter's carriage charges forward through hellish rain as our slower wagon follows pursuit. Though we're significantly slower and carrying more weight, Kronklich drives the horses to the point of no return. Our load has to be lightened.

Standing up, I grip the side rails to the riding seat and begin to step down toward the back of the wagon.

"Here," says Kronklich, putting the reins in my hands. "You drive."

The suddenness of his intention catches me off guard and I accidentally pull one of the reins. The team and wagon veers off to the left, nearly sending us into oblivion. The wheels rattle harder at the edge of the road.

"Keep her steady," says Kronklich, who seems not in the least bothered. Bending down somewhere behind me, I cannot see what he is doing. As he comes back up, there is a loaded crossbow in his hands. "Right then, keep her straight and true," he says. Patting my shoulder, he disappears to the back. I know we are too far for Kronklich to take a shot, but at the rate the horses are working, they will get us closer soon enough. Pulling right and left, I guide the oversized caravan wagon through the twists and turns of Decameron Forest. Looking ahead, I see Scepter headed for a tree. *Is he mad?* Yet no sooner do I ask the question, the vampire veers his team of horses and carriage at the last moment. One of his wheels hits a rock in the road, sending the back end up. Shovels and planks of wood fly out the back as he regains control. Scepter's ability at driving is stiff, sporadic, and suicidal.

Still focusing on driving, I recall our conversation back in Widow, *the rest of the Carnalreesee were headed to Sunstone, and Dorian was the driving force behind their momentum.* Scepter is headed for Sunstone as well.

"We can't let him reach Blood Mountain Pass!" I shout over the roar of wheels and rain.

"Of course," says Kronklich as his bow retracts and a bolt goes flying. It sails through the gap between both transports, yet falls short.

"Get closer!" yells Kronklich.

I give the reins another crack and the horses respond with more power. The wagon lurches again and Kronklich's body sways, yet never breaks stance. He pulls the string back again and loads another brass-tipped bolt. It strikes the wood framing next to Scepter's head with a dull *thwack!*

Scepter glares back at us. His hat covers all of his face except his chin, which is protected by his frock coat. I watch him crack his reins more, encouraging his mares to press on.

"The horses can't take this pace much longer. We will lose him altogether!" I shout, unsure if Kronklich hears me.

Another bolt ejects from the bow barrel and there is a loud smash of breaking glass. One of the lanterns spills its contents. Fire breaks out along the back of the carriage, blocking my view of Scepter. Kronklich fires another shot, striking the second lantern, knocking the metal frame from its hook. More flames erupt. If we cannot stop him, the fire will.

But Scepter never relents as the chase continues. With daybreak near, the gray light of the rain gets brighter. I dig my boots into the notches of the driver's basket, snapping the whip again, chasing the fireball on wheels. Where will Scepter hide? Where can he go? With his carriage on fire, he is doomed one way or another. Suddenly, I am caught in a black smoke screen and my vision is compromised. Chancing it, I guide the wagon slightly off the path only to pull hard the reins at the last second, missing a group of thick firs.

Through the gray mist, I see the large formation of rock rising from the thinning trees. Cornwall's Bluff. It marks the crossroads leading up to the high town of Delore or down to the valley of Blood Mountain Pass. The brooding rock gets closer and closer as the horses head forward. The fiery carriage slows significantly and our wagon catches up. The enormous fireball veers toward Blood Mountain Pass, toward Sunstone, the holy city. If Scepter reaches the pass, his carriage, despite the flames, will survive the treacherous descent. Our wagon will not, however. It will break into thousands of pieces of brittle wood.

Rounding another bend, Cornwall's Bluff comes into full view. A darkening shadow casts to the left of its face. With Scepter running his team straight for Blood Mountain Pass, and me directly behind him in close pursuit, there is no choice but to pull back on the reins as Scepter's carriage suddenly veers to the left with no warning. Two of his wheels lift off the ground as it arcs about, fishtailing out of control. I cannot pull the reins any harder, as the black stallions neigh with resistance, trying to follow suit after the burning carriage.

All of Blood Mountain Pass has vanished under a gushing river of mud. It rages with impassible fluidity. Red water washes down the side of the bluff with ferocity, mixing with large chunks of coagulated earth. It is a sure sign of winter's arrival.

Scepter struggles to keep control of his carriage as the wheels come down with a force, both snapping at the axles, and the carriage drops to one side, scraping along the ground like a wounded animal. Swerving left and right, there is nothing Scepter can do. The horses and carriage careen off the side of Cornwall's Bluff as does Scepter. I hear his voice screaming, cursing the air all around us, as he spins and turns hundreds of feet down, corkscrewing into a fate of deadly rocks and morning sunlight.

DAY SIX

CHAPTER
VIII

I WATCH AS THE LAST pieces of burning wood tumble down the mountainside, the remains of Scepter's carriage bursting among the rocks and disappearing beneath a sea of mist. If only I had said more. Asked more. I would have been closer to knowing the truth about Dorian. What exactly the Carnalreesee plan to do with him. But the opportunity has run its course and I seem to be out of options. My inquisition has abruptly come to a halt. The only lead being the city of Sunstone. They want to take him there, but for what? I have failed yet again, my love. I was onto something—a small ray of light in the vast world of horrible darkness. It is unforgiving and treacherous. And Dorian. Poor Dorian. I have this sinking feeling that—

I stare into the vast openness before me, out into the cold mist floating off the side of the bluff. My soul feels the same way, hovering over a chilled void. Aimless. Lost.

Using the trunk of a tree for support, I lean from the ledge, scanning the side of the cliff, looking farther down, as far as the mist will allow me to see. I wait at the edge, wondering if, any moment, Scepter will come soaring up, his blond hair whipping about his face and blood dripping from the corners of his mouth.

"I do not think he will return," says Kronklich, minding the horses. A light snow begins to fall as he tries to recover their state of shock. Steam seeps from their nostrils and froth drips from their mouths. They stamp the newly formed snow, mashing it into small puddles of mud and water. "There is nothing out there but barren rock and snow. If the fire doesn't kill him, he will perish in the snow-light."

Snow-light. Sunlight refracted from the snow. The effects of it are devastating to the vampire's flesh. I've never seen its effects in person but read about it in journals.

"You're right, Kronklich," I say, feeling fatigue washing over my body again. "There is no hope for him. Justice is served." My eyes wander to the bluff with its churning water. The red clay and rock seeps down the mountainside, engulfing the entire pass, sledging the road and into the valley. The way is now a river, blocked for winter. Scepter mentioned the Carnalreesee going to Sunstone. This was the only pass leading to the Great Carpella Road, which serves as the connecting vein for the Cordova Mountains. The only direct passage from the valley of Roland to the valley of Sunstone.

With masks off, our voices lose their nasally sound. Breathing in the fresh air, it feels good to be rid of them, to taste the cold crisp day without the acid at the tip of the tongue. Over my shoulder, the edge of Decameron Forest hangs in the distance. Its foreboding boundary of darkness lingers like a dark snake, hissing from the falling rain, waiting for those to venture into its domain. I have no plans of going back there, to melt away within its torturous realm.

Taking another deep breath, I try to calm my nerves. I look into the blotted-out sky, the cold sun doing its best to warm the ground below the cloud cover. It is a cruel fate—this hand I have been dealt. A piece of information taunts me like the devil in the distance. I know where my son is but have no means of getting to him.

Standing at the churning mudslide, I watch the brown and red swirls mix with one another, spinning into whirlpools of foam. I am useless and directionless on this side of the river. There is nothing to do now. What can I do? I have an arsenal of weapons at my disposal, but for what? I remember how the Bawaka pierced through Scepter's chest like paper, yet it did nothing.

I pull the Hand of God from my belt and hold it next to the Bawaka blade, comparing them, staring at them as if they will talk to me. How similar they are in size and shape, one proportionate to the other. Abandonment and frustration cause me to raise my arm back, the Hand of God dangling between my fingers. How very much I would like to be rid of the foul artifact, this little thing that's caused so much trouble.

"Raahhhhhh!" I scream in frustration. But something stops my hand. An unseen force with power greater than my own. I sink to my knees on the muddy bank, saturating my pants with cold water. Diana. My Diana. Is she back? I remember a time before, a similar instance when I stood at the edge of sanity within that darkness of Egleaseon's ruins, when blackness encompassed me like a veil and there was no light. I stood there watching the water's edge, much like I am now, losing my mind and sanity, vanishing away with the pale glow of fog.

I try to compose myself, my body hunched over at the edge of light and darkness, where Decameron Forest comes to an end and the gray-fogged sky fills its foreboding boundaries with dreary light.

I sense Kronklich as he comes to kneel beside me. His face is straight and unbending, a serious Kronklich, which is so unlike him.

"So. She is back, then," says Kronklich, never breaking his gaze from the churning mud.

Disbelief washes over me. Had he seen my beloved Diana the same as I once had?

"What are you talking about?" I ask, feigning my ignorance.

"It's good to know not all is lost within you," says Kronklich . "Love never dies, they say. The flame keeps burning. Such is the case now. Use the gift she gave you, Tenor. Love. It is more powerful than you know." His eyebrows furrow. "At times, when all seems lost, sometimes everything is lost. But. Now is not one of those times." Kronklich's gaze shifts to something far in the distance, beyond the edge of the forest.

"Kronklich," I begin. "You aren't making any sense. You've gone too long without sleep."

"Nonsense. Don't deflect. She's with you," he says, turning and looking at me. "That's good." He smiles and rises from the embankment. "We need all the help we can get."

Before I have a chance to say something more, he is back to tending the horses. I want to tell Kronklich that Diana is not just a memory, but real, that I've seen her and spoken to her, and kissed her and touched her.

I stop myself.

How could he believe me? She is dead. Dead as carrion in the road.

Death is final.

What I saw in the ruins, real or not, is something I'm not ready to share.

"C'mon, then," says Kronklich, hopping onto the wagon and bringing the horses around to the edge of the embankment. He looks down at me from atop the riding post. "We have your son to save."

I look at him with absurdity. "We can't drive Blood Mountain Pass. It's not possible."

"What other choice is there?"

There is a weathered wayward sign planted at the base of the crossroads. Two signs depicting familiar directions. I have been down both roads, but only one of them I dread traveling.

"There is another way," I reply reluctantly, pointing at the sign. "Delore."

Kronklich looks at me blankly. "Delore? You vowed never to return there."

"I know. But like you said, what choice is there?"

"Seems there is none."

"Indeed."

Memories flood me like a plague as I remember my time spent in Delore, arriving as a single man and leaving betrothed. Old Man Dora, the town blacksmith, hated me. Since the first time I laid eyes on his daughter, he was against me. Slandering my family name. Cursing the day I arrived. He harbored beliefs about hunters, that we were the reason so many people died, that hunters like me upset the natural order of things. Natural selection. But I tried reasoning with him, explaining monsters weren't natural in the world, and all he would do was laugh at me, tinkering around with his useless trinkets, ending our conversations with the strike of his hammer. I stayed my course, could not relinquish my desire, and eventually left with what he and I both cherished most. Diana.

"You mean to ride the Iron Carriage, don't you?" asks Kronklich.

I look at him blankly, my thoughts of Diana still lingering.

"It's the only steam engine in the Cordova Mountains, where passage by rails is deemed safe only three out of the four seasons."

"The very one."

"You know the fourth season is upon us," says Kronklich with an air of doubt. "The rails will be frozen, the wheels seized, and it's engineer left doubting. Not to mention the large glacial landslides known for burying entire villages. Remember those?"

"Yes, the risks are there."

A cloud of silence embraces us both for a moment. "Splendid!" says Kronklich, suddenly smiling. His nose and cheeks are rosy as he extends his hand to help me onto the caravan. "Let us embrace risk!"

CHAPTER
IX

THE JOURNEY UP THE MOUNTAIN path toward Delore is nothing short of cold winds and eagle cries coming from the Cordova Mountain peaks. The more we ascend, the dryer the air and the harder the ground become. Twice we are forced to circumnavigate fallen trunks of dead trees, dry-rotted from the inside.

The intense cold and lack of sunlight in the shadow of the mountain force us to pull our cloaks tighter around our shoulders, buckling forward to block the wind. In the distance, I hear the chime of icicles, nature's ever-reminding presence of winter.

It's been three days since I last saw Dorian, and my heart aches terribly for him. He's out there in the freezing cold somewhere, on his way to Sunstone, a prisoner to those treacherous fiends. How long would it take them to reach the great white city before it was too late? I still can't wrap my head around it. The meaning behind it. The confusion. Why my son? Why him? The Carnalreesee want my blood. Why not kill me instead? Why taunt me? The same four words enter my mind since the first time they were mentioned by Bronin and more recently by Caesar.

Blood of the father.

The words emit shivers like the cold all around me.

At midday I see the first lamppost marking the way to Delore. With its glass panes frosted over in ice, and the snow collected at the top mount in large clumps, evidence of the candle inside burns no longer. Poles made of bronze, I begin counting them, anticipating how many we will pass before reaching adequate warmth and shelter. My body aches with the cold. Fatigue has settled in, and I know Kronklich must be suffering far worse. He hasn't slept for two days and two nights. I watch him chewing on ebon root as he passes it into his mouth, forgetting the time, losing himself. The drug is going to kill him if he doesn't stop.

I am about to warn him of its harmful effects when I see the white smoke of cooking fire rising through the snow-covered trees. Everything is so bright in the refracting light of the ice. I raise my hand to shade my eyes from the glare. Gently, Kronklich brings the black stallions to a trot, adjusting the speed as to not alarm the townsfolk of our approach. Seldom do they receive visitors, living so high up in the mountains. The unwelcoming journey is far from any tourist's desire.

Unlike Widow, the outskirts of Delore are much different. We pass strong-looking men swinging heavy-ended axes. They split wood methodically while spitting over their shoulders. Each stroke cleaves a whole log in two, proof that strength lies in the hard-working class of this town. They glare at us with caution as the wagon bounces along, its creaking suspension bringing us unwanted attention.

The deeper we travel into Delore, the more our environment changes. Wooden cabins surrounded by fields of white. Cobblestone walls stacked high on to second stories. The tops of trees stick out from the thick snow. Bronze lampposts appear more frequently. Carriages with large black canvasses pass by, their drivers minding the side of the road. The road itself is riddled with ruts and holes from the constant wear of passing wheels and slush.

"Why do you think they use bronze for the lampposts?" asks Kronklich, speaking for the first time since we entered the town.

"I suppose to prevent replacing them all the time," I say. "Bronze slows the corrosion process."

Patting out his regent hat, Kronklich gazes about, seemingly intrigued by the quaint town. "Yes. Quite understandable. But where do they get the material? Everything is very bronze."

"You forget this is a mining town," I continue. "Most of the work is done in nearby caves. There is an abundance of copper and tin alloys, but neither of them holds well in the snow. That's why they mix the two to make bronze. It's the next best metal compared to steel." A driver pulling ore in a wagon passes us. "Bronze is the driving force of Delore, its commerce. Always has been.

"I remember visiting the taverns at night long ago, nights when I couldn't be with Diana. Most of the patrons where hard-creased workers. Miners with their pickaxes, drinking their aches and pains away from the day's intense labor. They taught me more than I needed to know about ore."

"'Tis a rugged lot, this town is," says Kronklich, sucking his teeth on the ebon root.

We ride through the main road of town, meeting more traffic than ever before. Seems anyone who can afford to stay out of the cold ensures it. Few people walk the snowy banks, and the few who do are wrapped in all manner of clothing. Men with top hats and thick black coats, women in long black dresses, thick woven shawls covering their pretty buns. It feels good to be around civilization again, even though it seems no one wants to talk. In fact, our presence in town seems to go unnoticed altogether. The people of Delore can't be bothered with the time of day. Maybe the cold has dulled their sense of decency. It was not like this last time I was here.

As the wagon turns along a bend, the center square comes into full view through the light snow flurry. Patches of red brick peak through the snow-covered rooftops of gray stone and mortar. Cones reach high into the sky, tapering to sharp points like fingers digging out of the snow. We pass a bank house, a butcher shop, and street-front inns, but the building I seek lies beyond this common area, past the slow trickling river, carving its way underneath the Hammond Bridge, past the white open field of Travesty Park. City Hall stands looming in the distance three stories high. Lined with countless windows, it is a sight to admire.

"I don't see a church," says Kronklich as he guides the black stallions onto the circle road of Travesty Park. Their hooves clomp along the cobblestones, matching the other carriages passing by.

"There never was one," I say, watching a large wooden cross move past us. Situated in the center of the park, it looms above, towering over everything in the square, higher than the trees, higher than the lampposts. Some people crowd around its base, huddling together, keeping warm. I notice two men placing logs at the foot of the cross, stacking them neatly and carefully as if the pieces of wood might break. Some of them look our way as we pass, staring at us with grim faces. I realize my fingers trace the iron bars on my belt, the Hand of God fastened securely to my side.

"Such happy people," says Kronklich sarcastically under his breath.

Despite the freezing cold, the smell of cooking meat lingers, forcing my stomach to churn. We would benefit from a decent meal and some rest. But the matter at hand is dire. Securing passage out of the mountains is crucial to finding my son. The train is the only way.

As the wheels of the wagon creak over Hammond Bridge, I hear the flapping of banners overhead. Marked in colors of black and red, diamond shapes decorate the flags. The familiar insignia of Delore is displayed all over the square. Wreaths made from rose stems cover the railing as we pass, preserved in frozen decorum. I cannot help to think some festival is being planned, and at the moment, I speak nothing of it. Kronklich gazes at the banners and wreaths, chancing a fake smile every now and then to let me know he is thinking the same.

Through a grove of leafless trees and cracked benches, we pull up alongside the massive City Hall building. Its three stories look down on us like a monstrous cave, covering us in its shadow. A circular fountain pool lies at the center of the one-way drive, circling the entire grounds. The water, still and flat, was probably one of the first things to freeze over when winter arrived. Countless carriages in their uniform black surround it now, nearly blocking it completely from sight.

All manner of people come and go freely from the oversized oak doors, pushing out from the inside as they pass through. Businessmen carrying ledgers are among the most present with their hair pulled back tight, tucked under top hats of varying colors. Climbing down from the wagon, we approach the building from across the drive, passing the important-looking men without so much a glance. Unlike the folks in the square, they simply move out of the way and continue on, some with a well-dressed lady on their arm, some with another man.

"Excuse me, my good man," says one of the young fops nearly running into me at the doorway. Attached to the man's arm, a beautiful young woman with long black locks curtsies. There is something alarming about her. Dark eyes. Porcelain skin. I find myself staggering through the doorway like a drunk as we exchange glances, shocked at the resemblance to Diana. For a moment, I drown in those eyes of twin abysses, and as I blink, they are gone, for Kronklich bumps into me, forcing me to step into the foyer of City Hall.

"Everything all right, Lord Wolfgang?" he asks in his formal public address. He begins adjusting the buckles of my dark leather coat, ensuring my weapons are hidden from sight.

"Did you see that woman?" I ask, looking back through the doorway. Had I imagined it?

"I did. You look as if you've seen a ghost."

Maybe I did. Was my beautiful Diana now among the living once more? Probabilities flash through my mind, thoughts of my dead wife moving along the ice-combed streets of Delore, walking around the town where she was raised by a blacksmith for a father. I find myself filled with strange desire. That woman—my Diana. *What is the matter with me?* I shake my head.

"Sorry," I say, putting my hand to my forehead. "It's nothing." I rub at my eyes as we walk into an immense first floor of long brown carpets and polished wood floors. Our boots tap along the hollow planks, drawing attention to us from all directions. I try not to think about what I saw, but my head keeps swarming with hope and doubt, back and forth like a game of lances. I am being foolish. She couldn't possibly be alive.

I take notice of the strange decorations covering the walls, the rafters above, and even along the mantle of the immense fireplace far off in the distance.

Masks. So many of them. Every kind imaginable lingering in doorways and off the back of chairs. Even the large winding staircase is covered in them. Hanging from every railing post. Blues, silvers, golds, reds. Every mask has its own dimension, its own number of holes to see through. Some have two circles cut out for the eyes and some with three. One has a large beak for the extension of an impossible nose. Others have large pluming feathers of white with glittered gold and amethyst. The colors clash with the integrity of the vast room, yet no one seems to care. With so many groups of business people dressed in black clustered together, it's impossible to tell who is who, especially the person I need to speak to.

By the bottom of the stairwell, a man standing at a wooden podium calls out to individual groups at random intervals. As they meet with the usher, he quickly has a word with them and sends them off, up the stairway to some other place, some other realm. I approach him without warning, catching the man off guard. His eyes widen in surprise and I know he is judging me. I don't care if I'm not properly dressed for the occasion.

"Byron Tremont," I say with confidence.

The old-looking man with white hair stares at me, holding his composure with a contemptuous gaze.

"Tremont. I need to see him. It's urgent."

"You mean Lord Mayor Tremont."

"Lord Mayor—what? I mean—yes."

"He is upstairs. Do you have an appointment?"

"An appointment?" I ask, stepping forward with agitation. I feel Kronklich's hand on my shoulder.

"Yes, that is what I said, good sir."

I grip the edges of the podium with both hands and rattle the foundation. "I don't need an appointment!"

Before the old man can react, I move to the stairs and begin ascending, despite the feeble protests behind me. I hear Kronklich in the background trying to calm the man. "It's all right, my good man. He is popular, I assure you."

I ascend the steps circling the wall of the chamber with the swooping vast emptiness to my right. Reaching the top, I am met by two scholarly looking men, one old, one young, and push them apart to get by, dividing them from their close proximity.

"Well I never," says the old man while the young one with long flowing hair scowls as if having eaten lemons.

The second floor is vast and intense. I have never seen extensive decorations such as these as I part from the stairwell and enter a large banquet hall. I take it all in. Countless support pillars erect into the high ceiling. Large oblong windows cover both extremes of the room from one side to the other. Sunlight glitters through the panes, reflecting off of silver and glass vases set on round tables covered in red cloths. Plates and culinary ware cover each table to accommodate a feast for an immense crowd. Along the far back of the chamber, tapestries of red and black diamonds emblazon the walls, countering the brightness of the room.

Slowly, I enter uninvited as servants stop to stare at me, wondering who I am and what I'm doing here. I ignore them, noticing the two large harpsichords facing one another by the windows. A man dressed in a fine gray suit sits at one of its benches while playing a soft melody, stopping every so often to lean forward to tune the pins. Nearby, a man holds a ladder for another man at the top, reaching out with one hand and balancing with the other, a measuring tape dangling from his fingertips. "Twenty-four quarters," says the man on the ladder while pulling a wax candle from his satchel at his side. He places it into the candle tube of one of the many chandeliers hanging from the ceiling at different heights. The chandeliers are different from one another other, and I realize these too have multicolored masks hanging from their bases.

Like the first floor, servants huddle together scattered about the chamber, talking to one another in deep earnest. But none stand out more profoundly than the familiar voice I hear across the room toward the back. I approach a man with his back to me who is guiding two workers in aligning a particular tapestry, a black cloth with red roses down the length of a molded pillar.

"A little more, almost, a little more—what are you doing?" The two workers stop to stare at me, ignoring the commands of the man with his back to me. The man turns around, following their gaze to match mine, and I come face to face with the man who will grant me passage out of this blasphemous town. His eyes are cold and blue and his short dark hair is cropped close to his skull. He wears a dark-gray tie knotted at his neck in a fashionable way, accenting the gold trim to his long captain's coat of deep magenta. The look on his face is one of sheer dread.

I nod. "Hello, Tremont."

Kronklich appears next to me with a cup in his hand. "That was a hell of a time. What a brash old timid man." He takes a sip from the cup. "Oh, hello. You must be Lord Mayor Tremont."

Tremont's face turns red. "Yes. So good of you to come." His words are flat, without expression, but they hang in the air as a threat.

CHAPTER
X

THE AIR IS DRY AND still as Tremont stares at the two of us. The entire banquet hall has stopped to watch and I feel three pairs of eyes burning through me like fire. Tension high, Tremont is the first to speak. "Seems our little reunion requires a little attention. Let us retire to somewhere more—private."

Tremont claps his hands twice and the planners go back to planning, the decorators go back to decorating and the musician continues tuning. I notice how the servants never bring their eyes to meet Tremont's gaze.

"Follow me," says Tremont, grabbing a crystal glass filled with ruby liquid from a nearby tray. I can tell by his tone he is agitated, but I don't care. There are far more pressing matters than hanging ridiculous ornaments for some ridiculous party.

Leaving the grand banquet hall of sparkling windows and floating masks, we step onto the winding staircase and continue up to the third floor, passing fewer and fewer people the higher we go. Never saying a word or turning around to check on us, Tremont continues to the top of City Hall. I glance over the railing from three stories. The activity on the first floor reminds me of ants working together to carry off bits of a sugar cube or pieces of an eviscerated insect.

We pass through a large door at the end of a hall and enter into an office of sorts with polished wood floors, cherry wood desk, and bronze-trimmed chairs. The entire room glows from candelabra light, for the windows lining the far wall are too small. A large sprawling couch with dozens of throw pillows adds the final touches. As we walk in, I immediately notice paintings of former mayors hanging along the wall near the door, waiting for spectators like us to observe and pay homage to the past. The last portrait is a lifelike image of Tremont with the paint done in a certain way to make him look younger. What the crazy old man downstairs said was true. Tremont was a lord mayor now.

"Please. Sit," says Tremont with the enthusiasm of a pigeon. He greedily takes a sip of his wine, swirls it around a few times, and then downs the rest. "Would you like some?"

I respectfully decline, as does Kronklich, who has already taken a liking to one of the bronze-trimmed chairs. I can tell he is waning. These past few days have driven us to near insanity. I remain standing.

Leaning against his desk, Tremont eyes me with great curiosity. "So. What unforeseen event has brought your cursed soul back to Delore?"

Standing near the window, I keep my distance so as not to cause alarm. "I don't want to waste any more of your time than you are willing to spare, Tremont," I begin. "Speaking plainly, I need your train for passage through the mountains. I need to get to Sunstone."

Tremont moves from the desk and over to his tray of replenishing liquids. He pours himself another drink. "Sunstone? What on earth for? On some holy quest—"

"My son, he's been kidnapped," I say, cutting him off.

Tremont lowers his glass from his lips. "Dear me, I did not know. Word has spread about Diana. But your son—is news to me. My condolences to you, old acquaintance." He raises his glass to me as if it's supposed to make me feel better.

"Tremont, there is no time to waste. Every day that passes, every moment that lingers—the gap grows between my son and me. The Carnalreesee have him. They are taking him to Sunstone. God only knows why."

"*God*. Don't use that word here. God is dead. God is the reason why things have come to pass in the first place. Bah! What good is *God*? Who is he? A puppet master. A ringleader. Nothing more." Tremont throws the drink from his glass into the fireplace. It flares instantly. With a sidelong look, he says, "The Carnalreesee. They should be dead along with Egleaseon. You made sure of that, did you not?"

"Yes, I thought the same, but they are very much alive. They destroyed my home. They destroyed everything."

"Hmph," says Tremont under his breath. "And to think, all these years, the words I preached meant nothing. Did I not say you would upset the balance of things? Piss off the wrong people? You. A servant of God. Slayer of monsters. All you've done is agitate them. You've brought this on yourself." Tremont pours another drink and moves to a window. He stares out as his hand turns white from gripping his glass. "You kill one vampire and ten more appear. They're like weeds." His head snaps in my direction. "Don't you see? It's better to appease them by letting things be. The natural order of things." His blue eyes sparkle in the late afternoon light. "Others say the same about you. People of this town. Your very own father-in-law."

The mention of Diana's father makes me flinch and reminds me again of the man who despised me, who forbade his daughter from leaving with me long ago. I have not seen him since.

"Best thing you ever did was leave this place, even if it meant crushing the heart of a loving father by taking away his only daughter."

Tremont's snide remarks agitate me. What does he know about monsters or love? He's never been outside this town. I look to Kronklich for advice but he shakes his head, never saying a word.

"I have no time for this. Tremont, will you help or not?"

"Yes, I will help, but under one condition."

"Tell me what it is and I'll do it."

Tremont stares out the window again. "Tomorrow night is the first cold moon of winter. There will be a celebration. The Festival of the Mask. You are to attend it."

I had a feeling Tremont would make some ridiculous request. Things haven't changed. I slam my fist on the windowsill, yet Tremont is unfazed.

"That is ridiculous! Why?"

"Because you think your God is everything. There are other beliefs in this world, other ways to gain favors. Tomorrow you will see."

The more Tremont explains things to me about his beliefs, the more I see he has no clue about anything. I know the rules. You have to have faith, this I know. It's something I've been lacking lately.

"Do it," Tremont presses, "or find another way down the mountain." He drinks from his glass again and places it back on the tray with all the other empty glasses. "I have things to attend to, so if you would please—"

"Fine," I say with reluctance. "Where is Master Engineer Gaskin? We'll need to make him aware of our intent and have him prepare the train for our departure."

"That won't be possible," counters Tremont.

"Why is that?" At this point, I want nothing more than to strangle Tremont.

"Because Gaskin is dead, killed in the wilderness beyond. Eaten by lechers." There is a pause of silence. I knew Gaskin. He was a good man and excellent train conductor. "Not to worry, though. I took the liberty to appoint someone else in the meantime. At least until we find a better replacement."

I cannot possibly imagine who would be more qualified than Gaskin to be the Iron Carriage's engineer.

"Who?" I ask, wondering how lechers ate Gaskin.

Tremont smiles. "Dora Eddington, your father-in-law."

CHAPTER
XI

I WATCH CITY HALL BECOME smaller as we ride over ruts through the square. I am thankful for leaving there when we did. A moment longer and I might have killed Tremont in his smug little aristocratic office with his red berry wine and ruffled sleeves.

"Of all the people," I begin saying to Kronklich, who is once again guiding us through the cold streets of Delore, "he makes his choice in favor of the old man. How could Dora possibly be qualified to manage the Iron Carriage? He is the town's blacksmith."

Kronklich, having tilted his hat just right, tucks his head down as he looks at me from the side. "Didn't you say he was an accomplished blacksmith?

"Yes."

"That his craftsmanship was well known?"

"Yes."

"That some would trade their sisters to sample a piece of his work."

"That's beside the point," I say, agitated. "Old Man Dora is a belligerent drunk. Always has been. I'm sure nothing has changed." I tuck my head down into the collar of my coat, trying my best to deflect the cold. A creeping fog has gathered since the time we left the government manor. It passes along the ground as if we were riding on a cloud. Just another typical day in Delore, the mountain town, one of the highest in elevation.

For a while, we ride in silence. Dark eyes enter my thoughts, as I cannot stop thinking about the woman I saw back at City Hall. The woman who looked like Diana. My eyes dart to the sides of the wagon, hoping to catch a glimpse of her walking amongst the crowd. I know I am being foolish, but my mind gets the better of me. The request made by Tremont was outrageous, my having to attend a foolish festival while my son suffers in the custody of vampires. But deep inside me, I want to go. Wonder. Hope. Possibilities. If everyone in town attends the festival, then she will be there. Suddenly, I find myself anticipating tomorrow night.

"You have that look again," says Kronklich, balancing the reins in his hands while scanning me with his eyes.

I shrug off my thoughts. "What look?" I watch the giant cross in the square go by again. The people from earlier are gone, and an abundance of wood remains.

Despite the way people carry themselves here, I cannot help admiring the town's beauty. With the sun lowering in the sky, and the shadow of the mountain forever growing, firelight from candles appear in windows. Through the fog, they look like golden orbs, floating in a sea of snaking mist. The trees remind me of enormous fingers pushing through the breath of a giant.

We pass merchants selling wares. Handmade wicker baskets. Fire-branded pots. Spare parts for wagons. One merchant is selling vast arrangements of flowers, varying from bright blues to dark-purple roses. What catches my attention the most are the thorn vines in pots growing over pieces of wood. I see neither buds nor hints of flowering petals. They are roses without heads. These are what I saw at the bridge. Wreaths made from their vines, frozen solid from being outside.

Suddenly, Kronklich pulls on the reins and the wagon comes to a sliding stop at the side of the road. He hops off before I have a chance to speak. "Just a moment," he says, ducking between two merchant stalls.

I glance around the street while remaining in the wagon, watching a merchant splitting wood for buyers wealthy enough to buy heating logs rather than chop their own. Two children come darting out of the thickening fog, swinging sticks at each other—*crack, crack*—the sticks echo along the stones, their parents nowhere to be found. Carrying a basket of small round nuts, an old woman walks by to my left with her head bent low. She stops and smiles at me, waving the basket in my direction. "Want some nuts, eh boy?" *Boy? How old does she think I am?*

"Not today," I say in the best modest tone I can muster. Going to see the old man has left me sour and hating everything around me, including this woman.

"That's a shame," she says. "That's a shame."

The wagon dips and suddenly Kronklich is back in the driver's seat. "They have it!" he says out of breath.

"Have what?" I ask without thinking, watching the old woman move on to a different person.

"Bergamot."

"Oh good," I say sarcastically. "Glad everything is in order."

Moving along the main street again, it takes a while longer till we reach the cobble-stone road that leads away from the main section of town. Turning onto the drive, our surroundings become significantly quieter. No bustle of the town. No sound of passing carriages. Just us and the creaking of our diminishing wagon.

"Are you sure you want to do this?" asks Kronklich.

I stare straight ahead, still thinking about what I will say to Old Man Dora when I see him. "No," I say in the dullest of tones, "but it must be done."

The road snakes back and forth, passing between rose-less thorn bushes and built-up snow banks. Small birds run along the ground, squawking at our approach. I know Dora likes to feed them, keep them around to warn him of advancing customers. How surprised he will be to see his son-in-law instead.

Bronze sconces decorate the top of a high archway as we pass underneath. One of them is turned sideways from a cobblestone missing. The wall, nothing more than to mark the property line, is disheveled and in complete ruin. Nothing has changed. Not since I left. Groundskeeping is neglected. The absence of workers I presume. Dora was always consumed with his work, not caring much for anything else, including his daughter.

We descend the small drive which leads to the front of the house, passing countless dead trees patched over in powdered snow. Vines curl and tangle most of the stonework framing the front walls of the entrance. Trailing along the ground, they reach to the tarnished green gate, which lays wide open, available for any and all to access the house's front atrium.

Kronklich brings the wagon to a halt. No sound breeches the drive except for the relentless squawking from the bush birds up the road. Snow falls around us as I step down onto the permafrost, crushing lingering weeds that managed to rise to freedom. Walking past the creaking gate, I make way through remnants of what used to be a flourishing garden. Bright sunflowers in the summer. Opal lilies in the spring. Diana loved this garden. All of it that once was is now covered in a thin blanket of white. Giant pumpkins never picked from autumn, lie dormant and tucked away in the corners, frozen in time until the return of spring.

A door made of thick gray oak is all that stands between the inside of Dora's home and myself. I knock twice and wait a few moments, glancing through dirt-speckled windows. My heart pumps heavily as I wait. The anticipation kills me, knowing any second the man who hates me most in the world will appear in the doorway. A bead of sweat trickles the length of my neck as my hand reassuringly passes along the Hand of God at my belt. Of all times, now is when God enters my mind. Even so, I do not think he could save me from the wrath of Old Man Dora.

I knock again. Nothing. I look back to Kronklich, who waits beyond the gate, watching, listening. I try the latch at the door, gripping its bronze finish and twisting. The door shims open, swinging in on itself, groaning deeper and louder than the gate outside. Stale air pushes against my face. Sun fading in the overcast sky thins the light coming in from the windows, and all I see is endless darkness within. I signal Kronklich and we move inside.

It takes a few moments for my eyes to adjust to the dim interior. Moving from one room to another, I pass old couches and dusty tables. There is a large fireplace across a room and a pile of stacked wood waiting next to it covered in dust. Candlesticks stand erect in bronze holders. Spiders creep along the wood molding of the doorways as I continue searching, passing through a kitchen where the pots lay stacked on one another and all manner of pug worms creep over the filth of rotten food. My hand goes to my face. I wish I brought the breathing mask.

Upstairs is the same, rooms full of emptiness, unattended furniture, and cloth-covered junk. I pass Dora's room, and then Diana's old room, daring not to enter, avoiding any sort of emotional breakdown that may come with the sight of it.

No sign of Dora.

Keeping quiet, I motion with my hand and Kronklich follows me out the back of the house. Weapons drawn, we enter the back grove that leads to Dora's workshop and follow the path leading between the massive fir trees. It will be night soon. Fireflies flutter about my face as I hurry, jumping over fallen trees and coming to a platform embedded in the ground. This is where Dora hammers big pieces of metal, smelting copper and tin together to form the bronze lampposts so readily seen throughout the town.

I point with my hand as we near the entrance under an awning. This too is all laid in bronze, now tarnished in verdigris from years of neglect. Putting my ear up to the door, I listen for a sound and hear soft shuffling from the other side of the door, then motion to Kronklich, *three—two—one,* and push.

The door swings open fast and I find myself face to face with the old man. He looks different than when I saw him last. Short in height and reeking of barley wine, he is hunched over due to a large curve in his upper back. White wisps of hair sprout out the sides of his head; the rest of his crown is bald. His eyes are wide and dark, and it is too dark to see his dilated pupils. A mixture of confusion and hatred contorts his face. "You? You bastard! Killer!"

The old man raises an axe over his head and chops down with deadly force. I leap back as the head is buried deep into the wood floor.

"Murderer! Vagrant!"

I duck as the axe swoops over my head, denting the bronze doorframe.

"You show your goddamn face here? Agghhh!" The old man swings again, although much more slowly this time.

I roll forward, avoiding his attack as the axe goes flying from his hands. "Blast!" he curses and begins kicking with his thick boots, trying to stomp me out like a fire. Rolling across the floor, nails poke at my back as I avoid the old man's attempt to snuff me from the world. *Patience, Tenor. Patience.*

"She died because of you!" screams Dora, He latches his bear-like hands around my neck and squeezes, lifting me off the ground.

"Dora! Stop it!" I try to say. Yet I can see a mix of hatred and alcohol redden his face.

"Dora—"

Kronklich grabs Dora from behind. "Now, now, good sir! No need for this!"

Dora's death grip releases and I gasp for air. Twirling around like a windstorm, tripping over water buckets, and knocking over metal bars, the old man tries to throw Kronklich from his back. Together they flail about the workshop, upturning tables and smashing through sawhorses.

Kronklich holds on to Dora like a spider, arms tangled around him, never releasing. Dora swings his fists at his sides, trying to knock Kronklich from his back, but the attempt is futile. Dora's energy is fading fast.

"A little assistance," says Kronklich as he and Dora sink to the ground, the old man panting, Kronklich never letting go.

"You bastards. You sons of whores..." says Dora through slurred speech. As I kneel beside Kronklich to help, the old man attempts one more time to lash out at me but misses entirely. His arm slouches to the side as he looks at me bleary-eyed. He continues staring as Kronklich, holds him fast from behind, arms wrapped around his shoulders and neck. He opens his mouth to say something, but nothing comes out except a deep guttural belch that could melt iron.

Kronklich looks at me, wondering what to do next, but I am just as lost. Sitting on the floor of Dora's workshop among empty bottles and empty casks of ale, there is no doubt as to how Dora has been spending his time lately. Low snoring comes from Dora's slumped chin.

"Well, that went well," says Kronklich, resting his head back against an empty barrel.

"We need to get him into the house."

It is a struggle carrying Dora's body up the path back to the house. With dusk nearly settled, it is no easy task finding our way through the hazy moonlight. Moving up through the back door and into the room with the massive fireplace, we place his body on one of the shorter couches. A cloud of dust settles over everything as he snores away, his arms and legs positioned exactly how we leave him. I stand over his body wondering what to do next.

"I'll grab some provisions," says Kronklich on his way out of the room.

Exhausted and tired, I begin making a fire. The least I can do is warm the old bastard, even if he wants to split my head open with an axe. We will have to sort it all out in the morning. His drunken state of affairs. His inability to run the train. Diana.

As I get a flame going, I hear a stirring behind me. Maybe I won't have to wait after all. Preparing myself for the worst, I turn to meet Dora, but he has simply turned over on his side so that his face is toward the fire. I grab a filthy blanket and place it over his shoulders and his scarred hand suddenly snatches it from mine, pulling it tight under his chin with a mumble.

Kronklich appears with two steaming mugs and extends one to me. I look at it questioningly.

"Not to worry, I rinsed it."

"Thanks," I say, sitting down and taking a sip. "The old bastard even hates me in his sleep." I watch Kronklich sit opposite from Dora, taking the long couch. Almost three days with no sleep, he deserves it.

Kronklich holds his own mug to his face and inhales deeply. "Ah, there you are. Thought I'd never taste you again."

I can't help but smile as I stare into the blackness of my own tea. With the fire roaring and filling the room with heat, it doesn't take long for the drowsiness to kick in. Nearly dropping my cup, I set it down on the table before me and begin removing my weapons, one by one, from my belt, stacking them on the table like tools on a workbench. Silver stakes. Short daggers. Long daggers. Bawaka. As I pull out the Hand of God, I pause a moment, holding it in front of me, turning it over in my hand, examining it from all angles.

"How does such a thing so small work so well against vampires?" I ask, and when Kronklich doesn't respond, I look over to see him fast asleep. "And yet you," I continue, picking up the Bawaka, "do not work any longer. Why now in a time like this?" I hold it next to the Hand of God, comparing them as if the answer is right in front of me. I realize I am having a conversation with my weapons.

"What does it matter?" I say out loud, feeling my eyelids becoming watery and heavy. Diana. Dorian. I wonder about them and cry softly to myself. Overwhelmed. Exhausted. It's so hard to keep going with so little hope to go on. "Be strong," I say, more to myself than Dorian, trying to calm the ever-growing sadness inside me. I place both weapons on the table with a thud and lean back into the lumpy couch. "I have not forgotten you, Dorian. Your father is coming."

CHAPTER
XII

THE WOMAN IN THE MASK. She is alone. Feet crunching through layers of snow. A short burst of winter air causes the lanterns high in the trees to sway. She looks up and then all around her. She does not see me. I am one with the surrounding forest, a black form in the shadows. She hesitates, stops, and then quickly resumes her steps.

Moving through the trees, I match my steps with hers, jumping from one branch to the next. Hood over my head, I am perfectly concealed, dressed all in black. No manner of man can detect me. The violin off in the distance taunts the air with its eerie sound, slow and melodic, drifting through the branches of the trees like an owl searching for mice. The masked woman's bravery seems to grow with each step, her pace quickening ever faster. Music and chatter wait in the direction she is headed, toward the town square. Just in time for the Festival of the Mask.

Closer and closer, my shadow moves. In her state of oblivion, she never suspects. I am only a tree length away and the violin player is closer. Her perfume grabs my attention in the downwind and I find myself unable to wait any longer. My predator instincts kick in.

I swallow her with my cloak, disappearing from the path. No trace. No sound. Only the long drawn out sound of the bow on string. We lie in the snow as she struggles against my restraint. It is hopeless for her. I am too strong. Misty breath puffs from under my hand as she tires herself.

I murmur into the back of her head. "It's dangerous to be alone out here in the forest." Her black hair smells of peonies.

Struggling, she stops from the suddenness of my voice.

I release my grip over her mouth.

"Curse you, Tenor. Always sneaking up on me." She turns over abruptly, her eyes coming to meet mine. So dark. So beautiful. Her black mask glitters from the lanterns above. She stares at me, waiting for me to say something, but instead, I bring my cold lips to hers, kissing as if it were the first time. Her lips are so warm. For a moment, I am lost to my surroundings. Nothing matters. The whole world could break apart into infinite pieces.

Reluctantly, I pull back and stare into her eyes again. They sparkle like black opals, moving back and forth as if reading my thoughts. I let out a cold breath. "It's not often a thief comes in the night and leaves empty-handed. Have you come to a decision?"

She raises a gloved hand to my cheek and already I see tears forming in her eyes. "I want to. I really do. But my father—"

I cover her lips with one finger. "Don't worry, my love. You are not ready. Waiting is a simple matter. I will wait an eternity for you if I have to."

I pull her up from the snow with ease. Under her thick black winter dress, she is light and petite. I remember times before, my hand passing along her rib bones and down to her hips. Her elegance is beyond all measure. Nothing stands in the way of my "D."

Without a second of protest, we emerge from the brush of the forest like foraging deer. Off in the distance, the man with the violin begins playing feverishly, striking double chords with his bow, a vibrant waltz native to the Festival of the Mask. Instantly, my hands are in hers and I lead us into a brisk jaunt along the trail, moving in circles and twirling her around like a doll. The skirt of her dress struggles to catch up with the rest of her but I don't allow it. Over and over, we canter along the gravel, coming to where the edge of the path meets the forest, only to reverse and repeat.

She doesn't stop laughing and I can hear her breathing heavily. The steam from our mouths meshes together in the night like silvery snakes. Bringing her into a dip, I look at my raised hand as if surprised, producing a white peony from the sleeve of my shirt. "A magic flower for my princess."

Slowly pulling her up, our faces come to join one another, but instead of kissing again, I bring the flower to her forehead and glide it down her nose to stop at her chin. She takes a deep breath and a smile spreads across her face. The look that will make a man do anything.

"Oh, Tenor, about my father—" she begins again, but then suddenly falls silent.

Strange. The music has stopped. We turn around to see the lone musician playing the violin. Yet he is no longer alone.

Three men stand close to him like dogs hovering around a helpless cat in a back alley. I watch as one of the hooded figures in red reaches out a hand. There is the clinking of coins, and the musician suddenly leaves—faster than any man I've seen run in these parts.

"Tenor—" Diana begins to speak, but I push her behind me, putting myself between her and the three men.

"Get back," I say to her, turning about to face the strangers, my cloak fluttering about me, Bawaka glinting in the lantern light. I stand waiting, watching the three approach slowly, the lead man slightly ahead of the other two. Arms tucked under their cloaks, I can tell they are armed with many weapons. Weapons of persuasion. One is armed with a crossbow and the other with daggers. The leader carries a long sword.

As they come to meet me in the center of the lane, they fan out to surround their prey, the lead man still in front. Under his blood-red hood, I see his lips pursed together tightly. In the still of the moment, light catches off the few fluttering snowflakes tumbling through the night air.

"Sorry to interrupt this lovely moment, Lord Wolfgang," the man says with a sarcastic tone, "but there are pressing matters you must attend to."

"And what matters are those?" I ask coolly. "Pray tell."

The leader looks dead into my eyes. "You leaving Delore." He pauses a moment. "Tonight."

I can't help but grin as the muscles in my body tense, knowing any second these men will be lying dead at my feet. I say nothing.

"So that is your answer, then?" The leader nods to the other two.

The flash of steel sets me into motion. I sidestep two quick strikes to my chest from a pair of daggers. The assassin to my right doubles back with both knives and lunges forward, arms extended. As he is left open and overcompensating, I take advantage, stepping to the side, thrusting upward with my knee, breaking the man's forearm *from the elbow down. One strike is all it takes. He attempts to stifle his cry of anguish but the bone protrudes from the break, tearing through the sleeve of his fabric. With another swift motion, I bring the Bawaka down, severing his arm. Blood sprays the snow-covered ground as the man withers, screaming.*

Gripping his stump of an arm, I pull him close just in time to protect my torso. A bolt pierces his chest, and his body becomes very heavy. The man with the crossbow curses in frustration and begins fumbling with his weapon to reload. After casting aside the lifeless body, I bring my blade down to split the crossbow man's head in two, but a long piece of steel interrupts my descent. A loud ringing echoes through the night air as my blade grinds against the leader's long sword. He braces his body against mine and forces me back.

Arcing his blade up and down, I parry, gripping the Bawaka with both hands at the center handle. I twirl it back and forth with every offensive thrown at me, catching the leader's blade within the crook of the Bawaka's pommels.

The leader moves fluid as shadow on water, barely disrupting the ground he treads. His footwork is superb. Penetrating the circle of my defense, he jumps into the air, bringing down the long sword with precision. Our blades collide again. Sparks light the night. The impact is jarring and the vibration knocks the Bawaka from my hands.

His forward momentum is strong and I fall down, rolling onto my back, jamming my boot into his stomach and cracking his ribs. I toss him over me, sending his long sword scraping across the gravel away from him.

Scrambling for the Bawaka, I reach and my hand is nearly pierced with a bolt. I shy away, rolling across the ground, avoiding the crossbow man's second shot from a hidden crossbow. Having missed, he casts it aside, drawing a short sword from behind his back. His teeth come together in a frustrated smirk and he rushes at me.

Weaponless, I wait for his approach. He slashes at my midriff and I jump back, scattering snow and gravel from the forest path. He follows through with a backhand swipe and I duck; the blade hums just over my head. With closed fists, I deliver two succinct strikes to his exposed underarm and the blade is in my hands. His confused look is answered with my counter, spinning on the spot and carving into his leather pants like a piece of mutton. Blood gushes from the wound as he staggers back, nursing it with his hands, agony escaping his lips.

A kick to my back sends me sprawling to the ground, yet I recover just as fast, turning around to face my foe. The leader. The long sword is back in his hands. He swings furiously, double gripping the weapon with tactical precision. I am at a disadvantage, my short sword against his long sword. I evade each of his attacks, parrying some and dodging others, slowly making my way to the Bawaka sticking out of the ground.

My eyes stay focused on him as I move, ensuring my intent is not discovered. Our swords collide and I step off his direct line of assault, moving even closer to my goal. The Bawaka is at my back. Perfect.

The leader moves forward, striking with rekindled energy. He is determined. I can tell. I give only a few inches as he presses his assault, taking one step back, then two. I feign falling down and as he raises his sword, assured he has bested me. My hand grips around the Bawaka and I pull, releasing it from the frozen ground and jamming it upwards through the bottom of the man's angular jaw. The blade breaks through the top of his head, forcing his mouth open into a look of surprise.

"Tenor!" calls D from behind me, and I notice the wounded crossbow man limping away from the bloody death scene.

There can't be any loose ends.

Standing, I pull the Bawaka loose from the leader's face and throw it, sending it forward like a spinning blade of death. There is a dull thunk as the blade strikes his back and the failed assassin falls dead to the forest floor. The only sound is the wafting music from the festival off in the distance.

Walking to retrieve the Bawaka, I scan the surrounding forest and swaying lanterns in the trees. The cool wind is nurturing to my slight sweat, but I have only just begun. Surely there are more. My body is warm and my blood is eager for more conflict. Usually, it is monsters I kill, yet today is no different. A man who would lift a weapon against me is no man at all, but a monster.

Delore. This godforsaken town. They are monster lovers with their backward thinking that monsters are a natural thing of this world. How very wrong they are.

There is a slurping sound as I pull the Bawaka free from the man's back. I feel warm hands grip my elbow, the soft touch of my D.

"Tremont will do anything to eliminate his competition," says Diana softly. Despite her fragile arms, she is strong and resolute as she turns me around. She looks into my eyes. "He won't stop, Tenor."

"Tremont thinks he can control me. He thinks he can persuade me to leave Delore. But he has no idea who I am or the blood that runs through these veins. I won't leave. I've already told you that. I will kill every last person in this town if anyone gets in my way."

Her eyes sparkle as she lets out a deep sigh. "I don't want bloodshed, Tenor. That is why I—"

I cut her off. "I'm not leaving."

She smiles. "That is why I've decided."

My heart suddenly stops; my stomach lurches. Will she stay? Here in this frozen wasteland? Among the cynical dogs of man, lovers of monsters and haters of God?

"I will go with you," she answers.

The sound of the festival bell rings off in the distance. The midnight tone. The Festival of the Mask has reached its halfway point. I try to make sense of her words. Did she agree to leave this horrible place behind? Old Man Dora. Tremont. Her home. Dora will never forgive me.

So be it.

Metal strikes metal. The bell chimes again.

I look into her beautiful face, through the falling snow, beyond the black glittering mask. Her smile widens. "Let's leave for Roland. Tonight."

Ringing fills my ears.

DAY SEVEN

CHAPTER XIII

SLOWLY I WAKE, RUBBING THE dust from my crusted eyes. The light coming through the stained windows forces me to squint. My vision is blurry for a moment as I recall my surroundings, remembering where I am, the strong smell of mold lingering in the stale air. Off in the distance, I hear the hammering of metal. Each strike causes me to wince in pain. I recall my Diana. The memory of her is fresh in my mind. The dream was so vivid. I can still taste her minty breath. Sadness lingers and I want to be rid of it, but the black mask and the dark eyes haunt me. I fear she will never leave my thoughts. I lift a hand to my forehead.

How long have I been asleep?

The roaring fire from last night smolders in the fireplace, its much-needed warmth nearly gone. Sitting up, my neck is stiff and my hand throbs. I raise my gloved hand and clench it open and closed, gritting my teeth, forcing the blood to flow once more. The room is much brighter than the day before, and suddenly, I am startled at how long I've actually slept. Was it midday already?

I flinch at the sound of ringing metal again. Glancing over the other couches, I see Kronklich sleeps soundly. No grunt or breath escapes his lips as his chest rises and falls under the many blankets. I notice his crossbow leaning against the side table, an arm's length away, just in case. His empty teacups are placed perfectly next to it.

Remembering the fiasco from last night, I reluctantly gaze at the couch where we dropped Old Man Dora down in his drunken state. There is a pile of blankets but no Dora. Immediately, my blood chills at the thought of him having run out on us. Where did he go? This man is going to be trouble, yet I need him. He is the only one who can conduct the Iron Carriage.

Standing from the couch, my hands instinctively go to my sides, checking for my weapons, but they are not there. I remember placing them on the table. Spinning around, I knock over my empty teacup, not disturbing Kronklich in the least. Nothing. The Bawaka and the Hand of God are missing, yet my daggers remain. My heart races. Where are they?

More hammering. It comes from outside. Glancing at the pile of blankets, a feeling of uneasiness washes over me. Standing over Kronklich, I hesitate to wake him. The man is exhausted from no sleep for three days. I leave him be and exit the back of the house, entering the grove once again from the previous evening.

The air is crisp and clean as beams of sunlight find their way through the large fir trees lining the path to Dora's workshop. Listening to the loud, dominant clanging of metal, I cover my eyes from the intense light reflecting off the snow-covered ground. Is the old man working? How could he be, considering how intoxicated he was?

Outside, it is warmer than the musty shade of the house. Quickly, I make my way along the snow-covered path, arcing my legs over dead fallen trees and sidestepping the shiny black ice now visible in the daylight. How Kronklich and I managed to carry Dora back to the house yesterday is beyond me. Still, I rush along to the large brass door with no handle and push. I am greeted with intense heat and the sound of hissing steam. Everything is a mess, as it was the day before when Kronklich and I wrestled the maniac to the ground, knocking over barrels and breaking crates.

I notice the old man right away across the elongated shop toward the back, completely engulfed in steam. With large thick gloves, an apron to protect his chest, and oversized thick goggles, the back of his balding head glistens with sweat. Arms extended, he holds a clamp dipped into a large vat of water and stands still, staring down into the container like a sentinel. I watch him with his back to me for a moment as the steam becomes too thick to see what he pulls out of the liquid. I watch him turn around. His roundish form moves with precise movement, his hunched back reminding me of a bank swindler working the desk, handling customers' dauntess. I am positive he does not notice me as he continues his methodical work, moving over to the large blacksmithing anvil and forge in the center of the workshop. That's when I notice what is clamped at the end of the tongs, submerged in the cooling water. The Bawaka blade.

Without thought, I am on him like a vulture, ready to bind him if need be. "Stop! What are you doing?" My hands grip the leather straps of his apron.

"Out of the way, boy!" he says, shrugging me off with little effort. He swings his hammer down onto the Bawaka like a barbarian, muscles flexing, his goggles reflecting each spark as it ignites on the steel pin. How is he working so hard and proficiently when he was so belligerently drunk last night?

Lying nearby on the table I see the Hand of God. "What are you doing with that?" I say in a stern voice. I move to take it back, but stop suddenly. The way he is focused on his work, I've seen that look before. Eyes dart back and forth, analyzing. Dora is, without a doubt, determined and resolute, but to what end, I'm not sure.

"You're crowding my space," he says, shoving me aside as he moves his large body around the anvil. "You may have gotten my Diana killed, but I sure as hell am not going to let the same happen to my grandson." Two more strikes on the metal blades and I see he has stripped the Bawaka of all its leather on the handles. "I heard everything last night. About your weapon being useless, which means I'm the only one who can help you." He shoves me aside again as I lean in too close to get a better view. "By fusing your holy relic there into the folded metal of the Bawaka, I'll be able to combine the two with my custom bronze mixture. I'll hammer it good into compliance and lace the newly forged blade with silver and steel. I'll make you such a powerful weapon, you can slay them all." He reaches for a rag and wipes at his sweating head, matting down the few silvery strands he has left.

For a moment, I'm not sure what to say. *How can I trust what he's doing?*

Dora suddenly chuckles to himself as he stands there watching me stare at the Bawaka with question. "Trust me, boy. After I'm done with it, no vampire will be safe." Gripping the tongs again, he lifts the morphed piece of metal off the anvil. "Now move, and stay the hell out of my way."

For now, I leave Dora to his madness, hoping my decision to let him work on my weapons is the right choice. But in all honesty, what good would it do me not to try? My options are limited, and it seems, despite all this misfortune, fortune has finally presented itself.

My face is blasted with cold mountain air as I step out of Dora's workshop. It feels good on the wounds below my eye, and for the moment, I remove the glove covering my blackened hand. It stings from the sudden cold but quickly alleviates after a few moments. I gaze skyward. Above the roof of the house, a blue hawk lingers in the air some distance away, caught in an updraft, spiraling up, and then down, searching for its afternoon meal. Beyond it, the purple and blue shadows of the Cordova Mountains loom high in the background with their snowy peaks and rigid glaciers.

I take a deep breath, letting the cold freeze my lungs, relaxing my body, and hoping for a moment of clarity. I try not to think about Diana, my sweet angel shrouded in darkness. Yes, I was the one to take her from her home, and I was unable to protect her from the forces of darkness in Roland. I did not know the Carnalreesee would come for my family and destroy everything I love.

Pain radiates from my clenched fist. My burned hand is wet from broken blisters and quickly I cover it back up. It will still be some time before it returns to normal functioning, despite how much horse piss I apply.

The hammering of metal sounds behind me, and I know Dora is back at it. Taking my leave, I crunch through the snow, making my way back to the house, enjoying the last few rays of sunshine before the overcast sky moves in to take over. I try to get the thought of visiting Diana's room out of my head, because I know I'll regret it, but it does me no good. Entering back into the stuffy house, I move past sleeping Kronklich and toward the stairs. As I rest my hand on the banister, a cloud of dust trickles down. I can't bring myself around to climb the stairs a second time. I stare up at the forbidding shadows of each step, knowing what lies beyond them... All the memories of my dead wife. Her room. The window I used to climb through. I find myself standing still, paralyzed at the bottom of the flight. Physically, I find myself shaking, yet it's not from the cold I feel.

"Look at all this filth," comes Kronklich's voice behind me. "How has Dora not contracted a disease living here? Well. Nonetheless, one's work is never done."

Kronklich's airy voice releases me from my depressing nostalgia and I find myself breathing again. Turning around, I see him stretching on the couch.

"First things first," he says, "a fire to light the darkness. If we sleep here any longer in this cold and desolate house, I fear we might become mushrooms!"

It's amazing what sleep does for the soul.

I glance once more at the stairs, and then turn away, minding my surroundings and trying to focus my thoughts on something else. "I'll get the fire going," I say.

"Suit yourself!" Kronklich says, chuckling to himself. "You were always better at it than me."

Kronklich and his jokes. Where would we be without him?

"Now, where to begin," continues Kronklich. "Oh, I know, the kitchen. I remember seeing salted meat and moldy cheese. Maybe I can make something of it."

I listen to pots banging and cabinet doors creaking as I place small branches and twigs into a small tent in the hearth. Reaching for moss kindling, I realize there is none, and the supply of wood used last night is greatly diminished. Grateful for having a reason to leave the house, I stand back up, stretching my knees and rubbing the backs of my legs.

A faint cry of disgust comes from the kitchen as I exit the house. "Good God, how disgustingly plump and fat the roaches are!"

I close the door gently behind me as I survey the frozen grounds. Icicles have formed along the awning surrounding the house, and in places, some have broken off due to their large size. With my weapons out of reach at the moment, I turn to go back inside in search of something I can use to cut wood with when, at first glance, I notice Dora's axe wedged into a nearby stump. It's the same axe he tried to split my head with. I frown at the memory as my hands grip the long wooden shaft. Under my gloves, I feel how worn and splintered it is. I can only imagine how rough the old man's hands are if I can feel it through leather gloves.

Hefting it onto my shoulder, I set out like a lumberjack, eagerly anticipating the swinging of a good axe and the physical labor it demands. The thought puts me in a less stressful mood for a bit, having not to think about Diana or Dorian. Fresh air. Cold snow. I smell it all around me as I grab the tethered rope to a toting sleigh and begin my trek through the surrounding woods. Moving beyond the outskirts of the town, the snow is thick and difficult to navigate. But soon I get the hang of it as I descend down a wooded hillside. It is peaceful moving farther and farther away from civilization. It is only a matter of minutes until I have fully removed myself from humanity. The trunks of the trees groan as the cold air whistles through leafless branches. Snow gathers in clumps at their forks and I see the occasional blackbird hopping along, scavenging the snow for frozen berries.

There is plenty of wood all around me. Every spot I come to will do, but my boots continue crunching through the snow. I feel energized and invigorated. I don't want to stop. I feel the cold on the outside force my internal organs to generate more heat. I keep walking, losing myself to the surroundings, losing myself to everything. Then the stomachache returns, reminding me of the reality I cannot escape. It's been a long time since I felt hunger like this. I press forward aimlessly, without direction. Searching. But for what? The walking feels good after having slept on the lumpy couch, but the horrors return. Four days ago, I watched iron spikes driven into my son's hands. Seven days ago, I was forced to kill my wife.

I come to a clearing, a little less cluttered with trees. As good as any place for chopping, I select a birch tree that looks dead, ready to fall over any day, and begin swinging, making precise cuts into the bark. Its hollow interior echoes around me, but I pay no mind. First a downward angle, then center. My third swing is an upward cut, and I watch the first piece of wood spin through the air and land softly in the snow. Over and over I repeat, letting my anger dissipate through each swing. I imagine Scepter's face as the tree, taking the full force of each hit. The head of the axe is loud and dull against the bark, causing the silence around me to listen to my work. I am disturbing the sanctity of the woods. There is a creak, a crack, and a groan. The tree comes crashing down, snapping its leafless branches in the process. A flock of bush birds scatters in the distance, squawking. I set to work, lopping the long tree into tangible logs that will hold a fire much longer than the ones Dora stockpiled.

As I load the last log onto the sleigh, my stomach groans again. My hand presses in to console it, and I take up the rope to begin my trek back. I think of the old man's disgusting kitchen, hoping Kronklich was able to make some headway with it. The last time we ate was yesterday at the market when we stopped for supplies. I hope Kronklich procured more than just tea.

Through the quiet of the woods, I hear the bush birds flapping their wings in the distance, settling down again after my disturbance. But something else catches my attention. A new sound. Crunching snow, not of my own.

Leaving the sleigh, I take up Dora's axe and duck behind the nearest birch tree, slowing my breath to minimize the blood flow to my ears. It is how to truly listen in silence when detecting all manner of things. At first, there is nothing, but as I wait longer, the sound of pumping blood fades and the faint sound of crunching returns. Tucking my head from one side of the tree to the other, I attempt to catch a glimpse of my target, yet see nothing. The snow is blinding. Everywhere is white. Some snow banks have collected three feet high. Crouching low, I maneuver from tree to tree, recalling the days when I hunted vampires in the woods, their hearing far superior to mine. Looking up at the canopy, I contemplate using the branches to walk on, but my thought quickly disperses due to the lack of leaves.

Something dashes in the distance and I spring forward. No thought. No hesitation. I run through thick snow, trees blurring past me as I move to head off my prey at one of the snow banks. Its pace quickens as does mine. Faster. Faster. My foot plants on a fallen tree and I jump, bracing the axe with my shoulder. Having the advantage of higher ground, I expect to see my target, but everything is white. In the next moment, I see beady blue eyes peering up at me with utter fright. I retract my deadly descent midair, casting the axe away and landing in a pile of powdery snow. Uprighting myself with my arms, I slip, falling face first. Rolling over, I wipe cold wet snow from my face, and at the same time, feel something warm and slick against my skin. A wet tongue licking my face. Startled, I shy away, causing the fox to jump back. It retreats a few paces and turns to face me, pink tongue hanging from its mouth. Its eyes stare at me, and I can think about nothing else except D.

The fox darts into the trees.

"No. Wait!" I call out, reaching with my arm.

Struggling to get up, I grab the axe and take off after the fox, following its footprints through the woods. I can't tell how long or far I run as my breathing increases. Time has stopped for me as I try desperately to find the beast, the fox with blue eyes. Everything is black and white as I pass tree after tree, oblivious to the branches hitting me in the face.

In the distance, I see it. I know I can reach it. Coming to an embankment, I leap over it in attempt to cross paths with the fox, but my boots never find purchase. I tumble down a sharp slope, sliding more than spinning, first turning on my side, then on my back, spreading my arms like an eagle to stop myself. My brief descent ends with hitting hard ground. Lying flat in the snow, I lift my head, straining my neck to see the fox trotting into a shadowy outcrop of stone steps and crumbling pillars. Raising my body to have a better look, I notice what the fox has climbed onto. A circular platform made of manmade stone. A ruin of sorts, complete with a rooftop formed into a steeple. Mossy pillars line its outer perimeter and steps lead up to a circular platform. A stone railing encases the platform, except for where the tips meet. The Rotunda.

I sink to my knees in the snow, gazing at the fox standing in the center of it. It looks at me as if smiling, its mouth open, tongue hanging and panting. I can't even begin to describe what I'm feeling. Shock. Wonder. Is this some trick of the woods? Or are the spirits really speaking to me? Words form at my lips, but I stop myself from speaking. I hold my arm out again to the fox, daring not to approach, afraid any movement toward it might spook it away. The words form on my lips yet again, and this time, there's no holding back. "Diana, is that you?"

The fox turns its head as if looking at something in the distance, and then looks at me once again. Its eyes seem to glow with radiance. *Could it be the glare from the snow?* I take a step forward and the fox doesn't move. But then, like before, as if it saw something in the woods, it closes its panting mouth and looks in the same direction. Another fox, similar in all ways but smaller, trots up to my fox, my Diana, and their noses touch. They do this for a moment until they both look at me in unison. The moment seems to freeze like the snowy woods all around us. Cold. Desolation. They are together, and I am alone. Then, without reason, they take off in a sprint, leaping over the stone railing off the back of the Rotunda, scattering an array of yellow moths I didn't see before. I move to chase after the foxes, reaching the platform as they take off through the woods. But I know it is pointless. Such speed. Such knowing. I stand lost in wonder at the sight I beheld, trying to make sense of it. But sense has left me. This isn't what I wanted. I was trying to get away from it all. Away from the pain. But it's no use. It haunts me wherever I go. Even here, far off in this small secluded wood of the Cordova Mountains. A moth lands in my hands and my memories come flooding back to me in horrible agony.

This is the place where we used to come, to tell each other stories and have picnics. She would rest her head in my lap while I leaned against a pillar, talking about knights and dragons in faraway places. We would break bread rolls apart and eat cheese fresh from the market, kissing, stealing sips of wine from each other's goblets. Sometimes we both would lie on the stone floor, wrapped in our fur blankets, gazing at the cold-weather clouds in the sky through cracked pieces of the ceiling, picking out the ones that looked like comets and the ones that looked like feathers. This was one of her favorite spots, where the moths would gather just before dusk to feed on tree sap and sometimes the salt from our sweat. I would watch her for hours as she held her hands out to them as if she was the fairy queen of the woods and the moths were her humble servants. Her black eyes would look at me, tantalize me, speak to me, and give me all the command I needed.

I move over to the edge of the railing, remembering now the vision I had in Egleaseon's ruin, where I found the buried rotunda in the catacombs, where my Diana guided me to it with her light, saved me from the darkness that threatened to consume me.

A cold wind blows through the trees as I look over the side of the railing, seeing a gravestone buried in the thick snow. The final reason this was her favorite spot: she could always be close to her mother.

The lettering on the epitaph is worn and streaked with black moss. *Katelyn Eddington. Loving wife and endearing mother.* She died when Diana was fourteen. I never knew the woman, but wish I had. She was more accommodating than most mothers of this day and age. Being there for D. Putting up with the old man.

Running my hand along the slick stone, I swear to myself this time I won't cry like I did in the catacombs, but already I feel moisture freezing in the corners of my eyes. I hold it back, and instead of giving into my emotion, I embrace the gift D has given me and yell into the solitary woods all around me. "Where are you, Diana? I miss you!" My voice echoes for miles, but no one hears it.

The trees. The moths. The stones. None of them have a thing to say. I turn on my heel and make my way down the steps of the Rotunda and back to my sleigh full of birch wood. I find myself smiling for some reason, for I can't stop thinking of tonight, the Festival of the Mask. This feeling keeps welling up inside me, that maybe, just maybe, I'll see Diana again. Never have I carried this much hope before. Even the thought of it scares me.

CHAPTER
XIV

DUSK LINGERS ON THE HORIZON as I make my way back to Dora's home. Although my pace quickens for many reasons: growing hunger, reclaiming weapons, and worrying Kronklich, having to see Dora is not one of them. But all things considered, there is only one real reason I can't wait to get back, and that is because of the mystery woman. Again the thought tickles me, that somehow, in some obscure way, Diana will be waiting for me at the festival. I ran into her already once when we first arrived at City Hall. Who's to say she might not reveal herself to me again?

Trudging through high embankments and maneuvering around dead fallen trees, it is a chore getting the stock of birch logs back to the house. The temperature has dropped significantly and the tips of my fingers, despite the gloves, are frozen. The cold even seeps through my boots. Still not having eaten, my body struggles at keeping itself warm and begins shaking. The thick leather coat isn't enough to handle the high altitude of the Cordova Mountains. So I do what I can and begin jogging through the snow, my feeble attempt at warming my body. Great spouts of breath break across my face as I stay focused on my return. Up the hill and farther through the desolate woods, I reach the outskirts of Dora's home while a heavy snow falls amongst the dancing fireflies. In the distance, I hear the hammering of metal. *That old bastard is still working on my weapons. I left hours ago.*

I pass his workshop, daring not to stop as I pull the tethered sleigh up to the rear of the house. Through the window, I see glowing candles and a somewhat tidier place than before. Opening the door, a gust of stuffy air presses against my face. The scent of candle wax fills my nostrils. I am numb all over, so I welcome the warmth and stench over the cold.

"Tenor! Good God, man. I was just about to go on a manhunt for you," says Kronklich in an exasperated tone. His crossbow is in his hands, and on his head, his reagent hat. "May the devil freeze over in his restful prison. You're woefully chilled. Quick now, inside." He begins shooing me toward the kitchen.

"The wood," I say, not realizing my throat is parched from the dry air.

"The wood can wait. Evening black, on the other hand, cannot. How long has it been since you've had it? Don't worry about the fire. I'll get it going. You go pour yourself a cup. Go on, go on."

Again he shoos at me like some disobedient child and I find myself obliging. I rub my hands together and admit a cup of evening black would do me well right now, something to prepare me for tonight. It's a wonder my head hasn't hurt all this time without it. I stop at the bottom of the stairs again before entering the kitchen, staring up into its haunting darkness. The flames of the lit candelabra on the wall waver suddenly, indicating the possibility of an unseen force. But the thought of a spirit passing through quickly diminishes. There is a gust of cold wind at my back. Kronklich has wedged the door open to bring in the firewood.

I admire the kitchen's new and improved state. Crates have been stacked and the barrels line the walls in orderly fashion. Porcelain plates and wooden bowls are laid out beside the washing basins to dry. At the far end of the room, a tarnished bronze stove radiates a fiery glow from within. I see its flames flickering between the slits of the ventilation slats. Coal is the fuel source, for a heaping mess of it rests adjacent to the stove on the wood floor. On top of the stove, the pot used to boil the evening black steams wildly, a sure sign the concoction is ready. Next to the pot, an assortment of eatable sundries simmers in a larger pot and pan. Whatever sort of meal Kronklich is preparing, the sight of sizzling meat makes my mouth water. It spits and bubbles with grease as I grab a porcelain mug and pour the sweet smelling aroma of the evening black.

Standing in the kitchen warms me significantly, for the heat from the stove is intense. I feel the numbness clearing from my elbows and knees, all the way down to my toes. It almost hurts to touch the warm mug I've poured. Sitting down at the only table, I relax my back by leaning forward in the creaking chair and resting my weight on the unstable table with my arms. The slight adjustment of my leather proofing under the leather coat releases the pressure on my spine. I feel better, yet feel naked, sitting at the table without my weapons. They've become a part of me, for danger seems to follow us everywhere we go.

Kronklich enters the kitchen with a broad smile decorating his face. "It's amazing what sleep can do for the body," he says, his words trailing off as he prepares our meals. "You know, I wonder how many days one can go without sleep using ebon root. The good thing about it is that it doesn't give you a headache after chewing it."

"I suggest you be careful. I've seen noble lords lose all they have over the drug." I say the words with heartfelt concern. It is true, but I have seen worse. Theft. Fraud. Even murder. I've seen addicted men and women kill to possess the black root once hooked.

"And caution I will take," confirms Kronklich. "What we both need right now is a full meal to offset the many days of malnourishment. We need to be ready for tonight. The Festival of the Mask starts soon. When the lamps light at nightfall, the debauchery will begin. The people of the town won't be themselves tonight, I assure you."

"Yes, I know," I say, recalling my vivid dream from last night. I had killed three of Tremont's assassins the night Diana and I left Delore many years ago. I remember the black glittery mask she wore. Those dark eyes from beyond. Again, I think of the woman I saw yesterday. She had those same eyes. Same hair. I can't but help think of the possibilities, that there's some connection—possibly a link between two worlds.

A steaming hot bowl of salted potato leek stew clatters on the table in front of me. It is followed by a large plate of peppered sausages, which Kronklich places on the table with two hands.

"It was a good thing we stopped in the town to get provisions," says Kronklich. "Everything in Dora's house was either petrified or carried away by some manner of insect." Kronklich smiles and begins serving himself some stew.

Everything smells so good, but Kronklich picks up my delay in eating. I see him eyeing me as he slurps up his first spoonful.

"Why so possessed, Tenor? You must be starving. I assure you, I've used only what we brought."

"It's nothing," I say, poking at one of the sausages with my knife.

"Nothing? Hardly. It's this place, isn't it? Nostalgia gets the best of us. Too many memories. Good ones. Bad ones. I don't blame you, Tenor. The thought of this place will never escape you. This is where your wife grew up, and where your father-in-law tried to kill you. Memories run thick, but don't let them deviate you from the path. Don't get, how do you say it, 'Bogged down.' We need to find Dorian and stay focused. Keep a clear head. It's essential that you do. That's why you need to eat. Come, come now." Kronklich slices a piece of sausage and stuffs it in his mouth. Juices drip from his chin. "Perfection."

Kronklich is right. The past is the past. My wife is dead and there's nothing to do about it now. And ironically, her father is willing to help. I want to tell him about what I saw at the Rotunda earlier, but wonder if he would even listen.

"Besides, we have to look at our situation in a different light," continues Kronklich. "No matter how much of a waste you might think attending this festival is, it brings us one step closer to Dorian. For some asinine reason, Tremont won't release the Iron Carriage to us without attending. So we do what we have to. Make the best of the situation. One thing we could do to offset Tremont tonight is show him how good of a time we are having."

"What do you mean?" I ask, but Kronklich takes another bite of a sausage and winks.

He chews rabidly in between his words. "By the way, I thought for sure Old Man Dora would come running once he smelled my delectable dinner. The poor sap must be starved."

I give Kronklich a doubting look.

"He couldn't possibly live on a strict diet of alcohol," asks Kronklich with a spoon full of stew halfway to his mouth. "Or could he?"

Having finished dinner, and after downing two more cups of evening black, I am wide awake and alert. The old man never came to eat, and suddenly, I have the urge to go check on him. It's possible he could have passed out in his workshop, drinking his barley wine as he always does. But I decide not to check. The bastard has lost everything, the same as me. So I know the pain he's in. I know the worry he has for his grandson. With Kronklich outside in the snow, readying the horses, I am left with nothing to do except stoke the fire. Each log I toss into the fireplace, I think more and more of Diana and home, watching the fire consume the wood like the memory of her burning body. With the sound of hammering metal gone and still no sign of Dora, I wonder where he's gone off to, and to what extent he's messed with my weapons.

I throw another log onto the flames and look over my shoulder to the banister of the stairs. The dark interior is waiting for me on the second floor. I don't want to do it. I can't do it. But something compels me. I've had this feeling since the moment we arrived. Maybe it's fear? Possibly curiosity? I've put it off long enough. I need to know.

Standing at the bottom of the stairs, I look up at the empty landing, casting all doubt from my mind. Slowly, I ascend, taking the candelabra on the wall with me, the familiar groan of the stairs never changing.

The wind whistles through the loose floorboards of the second floor, rattling in sync with the planked walls. As one of the founders of the town and all, Dora built this place on his own many years ago. It was through his discovery of the mines nearby that people expressed interest in this remote land, to begin with.

I didn't notice before, but the hallway is lined with stained mirrors and empty vases. The side tables, once brilliantly painted white, have lost all their lacquer and glow. The silver backings are peeling, and, neglected over time, the mirrors are now the color of urine. I wonder if the house was ever cleaned after Diana left. At one end of the hall, an empty door marks the old man's quarters, but the other end of the hall, where the small circular window overlooks the grove, in the back is the place I make way to.

Approaching Diana's door, my skin fills with gooseflesh and I stop. Turning to look out the window, I spy Dora's workshop in the distance. The dark holds nothing. I see no illumination of light or movement, which means he isn't there. I wonder where he has gone off to?

I focus on the door again. I place my hand on the handle and feel it's cold surface as I turn it. The chill passes through my glove and seeps into the marrow of my bones. Creaking from years of neglect, the door swings half open and I step through. Like a knife wedged through bread, the yellow glow of my candles penetrates the darkness. Everything is how I remember it from so many years ago when I visited her in the night. My eyes flash to the window across from the bed, the one she would always leave unlocked, which I climbed through countless times.

Across the room, a windowpane is frosted over from the cold outside. Next to it, her drawing desk and easel lie dormant. Slowly, I move about the silent room, my empty hand resting by my side, opening and closing, moving my fingers about, allowing the blood to circulate, feeling for something, anything. I notice the pottery collection she never came back for, mostly yellows and whites, the vases ranging from long cylindrical tubes to wide serving dishes. She always possessed an elegant style of class, enjoying the fine arts and crafting. How she loved to form the clay. It was really one of the only ways she and her father bonded. She would make the sculptures and he would fire them in his furnace. I wonder if those memories still linger in his alcoholic brain.

I move to stand before the easel and my heart pounds. Expecting to find a blank canvas, I find instead a masterfully painted image of the Rotunda. Our Rotunda. Mixed in greens, blues, and whites, the painting is stunning. I sink to my knees before it like an altar, as if worshipping a long-forgotten shrine. Paint brushes and empty rinse jars line the base of the canvas, supporting its weight. I told myself I wouldn't let this happen, but the tears come uncontrollably at the sight of the fox and the moths in the background.

"I'm so sorry, my love," I whisper, staring at the canvas, the stairs leading up the platform, the pillars supporting the half-crumbling ceiling.

"You think she can hear you, do you?" asks a voice from behind me.

I squeeze my eyelids shut, bringing my finger and thumb to the bridge of my nose. My anger starts to flare at the sound of Dora's voice. Now is not the time.

"She's dead, boy. You did that," he continues.

I turn my head to look at him, angrily. His finger is pointing at me.

"Best get over yourself," Dora says. His eyes are wide and judging. The wrinkles on his face are more angular than before. Did he age in one day? In one hand, he carries his axe, and in the other, a bundled-up piece of cloth. Over his shoulders, a thick leather coat worn at the elbows covers most of his round frame. A flat brown traveling hat covers his head. The brim is tilted down to the brow of his eyes, giving him an intense, menacing look.

"Come to kill me I see," I say sarcastically. I can't think of anything else to say. My emotions have taken over my soul at the moment.

The old man grunts. "Not yet. You have work to do." He holds the bundled-up cloth to me. His look of hatred doesn't change.

I stand and move before him cautiously, as if he were a venomous spider.

"Take it."

The weight of the bundle is familiar to me as he places it in my hands. The gleam of metal shows in the candlelight while I unfold the burlap cloth. Holding the Bawaka before me with one hand, I raise it up to the light to examine it better. It looks nothing like before, and the Hand of God is nowhere to be seen.

"This is Enivid," says Dora. "Its metal is mixed from your fancy Hand of God and the Bawaka. The barbed wire is coiled up inside the new bronze handle wrapped in moose leather. The blades," he points at the four razor-sharp edges, "I made shorter for master maneuverability."

I look at him speechless. The craftsmanship is incredible. The weapon is beautiful, although the name is strange.

"Enivid? What does it—"

Dora furrows his brows. "Don't judge the name, boy. Every fine blade has a name. It would do you well to remember it."

I try to remember the name, saying it over and over from the tip of my tongue.

"Enivid will kill any vampire it touches. Don't doubt me, boy. Wipe that look off your face. You're at the advantage now." Wiping his face with a hand, he wrinkles his brow.

"How is this possible?" I manage to ask.

"It's simple. When Enivid cuts vampire flesh, the wound becomes permanent. If you drive it through their heart," Dora closes one eye as he runs a finger across his throat, "you finish the job."

I remember the encounter with Scepter in the town of Widow. The Bawaka struck him true, yet it did nothing to incapacitate him. If what the old man is saying is true, the Carnalreesee will have something to fear. Still though, I find myself doubting the concept. Could it be done so easily now? Plenty of vampires died by the Bawaka before. What changed from then to now?

"Dora, how can I ever repay you—"

"Don't start with the ass-kissing. We all have our part to do."

Dora turns around suddenly as if to go, gripping his axe firmly with both hands. His curved back sticks out from his leather coat.

"Where are you going?" I ask.

He stops and looks at me. "Where do you think? I'm the master engineer. Someone has to prepare the Iron Carriage."

"But Tremont said—"

"Tremont can kiss my ass. Don't you worry about him. By the time you're done with your little party, I should have her blowing steam." He quickly looks around Diana's room, shaking his head. "Now, quit screwing off here, and go save my grandson."

CHAPTER XV

Stepping out of Dora's home into the cold night air, the crushing force on my lungs lifts. I take a deep breath and look to the sky. Dusk has been replaced with winter's first cold moon. Tremont's intentions haunt me from yesterday. His demanding words give me no choice but to go to this ill-begotten festival. So be it. I will play his little game and take up Kronklich's suggestion. We will make the best of it, pretend to enjoy ourselves and rub it in his face.

Looking elsewhere, I remove my thoughts from Tremont, the senseless ass. Snowflakes fall in fluttery patterns, drifting slowly through the darkness like petals from a flower. It feels like time has slowed. The trees in the distance have collected more snow than they can handle. The branches nearly touch the ground. Near where I stand on the front porch, a solitary torch burns on the wall, wavering softly in the weak breeze. Its yellow light illuminates the outlines of the frozen flowers and pumpkins.

Treading through fresh snow, I move through the archway and out onto the drive. Kronklich waits patiently with bridles in hand. Both horses are detached from the carriage. A yellow glow covers half of his body from a small oil lantern he holds in his other hand. Wet from the snow, his hat and leather coat glisten in the moonlight.

"So the old man lives," says Kronklich, smiling from under his hat. His breath spouts from his mouth in sporadic puffs. His eyes are set on my reconstructed Bawaka, now called Enivid.

"Yes, he's very much alive," I reply, handing Kronklich the weapon. He takes it delicately in his hands, exchanging the tethers and lantern to mine, and examines it like a new specimen.

"Finely crafted, I must say. Curious, how he blended the metals. Bronze with steel by the looks of it." Kronklich passes it from one hand to the next as I mount one of the black horses. Steam spouts from the stallion's mouth as it chomps at the bit. "It's lighter, too."

"Yes. Lighter, faster, more capable, and it has a new name, Enivid."

"Is that so?" asks Kronklich with a raised eyebrow. He looks back to the house and then to me again. "And the Hand of God, did you leave it behind?"

"That's where 'more capable' comes into play."

Kronklich eyes the blade with admiration. "Incredible."

"Now all we need to do is test it out." I have never been in more of a mood to kill vampires than now. Kronklich hands Enivid back to me and I tuck it away under my coat. "Well, on to the festival, I guess."

"Yes, quite so," says Kronklich. "I thought it was unnecessary to bring the wagon. It is an unsightly thing to bring to such an event." Kronklich eyes me mischievously.

"Really. Unsightly?"

"Well, you are a noble lord, sir. Etiquette must be upheld always, even in dire times." He says this while pulling the strap of his crossbow and cane over his shoulder.

"Yes. One can never be too prepared," I say, feeling Enivid beneath my coat.

With the flick of my wrist, we set out on horseback, going the way we arrived, passing through the ruined archway covered in moss and snow, and passing the sparkling white bushes where the bush birds no longer squawk their incessant songs. Following the worn path, we make our way along the long curved road, moving past frosted trees and rolling hills of white. The first lamppost we come to is dark and abandoned. Seems the lamplighters have not reached this far yet. I glance off in the distance toward Delore. The horizon is filled with the orange and yellow glow of burning oil, a sign that the Festival of the Mask has already begun. I hear the haunting notes of violins and the unmistakable sound of the bell master.

Picking up the pace, we begin passing groups of country folk walking along the roadside. Families and workers, single men and women. Even a few children walk alone. We pass a few slow-moving wagons carrying piles of fresh-cut logs, the wagon drivers behind masks of gold, black, and red, ears stretched out like a cat. Some sort of demonic imitation, perhaps? I remember seeing the piles of wood near the wooden cross in the center of the town. Are they going there now? Compared to my meager sleigh of wood collected earlier, with this much wood, they must have spent days cutting trees down. It has been a long time since

I was here for the festival; the townspeople's mannerisms have changed without doubt. The things they do, the things they celebrate.

The closer we get, the more people I see wearing masks and costumes. By the time we reach the outskirt of town, the scene is in complete chaos. Disheveled-looking men in rough leather coats wear large wooden masks similar to the ones I saw moments ago driving the wagons. They laugh among one another, swigging mugs of dark liquid together and taking long pulls. The common women gather together similar to the men, staying confined to their small circles, dressed in black-based fabrics trimmed in gold and reds. Their crudely made masks carry faint traces of scratches notched along the raised cheeks. Moss glitters in a stained red and blue; the pieces around the eye sockets are raised and exaggerated like those of tree spirits. But of all the participants, the most animated are the children. In full costume, they saunter around the streets and sides of buildings, laughing, dancing, throwing snow at whatever moves. Like some strange ritualistic dance, they give chase to each other in sync to the musicians playing the violins. Masked as monstrous depictions of willdermen, bears, and crows, they run from other children dressed as warriors bearing wooden swords and shields. A pair of sword-fighting children nearly runs in front of my horse, and my black steed raises its front hooves in response, nearly tossing me from the saddle. They laugh and run away as I try to calm my horse.

"Whoa, whoa," I say patting the beast on its thick black mane.

"Lord Wolfgang," comes Kronklich's sudden voice. "Is it only me who feels out of place or do you feel the same?"

There is no mistake the feeling is mutual. I nod, answering his question, when, off in the distance, I notice a masked man dressed in brown robes approaching. His pointy hat droops to the side of his mask, giving him an odd appearance. He is pulling a small cart behind him. "Sirs, oh sirs! Right here!" He points at the masks in his hands.

"You know," continues Kronklich, "I think we are the only ones here who are not wearing masks." He points to the vendor. "Maybe we should partake."

"No masks," I say as quickly as possible. "Tremont never said anything about wearing masks. I want everyone to know we are here."

I detect a faint hint of disappointment in Kronklich but the moment passes just as quickly as it comes. We leave the vendor chasing after us as we continue on, avoiding the growing mass of monsters and fairies. A group of women dressed in flowing gowns of torn cloth come skipping by, holding their hands to their mouths and snickering at us. The crafted wings attached to their backs bounce with each step they make. I'm amazed at the lack of clothing, despite how cold it is.

Having reached the town center that is Travesty Park, denizens of Delore have begun to create bonfires at random spots throughout the streets and parkways. I take notice of a group of men near a lamppost, huddled close together, smoking tobacco and rubbing their hands, laughing. Everyone is laughing, it seems. Aside from the few carriages rolling in the street, we are the only ones on horseback and without costume. Everyone we pass looks at us like the outsiders we are. Good. They can have their holiday. Let them see my distaste. Kronklich, on the other hand, is just the opposite. He tips his regent hat with a nod at every group of people we pass, who in turn, point and stare.

The sound of bells resonates deeply through the square suddenly, and I am drawn to it much like the crowd. I have always heard about the bell master, but never had the chance to see him perform. Picking up the pace, I nudge my horse forward, and Kronklich follows close by, never leaving my side. As the bells get louder, the crowd grows thicker. It is near the wooden cross in the center of the square where the magician of music has set up his strange mechanical device of pulleys, levers, and of course, bells—large enormous bells cast in bronze, and small ones as big as my fist. Sitting before his construct like the conductor of an orchestra, he is the maestro; bells sway at his command.

Positioned atop my horse, I have a clear line of sight to him, but others in the crowd are not so fortunate. They stand, shoulder to shoulder, shoving themselves as close to the bell master as possible. Unruly brutes. Such is the power of music, with its responsive effects and its ability to lure. I find myself drifting off to the beauty of the chiming bells and catch a glimpse of long, dark hair flowing from behind a mask. The woman does not turn around. Could it be? I swallow back the dryness in my throat. My mind suddenly flutters at the thought of my D being here. Leaning my weight on one stirrup, I begin to dismount my horse, wanting to go meet her in the crowd, but a strong hand grips my shoulder.

"We should keep going, Lord Wolfgang. We still have some distance before we get to City Hall. Don't want to disappoint our host now, do we?" Kronklich's gaze is a serious one, suggestive more than inquiring.

I shake my head, clearing the cloud in my mind. I look back to the woman with the raven hair, but she is gone. There is only a churning mass of bodies dancing to the music. No, of course it wasn't her. She wouldn't be out here among the degenerates and monsters. She would be where I found her. City hall.

"Let's go. I've seen enough."

As we move away from the bell master, something catches my eye near the base of the giant cross. On top of the wagons loaded with wood, figures dressed in red robes and gold masks toss the logs onto the growing piles of lumber. My blood turns cold as my hand positions itself over the outside of my coat, exactly where Enivid waits. The Carnalreesee. They're here. Out in the open. It doesn't make sense, and just as I'm about to warn Kronklich, one of them turns to face me. The mask is a depiction of a tragic smile, yet there is the absence of stag horns. My body relaxes. The rest turn to stare at us as if catching onto what is happening. I break the tension, forcing us on and away from this madness. I laugh to myself. *Heretics mocking the church.* I shake my head from the irony. *If only they knew it is true.*

As we leave the town square, the noise dies down, except for the drawn-out overtones of violin strings. Their ghastly moans seem to carry on and on everywhere we go, echoing off the walls of buildings and along the cracks of the cobblestone street. As we reach Hammond Bridge, the familiar sight of the red and black diamond banners reminds me of the gypsy wagon we rode. With no wind to breathe life into them, the flags hang limp like wilted branches. The wreaths remain the same, lining the cobblestone railing all the way to the other side of the frozen river.

With my nerves on edge, I waste no more time crossing. Galloping past black carriages with swinging lamps, I speed up, intent on seeing my Diana at this forsaken party. A fog has begun to settle on this side of the bridge, making it difficult to focus through the haze. Using the light from the lampposts as our guide, we slow our pace to a trot as we approach City Hall. The lanterns hanging from the doorway and the multiple lit candles in the windows are an intimidating sight, giving the mansion the appearance of a menacing dark castle. Snow banks as high as a man surround the premise, suffocating the leafless trees of the surrounding gardens.

Scattered groups of party guests line the front of the building, huddling close to one another, rubbing their hands and fingers, smoking tobacco. Securing the tethers of the horses to a nearby lamppost, we walk the side of the building, passing finely dressed entrepreneurs, who hold their masks in one hand while drinking from goblets with the other. Loud and obnoxious, they pay no mind to Kronklich and me as we pass by, hardly noticing us in the least.

A man dressed in black robes stands at the double closed doors, watching the outside meandering of guests coming and going. As we approach, his long-nosed mask turns to address me with its golden specks glittering in the lantern light. A deep voice resonates from underneath the mask, muffled from the lack of an opening for a mouth.

"Welcome, Lord Wolfgang. Your attendance is expected. Please enter as you see fit."

Hearing the doorman's deep voice, I wonder what sort of creature lurks underneath. A demon perhaps, beckoning the unexpecting to enter its death den. I take the words into consideration and pass through the doors, avoiding the masked man's gaze.

Like the burst of heat from a furnace, warm air greets us as we enter. My face tingles, thawing from the outside cold. The foyer, unlike the other day, is completely empty, no life anywhere to be seen bustling about with stacks of papers in hand or leather satchels tucked under arms. The doorways leading to other parts of the first floor have been roped off, corralling party guests toward the stairs. The keys of a harpsichord drift down from the second floor, carrying beautiful music made by two instruments calibrated at different octaves. It lingers, hovering through the air in the background of laughter and playful cries, like the opening of a play as the actors enter the stage. No one sees the musicians, but they're there. But it is not actors who descend the stairs and linger along the railing's banister. It is the masked party guests lucky enough to have received invitations. A multitude of design and color make up their attire. The women, dressed in long gowns accented in red, white, and black, the men, wearing their subtle black velvet suits and ties. The masks however vary greatly, ranging from purple butterflies to Dionysian expressions of the masquerade. A man in a blue glittery mask with long nose and one eye holds hands with a pink fairy accompanied with wing attachments and wand. They whisper into each other's ears, laughing, the white of their teeth glinting in the candlelight. There are other couples simply embracing each other, kissing, passing tongues along one another's throats. I see two men sharing a drink together, their faces close, one of them traces the other's cheek with a long fingernail. A woman wearing a pearl iridescent mask leads her partner by pushing past me at the foot of the stairs, undeniably drunk, for her movement is staggered and his is no better.

"Oh my! Heed my excuse!" she says continuing on, trying her best to make it out the front doors without collapsing.

I glance at Kronklich with uncertainty and he smiles back. We begin ascending, avoiding as many of the party guests as we can. Passing each couple, I see their eyes falling upon us, watching us from under their masked personas, eyes open wide, shaking their heads. I don't care if they don't approve of my attire. I smile at the thought of their disappointment. And with each step I make past them, they smile at me, happy as can be in their drunken state. Their wicked smiles mock me from under their flamboyant face protection. I press on, wanting nothing to do with these people, and only thinking of the woman I aim to run across. My heart thumps harder at the thought.

Coming to the summit of the second floor, I can feel the increase in temperature as compared to the ground level. More patrons crowd the balcony leading to the banquet hall. I begin pushing through them as if they were weeds. Oblivious to my presence, none of them respond to my touch. I pass a man slouched over in a chair near the railing. Arm and hand hanging loosely at his side. A crystal goblet lies on the floor with its contents spilled from the glass.

The doors to the banquet hall stand wide open, allowing all to pass through freely. As we approach, a woman trips and goes crashing down to the floor in the center of its threshold. Clutching at her ankles, she laughs uncontrollably through her yellow-feathered mask. The skin of her legs is exposed for all to see; the raised hem of her dress invites all the guests to view her undergarments. These people are mad, disorderly, and, above all, improper. I stand before the doors, contemplating how to enter into the realm of hell, where the demons within are waiting to defile me. I want to see my Diana. She is waiting for me in there. I know it.

The harpsichord rings out. The blare of heat presses against my face. Beleaguered with doubt, I look back at Kronklich one more time, and he simply smiles. Of course he does.

I take a deep breath and pass into the den of Satan.

CHAPTER XVI

I AM LOST IN A sea of colors.

I push my way through endless torrents of drunken patrons as they laugh obnoxiously, twirling in each other's hands, dipping their bodies elegantly, spit dripping from their faces. Eyes stare at me through gold and silver masks with long noses and one eye. Feathers plume from every angle. The women's garments dust the floor to the music, flowing from the back of the chamber. Not one, but two harpsichords release their elegant sounds into the air. The musicians duel one another at lightning speed with their backs to the audience, focusing on their music. The glass and silverware from the day before sparkle in the bright glow of the thousand candles. Everywhere I look seems to blur. Spinning feathers. Gleaming teeth. *How are they all enjoying themselves in this heat?*

I feel someone grabbing at my elbow, a woman in a blue-bird mask, urging me to dance with her. But I am not here to dance and so pull away harshly. She is hardly fazed as she grabs a woman passing by, running her hands along the curves of her body. I feel myself suffocating in this place. So much devilry, so much—sin.

Kronklich seems to be doing just fine. As if he were made of honey, the bees come flocking to him, men and women, touching his garments and passing around his hat.

"Oh my, sir, such dark and brooding colors your hat is. May I?" asks a woman reaching for his head.

Women's hands run the course of Kronklich's leather coat and the one puts his hat on her head, disregarding the plumed feathers on top of her own peacock head.

"This hat is so defined. So you. It speaks higher than the rest of the top hats here."

I can see the blush filling Kronklich's cheeks. He is unable to control his smiling. The groping and compliments continue. He is a sensation here, popular with the women and even more with some of the men.

"Well, really, it's actually a regent hat," begins Kronklich. "'Tis the native style to this region here, is it not?" Kronklich addresses all of them, but his question goes unanswered as they corral him away from me to some other part of the dance chamber to do God knows what. "No worries, Lord Wolfgang!" he shouts across the room. "All is in order." His voice trails off, drowning in the fast-paced harpsichord music.

Sweat beads off my brow as I make my way through the disorder, dodging past walls of spectators and nearly colliding with a server.

"Excuse me, sir. Compliments for Tremont's guests," says the man.

I stare at the tray full of red wine and send the man off with a wave of my hand. "I'll take water if you have it."

The man gives me a surprised look and bows away.

Damn, it's hot.

Seeing a gap part in the ocean of flesh, I break for the area near the windows; thankfully they are open. Cold air pushes through, alleviating the amassing body heat and burning candles. I don't doubt why the dueling pianists are near them. I watch them battle their way into the next melody, much darker undertones, foregoing the last bubbly tunes. They play even faster than before. The one closer to me rakes his fingers across the keys like a flock of carrion birds pecking away at the dead skin of crushed animals. Sweat trickles along his neck, disappearing into the high collar of his vest. Poor soul. I can't remember the music ever stopping since our arrival. Turning his head, I see the face of a red devil. His eyes are closed as his fingers hammer away at the keys. A fitting sight, the devil playing the devil's music.

"That one there is Ramses," comes a voice from behind me. "Messenger of music and delights. Good, isn't he?"

Wishing I had that cup of water, I slowly turn to face Tremont. There is no mistaking his voice.

"Hello, Tremont," I say in a barely audible voice, as my throat is so parched.

"So glad of you to come," he says with a perfect smile. "Enjoying yourself?"

I can't seem to find any words to say to him at the moment, so he continues speaking, first taking a gulp from his goblet.

"A bit overwhelming, isn't it? All the colors and such." I watch him hawking two young ladies passing by, their long eyelashes batting against their cheeks, giggling to one another.

"Ah yes, the sights can be a bit drastic, wouldn't you say?" His obnoxious laugh mixes with his slurred speech. He is dressed in a long white robe with knee-high leather boots stained a brilliant white to match. The mask on his face is a pure white sparkling beast of a creature, far more extravagant than those of the other guests. Long prominences stick out from the sides with white fur; altogether, he is a hideous sight to behold.

"Do you like it? I am a yeti from the Gebani Mountains. Terrifying, aren't I? The women simply love it." Tremont chuckles as he partakes in another drink. "Come, come now, Wolfgang." He gives me a firm slap on the shoulder. "We may have both lost the woman we loved, but let the past be the past. Let us not dwell. And look," he points to a crowd of people across the room, "not all is lost. See the woman over there? She has been watching you for some time now."

I see Tremont smile from behind his obnoxious mask. He bows to me. "I leave the matter in your hands. Farewell."

He turns to go, calling on the two young girls passing only moments ago. "Over here, my snow leopards, where have you been hiding?"

Buffoon. I turn to look at the woman Tremont was speaking of, and he was right, she is off in the distance passing glances my way, a bird perched in a forest of spectators. She is covered in a brilliant blue gown, which stretches tightly across her body, revealing her well-proportioned curves. The slit down her back exposes her white smooth skin, stopping just above the curves of her voluptuous backside.

As I look into the black glittery mask covering her face, I am drawn to her like a moth to flame. I find myself holding my breath and wondering. Could it be?

Fire burns in my chest as I slowly make my way to her, my eyes never leaving her captivating smile. I push party guests out of the way, uncaring of their reactions. I see a man dressed in servant's clothes approach me. "Water for you, sir." But words never leave my lips as I move past him, never stopping, not so much as a glance from me.

All this time she never moves, except to raise the crystal goblet to her lips, sipping the red swirling liquid inside.

I come to stand before her with nothing to say. Her scent is not of this world. The fire burns even hotter. "Dance with me," I say.

She smiles, setting her glass down, and puts her delicate hand into mine. Cold pinpricks shoot up my arm. *It's her, oh God, it's Diana.* I lead her into the chaotic swirl of dancers, placing my other hand on her hip, feeling for the prominence I so yearn to feel again, but there are so many people, so many drunken devils around me. I can't seem to focus. We spin and twirl to the upbeat tempo of the harpsichord, the demon pianist moving up and down the keyboard with his lightning fingers. The music moves through me. I feel it all the way down to my bones, pushing me harder, commanding me to pull my Diana closer to me than ever before. With our bodies pressed together, I feel her heat under my hand. She is beginning to perspire. Around and around we go, feet in sync with one another, so much like before, so much like the times when we were young, chasing each other in the snow, pouncing on each other like playful cats.

Spinning and spinning. The mask suddenly falls from her face and I am left staring into the dark eyes and porcelain skin of my Diana. My body goes numb. It really is her.

"Diana," I say, barely managing the word.

A strange look spreads across her face. "I beg your pardon?" With flush red cheeks and sweat dripping from her brow, she looks at me with question.

That look—seductive, scanning. We are no longer dancing. Bodies rush past us, bump into us. Forcefully, she squeezes my hand, pulling me from the crowd, beckoning me to follow her. She guides us to a nearby table. "Please, sit, sir. You are tired."

"No, I'm not. I am very much awake," I say, unable to stop my words before saying them. She looks at me confused, as if I have somehow discovered something she did not. "I don't understand," she says.

"Please forgive me. I thought you were someone…else." The pause in my voice seems to cause her eyes to dilate some.

She stares at me with her dark eyes, searching. "I'm sorry to disappoint you, sir," says the woman with empathy in her tone. "Was she dear to you?"

Was she ever.

Finding myself staring into this stranger's eye, I force myself to look away. Amazing. She is the striking image of D. "She was my wife."

"I see," says the mysterious woman while looking at the crowd dancing to the music.

"She's dead."

"Oh," says the woman, avoiding my eyes.

Awkward silence falls between us.

"I'm Belladonna," she says unexpectedly, standing and curtsying to me with her tight blue dress. The cleavage of her white breasts nearly pours out from her corset. Others are looking.

"I'm Lord Wolf—"

"I know who you are, sir. You are quite the celebrity." I'm not quite sure what to say to her words, and before I say anything, she adds, "I'm getting us drinks."

I grab her hand. "I'm not drinking."

"Surely, you wouldn't let a lady drink alone?"

"I'm not here by choice."

"Even the more reason to drink," she replies with a smirk.

Watching Belladonna's form sway back and forth is entrancing as she moves away. The smooth exposed skin of her back glistens in the candlelight. She disappears into the crowd and I am left alone, long enough to catch a glimpse of Kronklich across the room. He is laughing uncontrollably, surrounded by an audience of women. A man's man, he is no doubt capable of all things, including inducing the swooning of females.

I shake my head at the thought, turning around to watch the two pianists play their duet. Having performed the entire time since we arrived, their hands finally come to rest. They are met with applause as they rise to wave and stretch, bowing to those around them, and stepping away from their massive instruments. I find myself wanting to stand and applaud them as well, but I notice Belladonna making her way back to me, a crystal goblet in each hand filled with red liquid. Her hips sway and turn every man's head as she approaches.

"Seems we took a break at the right time," she says, handing me one of the cups. The thick liquid inside swirls around the glass, causing legs to form along its sides. The sweet aroma of berries rises from the lip of the goblet, causing me to salivate. "Here's to the dead and their peaceful rest," she says, raising her glass to mine. Holding my glass high enough for her to toast, the words she says seem to have an effect over me. Was my Diana truly at rest or was she still in my world, hovering near, always watching?

I take a heavy swallow, lost in my thoughts. The drink is sweet and smooth, like silk going down my throat. Overheated as I am, it warms my insides even more so. But I continue drinking in her company, despite her saying she is not my long-dead lover. We talk about all sorts of things: the young fop I had seen her with, how she was offered to walk with him for some ridiculous amount of dauntess. We speak of the aristocratic politics that seem to haunt the town with power struggles, and, of course, of Tremont himself. How more than once he advanced on her on separate occasions, approaching her with his privileged attitude.

"He is quite the spectacle tonight, is he not?" she says all too boldly. The wine must be taking effect. "He calls himself a yeti, but to me, he looks more like an albino ape." Belladonna laughs immediately and I find myself grinning. Maybe it's the wine affecting me, but in time, I find the company of Belladonna very agreeable. We talk for a time, watching people and deriding their costumes.

"Seems they let anyone in here once the wine starts flowing," says Belladonna, pointing to a patron wearing a red crow mask and black raggedy strips of cloth.

Not sure what to make of her comment, I notice the dark-clad figure make its way over to our table. It wears a red-painted mask with feathers and a long pointed nose extends from its face like a beak. A top hat rests on its head, which gives the figure an overall eccentric appearance. Immediately, I notice the painted-on teeth fashioned in a crude grin. At first glance, the mask shimmers in the candlelight in the impression of a bleeding face.

As the figure gets closer, I notice more details than I wish to examine. Something isn't right. The skin at the neck and around the eyes is black and crispy. Like burned scars, scars I've seen before. I blink my eyes a few times. Maybe it's the wine. *I am seeing things*. I blink again and the figure is gone.

"What's the matter, love?" asks Belladonna in her slightly inebriated state. Her hand is on my arm, fingering the bracer underneath my leather coat.

"It's nothing," I say, looking past her shoulder.

A chord is struck on the harpsichord behind me and the pianists begin playing their new song. Another duet, fast and harsh and sharp with high notes. I don't think it's a good idea to stay idle any longer.

"Let's dance," I say, standing and holding my hand out for her to take. As she places her milk-white hand into my glove, the red-masked figure appears behind her suddenly, placing a gloved hand on her shoulder.

I feel her body tense.

"Pardon me—hope I'm not interrupting. I was looking all over for you, Belladonna. I was beginning to worry you had run off."

Belladonna places her hand over the figure's hand while smiling at me. "Yes, Mr. Crow. I never left. I am still here."

"That's good. That's very good," replies Mr. Crow, patting her shoulder like a puppy. "And did you do as I asked?"

"Indeed I did, sir," replies Belladonna in a shaky voice. "I said I would not fail, and so I didn't."

I try to understand what is happening here as I watch the two of them converse, wondering why I am being ignored. A strange sensation passes through my body like drinking ice-cold water from the river. All at once, pain strikes my gut, and I bend over to keep from vomiting. A cold sweat breaks across my forehead as I feel my throat swelling. Opening my mouth to breathe more quickly, I see the sleeve of Mr. Crow's robe ride up his arm, revealing blackened skin like scars from the dread rain or worse, sunlight.

Looking up, I see Mr. Crow staring straight at me with his yellow eyes from under his red mask. I go to move my hand, but the slightest movement overwhelms me with nausea.

"Ha ha! Would you look at him!" says Mr. Crow in an excited tone. "He is rendered useless. Excellent work, my love." He kisses Belladonna's hair through the mask. She smiles and looks at me with pity.

"I knew from the moment I laid eyes on you, Belladonna, you would fit the part. How so much you look like Wolfgang's dead wife. What was her name again? Ah, yes, Diana. I knew he wouldn't resist your charms."

Mr. Crow slams his hand down onto my arm with a force no normal man could produce, pinning it like a helpless, weak animal. "How unfortunate situations can be sometimes. Isn't that right, Wolfgang?" The voice under the mask becomes evident to me, despite my urges to become sick. Mr. Crow is none other than Scepter.

He leans in close to me; the red nose of his mask nearly touches my face. "The taste of her sweet blood. How wonderful the look of terror was when I bit her. You should have seen it." He hisses into my ear like a snake. "The sweet agony. And to think you almost killed me." Lifting his mask, he reveals a puss-filled, blackened face. "Do you have any idea how long it will take for me to come back from this?" The mask goes back down. "Damn vampire hunters. You are like goddamn cockroaches. I will take payment now, compensation for all the trouble you've caused me."

I want to move, but every time I will myself to act, I feel my insides churn. It is horrible pain, worse than any broken bone or cut. I feel something like tentacles squirming over my organs and squeezing. I try to move my arm, but his strength is ten times my own.

Scepter produces an extraction dagger from underneath his robes and waves it around nonchalantly, as if it were a dinner fork. "Oh, and if you're worried about the poison killing you, it won't." He slams the dagger into my side, piercing straight through the underside of my proofing, inches above where Bronin did the same. I ignore the pain as I watch my blood bubble into the vial attached to the weapon. "Can't have you dying on me just yet. Your blood is a novelty."

My head spins from the poison, the wine, and the draining of my blood. The whole room seems to be a whirl as he pulls the blade from my side with a sickening slurp. I know he is smiling at me from under the mask. I can sense it. He leans in close again, allowing me to smell the metallic aroma on his breath. "Ahhhhh. Thanks so much, friend." He backs away slowly, stowing the dagger into the folds of his robe.

"You bastard," I manage to say, attempting to go after him, but I fall meagerly to the floor, unable to control my legs, gripping my side, trailing blood from the table to the floor.

A group of party guests move out of the way and a woman cries out at the sight of my blood.

"It's all right, friends!" says Scepter over the crowd and music, moving away from Belladonna and me. "I've come to do magic for you."

Where is Kronklich? I need him here. He needs to stop Scepter. He needs to get the vial of blood back.

Party guests gather around the spectacle, waiting for the magic performance to start, clapping their hands, and hollering over each other to be heard. I hear one woman say to another, "Do you think he is going to pull something from his hat?"

I want to shout at these people to warn them, but my voice can barely croak. I roll on the floor, trying to regain control of myself. At least the nausea has stopped.

The pianists continue playing. Their music wafts over the crowd in the background, mixing with the loud chatter of spectators. I see Tremont lingering behind Scepter in his obnoxious yeti costume, laughing and drinking at the spectacle as well, the two ladies he saw earlier under each of his arms. These people are daft.

I watch in horror as Scepter reaches into his robes and removes two bloodied spines dangling from his hand like rope. As he drops them to the floor, some of the guests jump back in fright while others try to get a better look. Bringing his wrist to his face, he reaches underneath the mask and tears at his wrist with his teeth, only to then extend his hand out before him, letting the fresh blood drip onto the spines on the floor. A few drops for each. Stepping back, he stands motionless while the spines on the floor begin to slither and snake like tentacles.

Blood mixing with bone, red webs coagulate across the spines, forming cocoons of fleshy skin and mucus. Growing. Extending. First, sinewy legs and arms extend from the conglomerate of flesh and bone, and then fleshy heads pop from the center of the masses. Monsters with gray muscular skin, sharp teeth extending from their snapping jaws. They survey the audience with their one yellow eye.

The harpsichords fill the chamber with fast melodies as the guests in the front begin pushing to get away from the horrors.

"Everyone! Your entertainers!" shouts Scepter to the unsuspecting guests. He extends his arms out before him as if presenting a spectacular performance. Reaching behind his back, he produces his golden scepter and twirls it with one hand, bowing low before his audience.

He turns to Tremont, whose face is whiter than his outfit. "Excellent party," he says, and then flees through the crowd.

"Scepter!" I shout, struggling to my feet and tripping, catching myself on a chair. I see Kronklich running to my aid.

"My God, man!" says Kronklich. "Bloody devil. Was that—"

I struggle to say yes, coughing uncontrollably and dry heaving onto his boots.

"What ever is the matter? You're sick. You need water."

"No," I say, regaining my composure some. "Scepter. Go after him."

I notice Belladonna is gone too.

"But the guests, Tenor. The bogarts will shred them like confetti."

I grab Kronklich by the hem of his coat, struggling to get the words out. "Blood…Kronklich. He has my blood!"

CHAPTER
XVII

CRIMSON STREAKS ARE EVERYWHERE.

Patrons run for their lives, jumping over tables and stumbling over chairs. A man defends against a bogart with a candelabrum but screams as its deadly jaws maul him. Blood spatters the face of a woman lying on the floor. Half of her face is torn away while the other half still supports the remains of her golden mask. Pink feathers once white plume from the top of her head. She cries, reaching out for someone to help. But no one can save her. They are busy fleeing, saving their own lives.

Fire spreads across the rugs as candles are knocked from tables. A man in a frock coat uses the broken leg of a chair to assail a bogart. The creature retaliates, clamping its deadly mouth over his arm, pulling, and shredding the fabric, flesh, and tendons from his ulna and radius. Never have I heard screaming like this before. It is deafening and sick. His suffering ends in a moment and the bogart moves on to its next victim.

"Kronklich!" I shout over shrieks and wailing. "We need to head off Scepter!"

"Undoubtedly!" replies Kronklich over the terror of fleeing guests, his voice barely audible.

A fiery curtain separates us as it falls to the floor. It trails black smoke, causing my eyes to water. My face and hand tingle from the close proximity of the heat, the scars of my wounds all too fresh in my mind. Backing away, the fire rages, consuming tables, chairs, and tapestries. The red diamond on the black field turns to a blackened-threaded mess. A masked man bumps into me, half on fire, running for his life. His screams rise in short breaths. He doesn't make it ten feet before the flames silence him.

I double back to make a new way to the entrance but it's swarmed with party guests. There is no telling how many people are trying to descend the stairs at one time. Some of them will die being trampled, some from suffocation. I don't see Kronklich and assume he made it out before the rush. I notice the windows to my left.

So much for the practical way.

Taking a deep breath, I run toward the windowpane, tucking my shoulder to smash through the glass, but the bogart stops me, grappling my leg. With proofing protecting me, I drag the weight of the bogart, one step at a time, but can't shake it loose. Reaching into my leather coat, I extract Enivid, twirl it with my fingers around the handle, and slam one of the points down through the top of its head. The blade pierces bone and flesh with a crunch and the abomination ceases moving.

Breaking off its teeth from my armor, I hear a sharp *pang!* to my left. Over and over, the banging of strings repeat. The second bogart is on top of a harpsichord, raking its claws at the pianist. As if noticing for the first time, the pianist cowers away, falling backward off his bench unscathed. The other pianist continues to play, lost in the passion of music. *These people are daft!*

Ripping the strings and breaking apart wood, the bogart tears free from the confines of the harpsichord, causing a cacophony to erupt. Standing with its sinewy legs, it gazes at the stunned pianist with its yellow eye, leaning over the edge of the piano box like a cat, peering and screeching. I grab the musician by the hem of his jacket and pull. The bogart pounces but misses, splintering the wood bench like a toy, and raking its claws across the wood floor, whittling it into chiseled spirals.

I see the fear I've come to know so well in the pianist's mask. All white corneas. Black dilated pupils. "Get out of here!" I yell, jolting the man from his frozen state. A heavy weight lands on my back, forcing the wind from my lungs. Countering, I turn over, causing the bogart to fall to the floor. As I roll and roll, the bogart clamors after me, slamming its claws through the ground with every reach of its arm.

Wood breaks. Splinters fly.

I don't remember the bogarts being so strong. They could easily break my arm with one clean blow.

Recovering from rolling, I stand on my feet, as does the bogart. Grabbing a broken piece of chair, I use it like a club in conjunction with Enivid, alternating thrusts and swings to overwhelm the monster. By chance, I catch its claw with the club and trap it to the floor. With precise agility, I lash out with Enivid, separating the bogart's arm from its body. It howls like a demon, casting its severed arm to the side like a piece of meat, and charges me.

202 | F.D. G<small>ROSS</small>

I am not fast enough.

We crash through the second-story window like a satchel of bricks, plummeting to the white snow below. Scrambling around in powder, I kick my legs and swing my arms, trying to free myself from the four-foot high snow bank. The bogart screeches next to me, struggling with the snow, unable to break free from its cold cocoon. As I roll out of the embankment and onto frozen grass, bystanders cower from my emergence, unsure if I am friend or foe. Without another thought, I stab repeatedly where the bogart flails its arms and legs, turning the white snow red. Enivid finds the bogart's head and it stops moving.

The night sky is full of clouds and white flakes as I limp along the side of the mansion as fast as I can to the front of City Hall. My eyes scan for any sign of Scepter, but my luck seems limited. The neighing of horses echoes from across the drive as patrons spew from the front doors of City Hall. Manic and chaotic, they scream as they run, clothing torn and burnt. Some still wear masks. I spot Kronklich out of the surging crowd. He is on a horse, leading another with no rider, galloping through a riot of people. It is a wonder how Kronklich doesn't trample any fleeting patrons. I ready myself for his approach, stowing away the blade into my leather coat and standing firm with my legs.

Kronklich races past me on his black stallion like a demon, tossing me the reins of my horse. I kick up from the ground, allowing the pull of the leather strap to give me momentum and land on my saddle in one motion. Situating my boots into the stirrups, I stare ahead, squinting from the dirt and snow kicking up from Kronklich's horse. Kronklich's crossbow is out, pointed skyward, waiting to take aim on our prey that is nowhere in sight.

I crack the reins hard, urging my black steed to run faster. Wherever Scepter is, we need to catch him. If he makes it over the bridge before we spot him, he will be lost to us. "Hya, Hya!" I urge my horse even faster, passing patrons on foot, some jumping out of the way in fear of their life. Trees pass by in a blur as Kronklich and I charge up the muddy road. Kronklich lowers his crossbow and fires. Through the bleary snow, I see a fast-moving figure on the back of a black horse. A long nose turns to look back. A red mask gleams in the lamplight.

It's him.

With legs crouched above the saddle, Scepter pushes his horse to the limit. In one hand he holds the reins and in the other, his golden rod, *Malice*, gleams in the moonlight. I watch in horror as he splits the skulls of the innocent along the way, their heads exploding like melons, their blood cascading onto the snow banks.

"Shoot his horse!" I shout to Kronklich ahead of me, hoping his next shot counts.

Loading his crossbow with one hand, Kronklich fires another bolt but misses. Scepter's laughs echo in the wind.

The sound of galloping hooves turns to hollow tapping as Scepter reaches Hammond Bridge. The flowerless wreaths along the railing are nearly buried in the collection of snow. The sound of the bell master playing his instrument chimes in the distance.

"Watch him!" I shout as we reach the beginning of the bridge. Scepter has nearly crossed. There's no telling what he'll do once he's on the other side.

As for the Festival of the Mask, it's as if we never left. Monsters and fairies dance in the streets as we charge over the crest of Hammond Bridge. Scepter's direction never changes. Townsfolk scream as he blasts his way through the audience surrounding the bell master, knocking over those in his path, trampling them like dolls. A child is crushed. A man loses his head. Blood sprays across spectators' faces. Screams are everywhere and there are so many. Scepter's laughter chokes the wind.

"The people!" I say, swerving from a bear-costumed patron. I miss another person dressed like a tree, erected on stilts for effect. Kronklich lifts back his crossbow, never pulling the trigger, and veers to the right as I go left, following the outskirts of Travesty Park to lessen the chances of hitting a victim. Split apart, I no longer see Kronklich though the swarm of people and trees. Scepter continues barreling straight forward, knocking over more victims and jumping through bonfires. Ash scatters into the air, giving him the likeness of a demon rising from hell. *How is his horse so fast? We're losing him.*

Unlike the desolate roads of the town bathed in dim moonlight, the town square is bright, lit with bronze lampposts and the blazing bonfires. Wild eyes stare at me through the masks of the townsfolk. They stop in their tracks as I pass, startled from my sudden approach. Some raise their hands toward me in ritualistic fashion. *What is this? What are they doing?* I dig my heels into the horse's side, hurting it, not out of desire, but out of necessity, attempting to escape the growing madness. The stallion moves faster and faster, providing the results I need, putting me farther away from the grotesque scene and closer to the bastard vampire that's killed more innocent people than I can count.

My eyes water as the cold wind burns my eyes deeper and longer than before. I pass a massive fire burning in the distance, larger than any bonfire I've ever seen. Made from planks of wood and pieces of logs, I realize it is no random bonfire, but a giant burning cross.

The fire rages uncontrollably, almost unnaturally, like a red glow burning in the cold blue-white of the night. The low murmur of chanting hums all around me as I gallop past black-cloaked figures, closer to Scepter, charging through the wood-covered square, arcing between snow banks and snapping low tree branches. What has gotten into the townsfolk? They must be mad, or maybe it's the effects of the festival.

Steam emits from Scepter's horse as I am nearly upon him. Closing in, I ready Enivid with one hand and crack the reins even harder. I see Scepter's long masked nose looking over his shoulder, searching for me. He tucks lower on his horse, snapping his reins to go faster. I feel my horse trembling underneath from the demand. *Come on, boy, hold out a little longer. That's it.*

The cold steel of Enivid glints in the moonlight as it races from my hand toward Scepter. Just as the blade is about to strike, Scepter careens to the right.

The blade whistles past them, missing a tree, and arcs its way back into my hand. He's too fast. I raise my arm again to throw, but pause. The sight of wood goblins and walking trees stays my arm. What the hell? The horse slows at the sight of them. *No, no, no! I'm losing Scepter!*

They seem to be coming from every direction, the minions and goblins. Big bears walking on their hind legs, black-cloaked figures with hoods over their heads. The monsters are everywhere, seemingly coming for me. The cold moon, the large round obelisk in the night sky sheds its light down onto the crowd gathering all around me. Surrounded, I feel the horse tensing under my legs. The coarse muscles in its side contract.

"Come on, boy!" I shout at the horse, but he does nothing. He stops suddenly, apparently overwhelmed by the intense crowd advancing in all directions. "Damn it, boy! Come on!"

I can't see Scepter through the crowd. My horse begins neighing, kicking its front legs into the air, stressing, tensing. Somewhere off in the distance, a loud bell sounds through the town of Delore like a great summoning. Its deep, resonating tone penetrates the night. I feel it in my bones. At first, I think of the bell master's instrument, but the sound is too invasive, so unmusical. It is something more. Something universal. Delore's clock tower.

Bong. It sounds again, signifying midnight. The cold-moon night has reached its peak. The advancing crowd cries out in response, surging forward, ever faster. I feel a wind blow from the west, the direction of the high peaks of the Cordova Mountains. I can only hope Kronklich has somehow managed to get past the devilish crowd. Even now, I watch pixies and fairies, once shimmering with golden glitter, approach with bare feet, hopping and skipping through the snow like deranged spirits.

Blood smeared across their chests and arms, some laugh as they run past me and my black horse.

Again, my stallion kicks high into the air as a man comes too close, startled by his bear costume. Hooves descend on him with crushing force, caving his chest in and snapping his ribs. The man's screams are feeble and replaced by a woman's ranting. The words are dangerous and I prepare for what comes next.

"He killed that man! Look at him! He's dead!"

A rock comes hurtling toward my head and I duck.

"You nobles think you're high and mighty and all that, don't cha?"

The mad people swarm me, sending my horse into frenzy. I desperately try to hold on, as I know if I let go or fall, things will not go well for me. Over and over, he bucks, trying to free himself from the demented crowd, as well as from me. Something hits me in the head and I lose focus for a moment, long enough for the stallion to throw me from the saddle. I am forced to the ground with a jarring crash.

Landing prone, hooves dance around me. Human legs kick me. I pull my arms and knees in to shield my body and vital organs. A boot hits my ribs and I cringe. I hear them batter my horse, clubbing it with whatever they have available at the moment. I think about Scepter, why he's so desperate to obtain my blood. His blackened skin flashes in my mind. Where is he going?

Another kick to my ribs. I clench my teeth. Is this the end for me? Killed by madmen in a town I hate?

Echoing off the mountains, a long piercing whistle blares through the night like a demon. Shivers travel up my arms as the kicking ceases. The whistle is long and drawn out. The townsfolk look around in confusion. I know that sound. It is Dora pulling the chord of the Iron Carriage.

One of the bear-costumed men pulls hard at my shoulder, managing to turn me over. I stare into his horrible red eyes and his breath reeks of spoiled meat. As he raises a clawed hand to slash my face, I jam a dagger through his throat and watch the blood drain from under his mask and down my arm. Kicking him off of me, I suddenly realize I know where Scepter is headed.

CHAPTER XVIII

A FLASH OF A BLADE. A deafening scream. I watch a man dressed in tattered furs and goblin mask grope at his dismembered arm. Blood spatters the brown snow around me as he squirms away through the slush of mud and ice. Townsfolk run everywhere as I hear the cry of a horse. My horse. The madmen of the town are destroying him, bludgeoning him with branches and pieces of splintered wood.

I am still on the ground getting kicked and see a black-cloaked figure advancing toward me, carrying a crude wooden cudgel adorned with rusty spikes. I cannot see its face. Darkness engulfs the hood of its robes. A cult leader of some sort? I back along the ground on hands and feet as the figure runs toward me. My shoulder blades hit something solid as I watch the figure raise its club, reminding me of Scepter, the way he swings Malice, taking the lives of women and children.

I raise my arms to defend myself and the figure descends on me, shouting into the night words I do not understand. A crossbow bolt passes into its face and there is a gurgling slurp.

Strong hands grip my shoulders as I watch the lifeless body slump over. I ready my dagger to sever the hand touching me, and look up to see Kronklich and his black horse staring down at me. "You look like you could use a hand," Kronklich says, smiling. Grasping his forearm, I clamor onto the back of his horse.

With the festival advocates surrounding us and the burning cross in the distance, the night seems to be alive with the devil. The bright glow of the square illuminates like a beacon in the night. Kronklich lets out a "Hya!" and the horse lurches into action. Its strong broad chest plows through degenerates in the street like a battering ram, casting them to the wayside. I hold on to Kronklich's coat with clenched fists while holding the blood-soaked dagger in my hand, waiting for the next victim.

We pass more townsfolk dressed as walking trees and jackals, monsters and demons. They enter into the square from the surrounding homes and shops like busy ants. Kronklich suddenly veers off the path, passing between buildings and down long alleyways. The orange glow of the town is replaced with the cold dark of stone and mortar. There are shadows lingering around every corner we come to. We pass fewer and fewer souls as we rush through narrow passages and low-hanging archways. The echoing sound of hooves ricochets off the bare walls of ruined buildings.

"Where are you going?" I ask, trying to keep my growing anxiety from escaping. "Scepter didn't go this way."

"Have faith, Lord Wolfgang. Have faith!"

I want to have faith, but every jolt from the horse sends pain up my side where Scepter stabbed me, reminding me that every decision made at this point moving forward is a crucial one.

Kronklich never turns to look at me. His gaze is focused straight ahead. All I can think about is Scepter and the vial of blood he extracted from me. The words "Blood of the father" resound in my head.

I need answers.

There is significant distance between us now. I have no doubt Scepter is headed for the Iron Carriage. Of course he would go there. Where else was there to go? Now that the winter solstice is here, it is the only way down the mountain through the blizzard. Agitation grips me. I should have made sure Scepter was dead after his carriage careened off the side of Cornwall's Bluff.

The whistle sounds in the distance again, closer this time, and I can't help but think of Dora. Kronklich berates his horse, forcing it to run faster. Snow banks, buildings, trees. They pass us by in a blur as we follow the only horse tracks leading out of Delore. Moments pass and the town falls away. The air bites the skin and the drifting snow cuts like tiny knives against my eyes. I reach into my coat and put on the goggles Kronklich salvaged from the caravan wagon before leaving for the festival.

Galloping through a stretch of flat snow, we come to a dilapidated stone wall that parallels the north side of Delore. I stare at a lantern hanging from a hook in the archway as we pass, its fire barely aglow. Never slowing, we pass a corpse buried in powder. The town watch. Blood speckles the white ground around his caved-in head.

Looking over Kronklich's shoulder, I see great plumes of white clouds rising from the mountains like silvery feathers. They glow in the light of the moon, easy to see. Eerie. A white aura shimmers off the snow-covered rocks and trees. The sight is breathtaking and surreal and—evil.

Silence lingers, waiting to snuff us from existence. The trees sway in the wind but I cannot hear them. The whistle in the distance blares again.

The Iron Carriage.

I feel the vibration through the air this time, warning of its departure. There is a terrible shriek from a horse nearby, but not one of fright. It is horrible and demented. Bloodcurdling. The sound of dying.

We come to a sharp turn. The road snakes toward the north mountain range, carving through large rock expanses like a scythe of black ice. Within minutes, the mountain swallows us up as we enter into the cold deep ravines. The snow becomes thicker and with each step the horse takes, its hooves sink deeper in the soft white cover. With the double weight on his back, the stallion struggles and stumbles a few times. We are forced to a walk and cross over Scepter's tracks, moving higher still.

Steam coils everywhere, filling in the tight spaces between jagged rocks and upturned stones. The path gives way to a massive opening in the side of the mountain. A yellowish glow and long tendrils of steam bellow from within like the mouth of a fire-breathing dragon. Hissing lingers in the air.

Scepter's tracks come to an end. At the entrance of the cave, a black horse lies motionless. Throat ripped apart just under its mane, its lifeless eyes remain open, dry, and covered in snowflakes. Blood trails from the puncture wounds into the cave, disappearing beyond the fading threshold.

This isn't good.

Scepter has fed. He is replenishing his strength slowly. I have seen it before. And the next victim—my thoughts immediately fall on Dora.

"We need to hurry," I say over Kronklich's shoulder.

Kronklich simply nods.

Old Man Dora is the only engineer in Delore, which means—

The train's whistle blares again, longer and louder than before.

Kronklich snaps the reins and the horse jerks into action. We enter the mine at full speed, racing along tracks embedded in the rock, swerving between mine carts, and ducking below stalactites. Torchlight glistens in the distance through the darkness. We ascend rock mounds and descend long dips in the cave floor. It is impossible to tell where the patches of black ice are. Long icicles hang from the rafters, supporting the low portions of the tunnel. They burst across our shoulders as we race to reach the Iron Carriage.

Entering a vast chamber, a blast of hot air greets my face. Steam is everywhere, thick, making it hard to see. The whistle sounds again, and this time it is accompanied by the squealing of metal grinding on steel. A loud burst of exhumed steam blasts from somewhere beyond the darkness, and slowly, another follows. The process repeats again and again, in slowly increasing repetitions.

"The train!" I shout. "It's starting to move. There!" I point over Kronklich's shoulder.

Off in the distance, like a giant colossal beast, the Iron Carriage materializes. Its wheels grind slowly along the rails. The train, made of iron, steel, and wood, stretches far beyond the torchlight, disappearing into the mine. Train cars link to one another, forming an extensive line of passenger cars and storage containers.

Over the squealing of rusty wheels, a voice sounds through the white noise, penetrating and distinct, yet it is disembodied. "Persistent, ever so persistent. And for a cause so utterly lost."

"Scepter!" I shout, sliding off the flank of Kronklich's horse. Landing on the ground, my boots crunch through gravel as I run for the train. My proofing and leather coat creak as I plant one foot on a rising step and leap over the side railing. "Show yourself, Scepter!" My eyes dart around. Searching. Seeking. "Show yourself!"

Laughter echoes far ahead of me, beyond the light of the train cars. The bastard is hiding in the shadows somewhere, waiting. Slowly, I draw Enivid from my coat and hold it before me like a ward of evil.

"You are not quick enough, Wolfgang. Trying to stop me is, well, how do I put it, not possible." Scepter's words are conniving and followed by more laughter. I hear the footfalls of clattering boots along the metal gangway. "Constilla. Constable. We have guests!"

Constilla? Constable?

Movement from behind causes me to react. I draw my arm back to throw Enivid but stop short at the sight of Kronklich climbing over the railing. He is still wearing his regent hat, and his leather coat is open, exposing the arsenal of crossbow bolts quivered around his waist. He holds his weapon before his face as he wipes the frosted windows with his sleeve, peering inside the glass of the first passenger car.

Subtly, I feel the movement of the Iron Carriage rumbling along its tracks and watch our horse slowly fade into darkness. I feel the rusty bearings vibrate through my feet and ankles. Rocks and torches creep by in the dark like hovering ghosts as the sound of squealing metal fades to the sound of wind. The steam clears as momentum picks up. My hair and the tails of my coat begin flapping. As the Iron Carriage rolls through the dark cold, the glowing lights of the cast bronze lamps begin to illuminate. At first, they are too dim to notice, but then slowly they brighten, as if the intensity of light depended upon the speed of the train.

I need to find the old man. Sense tells me he's at the front of the train being held against his will by this Constilla or Constable, forced to operate the train. But another part of me says the old bastard is stubborn and most likely being beaten to death. Despite my dislike for Dora, despite his ill temper toward me yesterday, he's helped me, and that is enough.

The train creaks and rattles as if it were going to fall apart. The links and chains binding the cars jingle from constant motion.

"Scepter!" I shout for a second time. "You coward. Come and face me!" My eyes work the darkness, straining. "Why do you want my blood? Why do you want my son? Answer me, goddammit!" Yet there is no answer. Only the sound of wheels grinding on railroad tracks.

Ta-ta, ta-ta, ta-ta.

I feel the anger shoot through me with hatred. I need to get my blood back from Scepter or I will become subject to some estranged fate. This I'm sure. It is the same as when Bronin betrayed me by piercing my ribs with that foul contraption, the extraction dagger. He wanted my blood, tried to take it and failed. It is no mystery the Carnalreesee want my blood. But the question lingers. Why?

Kronklich comes to stand next to me, shoulder to shoulder, not uttering a word, his crossbow pointing at the next car. I watch his eyes focus, never breaking concentration. Motioning with my hand, I signal him to go around the right flank of the passenger car while I go around the left. The car itself displays glass windows and drawn curtains.

As Kronklich goes around the corner, I keep talking out loud to keep the attention drawn to me. "Since when did you start naming your creatures, Scepter? Constilla. Constable," I say mockingly. "Are those names for your bogarts?"

I continue moving along the side of the passenger car, looking for any sign of movement. Every window is frosted over. The cold in the mining tunnel is severe. Much colder than outside. My coat protects me from the wind for now, but if the train picks up speed, it will slice through me like a dagger.

Coming to a curtain-less window, I creep just below the windowsill and peer inside. Like the rest of the windowpanes, it is covered in a thick haze of frost. I chip at it with the edge of Enivid and look again. An ashen face stares back at me, still and devoid of life. Skin flaking from its forehead and cheekbones, its graying head rests against the glass in eternal slumber. I look beyond the corpse in the window and see the whole passenger car is full of the same. Bodies everywhere. Death and darkness. Scepter must be hiding in there.

The bronze lamps of the exterior passenger car barely give enough light to see. The channel rod running the length of the entire Iron Carriage buzzes below my feet, constantly humming, constantly vibrating. The light is the same light I remember from Egleaseon's ruins, the pressurized sodium lamps channeling electricity through conduits. A rotating turbine must be somewhere on the train.

Quickly, I continue, checking in each window until reaching the end of the passenger car. Peering around the corner, I find myself staring down the barrel of Kronklich's crossbow.

"Find anything?" I ask, looking ahead of us at the next few train cars. There are open containers filled to the top with minerals gathered from the mine. Copper. Iron. Silver. The mounds seem endless.

"Nothing. Only the incessant sound of rattling chains."

I look between the connecting link of the passenger car and the container holding the glittering silver mound of cargo. Chains dangle loosely between the platforms, swaying with each bump of the tracks like wind chimes.

Ta-ta, ta-ta, ta-ta.

Focusing my attention back on the passenger car, I point Enivid toward the door. "In there." The door is made of a thick red wood, enough to insulate the interior of the car from the cold exterior. A large window rests in its frame, and the ice once covering it has been disturbed.

Kronklich tips his hat down and raises his crossbow to his shoulder. We hear more rattling of chains. My grip tightens on the leather handle of my blade as Kronklich moves forward and places his hand on the latch. I watch his grip tense on the handle, but he doesn't move it.

"Bloody hell, it's stuck." Kronklich moves closer, resting the stock in the crook of his elbows while gripping the latch with two hands.

I feel something cold wrap around my neck suddenly. I try to react but it tightens just as fast, constricting my throat. I can't breathe. My free hand goes to my neck but I am unable to make a sound. *Air. I need air.* There is a heavy pull at my chin as I feel my body lift from the ground. Legs kicking and arms flailing, I can't do anything except let go of Enivid. It clatters against the metal catwalk with a loud bang. *Air. I need air!*

Pressure building, blood throbbing, I come face to face with my assailant, gold mask covering its face. It is the same mask Bronin wore, the same one the Carnalreesee wear. My vision is fading. It winks in and out. If I don't taste oxygen in the next few seconds, I will lose consciousness.

The masked figure bunches a fist full of chain in his hand, pulling the links around my neck tighter. "Quite the humorous one, aren't you?" The voice is muffled and deep like that of a man. "Take a good look, Wolfgang." The figure motions to itself. "Do I look like a bogart?"

Inside, my body is screaming. I want to kill this monster, but I need answers. My lungs need to breathe, but they can't. I stare at the red eyes underneath the horrible mask. There has to be something. A sign. A weakness.

But there is nothing.

My soul fills with angst as the Carnalreesee laughs beneath the mask.

CHAPTER
XIX

HANGING FROM THE TOP OF the passenger car, the rusty chain around my neck constricts me as I dangle in mid-air. Black spots spatter my vision as I sway back and forth before the large Carnalreesee with muscular arms.

"They told me to spare your life," the Carnalreesee says, its voice muffled behind the mask. "They told me, 'He is the key to the future, a mighty and noble lord,' but I see no lord before me. I say what's the point in keeping you around? We have your blood already." Its muscles flex. Pressure rushes to my brain. My head feels like it will explode.

The Carnalreesee pulls me in close to take a bite out of my neck, but an arrow pierces its flesh, right between the elbow and wrist. It stops suddenly, letting out a noise that sounds like annoyance.

The vampire stares at its arm, then turns to look at Kronklich down below. A growl rumbles deep from its chest and pulls on the chain around my neck in response. I feel my body rise into the air, then swing down with immense force. Pain radiates across my face as my body collides with glass and wood. Fragments explode on impact as I am sent through the door of the passenger car, rolling and sliding across the ground like a corpse. With the chain no longer constricting my air passage, my first gasping breath fills with the horrid stench of death. It assaults my nostrils, causing me to gag and cough uncontrollably. Breathing in fumes of decay, my vision wavers back to reality.

Dead bodies surround me. They are stacked on one another in piles, having been thrown into the passenger car like rotten meat. With backs exposed and spines ripped out, they are similar to the gypsies we encountered days before at the forest camp. Women, children, men. Ruthless. Merciless killing. They are townsfolk from Delore. As if snatched right off the street, unsuspecting and vulnerable, some still wear masks from the festival.

Looking through the broken window, I see movements of shadows dancing in the dim glow of the lamplight. Arms and hands flail. A cane sword thrusts forward and then swipes. A chain whips about like a snake, the same chain that moments ago nearly strangled the life from me. Rising to my feet, I reach for Enivid, but then remember it's not there. I dropped it to gain precious seconds of oxygen. I feel for the curved dagger stored behind my back and touch its sticky handle coated in blood. It will have to do.

What's left of the passenger-car door explodes as Kronklich barrels directly toward me. When I catch him in my arms, he raises his head smiling at me, the regent hat still sitting on his crown. "Quite a nifty weapon that one has," says Kronklich, gripping my shoulders. "Watch out!" he cries.

We dive into a pile of bodies just as a chain with a black hook passes through the threshold like a cannon shot, slamming into a cadaver at the back end of the car. Just as quick, it retracts like a snake on the ground, flicking and snapping with the body still attached, rattling and jingling. "Like the butcher in the meat market, that one is," concludes Kronklich.

The muscle-bound Carnalreesee steps into the train car through the splintered doorway, crushing broken glass under its menacing boots. By now, I can only assume it is male in nature.

He stands nearly seven feet tall, surveying the contents of the car like a hunter sent to flush out prey. His mask is still in place; a leather vest covers his chest, and dark leather pants cover his bulging legs, which are the size of small tree trunks. A thick haughty belt wraps around his waist and comes to meet at an ornamental sun fashioned from gold. His boots rise past his kneecaps, reminding me of a gladiator ready for battle. Buckles and large steel rings are stitched into his clothes in a mismatched array of bindings. His snake-like chain, black as obsidian, intertwines through the rings in no particular order. He lets out a deep laugh as he pulls up the rest of the chain with the terrible black hook like a fishing line, catching the body in his hand and removing it like trout from a stream. "You can call me Constable," says the vampire with purpose. "Ward of the Carnalreesee." He tilts his head to the side. "Not that it matters. I make sure our affairs and assets remain in the interest of our master."

I scramble to my feet, as does Kronklich. "And what are your interests?" I ask hoarsely, choking back the bile in my throat, massaging the area of my neck where the chain strangled me.

"To ensure the resurrection of my lord," responds Constable, his eyes hidden in the shadow of his mask. The gold shimmers along the floor and ceiling in the lamplight of the train.

His answer confuses me. I try to make sense of it, but the absurdity of it infuriates me. "Resurrection? Of whom? Egleaseon?"

I notice Kronklich move behind me and feel Enivid push against my fingertips.

Constable nods.

"You're mad," I respond, half serious and half laughing.

"So I've been told," says Constable tensing his muscles. He pulls the chain tighter across his body, forcing it to constrict him like a snake.

"What does my son have to do with it? Why are you taking him to Sunstone?"

Constable's gold mask cocks to the side. "Sunstone has everything to do with it. It's where it all started."

More riddles. I can't stand this game Constable is playing, but I have no choice but to feed into his whims.

"Where *what* started?" I ask, thinking hard on his words, but unable to make sense of them. The only relevance to Sunstone is that it is the capital of Ashton and is the location of the top religious sect. I stop suddenly, feeling sick to my stomach.

Constable releases the chain from his body, letting it hang loosely to the floor.

"How deep does the church's betrayal run?" I ask desperately, pressing further with my questions.

"Enough talk," says Constable, moving forward with lightning speed, bringing his chain around like a whip.

Kronklich and I separate from the middle, jumping out of the way of the menacing meat hook launched in our direction. It ricochets off the floor of the passenger car like a rabid atter, skittering and snapping back and forth. Sparks fly as metal collides with metal, tearing into moth-eaten couches and mutilated bodies. Pressing up against a window, I move to the side and crouch as the chain hook rakes a plush chair, lops the head off a corpse, and smashes through the side window. Hiding between two seats, I listen as Constable directs his assault to Kronklich. The rattling of the chain slides across the floor and swooshes into the air. There is a loud clang, the breaking of another window, and the frustrated voice of Constable…

"At least you're making good sport," says the oversized vampire. I hear the ripping of a seat attached to the floor and it is followed by a loud crash.

I chance peeking over the chair, seeing if Kronklich is all right, and retract my body instantly just as the chain swoops overhead. I roll back into the center aisle of the car as Constable follows through with an overhead flick of his wrist, bringing down the chain to demolish the chair I was hiding behind.

As he is vulnerable, I rush Constable with both hands on Enivid. But Constable anticipates my move, running faster than I can see to the corner of the passenger car. All in one motion, he unleashes the chain in a direct attack, shooting it like a spear straight at my chest. Jumping back, I thrust the blade into the length of the chain and twist, turning it around and around, entangling the links, and then pulling hard.

Constable staggers forward suddenly, bending at the waist with the entire chain wrapped around his body. He curses. Kronklich rushes forward, drawing forth his blade and slashing through Constable's mask. Quickly, he follows through, ramming the cane sword into Constable's shoulder.

The giant brute hardly flinches as half his mask falls to the floor. Blood trails down his face. Placing one of his large hands around Kronklich's neck, he lifts him off the ground and tosses him through the broken doorway like a toy. The gaping hole in Constable's body closes up quickly. Normally, a sword strike like that would sever a person's head from their spine.

Constable leers through half of his mask with his one visible eye focusing on me. The exposed half of his face is smooth and perfect with a chin chiseled to a point. The muscles in his jaw flex over and over like a beast salivating over meat. Still grappling his chain, I realize my plan wasn't the greatest as he begins reeling me in like a freshly caught fish. The hook on the end scrapes across the ground with each tug.

I pull at the Bawaka, trying to wrestle it free, but it doesn't move. As the train bounces along subtly, speeding through the dark tunnel of the Cordova Mountains, I look around for something useful but there is nothing. I see half of Constable's smiling teeth in the closing distance.

"There's no way around it," says Constable. "I'm going to break you piece by piece, starting with your legs. Just like I did with that old man." Constable laughs. "You don't need legs to conduct a train."

My blood runs cold at the thought of Dora's legs bent in horrible ways. Anger takes hold of me and I snap. Energy surges through me, starting from the palms of my hands and working its way up into my shoulders. I feel the rough leather handle of Enivid burning the inside of my palm.

"What did you do to him!" I scream, pulling Enivid with all my might. A loud ringing penetrates the air as Enivid cuts through Constable's chain, sending pieces of metal shrapnel flying.

The look on Constable's face is one of astonishment as I run for him, spinning my blade back and forth. We are shoulder to shoulder. He comes to life just as I engage him, bringing my blade of death before his face. He leaps back, whipping his chain into motion before him like a transparent shield. The air hums as our weapons spin. My blade, his chain. He lashes and I parry. He advances with both hands stretching the chain to grapple me, but I duck and strike low, cutting a gash into his leg. He howls this time. The smell of burning flesh fills the rushing air of the train car. Just outside the threshold, I see Kronklich crumpled next to the storage container of silver ore. "Kronklich!" I shout, but there is no response.

Constable groans as I watch him place a hand over the fresh wound, feeling it, tasting it with his fingers.

And yet, it doesn't close up.

Constable's eyes glow red. "You'll pay for that," he threatens.

With my thoughts completely engrossed in Dora and Kronklich, I rush forward with maleficence pumping through my blood. *Diana, I couldn't save your father. He is dying. He is suffering.*

Constable's rancid breath hits my face as he catches my downward thrust with Enivid in the fold of his chain. I feel it grinding into the links, creaking from the force of my anger like before.

"You really do want to kill me," says Constable, nearly whispering.

Half a chain link pops.

"That's quite the weapon you have there."

I try to block out his taunting words. I can't let the anger control me. It's what he wants. The focus of his intentions lingers with every foul word out of his mouth.

"Wolfgang. The mighty hunter. Not strong enough to save his family, though. All of the people you ever loved have been taken from you, haven't they?"

The other half of the link pops.

Constable's eyes widen as my blade cuts through the chain, passing into his shoulder, and severing his arm off completely. Fire bursts from the stump as his arm flops to the ground in a bloody mess.

Constable screams and wails like the demon he is. His eyes blaze redder than before as he grabs my throat with his other hand and squeezes. Again, I cannot breathe. What seemed like a good idea moments ago has gone terribly wrong. Constable roars as he lifts me three feet off the ground and slams me against the roof of the train car. His power is still so strong. How is it possible?

With another scream and finishing motion, he sends me sprawling through the side window of the passenger car and out into the freezing cold wind.

CHAPTER XX

THE WIND STINGS MY FACE as I am ejected from the side of the train car. Arms out, Enivid in hand, I reach for something, anything, using it like a grappling hook.

My momentary flight comes to a jarring halt as I latch on to the side of the train, right where the bars of the railing meet the metal gangway. Inches below, the soles of my boots skim the surface of the tracks rushing by. I struggle to keep them aloft in fear of having them ripped from my body.

The train rattles and bounces.

Ta-ta, ta-ta, ta-ta.

I see the cold moon high above. The Iron Carriage has moved beyond the mountain tunnel and is now barreling along the jagged cliffs of the Cordova Mountains.

I try with all my might to pull myself over the railing to safety, but the force of inertia bears me down.

The tracks rush by.

Ta-ta, ta-ta, ta-ta.

Wrapping both feet along the bottom bar of the gangway, I use my arms to inch myself forward, battling the fierce wind and snow stinging my face. The cold burns through my gloves.

My one hand, blistered and blackened from the dread rain, is stiffening up, seizing almost completely. I curse the night air as I try to hold on by wrapping my arm over the bar.

Off in the distance, through the noise of rushing wind and hissing steam, I hear swordplay. Loud sharp rings echo through my ears. A dark-gray regent hat blows past me, nearly hitting me in the face.

Kronklich.

I ignore the freeze biting through my leather coat and try bringing my legs over the railing. I fail.

Looking ahead under the glow of the train lamps, I observe an anomaly in the distance, dark and massive, approaching fast.

Again, I try to lift my body over the railing, but it's no use; the force of the train is too great. Wedging myself between the two railing bars, I try another way, exhaling as much as I can, shrinking my torso so the proofing under my coat has the same contour as my body. Tensing my muscles and straining my neck, I push against the bars and exhale even more, just as a large stony mass passes me in the darkness. The wall of the mountainside rushes by, fraying the sleeve of my coat like grinding salt.

Rolling onto my back, I breathe in deep, letting the blood rush back into my extremities. I listen again for the sound of swordplay, but it has stopped.

Quickly, I rise and run the length of the passenger car's exterior. Charging forward with Enivid in hand, I hope it's not too late for Kronklich. His sword won't be enough against Constable, even if the vampire is missing an arm. I stop in the doorway where I last saw Kronklich lying unconscious on the floor, yet it is empty.

Standing in solitude, I bob up and down with the cadence of the train.

Ta-ta, ta-ta, ta-ta.

Moonlight illuminates my surroundings like an eerie ghost land. The containers of silver and iron glitter.

"Kronklich!" I call out, yet there is no response.

I try again. "Kroooonklich!" but my attempt is useless. Where could he have gone?

Anxiety grows inside me as I leap onto the open container of silver and begin navigating my way from car to car, shifting through mounds of metallic ore, hopping the short gaps from one container to the next.

"Kronklich!"

My boots grind through minerals as I fight to keep my balance. A sudden stitch in my side reminds me of the wound where Scepter stabbed me. I need to be more aware of my condition or else I'll bleed out from opening the wound again. What good would I be to those in need of me if I were to die? I dismiss the thought. I have no time to entertain death.

Landing on the next train car with a *clang*, I listen intently, cocking my head to the left and right, trying to make out sounds other than the running of the tracks and the chug of the steam engine. I hear the soft sound of creaking metal. The passenger car before me has a door leading into the back of it and two metal gangways that circumnavigate around the exterior. The door swings freely on its hinges, banging against the wall repeatedly. Quickly, I advance, thrusting myself into the darkness beyond. Moonlight pours in through filthy windows, revealing shredded passenger chairs and couches once covered in fancy fabrics. Tables and cabinets lie on their sides as I move forward, searching behind every shaded corner. Clouds of dust coil low in the shafts of light. Glass crunches under my boots as I move to stand before the door at the far end of the car. Without waiting, I smash the door open with a loud *bang* and am greeted with outside air again.

I come to another passenger car. The howling wind sends snowflakes blowing past my cheeks as I glance around. Realizing there are no walkways to move around the exterior, I am left with the options of going through the back door of the next passenger car or up the wrung ladder to the roof. I decide on the door, ruling out the possibility of a one-armed Constable ascending the ladder if he could avoid it.

The inside is stuffy. It reeks of candles and death. Throughout the center aisle, ghostly images of pale-skinned women stare back at me.

Hollow eye sockets. Shriveled skin. They do not react to my arrival. Are they real? Clothed in fine dresses, the colors and styles are more than extravagant. Some are elegant. Some are absurd. One of them reminds me of a cross between a peacock and a thrush. Blood drippings run down the front of the dresses, ruining their purity. Only the arms of the bodies sway to and fro with the ambience of the train. Yet still, they stand erect somehow, and as lifeless as they appear, I approach them cautiously, waiting for them to react to my advance. One by one,

I pass them, five dead girls in all, with their long hair askew and cast to the sides and front of their faces. It isn't until I pass the first one, dressed as a yellowish tart cake, that I realize how they are able to stand. A long wooden pole has been shoved through their bodies, entering through a large gaping hole in the back and emerging out the front of the throat.

I back away, startled by the brutality, trying to keep my composure.

Searching the passenger car for answers, eyeing the storage shelves above, I pass my hands over chairs, feeling for something. The shelves are lined with burning candles and skulls. Trails of wax drip down in the form of stalactites, making a damp, dark cave of the gruesome scene. I pull at the collar of my coat, relieving the thick energy hovering in the air. I try to make sense of the murdered girls before me. Who would do such a thing? I imagine they too were victims from the Festival of the Mask.

The room is filled with a voice unexpectedly. "Aren't they beautiful?"

Seductive, attractive, and melancholy; the voice is feminine. My spine tingles despite the uncomfortable heat growing underneath my armor. The voice continues, "I particularly like the one in crushed red velvet. The stain doesn't show quite as much."

Slowly my eyes move to the back of the compartment. There, in the glow of candlelight, perches a thin woman with nut-brown hair on a couch, dressed in a lacey white undergarment. With only half of her body in the light and the other half in shadow, I can somewhat make out that she's holding a woman in a blue dress. Ribbons lace the blonde hair spilling to one side of her bloodied forehead. Eyes missing, gouged out like the rest, the other side of her face is crushed, caved in as if brutally beaten with a cudgel.

"I know. I know. I wish Scepter were more careful with them," the half-naked woman says, nudging the corpse in her arms in my direction as if I should sympathize with her. She drops the body to the floor with a thud and her red eyes fix on me. "Doesn't matter. Her dress was horrible anyway. Blue is not my color."

«You're sick,» I say, slowly maneuvering my feet into a ready position.

"No, I'm Constilla, one of the six Carnalreesee." She pauses. "No. That's not right. Let me correct myself. Five Carnalreesee. You killed Caesar." Constilla glares at me like a piece of meat. Even now as she climbs off the couch, white fangs extend slowly from her lips. "How did you do it?" she asks. "It's impossible to kill us. Our power comes from the one. Blood of the father."

Blood of the father, again? The words haunt me. Tease me. I want to answer her, but I am inflicted with the purest hatred toward the Carnalreesee in every way. Constilla has desecrated these innocent women. Defiled them in unspeakable ways. "How could you—" I pause, shaking with anger. I can't even finish my question.

"What else could I do?" she continues. "Scepter wanted their spines and I needed them to model my dresses." She smiles. "My collection is to die for."

I cannot comprehend the reasoning behind this monstrous beast's action. No remorse. No *feeling*.

I throw Enivid with rage. Disgust fills me, unlike ever before. I remember my dead wife and the disappearance of my son. But my actions are sloppy, and as the four-pointed blade spins its way toward Constilla, she leaps into the air, flipping her body upside down, and clings to the ceiling with long black talons. Her fingers and toes are no longer present. Enivid comes back to me as Constilla spiders across the ceiling, staying in the shadows of the candlelight. I watch her scramble toward me as dark lines spread across her pale cheeks. Within the shadow, her eyes glow red, hovering as if suspended in air. I throw my blade again and she maneuvers out of the way, springing down from the ceiling just as the blade skims off the metal roof. There is a flash of light, then sparks, and I am forced to the ground. I hear Enivid skim across the floor as the long talons try penetrating the proofing hidden under my coat.

For such a small vampire, Constilla's power is great. Her weight is heavy as she pins me to the floor, her fleshy white breasts in my face, her sickening smile revealing more than two sharp fangs. Her mouth is full of razor-sharp teeth. Pieces of skin and cartilage hang loosely between them. "You have a pretty face," she says. "Yours would be a nice addition to my collection. You could model my husband Constable's clothes for me. Have you met him?" She retracts one of her claws from my chest and brings it before my face. "Of course, those eyes won't do." She thrusts down with her black talons, denting the metal floor as I turn my head at the last second. Again, she strikes, missing my face and nicking my hair. I hear the frustration in her throat. "Quit squirming around like a worm!"

She tries again, but her thrust ends with one of my daggers through her hand. Blood spurts across my face as I roll away. She tries to grab me with one of her spider-like legs but misses, knocking over a dead girl in a cream dress. I tuck my body between two chairs, using them as an obstacle to slow Constilla down.

One by one, she begins ripping the couches from their foundations, sending nails flying and tearing holes in the floor.

The clacking noise of the tracks becomes louder and the whistling of wind invades the interior of the passenger car.

Ta-ta, ta-ta, ta-ta.

"Don't try to hide from me, worm. Come out and squirm around a bit."

The chair in front of me suddenly launches into the air and slams into the ceiling above, cracking the roof and knocking over candles in the storage compartments. The pressure in my ears suddenly increase, forcing me to swallow back the sharp pain at the back of my jaw. A freezing wind whips through the passenger car, wailing like a ghost, blowing out the remaining candles. Suddenly, it is totally dark inside.

I scramble across the center aisle, ducking between more couches, but something ensnares my leg. One of Constilla's claws. Both chairs on either side of me rip from their foundations as she positions her body over me like a fly caught in a web.

"Naughty, naughty, worm."

The scent of her decayed breath hovers around me like a cloud, finding its way into my nostrils, forcing me to gag. She tosses me by the leg, sending me through the air like a puppet. I slam into the back of the train car, feeling my brain rattle. The stitch at my side burns like fire. Sore, bruised, and disorientated, I try to collect myself while watching Constilla scramble across the ceiling toward me, the claws on her hands and feet tapping against the metal roof like pelting rain. "Some hunter you are," she says. "All soft and no resilience. You're not proving to be much fun at all."

Constilla mocks me as if I am her personal plaything waiting to be eaten. If I am to beat her, the odds need to be in my favor. Finding myself trapped in this train car is making it that much harder. I need to escape or I will die. It's that simple.

Her talons continue to tap against the metal as she approaches, nearer and nearer. My eyes desperately search for Enivid but I can't see it in the lingering darkness. Only a few swirls of smoke illuminate through the pale moonlight shining through the windows. I see Constilla's eyes getting closer.

Through the blackness, as if someone or something were watching over me, a sliver of light appears in the distance like a dancing orb. It glints with the reflection of steel.

"Aww, poor little worm," comes Constilla's steamy breath directly above me. "You're scared aren't you? I can sense it. Allow me to comfort you."

She turns me around to face her, to look into those horrible blood-red eyes, growing bigger as she lowers her head. I watch her face spread into a grin, and then the razor fangs begin to show. "A kiss from my lips will bestow you everlasting life."

"I would sooner die."

Pulling the dagger from my belt, I plunge it deep into one of her eye sockets, then the other. She screams in a fit of rage. Blood gushes onto the floor as her arms flail about, batting me away from her, and making me abandon my dagger, still lodged in her face. "What did you do to me! I can't see!"

Now is my chance.

I dive forward just as I feel the rush of air pass my body. Landing on my side, I pull myself forward on elbows and knees, reaching until I feel the metal and leather in my hand.

"I'm going to kill you! I'm going to kill you!" screams Constilla behind me. Malice seethes from her mouth with every passing word. She is enraged and unpredictable, and blocks the way I entered the passenger car.

Doubling back, I dash down the center aisles, passing the bodies modeling Constilla's dresses, and finally reach the other end of the passenger car. I try the handle, but it doesn't budge. Turning around, I watch Constilla thrash about the interior, hair tossing back and forth, blood spattering the windows and walls.

Quickly scanning the room, I see my only option to escape is through a window, but I'm not sure my strength is enough to break through. The windows are made to withstand the extreme cold and gale-force winds while the Iron Carriage makes its way through the mountains. I lift one of the upturned passenger chairs and throw it awkwardly at a window, but it bounces off pathetically.

Constilla begins making her way toward me, sniffing the air with snorts from her nose, and slicing the atmosphere with her long claws. "I'm going to kill you, then drink you, then eat you! Slowly, I will suck the tender marrow from your bones, down to every last drop. There will be no sharing." She laughs hideously.

I lift another chair to throw at the glass, and that's when I notice the bent panel on the floor. Peeled away like the flesh from a fruit, the chairs Constilla uprooted left large gaps in the metal ground. Securing Enivid to my side, I crouch and begin pushing and pulling on the damaged metal in every direction possible. More air fills the passenger car from outside. Wind whips at my face, blowing my hair about wildly.

"What's that sound? What are you doing?" I hear Constilla's claws tapping closer. "You're leaving? No! You can't leave!"

In a final attempt, I push on the piece of metal flap with all my might, creating a large enough hole for my body to fit through. The tracks below rush by.

Ta-ta, ta-ta, ta-ta.

Gripping the edges of the torn metal, I hear claws scraping toward me as I drop through the gap. The jagged edges cut into my gloves while I strain my body to keep my legs from touching the ground below. The stitch at my side aches as I struggle to swing my legs up to grapple the bars running along the underside of the train.

Ta-at, ta-ta, ta-ta.

Long black claws plunge through the gaping hole, trying to grab a hold of something, anything—me. I hear Constilla shouting with frustration from inside the train. "Nnnnaaggghhhhhh!

Just wait till I sink my fingers into you, worm!" There is a loud thumping against the inside.

I need to move fast, but navigating the underside of the train is no simple task. The way is riddled with bars connecting to other bars in multiple directions. I can hear the loud hum of the electrical conduits channeling their energy to the lamps on the top side of the train.

Suddenly, a black talon bursts through the floor just inches from my leg. Hand over hand and blood pressure rising, I start sliding my way along the bars like an insect. I hear Constilla's frustrated voice muffled in the distance, but I can hear it distinctly through the roar of the wind. "Missed? You must be right here." Another talon pierces the metal close by. I wonder how she's judging my location. Sound? Vibrations?

I place my hands on another bar and strain as I transition to the next, feeling the burn in my core and the wound at my side. There is cracking and grinding just above my head, and I pull myself to the side just as the metal floor breaks apart again. Not one hand but two rip through.

Constilla is laughing at me. Her hands grip the sides of the freshly torn portal and begin pulling two plates back with amazing strength. I watch as her face bends closer and closer to the opening. The mangled gore where her eyes used to be press right against the frayed edges of the opening. "Is that you, worm? Is it? I can smell you're close. I can taste your fear." A large purplish tongue protrudes between her sharp fangs, lapping the sides of the hole like a snake slithering through jagged rocks. I can do nothing as it passes over my face, touching the gashes below my eye and lapping my ear. "Ah, there you are, worm. Blood of the father."

There is nothing I can do while I hold the bar. If I let go, I will become mangled in the wheels of the Iron Carriage.

"Time to end this little game," says Constilla in a hoarse voice. Unable to move back, I watch as she reaches with one of her arms to pluck me from the underside of the train.

A loud steam whistle suddenly blares somewhere in the distance toward the front of the train. It resonates loud and long, echoing down the mountainside.

Constilla's hand stops. "What is this?" Her voice is a crackle from above. "Not now, not now!" she screams. Constilla's hand retracts through the hole and out of sight. I am left holding on for life, alone and hovering just above the rushing tracks of death.

My mind races at the thought of Old Man Dora pulling the whistle cord to distract the Carnalreesee. But did he know we were on the train, and was it even him? My thoughts jump to Kronklich. Maybe he managed to find his way to the front of the train and rescue Dora and was now signaling me to come. Regardless of its origin, the whistle altered Constilla's course of action. And not necessarily for the better.

Slowly, methodically, I begin making my way forward, one iron bar at a time. The cold wind slices through me like a knife, but I don't care. I need to get to my comrades and stop the Carnalreesee with their hellish plan. Sliding my legs along the freezing cold bars, I make way toward the front of the train, slowly, yet surely. With Constilla well on her way, it is a race now to the front of the train. Constilla versus me.

I need to get to my comrades before she does.

CHAPTER XXI

IT IS NO SURPRISE THAT my body is not cooperating. I will it to move faster, but hanging upside down drains the blood from my arms and legs. I feel the tingling sensation spread through each limb as I struggle to hold on. With the tracks rushing by and the wind piercing my body, it would be so easy to let go and end my suffering. All of this strife and struggle stemming from the core of my body, so physical, so real. I can't understand why I want to give up so suddenly.

Determination forces me to continue. I pull myself along the rusted pipes under the train faster now and clasp my hands onto the side of the gangway. I'm not entirely sure how far I traversed. I've come closer to the engine room, this I know for sure. I can hear the roar of the furnace close by. The first car, like all trains, is the locomotive, which serves as the driving horse of the Iron Carriage.

Pulling myself up, I roll onto my side and stare at the large plumes of steam blowing into the night sky. Breathing in the cold air, I am thankful to no longer be suspended above the menacing tracks. Even in this position, I still feel the fatigue and urge to just give up. Maybe it's the hopeless, impossible odds against me at the moment. Maybe it's from the wicked pain from my blackened, pustuled hand, covered in the leather glove. Maybe it's the scars on my cheek that burn from the intensity of the cold. All of these inflictions add to one another. And how they are so very real, so devastating.

The train speeds on through the dark country of the Cordova Mountains, relentlessly, with bearings squealing and lamps flickering. The tracks get worse as I feel every little bump the train runs over. There is a reason why the use of the train is banned during the winter times of the year. Snow and ice. I imagine thick layers of white covering the tracks and the impact of large frozen boulders. I close my eyes for a moment's rest.

Thoughts of a fireplace crackle at the back of my mind, a warm hearth of redwood and birch, oak berries and bergamot steaming in the kettle. Books along the walls of my study flush my memories in a painful way. Every facing side, different colors, thick bindings, and frayed tattered edges.

I see her again. Her soft body lying on the plush purple couch. Her white linen dress, her black hair sprawled over the throw pillows.

"Have you come to torment me again, my love?" I ask her.

Her eyes are so dark, her nickname used to be black beauty when she was young.

"Curse you, Tenor," she says to me. "Look, I've brought you something."

There is a teakettle and cups and saucers laid about the table of black wood. She stands, revealing her tender form to me. Leaning over, I watch her tender breasts through the linen as she pours me a cup of, what is it? Morning black? Bergamot? The liquid is dark, but its aroma I cannot smell.

"Please, Tenor," says her gentle voice, "you must warm yourself. You will catch a chill. Do it for me."

Kronklich suddenly appears from across the room. "Lord Wolfgang, I have brought what you requested. Freshly brewed red—"

"Kronklich? What are you doing here?"

The black beauty that was once leaning over me is now kneeling before me. "What's the matter, Tenor? You're not thirsty?"

I knock the saucer and cup from her hands, spilling the dark liquid across the black wooden table. Her eyes are wide and full of emptiness. Something moves across the table. Tiny black spiders trail from the inside of the tilted cup, scattering across the table like ants.

"What devilry is this? What sorcery?" Somehow I grab her by the back of her hair and pull her close to my lips. "How dare you." I want to reach for my dagger or Enivid, but I can't feel my arms. My hands are numb.

"Ouch, Tenor, you're hurting me," pleads the woman.

This is not my Diana.

This is not my black beauty.

A teakettle whistles somewhere off in the distance.

Ta-ta, ta-ta, ta-ta.

I come out of my unbidden thoughts and remember the menacing tracks below me rushing by. My body shivers from the icy wind relentlessly cutting through me like a scythe. Although feeling has returned to my limbs, my heart is cold and empty. I immediately think of Belladonna, the woman who looked like my D at the Festival of the Mask, the one who fed me the drug, who smiled her smile, who smelled like her. Black hair. Beautiful lips.

Evil has so many forms.

How could I so easily be influenced? Diana. She gives me strength, and evil has found a way to attack the very power that drives me. But why? How has my mind betrayed me?

The steam whistle blows defiantly loud again, and the moon blares its pale light, causing the train to glow an ashen white. Weary of Constilla, my eyes, darting back and forth, search every shadow and corner I come to. The image of her pale face and gouged eyes makes me paranoid. I cringe at the thought of her grotesque purple tongue running the course of my face again. I can't stop thinking about Diana and Kronklich and Dora as I run along the gangway, getting closer to the front of the train. The thought of more death on my hands fills me with strife. If only I were stronger. If only I had the foresight to predict any of this.

There has been so much loss, and I am lost. That sense of futility overcomes me again and I have to fight it, to push it out of my mind and just continue with my purpose of saving the people I love.

I still don't know where Kronklich is and that worries me, despite all the times he's disappeared before. This time feels different.

I find myself slowing to a walk. Looking around, I see I've arrived at a gruesome sight. Corpses lie scattered along the gangway here and there, but not of the human kind. Gray sinewy monsters lie motionless. Strewn about the metal grating, some are without heads, while others are missing limbs.

Bogarts. Their yellow eyes stare at me in a petrified gaze as I slowly advance through the carnage. One of them is still alive, twitching where it lies. It tries to raise its head from the floor as ooze drips from its sharp teeth. There is a long gash in its side and its hands and feet have been hewn off.

Such brutality.

Such malice.

I wonder if Kronklich did this in his fight against Constable, or was this the work of Constilla? I stab the bogart through its brain and press on.

More corpses appear in the dim light. An arm severed here. A leg chopped there. It's as if a lumberjack was set free in a forest. But what grabs my attention the most is the caved-in face of a bogart's corpse. Brutally beaten, the wound shows similar evidence as if its skull was smashed with a hammer. Blood decorates the walls and windows of the train car. Moving along the gangway, I clear each remaining car until I reach the last. Standing at the front of the train, I stare out into the vast countryside. Wind stings my eyes as I see beyond the flurry. The snow comes down in droves, and through the hazy white, I see the large dark forms of the Cordova Mountains moving slowly in the distance. The train glows as it enters a tunnel.

Drawing Enivid in one hand and the dagger in the other, I move before the opening leading into the engine room. A bogart, lying dead against the wall, displays a massive gash in the center of its face. Blood spatters the wall and its single eye is split down the middle. The blood trail leads through the opening, beckoning me to come forward. I take a breath and pass over the threshold.

The room is hot and smoky. A bright reddish glow burns from the smoke box at the front of the room. Its light is dim and makes it hard to see the piles of soot and coal scattered around its large opening. The thick metal door groans slowly back and forth with the movement of the train. Despite the heat generating from the coal oven, a hatch in the center of the ceiling lies ajar, allowing drifts of snow to twirl their way into the car and melt on the floor. A metal ladder rises from the floor to the top, which allows the conductor to survey his horizon on an as-needed basis. Shadows cast about the many crevices and corners of the room as the train jolts along the tracks. Lanterns hanging on either side of the room rattle, spilling some of their burning oil onto the floor. Despite the room's claustrophobic ambience, I am thrown off by its emptiness. No one is here. Not a soul. I stare at the long chain hanging next to the control panel, where the mechanisms to drive the train wait unattended. Whoever pulled the chain to sound the whistle is no longer here.

I take a few steps inside and feel something strange. It hovers around me like static electricity. My eyes search the interior frantically, but they fail to find a source. I listen to the roaring inferno of the furnace behind me and feel its welcoming warmth. I long for that fireplace I dreamt of earlier, but remain alert, stepping back and forth over loose piles of coal. Eyeing the ladder for a moment, I move to climb it, but as I place my hand and boot on the first rungs, I hear an odd sound come from the back of the engine room. Stepping down, I advance toward one of the corners loaded to the ceiling with crates and barrels and move toward the darkness slowly, anticipating Constilla jumping out at me any second. Little does she know I am ready for her. I raise Enivid ever so slightly as I push against one of the barrels, knocking it to the ground. It hits the floor with a loud crash, sending coal and black dust clouds along the ground.

"There's no use hiding. I know you're in there," I say to the corner of the room, to the darkness. I hear more scuffling and scraping and can't wait any longer. I tear away the remaining barrels in a fury, one by one, hoping to catch the wicked bitch off guard, and suddenly a loud scraggly voice shouts my name. "Tenor!"

Instincts cause me to duck as the edge of an axe soars over my head, displacing the air around me in a gust of wind. Dodging to the side, I look up just in time to see Old Man Dora bury his axe into the forehead of Constilla. She lets out a startled cry as her body convulses from the metal splitting the fibers and muscles in her head. Arms falling to her sides, she crumples to the floor.

Without a second thought, I jump on top of her with Enivid and plunge the holy blade straight through her despicable heart. She screams as fire bursts from the wound. Flames issue from her hollow eye sockets as her head twists back and forth in spasms. For a moment, I think her head will pop from its foundation, but it soon stops, and I feel her substance underneath me begin to transform. Her body and flesh wilt to a papery membrane, which shrinks, fitting tightly over her skull. Old age takes her in a minute, and then her bones dissolve to ash.

Slowly, I stand, brushing the dust away from my clothes. Turning toward Dora, I see he is busy stabilizing himself on one leg, leaning on his axe and holding on to one of the barrels. He is grinning.

"Think you're the only one who knows how to do it?"

I have no words for the old man as I stare at him. He is alive and breathing, and speaking, yet his leg is destroyed, bent and broken at an impossible angle. It is true what Constable said, his warning of harm to Dora, and I find myself wanting to drive Enivid straight through his skull even more than before.

"When I heard the whistle blow, I knew something wasn't right. I started making my way here, emerging from my sanctuary of crates and staying in the shadows," says Dora.

"So it was you who left the trail of bodies behind," I say in disbelief, eying his leg again. It is twisted in such a way that I can't imagine him staying conscious for any length of time.

"It will take more than a broken leg to take this bastard down," says Dora wincing. The cracks in his wrinkled face are more pronounced than ever before. "I may be old, but my heart is stubborn. Some say it's so cold it's made of steel. Ha! Would you believe that? I am a bloody blacksmith after all."

Somehow Dora manages a slight chuckle, but ends in a fit of coughing. He loses balance but manages to keep himself from toppling over.

"Goddamn brute. That big one with the chains did this to me.»

"Don't worry about him anymore," I say. "I cut his arm off."

Dora's eyes widen at my words, then he nods his head. "Well good. Might've been better if you cut his head off though."

"Really didn't get the chance to," I say, somewhat annoyed. Damn Dora's expectations, always judging. I try to stay focused. "Kronklich and I were separated in the fight. I've been looking for him. Have you seen him?"

"What, your strange friend who talks funny? No. But it was probably him who blew the whistle." Dora starts hobbling his way over toward the smoke box and controls at the front of the engine room. "They really made a mess of this place, didn't they?" He pokes at the piles of coal with his axe and slams the furnace door shut.

"What are you doing?" I ask, as he begins tugging on one of the many levers.

"What does it look like I'm doing?" Dora pulls with all his might on a lever, but it doesn't budge an inch. "Damn," he grunts. "Bloody bastards seized the brakes."

I look at him as he looks at me. "You can't stop the train."

"The hell I can. I'm the engineer of this runaway death trap. If you haven't noticed, the vampires have us going full speed through the Cordova Mountains. Mark my words, there's a glacier just waiting for us out there."

I follow his hand as he points out the front windows. The silver moon burns through a layer of gray overcast clouds as the dark shadows of trees pass quickly in a blur. We are no longer in a tunnel, and as Dora's eyes search mine, I can see the pleading look on his face, one of desperation and reason. I understand his cause for concern and why he wants to stop the train. But we can't stop. Not now. We've come too far. "The Iron Carriage is headed straight to Sunstone. It's where Dorian is being taken."

Dora looks at me with his beady little eyes. I think it's the first time I've seen them sober. With a determined look and clenched jaw, he grinds his bottom teeth, as if chewing on something. "In that case, we're going to need more speed," he says, throwing his axe to the side and snatching up a nearby shovel. He opens the furnace door, spits into his hands, and begins shoveling piles of coal into the furnace with a renewed vigor. With every pile that enters the oven, the fire burns brighter and hotter. Dora sweats before the smoke box like a minion slaving before its demon master, feeding it more power with every shovel full.

Even though he is a short, squat old man, his muscles bulge and glisten in the furnace light. I stand there a moment, admiring him despite his stubbornness and lack of sensibility. I watch him work with the pain he must be enduring, showing no lack of passion for his grandson. I know he loves Dorian to no end, even if he truly hates my guts for having stolen his daughter from him all those many years ago. At least he is able to look beyond hate and set aside his differences in these dire times.

I smile.

Shouting somewhere off in the distance carries on the howling wind. A voice full of anxiety and command wafts down through the open hatch in the roof of the engine room. Dora continues to shovel as if hearing nothing.

Slowly, I approach the metal ladder leading up. "Do you hear that?" I ask, but Dora continues as if he hasn't heard me.

The voice comes louder this time. "Wolfgang! Come out wherever you are!" the voice teases over the abrasive wind.

Looking back one more time, then ascending the ladder, I leave Dora to his task. He is lost in his work. *He will be fine. I'm sure of it.*

The voice comes again in the wind. "Better hurry up, Wolfgang. You have about ten seconds before I cave your friend's head in with the tip of my scepter."

CHAPTER
XXII

WIND BITES MY FACE. GALE forces push against me, battering my body back and forth like a thicket weed. It is cold and freezing on top of the train. Already I feel the shivering force its way through my body. I've been in this situation before. The time I fell into the Faust River. The psychotic waters of the damned. That horrible curse feeding into Egleaseon's ruins. My lips are frozen. Already I cannot feel them. I try to form words to shout across the rooftop, but nothing coherent emerges.

Across the way, through the haze of snow and silver light, three figures wait for me. At first, it is perplexing, the way they are standing in such awkward positions. But soon I realize that not all of them are standing. One of them is kneeling. And that one is Kronklich.

Body bound by a coil of chain, he waits motionless, gagged at the mouth by the same chain imprisoning his arms and legs. I'm too far away to tell if he is all right, and as I approach slowly, ensuring my footing won't send me to my doom, the other two figures do not move. One of them stands tall and erect, a golden scepter in its hand and a red-nosed mask covering its face, and the other remains somewhat slumped over, grasping a shoulder where an arm used to be.

"So glad to have you join us, Wolfgang!" shouts the red-masked villain from afar. I can barely hear Scepter over the loud wind and the roaring of the wheels along the tracks.

"Let him go!" I shout back. The metal roof is stiff with ice. I've only taken two steps and I can feel its slickness. Every couple of feet, a pipe juts out of the roof. Steam rises from their open ends in a steady stream of white smoke.

Laughter comes from Scepter behind that awful mask. "Let him go? Let him go?" There is more laughter. "You think we've come all this way, you and I, to just *let him go?*" Scepter turns his laughing head toward Constable. "All right!"

There is a grin on Constable's face as he lets the slack out on the chain wrapped around Kronklich.

"No!" I scream.

Kronklich's body slides along the rooftop, hastily away from Constable, nearly slipping from the train. Constable pulls suddenly with his one arm and the chain goes taught, suspending Kronklich off the side with the black hook of the chain buried deep in his leg. The chains wrapped around Kronklich's body strain again and he lets out a cry of agony. Blood trails from the wound in his leg.

Scepter's laughter is maniacal as the train jerks suddenly and I drop to one knee. The glow of the moon reveals the tops of trees rushing by.

"It doesn't have to be like this, you know," shouts Scepter, pointing Malice at me like some demented warden. With neither of his hands holding on to the train, he never loses balance. Cloak snapping in the wind, he produces a crossbow from behind his back and aims it toward me. "You could just give me what I want and we'll call it an evening. What do you say?" He fires Kronklich's bow, and the bolt ricochets off the metal roof with a ping.

"What do you want?" I ask in desperation. "You already have my blood!" It is no surprise to me Scepter is mad. How he chose to interact and negotiate is absurd.

"Yes, this is very true! I do have your blood. But I've come to a certain dilemma that I can't wrap my head around at the moment."

I watch as Scepter shoulders Kronklich's crossbow and reaches into the folds of his robes. He removes a dagger from it, long and needle-like, crude and menacing. I've seen that knife before. The extraction dagger. He tosses it toward me like one would throw a treat to a dog. It slides across the roof toward me, stopping at the base of my feet. "I'll be needing more of that blood."

I look down at the contraption lying before my boots. So many times I have been stabbed with it, felt its piercing blade enter my flesh. There is an empty vial set in the handle while three more rest beside it, bound together.

"Isn't one enough?" I say, placing my foot over it so it doesn't fly off the side of the Iron Carriage.

"Hardly," says Scepter as he slowly makes his way toward Kronklich, still suspended off the side of the train. "Think of it as insurance." I watch Kronklich struggle for the blade sticking out of his leg, but he can't reach it. Constable's chain holds him fast.

"And if I say no?" I cringe from my own question. I know what Scepter is capable of. I know what he will do if I say no. But I need to buy time.

Laughter pours from Scepter again, only this time, it is low and sinister. "Would you really say no to me, Wolfgang?" He stops before Kronklich's body where it is braced against the metal engine car and lowers Malice to Kronklich's wide-eyed stare. He raises his scepter like a club and swings, breaking off one of the metal pipes instead of bashing Kronklich's face in. A burst of steam explodes from the sudden release and hisses a steady stream of furling clouds. Scepter laughs. "I couldn't possibly miss again." He raises Malice once more, bathing it in moonlight.

"No! Wait! I'll do it," I shout across the roof.

I am out of time.

Bending down, I collect the ridged contraption in my hand. The metal is cold along the blade and the handle is ribbed with wire binding. The glass vials tinkle together as I hold the dagger before me like a poison. Am I really going to insert this into my body? The memories of Bronin and Scepter stabbing me with this dagger come back to me. I look over at Kronklich, swaying helplessly off the side of the train, suffering, black hook sticking out of his leg. Constable grips the chain with his one arm, twisting. There is a look of pleading in Kronklich's gaze. Not one of mercy, but one of not giving in. He shakes his head and I am left in despair. He is my friend, my only companion. Pointing the dagger inward toward myself, I look at its serrated blade one more time, pausing before plunging it into my side. I see Scepter's eyes glowing triumphantly as he watches me through the snow flurry. I can still see the parts of his caked black skin from under his mask.

The whistle of the Iron Carriage suddenly emits a burst of steamy smoke, deafening my eardrums with its piercing sound. I am thrown onto my stomach as the whole train shakes. Keeping myself from sliding off the roof, I use the extraction dagger to anchor a hole into the metal and brace myself in place. White powdery snow blankets everything around me like a celestial spirit. It is cold against my face and body as I try to shake away the excess snow caught in my eyes. *What the hell just happened?*

"Snowdrifts!" shouts a voice from below, a voice that could only come from Dora. Trying to get a grasp of the situation, I look over the sides of the train to see the train has entered another pass through the mountains. Rock cliffs fly by quicker than I can make out. Streaks of white pearl saturate my vision. Pulling myself back to the center of the roof, I take a deep breath. I fear the worst as I look over my shoulder where I last saw Kronklich. He is there, but Constable is not. He is beyond Kronklich, straining to hold on to the back train car with his one arm and hand. The chain, no longer in his grasp, flaps loosely from his body like a wild tentacle. His head moves back and forth frantically. I realize suddenly, Scepter is missing. Did the snowdrift knock him from the train?

"Kronklich!" I shout, uprighting myself to a crouching position. "Are you all right?" I see the chain has gone slack from his mouth.

"Tenor, behind you!" warns Kronklich.

But it is too late.

A sharp pain issues from the center of my back as I stumble forward, slamming face first onto the metal roof. My skin burns as my face scrapes against the ice.

"Did you really think a little snow would stop me after what you did to me on Cornwall's Bluff? Forgetful, aren't we?"

I turn around to see Scepter walking toward me, twirling Malice in one hand and holding his other hand out to the side. The moon's large orb hangs low in the sky. There is a faint strip of pink on the horizon.

"Let me help you remember." Scepter slowly peels the red mask from his face, revealing the blackened pustuled burns from when he was left to die in the sunlight. Pieces of burnt flesh stick to the mask as he tosses it from the Iron Carriage. Despite his entire face having been burnt to a crisp, there are some parts that have begun to heal. Only his eyes and teeth remain their true color.

Scepter smiles. "The extra vials of your blood were a safety precaution, just in case I lost the one I already have. But I have reconsidered killing you due to the elevated state of things. Martyr, will just have to live with it."

Martyr. Another name. Another vampire to kill. More plans in the making I am unaware of. The intent of the Carnalreesee extends further than I thought.

"The time has come for your departure, Wolfgang," says Scepter. He stops twirling his golden baton and the smile vanishes from his face.

There is no time to think. Scepter swings and I leap back, minding the footing along the icy roof. Snow-covered rocks and trees rush by as I regain control. The cold wind snaps my hair and coat about my body. Over and over, Scepter swipes at me, missing and denting the floor of the roof.

Halfway between the front and back of the engine car, I squint into the snowy wind, watching the backdrop of the mountains rush by. Scepter is only feet away from me. "You're going to make this difficult, aren't you?" he says, pressing his attack, never losing a step in his stride. He swipes the air before him for good measure. "I'm going to crush your head into a bloody pulp. It will be glorious watching it explode like a melon."

Crouching low with both arms extended, I retrieve Enivid from my hip and wait for Scepter's next move. "Kronklich!" I shout over my shoulder, daring not to look away. "Are you all right?"

"Never been better, sir," says Kronklich feebly through the rush of the wind.

Scepter's laughter penetrates through the roaring air all around us. "Really. I thought the great mighty hunter would learn his lesson by now. You can't use children's toys to fight a vampire," he says pointing to Enivid. His mouth is full of white teeth, contrasting with his blackened face. "This is going to be fun."

Scepter leaps into the air, bringing Malice down with a thunderous force. I jump back as he breaks the rooftop apart with a loud bang. Pieces of metal shrapnel fly into the wind. My boots lose traction and my leg slips off the side. Using Enivid like a hook, I save myself from falling to my doom. There is a humming by my head as Scepter attempts to smash my brains into the side of the car. "Just like the festival games! Crush a skull, win a prize!" The club hits metal again. *Clang!*

Using my upper body, I brace against the wall with my forearms and swing the lower half of my body up, kicking Scepter square in the face. He staggers backward as I land on the roof. I go on the offensive, keeping my stance facing to one side. Lashing out with Enivid, I slice at Scepter, curving my blade back and forth, low to high. He moves with ease, dodging my blows, and extends a fist into my abdomen. I am sent sliding across the rooftop, gasping for air.

Choking and coughing, I force myself to stand. Again he advances, walking straight toward me without a care in the world. "Like I said, Wolfgang. Toys."

Arcing my arm and wrist inward, I throw Enivid like a disc, sending it speeding forward like a deadly missile. Scepter bends backward, arcing his spine in an unnatural way. Enivid skims over his torso and makes an upward turn. Scepter recovers with lightning speed and smiles as he steps to the side, smacking Enivid with Malice on its return flight. Enivid falters, skitters, and scrapes across the ground until it punctures the rooftop stopping inches from me.

The trains whistle blares relentlessly behind Scepter. "How quaint!" he shouts over the sound. "Your silly little distractions won't work on me. I guess the old man is still alive." But I know what Dora is doing is not a distraction but a warning. I look frantically for something to hold on to and realize there is only Enivid before me.

The train shutters violently. The repercussion engulfs everything in a blanket of white.

Bending my head as low as I can, white powder bombards my shoulders and back, tearing at my skin. I feel the cold snow whipping at my face and legs, trying to strip me from the train top.

I dig in deeper.

Plowing through the snowdrift lasts only a moment, and then the air clears again and I can see the light of the pale moon.

Looking up, Scepter is gone. My anxiety immediately calms when I see Scepter struggling off the side of the train. Holding on to Malice, braced by two steam pipes, his legs dangle as the train races through the early morning twilight, never stopping and gaining more speed.

I pull Enivid from the rooftop. Now is my only chance.

As I take my first steps toward Scepter, I am filled with relief knowing that what I have in my hand will finally end this devil hanging from the side of the train. So lost in my hatred toward Scepter, I ignore the voice coming from behind me. I do not have time for any more distractions. I need to claim what is mine. The family tradition. The death of the vampire.

"Wolfgang. Help me," comes the voice again.

No. I try to block out the voice. Scepter is right there. His foot is caught in the steam pipes. It will be so easy.

Listen to your friend.

I turn suddenly at the voice in my ear, but there is no one there. It was a woman's voice, I'm sure of it. Instead, I see Kronklich hanging off the side of the train.

"Kronklich!"

I move quickly, coming to his aid. He is barely holding on to the torturous chain that is now saving his life. Any moment he will fall. "Hold on!"

I reach down and he takes a hold of my arm. Slowly I pull him up onto the roof.

Kronklich moans in pain. "I was wondering if you were going to save me," he says in short breaths, smiling.

"You fool. You think I would abandon you?" Up close, I can see the black blade sticking out of his upper leg. It is lodged in deep and the blood has frozen over. "How are you feeling?"

"I must say, at the moment, not too bloody good." He grits his teeth as he adjusts himself into a less painful position.

The train begins turning to the north and in doing so, the steam stack issuing from the smoke box smothers us in vapor. Visibility suddenly becomes an issue. It will be difficult to drag Kronklich, cold and rigid, to safety. The roof is slippery and I can't find solid footing to brace my body. "You're going to have to give me your other hand as I pull you along."

As Kronklich reaches for my other hand, I am pulled back suddenly.

I can't breathe.

The familiar cold of metal restricts my throat, pulling tighter and tighter. I hear chain links rubbing together.

"You killed my wife," rasps a voice in my ear.

The image of Kronklich slips from my vision as I struggle to obtain air.

"I loved her very much." The chain constricts tighter.

I am pulled back from the edge of the engine car and forced to stare into Constable's face. He holds the chain around my neck with one hand as he leans forward, striking me in the face with his forehead. The pain coupled with the lack of oxygen blurs my vision as I spin around delirious. Refocusing, I stare at the many chains and hooks wrapped around Constables body.

I remember Enivid is still in my hand. Squeezing the handle, I stab carelessly, trying to catch Constable in the wake. But my assault is blocked and something strikes my hand. Enivid drops from my grasp, clattering noisily upon the rooftop.

"Close. Very close," says Scepter as he comes to stand next to Constable. His red eyes glare at me, but I look away. "Don't kill him just yet. Let him breathe."

Constable pulls the chain around my neck, forcing me to look into the face of the one I loathe more than anything, but then the slack increases.

"What's the matter? Having a hard time looking at my face?" Scepter's long, slender fingers clench my jaw as a parent might scold a child. He leans closer to me. I can see the burn scars all over his cheeks and nose and forehead. They are shiny and black, glistening in the moonlight like silver veins. Clear liquid oozes from the many cracks in his face as he smiles with his white teeth. "Like I said before, it will take more than the mountain snow to defeat me." He strikes me in the abdomen with his fist and my body shudders. A metallic taste fills the back of my throat and rises to my lips. Scepter takes a deep breath close to my face and licks the blood dripping down my chin. "Ahhhh, blood of the father. I hate when they prove me wrong. Your blood *is* strong."

Scepter thrusts a hand into my side where he stabbed me with the extraction dagger at the party. The pain is excruciating as he wiggles his fingers under my proofing and flesh, the nails of his finger scraping parts of my fascia. "Nnnnaggghhhh!" I shudder between my teeth. The feeling is torture and Scepter enjoys every second of it. "Like the pain, Wolfgang? You killed two of the Carnalreesee and almost a third. The price for assailing a Carnalreesee is death. Did you know that?" His fingers work their way in even more. I can barely stay conscious from the pain.

Stay strong, my love.

The voice returns. Is it inside my head or is it real? I look around, rolling my head like a madman, frantically searching for the source, but Constable racks my head back with the chain again.

"What are you doing? On your knees!" commands Constable, kicking me in the back of the legs.

Looking off to the side, I watch the horizon of mountains and snow whirling past with great speed. My head fills with thoughts of my beloved Diana. Was it her? "I am strong, my love," I blurt out.

"What's this?" asks Scepter.

"He's gone mad," responds Constable in a low chuckle.

I stare straight ahead, straight through Scepter's hideous form as if he were invisible. There is a light ahead, like a floating orb, moving toward me, bobbing up and down ever so slightly. I wonder if they can see it. "I'm strong, my love. I'm strong."

"Not strong enough," says Scepter, jamming his fingers into my side again, yet I feel nothing. "The pain is finally setting in." He removes his hand from my side and slurps at the red stains dripping from his fingertips. "Now, where is that dagger? I think I will need another vial of your blood after all."

From the front of the train, the main whistle blows out a plume of steam once again. The howling tone of the steam echoes off the surrounding precipices thousands of feet up. Immediately, it blasts a second time, the usual warning of the conductor when trouble is afoot.

Scepter turns to his side and yells. "Goddammit! Can that old man get any more annoying? I'm trying to do something here!"

The whistle somehow tears me from my disillusion. Its piercing sound rattles my brain, adding to the already throbbing ache from the loss of oxygen. Whatever Dora is up to, I am thankful for it. Each blast of the whistle seems to pump life back into me. I check into reality and remember the modified weapon in my hand, the one Old Man Dora made so it could serve its justice on those who deserve it.

And I am partial to justice.

The chain is slack around my neck. I can breathe and I can move. I force Enivid down into the floor, piercing Constable's foot, through and through. Fire bursts upward like a fountain of flame. The chain unravels from around my neck and I turn around to see the surprised look on Constable's face, and then cut two more times. Once on each of his legs. Fire emanates from the wounds. Constable screams, and as he tries to grab me with his one arm, I exact my final blow at his waist, removing his upper body from his lower in a burning fire. Constable, now in two pieces, topples over, tangling in his many chains. He grips one of the chains, the one embedded in Kronklich's leg and pulls as his torso slides along the rooftop.

"Kronklich!" I shout, diving forward and reaching. Kronklich's hands land in mine as his body is pulled from Constable's chain. Kronklich lets out a cry of pain as the hook dislodges some. "Hold on, Kronklich!" I see that look in his eye, the hawkish look of determination for me to let him go.

No. Not now. Now is not the time to die. I remain strong, bracing my body to withstand the weight of Constable's torso.

Scepter's voice comes from behind me. "How come every time you want something done, you have to do it yourself?"

I turn to see Scepter rapidly approaching, Malice in hand. His face looks more burnt than ever before; every crack is exaggerated.

Behind him, beyond the front of the train, I see it—an enormous wall of white, a glacier across the tracks. I see now why Dora was blowing the whistle over and over and over again. He wasn't distracting. This time he was warning, not just me, but everyone.

"Wolfgang! Look out!" shouts Kronklich.

I shift my body to the side, having no choice but to release Kronklich's hand, as Scepter brings down Malice, bashing the rooftop into pieces, breaking the chain holding Kronklich's leg. I watch Kronklich and Constable fly from the rooftop as the tension unravels. I turn over just in time to see Scepter come for me, but I am quick to use Enivid, bracing his attack. Our weapons spark as they collide, but Enivid holds and Malice holds and I stare into the hateful red eyes of Scepter.

The air is suddenly filled with a thunderous roar as the train makes contact. The whole world shakes and is consumed by a terrible white. Snow and rock swallow everything. Impacting everything. Crushing everything.

And all things that once were light, now become dark and buried, for nothing can escape the force of nature.

CHAPTER XXIII

DARKNESS.

The cold void.

I feel nothing. See nothing. Emptiness is all around me. Yet, somehow, something lingers. A thought perhaps. Or possibly an emotion.

Someone is here.

"Hello?"

"Yes?"

"Am I dead?"

"No."

"But I can hear your voice."

"Of course you can."

"How is it possible? Where am I?"

"It does not matter where you are, only that you are."

"Are? What does that mean? Why can't I see you?"

"Curse you, Tenor. Now is not the time to worry about such things."

I know those words. It's her. It's really her this time. My beautiful Diana.

"*My love. Where have you been?*"

"*With you.*"

"*I thought you were gone forever.*"

"*Never.*"

"*But why can't I see you?*"

"*None of that, sweet love. No more. Now is time to rest. Only rest now.*"

Delicate fingers caress my head. I feel them at the base of my skull, right at the occipital. They run up the back of my scalp, twirling the curls of my damp hair. The rich smell of peonies fills my lungs. I try to open my eyes but the lids are too heavy to lift. I want to grab onto her like a floating vessel in a vast ocean. Like I've done so many times in the past. Kiss her, caress her, but I can't. I am held fast by the void of nothing. Floating in oblivion. Is this what death is like?

"*But you are not dead. You must rest now.*"

"*What are you saying? I don't want to rest! There is no time to rest!*" *I shout, my voice echoing.* "*There are things that must be done!*" *I try to recall those things, but find myself drawing a blank. Why can't I remember? What is happening to me?*

"*Rest, Tenor. Rest.*"

I hear Diana's voice close to my ear. I feel her hand running through my hair again, this time, from my forehead to the side of my ear.

"*No. Damn you. You're not her. You can't be my D. Demon. Monster!*" *My eyes struggle to open and my vision remains empty. Why can't I open my eyes?*

"*Rest now, Tenor Alvadine Wolfgang.*"

And so I vanish.

My mind wanders to a different place. A place of darkness, but not a darkness like the void, but a darkness natural to the world of the living.

Nightfall.

Moving through a field of corn stalks, I take heed of the pumpkin and squash impeding my advance along the dirt row. Such a clever boy. He is trying to detain me, corral me into a place I cannot escape from. But I break to the right, crushing cornstalks under my straw-covered boots. I use my straw-covered hands to push back the husks so I can have clear sight all around me.

In the distance, I see a soft yellow glow making its way toward my direction like a hovering ghost. Every now and then, the light is lost in the foliage of the stalks, but I wait, motionless, inhaling and exhaling in shallow breaths.

Standing completely still, I wait, raising my arms to the side and grabbing two stalks beside me. I look to one side to see a man dressed as I am. Dark-blue coat, straw coming out of his legs and arms. Perfect. He will never suspect.

A caw from above alerts me to a crow. Its wings flap menacingly near me and it swooshes as it dives. Feathers beating in my face, it lands on my outstretched arm, inches from my face. It blinks at me once, then twice. Goddamn bird. Go away. What good are the wicker men if that can't keep the blackbirds at bay? I motion to shoo the cursed thing away but stop.

Cackling in the distance draws my attention. Laughter.

"Though these fields are filled with monsters, Mother, fear not. I will protect you."

"I'm sure you will, Lord Dorian. The kingdom will never be safe without your valiant efforts."

Now I hear giggling. The cracking and rustling of wood and straw. "Hya-ah!" Shouts the young voice. "Die beast. You shall rise from the grave no more." I hear another sound of wood against wood and the splattering of a pumpkin when the crow on my shoulder suddenly caws in my ear.

"Stupid bird," I rasp at the cursed thing, shrugging my shoulder to make it fly away, but it doesn't budge. I start shaking more violently to increase the effects but stop suddenly, realizing the potential of giving away my location.

"Quietly now, Mother, did you hear it? The beast lingers just within these parts."

I can't see them, but I know they're getting closer. Each footfall crunches in the undergrowth. Closer and closer they get until their noisy approach abruptly ends. I can no longer see the glowing yellow. Clever boy. Covering his tracks. I listen to my surroundings. Within the silence, the rubbing of stems, leaves, and crickets dominates.

There is a sudden burst of the cornstalks and the voice of a forceful "Hyaaa!" As I watch the blond hair of a little boy emerge from the brush like a cat, he pounces on his enemy, using a wooden sword to stab and slice at the wicker man next to me. The wicker man doesn't make a sound as the boy lays into him, stroke after stroke, using a series of blows that, were it a real sword, would shred the straw man into pieces.

Dressed in a tailored coat, embroidered with red and black, the boy wipes sweat from his brow, despite the cool autumn weather.

He looks rather disappointed and glances back at the one he calls mother.

My heart beats at the sight of her but I dare not move. Long raven locks fall around slim shoulders. A dark-gray dress presses against her body. I watch her console our son. "A most valiant effort, Dorian. Well done."

He smiles at her as he lowers his guard. I told him about that.

Never let your guard down.

Ever.

I emerge from hiding like a ravenous monster, wailing and growling, stomping over the cornstalks, rustling the grass, and shaking the straw in my hands.

They scream in fright and take off running through the field, away from the treaded path.

Good. They will become lost.

I can hear their breath as we run together. I control my own as I move to head them off. Leaping through patches of corn stalks, I see the tops of husks shaking back and forth violently. I charge forward through the dark, the crickets around me chirping louder as I push aside leaves.

Breathing the cool air, I take in the rich smell of smoke off in the distance. Kronklich is at the manor preparing our meal of roasted lamb and shredded pork topped with rosemary splints and garlic salt. There is no doubt he and Joachim are exchanging qualms about the placement of dinnerware—near the thicket of trees, or out in the open along the rolling slope behind the manor. The hill ends at the wall that meets the cornfield. And there upon the stone, large flat pumpkins with carved faces glow with sinister smiles. I can still hear

Diana's worries inside my head about Dorian's exposure to monsters at a young age, but who am I to withhold such illusions? He likes them. Always has, and by no means was I going to stop him. It's in the blood. The boy has talent, possesses the makings of a hunter, the hunter that will one day replace me, just like his father, and his father before.

I stop running, listening to my surroundings. The sound of breaking undergrowth isn't far. They are headed for the rows of pumpkins. I see the glow of candlelight through the endless dark.

Quickly I dash, casting the straw hat from my head. I push matted yellow locks from my face as I enter the clearing, breathing heavier, but still quiet, stopping before rows of squash. Yellows. Reds. Oranges. Glowing faces of fire stare back at me. I hold my hands before my eyes and open my mouth, feigning terror of the hideous soldiers before me. Dorian's army, strategically placed to bar my passage. They will destroy me if I do not retreat.

I hear footfalls approaching behind me. I turn around, hiding my smile from their searching eyes.

Casting my head back, my teeth gleam in the night as I let out the most menacing monster growl I can muster, howling into the night sky at the moon high above and all the stars watching. Clouds of cold breath waft from the warm moisture of my throat. I lower my eyes on them, Dorian and Diana, standing defiantly before me. Menacing grins of their own decorate their faces as Dorian motions his mother to stand behind him.

"No more, beast!" shouts Dorian. He holds the wooden stick before him like a sword and the closed lantern like a shield. "Go back to the shadows of darkness whence you came. There is no room for monsters like you in this world. Me and my men will hunt and destroy every last one of you."

My crystal-blue eyes gaze into his glossy blacks, and then focus on Diana. She is trying her mightiest, it seems, to stifle a well-hidden laugh as Dorian continues to glare at me seriously—his intention to slay the scarecrow before him.

"You have no power over me, boy," I say in a scratchy voice. "You are in the crow's kingdom here. Your puny stick is no match for the Wicker King." I open my eyes wide, staring down into Dorian's visage of fair skin and light brows. My intimidation doesn't seem to work as he stands between his mother and me. His black eyes squint closer together suddenly, as if questioning my next intention, and so I know I am out of time.

I run forward with my hands open like claws and move to grab Dorian, but at the same time, he drops the stick and reaches for the lantern, opening its closed shutters. Instantly, I am bathed in a golden light, bright and menacing. I cry out in exaggeration, feigning agony and stammering back with my legs and hands cowering before my face. "Aggggghhh! The light! The light! You tricked me, Dorian!" I move backward as quickly as I can, one step at a time, remembering how many steps it was to the pumpkin soldiers on the ground. I count the last step and feel the back of my heel hit something hard. Down I go over the row of pumpkins, falling back onto my elbows. Dorian stands over me, holding the lantern high over his head as he points the stick at my chest. Inside, I am filled with pride.

"Wicker King or not, my quest has been fulfilled. Your time in this world is over, monster," Dorian says, raising his stick before me.

"Noooooo!" I shout in my best monster voice. Dorian beats me lightly with the practice stick, over and over, as I clutch my chest and whine in pain. And then, as quickly as I started, I stop, lying motionless on the ground quietly, waiting for him to come closer.

"Mother, do you think he is dead?"

"I don't know," says Diana. Her voice is soft and delicate. "Let's check together."

I hear their footsteps come closer. The stick pokes at my back.

Growling, I come to life, grabbing both of them and pulling them down to the soft earth with me. They yell in fright as I hold them down, tickling their sides. Their fear turns to laughter as I continue growling and poking their stomachs.

Having tortured them long enough, I turn onto my side and stare up at the dark sky, listening to Diana and Dorian catch their breath as they try to calm down. How beautiful the sky is with its glittering grove of stars in a sea of blackness. My eyes fall on the giant moon floating in the emptiness, its crescent shape curved like a scythe. Lying in the mess of leaves in the middle of the cornfield, I stretch out my hands before me, making L shapes with my fingers, and begin measuring stars adjacent from the moon. One by one, I connect the dots, counting the weeks left till the winter solstice. I already know when it is, but as I turn my head toward Dorian, he is doing the same as me. I smile. Children really are like sponges.

I look to the sky again and my arms are getting heavy. I imagine the leather bracelet as the source of fatigue, but I rub the other wrist bare as a bone, wondering if Diana is wearing hers. The smell of peonies fills my senses as she nuzzles her hair into the side of my neck.

I feel my arms becoming numb and lower them and feel her hand wiggle its way into mine, entrapping bits of leaves and dirt.

I take a deep breath and watch the sky intently. "What is it you want most in life, if you could have anything in the whole world?"

Dorian is first to answer. "That's easy, Father. To be strong and resolute as you. I'm going to be the best hunter the world has ever seen."

Strong ambition, but he is young. There is still so much more I have to teach him. The world is full of deadly intent. He will have to face more than just scarecrows and pumpkins.

I squeeze Diana's hand. "What about you, my love?"

Her initial response is to move closer to me, even though that's hardly possible. I wait patiently and eventually she answers. "To ensure both of you outlive me. Living without my boys would be a fate far worse than death."

I feel her raise my hand to her lips. The softness of her skin reminds me of her tenderness, even though I need no reminder. She haunts my thoughts day in, day out, with no rest in between.

I fall silent for a time, enjoying their company, enjoying the reality I have with them, this moment of tranquility and peace, where there are no monsters to hunt or vampires to slay. I watch the heavenly sky and stars like a scientist at research, wondering why some shimmer and fade, wink into and out of existence.

Something rustles next to me.

"What about you, Tenor?" asks Diana.

"What about me?"

"You never said what you wanted."

"No, I suppose I didn't. But it's never too late to say the things we want in life. They either come to you, or they don't. That's just the way things are."

I begin to utter useless words, but something stops me. A light. A brilliant burning light in the sky, streaking across the world, leaving a trail of glittering sparkles and dust. It's over in a moment, and as I break from its trance, I finally speak the words I wanted to say. "What I want most is for us to be together forever."

Suddenly, all the feeling in my body starts to fade as if I'm sucked from a world of warmth and emotion and into a place of evil.

I have no control. What is happening to me? This isn't what I want. I want my family. I need to be with them. Stop this. Stop pulling me! Leave me be! Further and further, I am pulled away. The field. The sky. The lush ground surrounding my loved ones. Dorian. Diana. Come back to me! I can't be without you!

The world I once knew is gone.

Emptiness.

Darkness.

It is as it was before. A plain of nothingness. An inescapable black hole.

"Stay in the nothing, Wolfgang, and you will become nothing."

"No! What are you doing? What are you talking about? I don't want to leave!"

"But you must, or all will be lost. The realm of death is no place for the living."

I can't go on like this. I'm weak. I need strength. What is she talking about? This demon mocks me. It can't be my Diana. She *would stay with me. She would comfort me. She was incapable of abandonment.*

"I would never leave you, my love."

"Take me back! I don't want to leave! I can't do this without you. I need your strength."

"And so you shall have it."

Orbs of light appear in the black, empty void. At first, they are far away like the stars in the sky. Dozens of them. Hundreds of them. They spin and twirl through the great distance toward me, like a nebula of shooting stars. The closer they come, the warmer it becomes. The cold slips away from me like melting snow against the fire. The spinning turns into spiraling as the orbs of light come faster. Blending into each other, they begin to form one, growing in size as the light glows brighter and hotter. The hundreds turn into dozens, and the dozens turn into few. I feel a tear streak across my cheek as the hot wind blows against my flesh and ravishes my hair. The orbs float before my face, moving into one, and I am left blindly staring into it, pulsating with energy and life. It flickers once. Then twice.

Soft buzzing fills the air and I slowly open my eyes.

DAY EIGHT

CHAPTER
XXIV

THE ORB OF LIGHT. THE orb of death. Which fate is worse is hard to say. The cold is so very cold.

It is the first thing I recall.

Enveloped in a cocoon of snow, I can't feel my body, but strangely, I am aware of it. The chill is numbing. My vision focuses on the light of a glowing orb, one of the many round lamps from the Iron Carriage. Broken beyond measure, the glass ball buzzes and flickers with its dying light. It sputters and sparks from the bronze conduit broken at the base. Similar orbs lay strewn about, demolished beyond recognition, dark from the loss of power. I hear the creaking of metal nearby, but everything hurts as I try to move. Pain is unkind to me as I strain to see where the noise is coming from. Spasms shoot up and down my neck, moving their way into my arms and shoulders.

I work through the pain slowly until my head finally moves and realization sets in. I am perched against a tree, half buried in a snow bank. Wreckage from the train surrounds me. A brilliant fire blazes in the distance, ejecting plumes of smoke and steam. It must be the smoke box from the locomotive.

The last thing I recall was the roof of the train, fighting Scepter to no end, and at the last moment, Kronklich and Constable were blown from the train, the wind having taken them into the winter's oblivion. Were they even alive still? And Scepter. Where was he?

Working through the fog in my head, I recall the dream still vivid in my mind, of seeing my family again. It was such a long time ago. Kronklich and Joachim, Dorian and Diana.

How utterly alone I feel.

The creaking high above turns into a loud, obnoxious groan. Body tensing, I use every ounce of my strength to break free of my frozen prison as a piece of railing from the train comes crashing down inches from crushing my body. Breathing heavily from the effort, I stare at the wreckage as the snow trickles around me like ash. Steam puffs from my face in small billows as I recognize the pinkish glow of dawn streaking across the darkened sky.

Wreckage from the train is everywhere, passenger cars stacked upon one another, tracks and wheels bent and twisted into deformed sculptures of art, mangled from the sheer power of speed and collision. Shattered glass glitters yellow in the glow of the fire. It's a miracle I'm alive. To one side of the decimated train, the towering height of the mountain precipice looms. It is so high and dark, my body shivers at the thought of the walls closing in on me. Collecting myself from the snow like a forgotten winter beast, I stagger forward as if learning to walk for the first time. The snow is thick and my boots sink like heavy rocks.

Chains sway in the wind some distance away. The rattling makes me uneasy, reminding me of Constable's chain around my neck. The chains hang from a passenger car suspended by two others, forming a sort of veil that I must pass through. There is no other way around.

The metal panels creak as I bend low to pass under the cave of train debris, pushing aside the chains, remaining ever mindful of their origin. Chains snake through shattered windows and open roofs. Railings are bent at odd angles; I can only imagine that no one survived. My heart fills with dense weight at the thought of seeing Dora or Kronklich's decimated bodies. Yet I move on, despite what I might find.

More fire.

More metal fragments.

As I emerge from the tunnel of wreckage, a new wind pushes against my scarred face and leather coat. Immediately, I notice the extent of the damage strewn along the mountainside, for what seems a mile long. The passenger cars lie buried in the snow, caught between shattered tree trunks and cracked rock faces. With the wind and snow blowing harder on this side of the clearing, everything has become buried deep in the snow. The caw of a crow sounds somewhere in the distance, echoing off the cliffs, and I wonder at the possibility of life in this desolate place. A gust of wind sends clouds of black smoke curling through the clearing. The carcinogens force me to cough and burn my lungs along with the cold.

I have only gone a few paces when I notice specs of red splashed through the snow. Immediately I look up, scanning my surroundings for anything, anything at all that would lend some sign as to the whereabouts of my comrades. Close by, a large train wheel lies on its side, half covered in snow. The mounds of powder throw me off in every direction I look. They play tricks on my mind. Perhaps I have seen too many dead bodies and am afraid at each new view. But then I see it, a hand sticking out of the snow, holding a chain within its bloody grasp. Leather coat sleeve, disheveled hair. The only thing missing is his hat.

My mind collapses into a terrible place as I rush forward, throwing myself down beside Kronklich and begin shoveling snow away from his cold body. As I uncover his torso and legs, I see there—within inches of his being—the treacherous black hook lying in the red-stained snow. The cursed blade Constable used to keep him still. Somehow, Kronklich managed to pull the blade free. Seeing his eyes closed, I reach for his neck for a pulse, but it's too cold to feel anything. There is a light blue tinge to his complexion.

"Kronklich!" I say, shaking the collar of his coat, but there is no response. "Kronklich!" I push away the flakes of snow collecting on his mustache and unshaven face. His stubble has grown into a thick shadow since we left Wolfgang manor. I lift his head to feel if he is breathing and back away in horror at the sight of black stains frozen to his chin. Caught off guard, I am baffled, wondering if he is dead. From somewhere behind me, the cold air is filled with laughter.

"Looks pretty dead, doesn't he?"

Immediately I turn to face the voice, the voice so cold and full of malice.

"The poison should be well through his system now," says Constable. Mangled beyond recognition, he is suspended off the ground by his own chains. His upper body hangs loosely, pierced by the bent up rails and plates of metal from the train wreckage. His lower half is nowhere to be found. With half of his face torn off, he continues to laugh as I approach. A constant flow of ruby liquid drips from his blue lips.

"Death. It's what makes humans weak and vampires strong. A fair trade, wouldn't you say? Your friend for my wife."

There is nothing fair about it.

I stare at the long chain trailing from his hand, passing along the ground over toward where Kronklich lies still in the snow. The thought of Constable's menacing black hook inside Kronklich's leg fills me with dread.

Poison. I should have remembered the origin of the Black Blade. Long ago kings paid mercenary cults dedicated to the art of killing. Black Blades ensured their prey never escaped. Had Constable been one of them? Seems the influence of the vampire has spread far worse than I thought.

I try to keep my composure, but the bad memories begin flooding my brain like a plague. Thoughts of driving the stake through my wife's heart flash in my mind. Anger swells within me, and each step I move closer to Constable, the more I want to hurt him and make him suffer.

Constable smiles at me in his wretched state. "That's it, give into the hate. Makes the blood stronger in the end."

I have no time for words at the moment.

Pulling his head to the side, I stab one of his eyes with my dagger, dislodging it from the socket. He yelps in pain as his head shakes back and forth. Blood spurts from his face.

The questions will come, eventually. I just need a little more time. A little more closure.

Pulling the dagger out, I stab a second time, straight through the cheekbone of his smooth face. I watch the purplish veins spread over his moist face. His other eye searches around spastically as he screams, but the screaming soon dies off and he is back to laughing. His actions cause his torso to move back and forth, like a piece of meat swaying in the butcher's shop.

"Do what you will," he says, laughing at my torturous behavior. "It doesn't matter. I will come back stronger than ever. You'll see."

I laugh. There is no coming back from Enivid. It matters not what a vampire says. They can't be trusted. Kronklich is dead. Dora is dead. Those things are certain.

I pull the dagger from Constable's face and bring it before his one good eye.

"Wait," says Constable, his torso shaking with each word. "Your son."

I pause, staring at the dagger. I watch the blood travel the length of the blade. The blood of an immortal. "You won't tell me anything," I finally say.

"You don't know that."

"I know that vampires lie."

"What if I told you he is serving one of the noblest causes a boy could make?"

"Noble? You know nothing of nobility. Nobility comes with a price."

"Precisely."

Suddenly, I find myself reluctant to end this monster's life. For some reason, he is giving me information. I need to know more.

"What noble cause is my son serving?"

"Why, to ensure the return of our master. Only he can save us all." Constable's remaining eye sparkles in the growing dawn. His teeth gleam whiter than ever as he smiles. "Blood of the father. Blood of the son."

Thoughts of Egleaseon enter my head. What did he mean "save us all?" Save us from what exactly? My blood. Dorian's blood. More vampire riddles, and yet I am no closer to knowing the truth.

Constable is buying time.

"Spare me the lies, wretch. Your words are meaningless. I will find my son and kill every last one of your cursed kind, even if it means dying in the process." I clench Constable's throat and lift his decimated remains before me. With Enivid in hand, I poise the holy weapon before Constable's heart.

"Foolish mortal. The Carnalreesee aren't the only ones bearing a curse. You too bear a curse. You are doomed, Wolfgang."

I can't listen to another word and slam Enivid into Constable's chest. The weapon slides through his skin and bone with ease, severing his curse and ties to this world once and for all. All the years of life return in an instant, yet retract just as quickly as they come. As I watch his skin melt away like sand, I see Constable's body change from muscle to bone, then to dust.

Looking up to the sky, I try to imagine the spirit of Constable rising up toward the heavens, but I know that image is false. He is not going anywhere above here. He is going downward, to the same place I know one day I will visit too.

Walking back toward Kronklich, my eyes fill with water at the sight of his motionless body, his one hand still clutching the horrible chain with the black hook. Kneeling beside him in the snow, I wonder where he is at right now. Surely, God would consider such a great man for his kingdom. He was so versatile. A doctor. A coachman. A hunter.

Bowing my head, I cannot avert my eyes from the horrible black stains covering his mouth. Even though I know he is dead, I lean forward to check for his breath. Placing my hand on his forehead, I push back slightly and lean my head close to listen.

Nothing.

The echo of silence lingers.

Letting out a terrible sigh, my forehead rests on his shoulder as I begin crying. It is real now. My best friend is dead and I feel alone and cold. I wonder about my beloved Diana. Why is she not lingering close by to comfort me in this time of suffering? Has she abandoned me the same as God?

Dreary clouds drift toward the east, passing over the high cliffs of the Cordova Mountains, blotting out the pink glow of dawn. Slowly, it makes its debut. I listen to my surroundings. The slight breeze of snow falling. The creaking of metal. The buzzing of electrical currents. The crackling of dying fires. Again, somewhere off in the distance, I hear the crows call, echoing off the rock face like disembodied spirits.

Leaning back on the haunches of my legs, I wipe back my tears, listening to the life around me, even though life has abandoned my friend.

Suddenly, a hand bursts from the snow and grabs my arm with a fierce grip. Filled with terror and shock, I nearly fall over, unable to move.

"Tenor!" gasps a voice. I watch in disbelief as Kronklich falls into a raging fit of coughing and spitting, gasping for air, and rolling over to his side to discharge something small and black from his mouth.

CHAPTER XXV

"Water," whispers Kronklich into my ear as I lean closer to hear. "Water. Please."

I grab a handful of unspoiled snow and place it on Kronklich's cracked lips. He laps at the frozen water, moving his mouth and tongue as he comes to.

I watch his eyes blink as they move back and forth. He wants to speak, but no words come out. Leaning down again, I barely make out his whisper.

"Pocket."

I see him trying to move his hands, trying to get the blood flowing back into his palms, clenching the chain still wrapped around his fingers.

"Pocket."

"Yes, pocket. Your pocket?" Patting down his coat with my hands, I realize what he means. Undoing the brass buckles, I reach inside, feeling for anything he might be referring to, and there I find a small hidden fold. Within the secret compartment, I produce a small leather pouch and dump its contents. Three bunches of a dark substance land in the palm of my hand. They are rough in texture and contain a heavy earthen aroma.

His eyes light up at the sight of ebon root and suddenly I realize why. Examining the ground beside him, there are chewed up remains all around him, staining the snow a dark charcoal. The same color as the stains around his mouth.

"I should have known," I say, taking one of the new pieces and placing it in his mouth. He starts chewing and there is an immediate effect. "You are just full of surprises, aren't you?" I say, wiping back my tear-streaked face.

"Not surprises, Tenor. Preparedness," Kronklich croaks.

I can tell his throat is beyond dry and encourage him to eat some more snow, despite how cold he is probably feeling.

Pulling his torso upright, he groans from the effort, and then, being the doctor he is, begins examining his leg where the black hook laid waste to his leg. The wound, coagulated and cold, has deep black lines spreading from it like roots of a tree, spidering away from its center.

"Doesn't look good, does it?" Kronklich says with an airy voice.

Listening to him sucking on the snow with his lips, I am amazed how responsive and alert he is despite the state he was in moments ago.

Pulling his bag from the snow, I rummage through it, taking account of our supplies, which have dwindled considerably. A few apples, a loaf of bread, some cheese. Finding a bandage, I wrap his leg tight in the event his leg starts bleeding again. I notice Kronklich looking over my shoulder.

"I take it Constable is no more? Last I remember, he was laughing at me when I pulled the hook from my leg. I must have passed out from the pain."

Glancing at the hanging chains swaying in the wind, I try not to think about the anger Constable invoked in me. If anything, I feel better knowing there's one fewer vampire in the world.

"Were you able to find out any more information?" Kronklich's eyes are searching as he looks into mine.

Recalling the conversation I had with Constable is convoluted with my fantasies of torturing him. Making him cry out in pain was enjoyable. The thought of it still comforts me. Kronklich continues to stare at me, waiting for an answer. "Nothing from what we already know. He was pompous and uncooperative." I leave out the details about the cursed comment from Constable, for I don't fully understand it myself. Vampires are devious monsters. He could have been trying to plant a seed in my mind.

"We need to find Dora," I say, brushing the snow from my coat. "Think you can walk?"

Within moments, Kronklich is on his feet, chipper as ever. He staggers around a bit, acclimating to his injury and using his cane sword for support.

"Good as new," he says, hobbling his way out of the clearing.

I notice he managed somehow to get his crossbow back. I'm amazed at the stamina and the resourcefulness the man possesses. Pressing on, I follow after him, ducking under another passenger car tilted at an angle.

Gaining the perspective of the train wreck is a horrific reality. Could Dora have survived the crash too despite the carnage surrounding us? Parts of passenger cars have been ripped in half, cast alongside the mountain precipice in odd angles and directions. At one point we come to a glittering field of silver, a monetary value worth the purchase of a new estate. We circumnavigate around the spill, paying no heed to the treasure horde. With no real direction to choose from, our path is ever forward. We leap up through open cargo doors and passenger thresholds, pass torn couches and chairs, and move alongside shattered tables and storage trunks.

Kronklich's energy remains high as we continue, the miraculous ebon root doing its job, keeping him alert and focused. I'm not entirely sure about his condition, but he assures me he is well. Coming to a stop, we stand before a passenger car flipped completely upside down with its roof caved in and windows blown from their supports. I am weary of its dark interior and calculated height, knowing it will be difficult for Kronklich to climb. The sound of cawing birds surrounds us as a flock of white-feathered crows swoop toward the train car. Undersides covered in blue-gray feathers, some of the birds land on the twisted wheels of the train car while others pitter-patter on clawed feet along the broken conduits. Having no idea how far we've traveled, I wonder about their presence so far away from civilization. Much like the atters in the woods, they are scavengers, always hunting, always hungry. Their white beaks are stained red from the blood of their prey. For a moment, I consider the odds. There are so many of them and only two of us.

"Quickly now," I say to Kronklich, grabbing hold of his hand and hoisting him onto the reversed side of the platform. Temporarily sheltered in the darkness of the train car, I hear the *tap-tap* of crow's feet clicking above us. Glancing around the interior, I see nothing that would draw their attention except the bones of the long since dead. But as I watch Kronklich tighten the cloth wrapped around his leg, it becomes very clear to me why they've come. "Your leg. They can smell the blood."

Kronklich screws up his face in a way that shows disbelief and waves his hand about, addressing the air. "Preposterous!" he says in a harsh whisper. "How long have we been out here?"

I shake my head, knowing he doesn't understand. "It doesn't matter. They can smell blood for miles. Harsh conditions call for drastic adaptabilities."

There is a sharp cry in the distance followed by shouting and yelling. Kronklich's eyes open with ferocity as he looks at me with question.

The voice could never be forgotten.

Old Man Dora.

Sparing not a second more, we exit the train car, sending the ice crows into spastic flight. Doom caws around us as we run along the snow bank. In the distance, beyond the drifting snow, I notice the ice crows flocking to the side of another mangled train car. Squawking and flapping their wings, they hop along the snowy ground covered in blood. The worst, I fear, is true. Among the rabble of frantic birds, Dora lies exposed to the scavenging crows, unable to do anything but scream at them. His arms and legs lie limp to his sides and a long metal pipe pierces his belly. The few crows able to get close enough to his hellish screaming fight for a chance at his entrails. They pull at his sinewy insides and peck at each other's thin legs to prevent each other from stealing the meal.

"Goddamn fiends! Be gone with you!" Dora spits, baring his bloody teeth at the closest bird, unable to do anything as it continues to feed. On the ground next to him, I notice the remains of an ice crow lying motionless in a pool of blood and feathers, neck twisted at an odd angle.

"Arrrgghhh!" Dora yells again as another bird comes within a breath's distance.

I brandish Enivid, feeling its strength rush through my arm as it leaves my hand. The blade spins straight and true, slamming into the crow's small body, speckling the snow with more blood. Pierced through and through, the bird lies motionless, impaled upright in the snow.

We do our best to run before the flocking crows. They caw furiously as they take flight. Feathers scatter everywhere. Kronklich is slow coming, pulling up the rear, and swinging his cane, shouting, "Hya Hya!" The ice crows fly a short distance before landing in the nearby trees, pecking at each other, trying to find a good spot to watch what we're doing from the distance.

Dora coughs as I kneel down beside his destroyed body. I want to help in some way, but I know it is too late.

"Got one of those bastards. Did you see?" Dora smiles and coughs. Blood leaks from the side of his mouth as I watch him breathe heavier and heavier with each gasping breath. "I thought the lot of you were done for. The train. I tried to warn you."

Although he is unable to move his arms and legs, he is somehow able to move his neck. He looks off to the side of him toward the patch of thick snowy trees and says, "Saw the bastard take off that way."

I look at Kronklich, who is already on guard, aiming his crossbow at the trees. Scepter escaped through the forest. Could he have gotten that far?

"Don't speak, Dora," I plead.

He bursts into another fit of coughing. "The hell I won't. I'm going to say what I want before I die, you son of a bitch."

There it is, the same old Dora I've always known. I look upon him with empathy, imagining the whole of his existence, after all this time, being snuffed out in the moments to come. All of his work, his craftsmanship, his ideas, lost forever. My eyes fall on Enivid, sticking out of the snow and the dead ice crow. Never will such a relic be created again.

"Take care of it," says Dora, "Cherish it. Treat it as if it were my daughter. Can you do that? Huh, Tenor? Can you?" His breaths become shallower.

I look on his dying body, wanting to do something to ease the pain and suffering, but we are in the middle of nowhere and his wound is too great. Ebon root won't stop the bleeding from the large hole in his abdomen. He was always boasting about how the natural order of things were paramount, how things should take their due course. The irony. Now nature will claim him.

Struggling to breathe, Dora whispers my name again, hardly a breath.

"Tenor."

I lean in closer.

"Damn you, you bastard. Save my grandson."

Crows caw in the nearby trees.

CHAPTER XXVI

I PULL ENIVID FROM THE red snow and stand before Dora's lifeless body, lowering my head as I hold the holy weapon before him out of respect. Only the sound of wind rustling the leaves confirms there is still life in this realm of death.

So it is done.

Just as all things live, they die; the vicious cycle continues on and on, never judging, only taking and giving.

I look at Kronklich as he comes to stand next to me, the shovel used for coal in his hand.

"There is no time for that."

Kronklich gives me a horrified look. "We aren't going to bury the poor fool?"

"Scepter can't be far off. He still has my blood. We have to stop him before he reaches Sunstone. The Carnalreesee have my son and my blood is the key to their plans. The words 'Blood of the father.' The Carnalreesee repeat it over and over. Why would they keep saying it if it didn't mean anything?"

"But Tenor, we are in cursed lands out here. The old man might rise in death or perhaps worse."

Suddenly, I am reminded of my beautiful Diana on that fateful night when I drove the stake through her poor delicate heart. Curse the vampires. Curse God. Curse them all.

I have my D now.

She gives me strength.

With Enivid in hand, I step forward and ram its sharp blade through Dora's forehead.

"There." It is a strange feeling, desecrating the father of my beloved, especially the man who hated me so much. I shudder at the thought of where he is now. Some place cold and devoid of drink. Would he reunite with his daughter?

The ice crows around us frenzy into excitement at the spilling of Dora's blood. Looking to the trees, I know very well once we leave this place, they will have their way with his corpse. But by no means will it be the last time we see the ice crows. They will follow us everywhere we go. We will need to keep moving.

"Let's go."

Coming before a wide vast clearing of trees, we linger at the edge of Decameron Forest, a cold and desolate fortress of ancient trees. With canopies running wild and thick, the snow caught within its heights blot out the sun. Eternal darkness waits for us within. A strange energy wafts from the essence all around, almost as if the dark empty spaces of the woods were alive with the shadow. For a moment I feel it calling to me, beckoning me to come forth without warrant nor care, and so I take a few steps. I feel a hand across my chest.

"What is it?" asks Kronklich, looking at me curiously.

I blink my eyes and rub my forehead for a moment, staring beyond the shade of the trees. "This place is a nightmare," I say. "Egleaseon's influence is strong here."

"This far from his ruins?"

"Decameron Forest spreads all throughout the Cordova Mountains. Its roots go deeper and thicker where the vampires reside. Egleaseon's power lingers over this land still. These mountains and everything around them, cursed. Even where we lived—Wolfgang Manor, Roland, Cordova Woods—was an extension of this forest. Tendrils, if you will."

"Interesting. And to think I knew all the geography of Ashton."

I look back at the train wreckage, and then to the path before us. Without horses to carry us and with minimal provisions, the challenge ahead of us will be a daunting one. But the same reasoning pushes me forward. What choice is there? I must save my son. For the sake of the living and the dead.

Despite the condition of his leg, Kronklich crouches low to the ground, searching for clues. He passes his hand through the snow a few times, sifting through it, and then holds it close to his face. Standing, he wipes his hands on his coat and holds out a petrified leaf. It is damp and discolored a reddish brown.

"My thoughts conclude blood," he says, looking up toward the canopy of trees. "It could be from an ice crow. Or maybe not. Let's take a look." He motions with his hand, pointing to a thicket of trees in the distance; the way is full of darkness, despite the day's morning light. The tree bark is dark and filled with cracks while the roots, thick and gnarled, swirl upward in great curls and loops like a river of snakes.

As we approach the grove of trees, they come closer together, forming a natural hallway. We follow through them with Kronklich in the lead. Pressing on into enveloping darkness, we move past long, thick icicles falling in cascades of glittering ice. Inside the clearing, the smallest slivers of light penetrate the deep forest leaves from above.

Rays of hope in a dismal realm.

The soil is free of snow here and there are fallen trunks, rotted from the inside. On one of the birch trees, Kronklich discovers a red handprint smeared in various spots up and down the trunk.

"He maneuvered like this, and then placed his hands like this," explains Kronklich, dancing around the tree. He stops and looks off in the distance. "This way!" He dashes from the small clearing and out of sight.

"Kronklich, you shouldn't be running around with your leg like that."

He pays no heed to my concern and so I follow him, taking notice of the stillness of the forest, the tranquil peace in a place so devoid of life. Traveling a small distance, I catch up to Kronklich who has stopped in the middle of his hunt. He is crouched low over something, and as I look over his shoulder, he is holding a mass of some sort, bloody and disfigured. White feathers jut out from it in odd angles and there is the evidence of small bones.

"Just as I thought," he says, examining the small carcass in his hands. "He is feeding, regaining his power. As long as he sticks to small prey, we should be fine. If he finds something more substantial, something larger, he will regain his full strength in a short time." Kronklich drops the dead ice crow and looks up at the branches blocking out the sunlight. "If Scepter stays in the forest, he will survive the daylight."

"I have no doubt about that," I counter, eyeing our surroundings. "But despite the shade of the forest, Scepter will need to find a place of sanctuary. No vampire can go all day and all night without lying close to the earth at some point. We must strike him down during the day, when he is most vulnerable." I glance around at the surrounding forest. "If we can find him."

Looking back at Kronklich, he is watching me intently as if waiting for more. "Scepter is no fool. He is powerful and intelligent and mad, all at the same time. He could be watching us as we speak."

But the day lingers on with no further trace.

The sun travels its linear path across the sky and dusk will come sooner than expected. Despite no luck in finding Scepter thus far, the day isn't completely lost. Twice we spot atters chattering their way through the gnarled branches of the forest, stopping to watch us pass through their sanctuary. Moving through a glade of high snow banks, Kronklich discovers a deer and hunts it down, procuring its meat and adding to our already-low provisions. The task is menial, and taking only what we can carry, we leave the deer's remains for the ice crows to feast on.

Still, the birds follow us everywhere we go.

Coming to a clearing of rock formations and very old-looking trees, much older than the ones at the edge of the forest where the branches touch the ground, we investigate the ancient ruins of what once was a place of some significance. As to what it was, I cannot recall, except that something nags at the back of my mind, telling me I know of this place. There are strange symbols etched in the crumbling stones, signifying an old language that neither of us can decipher. Long, thick roots hold the stones together. Pillars once standing tall have toppled over on each other, leaving a cascade of broken rubble and uprooted trees.

We check every hidden opening tucked away between the stones. We look through every foundation of every tree facing the ruins. We are greeted only with death. Cadavers of passing gypsy parties stripped down to nothing but bones. Their remains mixed with those of animals: foxes, atters, deer. Satchels ripped apart. Barrels over turned. We find nothing useful in this abandoned sanctuary. Where was Scepter hiding? The thought of revenge saturates me. The need to sever his head runs through my blood like a drug.

Time is running out. Night approaches fast as the lasting auras of orange and pink reflect onto the gloom of the snow. Full of exhaustion and hunger, I try not to think about the churning pain in my stomach or the sizzling of meat over an open spit. Squinting through the fading light, Kronklich nudges my shoulder and places a torch into my hand. The warmth feels good despite the tingling sensation from the scars on my face. He points with his own torch to a portion of the ruins I did not notice before. Mortared stones pieced together in unison, forming structures that could provide shelter from the elements, for a human or vampire.

Weapons drawn, we approach cautiously, treading lightly through the powdered flakes on the ground. The ancient roots frozen over with ice glisten in the firelight as we pass. We enter what was once long ago, a courtyard full of demolished walls and ruined archways. Solid wooden doors bound in iron lie on their sides next to huge openings leading to nowhere. Each building is a mystery; each passageway, a guess. As we encounter each threshold, the dead silence greets us like an old friend. Smoke rises from our torches. Steam clouds from our mouths. The ceilings have fallen in on most of the structures and some of the rooms have missing walls.

Pausing before one particular opening, I take a moment to view the chains hanging from the sides of the archway, oxidized and black. Its crest hosts the skeletal remains of some poor soul, dangling loosely from the top, bound in snaking links of metal. It reminds me of Roul's last recitation at Egleaseon's ruin, about the poor girl chained to the castle's parapet, her insides exposed to those passing by, the gruesomeness of it, the brutality. I am filled with a sense of knowing and dread as I back away from the suspended skeleton. This place is cursed.

"We are treading on unholy ground," I say, breaking the utter silence.

"I beg your pardon?" asks Kronklich coming to stand next to me, bearing his torch for more light.

"This castle belonged to the late King Stellamane of Burgery, an aristocrat vampire sired by Egleaseon centuries ago." I move closer to the wall to examine the red streaks covering the stones. "Countless blood has been spilt in this castle. It is said the walls were painted red with the blood of his tortured victims. This place has seen pain," I say, running my gloved hand over its slick surface, "*it* knows pain, the same as Egleaseon's ruins. The stones covered in blood were used to create a living castle, a castle capable of terrorizing the land and its people. It was Stellamane's intent from the beginning to create a similar castle to Egleaseon's, a fortress of doom and death, yet stronger."

"Can a vampire surpass his creator in power?" asks Kronklich.

"No," I say with a sigh, "But Stellamane was different. He was mad and obsessed with science, and mad enough to cause Egleaseon worry. So he killed Stellamane. Crushed the walls of his castle and used him as an example. After piercing his heart and severing his head, Egleaseon cast Stellamane's remains into the abyss, a place known as the Devil's Drain. I recall the place not being far from here."

"Intriguing on all accounts, Tenor," says Kronklich in a matter-of-fact way. "So what you're saying, then, is that this place is not only cursed, but *haunted*."

I glance around at our surroundings, transfixed by the torn curtains, the shattered vases, and the molded rugs. "You could say that. But in reality, it makes the best logical place for a vampire to hide." Still, at the mention of the word "haunted," immediately my thoughts fall on D. My desire to see her again is strong, but the recollection of my recent dream has made me wary. Has she been taken over by some unseen force? A demon posing as her in the netherworld, working its dark powers to weaken my state of mind?

I shake off the thought, wondering if I am borderline insane.

We move on, examining more walls. Just as I thought, every stone is covered in blood from the past. In some places, the blood is so thick, it has soaked into the mortar between the stone, changing the color from gray to red. I have heard of residual haunting, where the remains of those long dead somehow linger in the place of their death, trapped for eternity until the place is cleansed or removed.

"Look, Tenor, over there," says Kronklich, having moved far ahead of me.

In the distance, beyond the glowing light of our torches lies another building, circular in nature, dilapidated and crude. It is the remains of a tower having once stood tall long ago. Crushed stones and rubble decorate the foundation like a memorial. Dashed among its rocky base are the remains of the dead, bones commingled with rocks and dirt, forming a loose barrier of unstable ground. It is not the ice crows perched on the walls that draws my attention, but the incredibly large wooden door blocking the way inside.

Signaling to Kronklich in silence, I motion for him to be at the ready, but his crossbow is already level with the door. Moving close, I approach the giant portal with caution, taking notice of its construction, the triple layer of wood separating me from Scepter. An old, thick, oxidized half-ring serves as its handle and it looks as if it's been untouched for centuries. I dare not touch it now for icicles have formed along its bottom, preventing me from gripping it without making noise. Remaining silent is a challenge as I push on the door with my shoulder. I realize it is nearly impossible to move; it will take more than my own brawn to budge it open.

I glance toward Kronklich for assistance and he is at my side within moments, shouldering his crossbow and keeping his cane sword ready. Mouthing the words three, two, one, we press on the door, forcing a horrible groan from its hinges. *Great.* Barely a slit open. We push the door again and the old door wails in response, leaving just enough room to squeeze our bodies through.

What was this place? I try to make sense of it as my eyes adjust to the pitch black inside. Skeletons suspend from the rafters and walls like welcoming decorations. Great stone basins once used for torchlight lie on their sides, cracked in places, having exhausted their use long ago. This place is a medieval tower of damnation. I am left taking it all in as Kronklich circles the room, passing his torch to and fro through the darkness, making shadows dance around like tiny devils. I watch him as he remains focused on the task at hand, ignoring the desecrated grounds around him.

"He is gone," says Kronklich, descending a set of stairs leading up to a broken ledge.

The skeletons sway from the draft coming through the open door. The crows outside continue in their cacophony. I slam the door shut using my body. The force of it shakes the old walls, sending bits of stone and icicles down around us. Listening to the muffled cries of the ice crows, I close my eyes momentarily and take a deep breath.

We missed our chance.

Scepter is gone.

Whether he was here or not, it is too late. With no blood trail to follow, he could be anywhere by now, gone in any direction, even back the way we came from for all I know.

Numbed with having lost my prey, I sink to the floor in defeat and exhaustion as Kronklich begins fussing around the circular chamber, rummaging through its old contents of splintered beams and frayed ropes. Some of the hanging skeletons fell and broke apart across the rubble long ago.

What will we do now? Our mission of saving my son has taken a horrible turn for the worse. The situation we are in is no longer about rescuing my son; it's about survival. What good am I to Dorian dead? Here, lost within the Decameron Forest, we have no direction or plan. We don't even know where here is. It will be a miracle if we survive this cold.

"Now, I know what you're thinking, Tenor. I know that look better than anyone," says Kronklich from across the room. His arms are full of wood. "Death. Moldy dark and uncontested death. That it waits for us in those shadows."

He eyes me with a certainty that only means a lecture is coming, one I surely will not care for.

"We may not be immortals like the vampires," continues Kronklich. "But we are human, after all." He bends down before his new stack of wood and pours some flask oil over the frozen beams. Sparks light up his face in the dim glow of the chamber. "And humans are damn right resourceful," he says, bringing flint to steel again, "and resilient," another flash, "and modest." His final spark ignites the makeshift bonfire and the room explodes into a brilliant light.

"Modest?" I ask, gazing into the fire from the bizarre statement.

"We will give Scepter a chance. Yes. A somewhat head start while we regain our strength."

I shake my head at Kronklich. What is he talking about? I watch him lay strips of deer meat over the open fire, meticulously wrapping them around thin pieces of wood.

"He is gone, Kronklich. The trail has literally gone cold," I say, pointing to the walls around us, and then fastening the buckles of my leather coat.

"Not cold," he replies. "Blood, Tenor. There is always blood. Scepter will feed and the trail will reveal itself to us yet again."

The smell of deer meat fills my nostrils as I try to agree with Kronklich's insane optimism. What would I do without Kronklich?

Moving closer to the fire, I welcome its warmth and enjoy the succulent meal Kronklich provides for us, despite burning my fingertips on the sizzling grease. Having found an abandoned helmet, Kronklich uses it to melt snow over the fire to create drinking water. Thinking twice about our location, I wonder at the possibility of hallucination as the cold water trickles down my parched throat.

With things seemingly in order and our bellies full, I watch Kronklich settle down for some sleep paying no mind to the skeleton lying beside him. It is a funny sight, seeing the living and the dead lying down together, backs turned toward each other in such a way. I want to laugh about it, but my mind is too riddled with depressing thoughts. I find myself unable to sleep at the moment and take first watch. Resting my head on a block of wood, I stare up at the heights of the old tower, focusing on the bones of the skeletons. With the fire burning high, I sink into deep thought of Dorian, blood of my blood, and his whereabouts. He is lost to the evil out there somewhere on the mountainside. Would he ever forgive me? I wonder about his condition and the possibilities of his death. My mind is plagued with the horrible sounds of iron breaking through stone, the spikes driven through Dorian's hands and feet, wounds becoming infected, the scars embedded forever in his mind. Suffering. Pain. The memory is vivid and I try to shut it out, but can't. Curse the Carnalreesee.

I don't want to think these negative thoughts, but how can I snuff them out? I am surrounded by death everywhere I go, reminded of it every second of my existence. They have him, and Scepter has my blood. Maybe Dorian is safe until he and my blood are united. Maybe there is still time.

Engrossed in the silence, the caw of an ice crow startles me from my thoughts. Looking up, I see the cursed thing staring at me with those horrible yellow eyes, nestled within the crack of the wall. Its head moves back and forth methodically as if examining me. Something is in its mouth. A nut, perhaps? But as my eyes focus through the dim light, I realize it is nothing of the sort. With clawed foot, the bird sets the bloody eyeball down and begins pecking at it, mashing it into jelly with each strike.

"Goddamn birds!" I hiss through clenched teeth. I pick up a stone and throw it at the crow, forcing it to abandon its meal. Madly, it goes squawking into the night. I listen to its cry echoing in the wind as it calls out to its friends in discomfort. Damn those birds, they should be asleep by now. Maybe they are attracted to the light.

I glance over at Kronklich, who has not stirred. He is fast asleep. Good.

With the crow gone, I lean back onto a stone, resting my spine against its hard, uneven surface. Drowsiness settles over me as I fight to keep my eyes open. *Stay awake, Tenor. Stay awake.* I focus on the skeletons hanging from the walls, staring down at me like some poor fools awaiting trial. What sort of tortures did they endure? Were they boys or girls? Probably both. The horrors they witnessed, the things exposed to them. I shiver at the thought of their spirits coming down to haunt us, or worse, possess us. Effectively, it keeps me awake, at least for a bit.

Sitting in the quiet of old dead things, surrounded by the decayed ruin of long ago architecture, my body finally calms. My hand, clenched over the handle of Enivid, rests comfortably on my chest under my leather coat. Even though the horrible crimes committed here came to pass centuries ago, I am still overcome with uneasiness that someone or something is here.

The cold breeze whistling through the cracks of the old tower reminds me of ghost voices, lamenting their woes to those who would listen. *I am listening*, I say to myself and to them. *Right now. Can you hear me?* But their response is distorted and I am unable to speak any longer, for the numbing dark sends me into depths further than the unknown, further than the black oblivion.

I sink into the realm of sleep.

CHAPTER XXVII

The creaking of lanterns.

The clanking of metal.

Light casts its shadow like a somber dance across the snowy plain. I struggle to keep upright through the thick snow. Horrors walk before me, pulling my body with rope, leading me somewhere through the darkness. Skeletons dressed in armor, methodically keep time with each other. Heads focused forward, they never turn to look at me.

What is this place?

"Release me!" I shout, but they do not respond. I try again, "Where are you taking me?"

One of the skeleton's head turns toward me and it points with its bony fingers, never stopping, always moving. "There," it says with a disembodied voice. It comes not from its closed mouth, but from the lantern swaying from its elbow. "To the pit with the others."

Others? It is the first time I notice there are others walking ahead of me, led by more caretakers, bound in more rope. I remember the caretakers from before. Roland. Egleaseon's *ruins. What are they doing here, and where is here?*

The others are naked bodies walking barefoot through the snow. Young girls half beaten and clawed. I can see the bright festering wounds along their legs and backs. Some of them still drip fresh blood from their crowns, the backs of their heads torn, hair missing.

"Goddamn you! Release us at once!"

Another caretaker speaks, unaffected by my retort. "There is no releasing of the mighty Lord Wolfgang. Only the waiting and coming of his death."

I struggle against my bonds and cringe in pain, for the more I struggle, the more the rope squeezes. It rubs into my wrists, breaking the surface of my skin like coarse salt. The pain is excruciating and I find it hard to breathe. I stumble on a hidden rock buried in the snow; down on my knees I go, forcing the march of the living and the dead to stop cold in its tracks.

"Get up," says a hollow voice behind me. A sharp poke to my back forces me to stand. In doing so, my wrists pass before my face, and that's when I realize the rope binding my wrists is nothing like rope, but thick twisted knots of human hair, hair from girls marching in the line. Pieces of skin remain attached at places along the strands. Caked blood and brittle ends.

Poor unfortunate girls.

Slowly, we shuffle along in silence for a time while some of the girls whimper from the cold, shivering to no end. They are suffering and their fate is sealed. They will either die from the cold or at the destination where we are headed.

The pit.

The thought of its existence eludes me. Just what is it? Trying to focus, I ignore the pain from my wrists, but it's useless. The cold has *seeped through my body. No coat, no proofing to keep me warm. I am naked like the rest. Even Enivid has vanished. Who amongst the caretakers has it?*

Suddenly, the march stops as the wind picks up. It bites through my soul, forcing me to contract my arms and legs inward.

"Get up," says a caretaker. Its lifeless face stares down at one of the young girls lying in the snow. Skin stretched over bones, she is too weak to continue.

The glow of the lantern rises to the caretaker's side. "Get up. The master will not take kindly to the weak. He needs strong blood."

But the girl does not move.

Weak and bound by human hair, I am unable to do a thing for her as the caretaker thrashes her with the metal lantern, over and over, saturating the snow with blood. "No!" I croak, coughing on my saliva. The horror of it is unbearable, watching the caretaker commit the carnage, bony teeth protruding, smiling. It is a lost soul obeying the commands of its master. There is no mercy here.

The girl hardly cries out after the first blow and never rises again.

The caretaker drops the lantern beside her lifeless form, its hollow eye sockets waiting and watching. The glowing light within seeps beyond its confined prison and snakes its way into the opening of the girl's skull. Like a possessed demon, the girl rises, slowly moving as if learning to walk for the first time. She turns her head toward me, showing me her glowing eyes and naked form. A smile spreads across her face before she turns around and walks away through the snow, disappearing into the darkness.

I shut my eyes, trying to banish the image from my mind, but I fail horribly. Evil prevails all around me. There is no mistaking it.

Like ruthless tyrants towing their property to the next slave buyer, the armored skeletons lead us onward through the frozen tundra. They march us through the dark cold, toward the destination, a place called the "pit." A light spreads across the sky off in the distance, faint yet apparent. It then winks out. This is enough to catch my attention. I feel a strain in the hair holding my wrists and raise my head to look. We are getting closer. I dread each step toward the large black hole in the earth, a dark cavity surrounded by high snow banks. Chills pass up my spine as we approach closer, never stopping until we reach the lip of the abyss. A horrible stench rises from its depths.

One by one, the caretakers line us up, allowing us to see what fate waits below, but as I look, I see nothing but empty blackness. It does not matter, however. I know what waits down there. Death. The reality of an inescapable nightmare. I see no way down, no stairs or rope, and as each of the girls steps to the edge to examine her fate, one of the caretakers raises its lantern.

"You first."

Terrible screams rise from the girls as the caretaker pushes one of them into the pit. The girl disappears into the darkness in an instant. There is nothing I can do or say. I am a helpless bound prisoner. Where is God's mercy? Remembering his cheek has turned from the people of this world, I bite my lip, cursing myself for thinking those thoughts again.

A flash of light—I look toward the sky and there is something descending, an orb of luminescence—speeding like an arrow. But despite the fire in the sky, the girls continue to look down into the pit, listening to the bones of their sister breaking and cracking, their fear growing. What horrible monsters wait down there?

"Next—" says the caretaker again.

Another girl screams as she is sent down into the pit.

A murmur rises from the remaining girls. Shivering and pale, some of them drop to their knees in the cold snow and begin mumbling, lips trembling. I wonder if they are praying or begging for mercy.

Looking up, I check for the light again, hoping it means something, a light in the darkness, but there is nothing. The sky is cold and ominous, the same as my thoughts.

Slowly, I rise to my feet, pulling tension on my shackled wrists, drawing the attention of my captors.

"It is not your turn, Wolfgang," says the hollow voice of the caretaker.

"I'm not waiting for my turn," I say, stepping off the ledge and into the darkness. Still holding on to the rope, the caretaker is pulled down into the pit with me, falling right behind me. Its white-bluish light parts the blackness of the pit the whole way down. I don't know what I'll find in this hell, but I fall freely and willingly, hoping I can get to the girl before it's too late. The caretaker says nothing as it descends with me, waiting for the impact I can only imagine at the bottom.

Within moments, my boots land in gravel and I am engulfed by rock and dirt as I tumble down an earthly slope. The caretaker smashes into bits. Its spinning lantern casts light and shadows in all directions. Tumbling and rolling, I am reminded of the descent in Egleaseon's ruin, passing along the dirt floor filled with worms and roaches.

Sliding to a halt on my back, I glance to my side to find the girl cowering at a wall toward the side of the pit. My wrists are no longer bound by human hair.

"Come, girl," I say, extending my arms to her. But she doesn't come, shaking her head wildly instead, looking around as if she can't see. I notice blood streaks coming from her hollow eyes. What the hell? The blue light of the lantern allows me to see through the darkness, but I do not want to see anymore. This place is death and chaos, and I want out.

Attempting to stand, I am suddenly gripped by cold hands bursting from the ground, exploding the earth around me like small fountains. Lifeless flesh gropes at my arms, tearing the skin from my muscles. I scream, but no one is listening. Not even the girl. She clamors against the wall, trying to escape her earthly tomb. There is nothing for her to grab, nowhere to put her feet. I hear her nails scraping on the rocks.

Unable to move, I am surrounded by the undead. Lechers rise from the earth, half rotten and reeking of decay. Yellow pus drools from their mouths. Moans of sadness escape their peeling lips. They are hungry and I sense their desperation, their hunger to feed on my warm living flesh, the blood pulsating underneath my naked skin.

"Girl! Girl!" I seethe, trying to gain her attention, but a lecher pulls her down. It claws her legs and strips her of her last worldly possessions. She cries in agony as more lechers swarm her, ripping into her body, tearing away piece by piece.

"No!" I yell in frustration unable to do a thing about it. Infused with rage, I feel nothing as the lechers chew on my body. In the distance ahead of me, I see ghostly images hovering their way toward me. Specters with tattered remains flowing in the unseen wind. Their eyes glow white as they come closer, never stopping, never changing direction.

"Take me! Kill me! Spare the girls," I plead, but they seem not to care.

Beyond the veil of the shadow, a large figure emerges from the void like a giant golem, gleaming in the bluish light. With a golden-greenish tinge of iridescent glow, the top of its head glints through the darkness with each step. A crown sinks low over its bony skull. Two long blood-red canines extend from its mouth. With no flesh encasing its body, I see every bone connecting to the next, ribs attached to vertebrae, vertebrae to appendages. Wearing a brown tattered robe over its bony shoulders, the atrocity never sways its gaze from me as it walks. Its white eyes stare me down. Long fingers extend from its wrists, coming to fine points like great talons. The arms hang loosely to its side, swaying with each giant step it takes. For a moment, the lechers holding me down stop feasting on my skin.

One of the specters speaks. "Knave, stand before your king."

I find it almost impossible to move. In such a weakened state, I haven't the heart to stand, let alone, obey.

"You will stand," commands the specter, and it moves forward, engulfing me with its freezing presence. There is a tight grip at the back of my neck, paralyzing me. Static impulses force me to comply as I rise from the ground, not of my own bidding.

"Now that you have acknowledged our king, kneel to pay your respects."

Sharp pain rakes across the back of my legs, forcing me down on both knees. The ground is wet with blood. I can feel the insects biting me, making their way up my legs.

The crowned skeleton moves closer to me, staring me down with its ghastly eyes. They never blink, and its fanged mouth never moves. "Blood is the essence of power," it says, "and without power, one becomes useless."

A strangeness fills my mind with the perplexing words, like a familiar thought that comes back to haunt you.

"Useless is unacceptable. Power is everything."

I have heard those words before.

A daunting reality sets in as I recall the same words repeated by the vampire Roul.

"Do you know who I am, mortal?"

Not of my own volition, I am forced to look into its wavering eyes of white. "Stellamane," I say, barely a whisper.

"Almost correct," says the skeleton king, forcing his fist into my stomach and making me wretch from the blow. The specters surrounding me laugh.

"You will address me as King Stellamane." More laughing ensues, but this time, Stellamane joins in. His cold dead hand extends to lift my chin, turning it this way and that, as if examining a fresh piece of meat. "Fortunately for you, you are not useless. You have power, and that power I will have."

My thoughts become flooded with the words Bronin spoke. Blood of the father. Of course. Why didn't I think of it before? "You want my blood just as much as Egleaseon does, don't you?"

"Egleaseon is a fool," says Stellamane patting my cheek with his cold bony hand. "To think the salvation of vampires lies within the blood of the Wolfgangs." Stellamane chuckles. "Fools. All of them. Blood comes and wanes, thick at first, then thin over time. It dilutes the power of the vampire." He releases my face and I slump back to the ground where the lechers grab me again. He steps away and turns around to where his back faces me. "Blood is useless to me now. What I seek is far more precious, and far more lasting." Turning around, he rushes up to me in a flash, placing his hand on my forehead.

A chill passes into my face from his touch, and instantly, my body weakens. I feel my life force draining from me.

"I will have your soul."

But something counters his words, echoing through the chamber in a whisper.

"No, you won't."

A brilliant light explodes somewhere behind me. A ball of fire charges forward, burning through corpses and ghosts, obliterating everything in its path. The ghost entities howl in response, and the howl echoes around the pit in a deafening screech. I catch the glimpse of some other being spinning through the chamber in a trail of mist and fluttering moths, too bright to see their true form. Over and over, their light collides with the lechers and specters, destroying them one at a time in brilliant cascades of light.

With Stellamane's hand still on me, I feel my energy fading fast. I want to speak, but the words I wish to say have vanished. Suddenly, a glowing sword emerges from thin air, striking against

Stellamane's arm. It holds fast against him as if trying to force him away from me.

"What is this?" asks Stellamane's hollow voice.

The same question races through my mind as I watch the shape take form. A thin, pale woman stands beside me, her jet-black hair blowing in wisps around her face like fire, a wreath of mauve peonies decorating her crown. Is it her? Is it really her, or is she the demon following me all this time? Something is different.

"Release him," she says in a powerful, resolute voice.

"Never," says Stellamane; his face moves ever closer to mine.

Gripping the sword with both hands, she pushes harder, yet Stellamane resists. The iridescent moths pour from her body, passing through her hair and eyes and mouth, then passing before Stellamane's face in a torrent of confusion.

"Whore of gods. Your tricks are petty." Backing off momentarily, Stellamane raises his arm again to strike. "I will have what is mine."

Able to finally speak, I am left speechless as my beautiful D moves between Stellamane and myself, the cheeks of her smooth face smiling at me.

"Leave this place, Tenor. Leave now." Her voice is frantic and I feel terror inside as Stellamane strikes her back. The concussion of the blow passes through her and into me, shaking my body violently. I reach for her, but my arms pass through her body like ice. She shakes her head, mouthing the word "go" as she shuns my second attempt to grab her.

As Stellamane raises an arm again, she turns to face him with sword in hand, and the two of them collide. Another burst of energy *surges from their impact, and I am sent sprawling through the dark, shaking violently and out of control. I hear Stellamane in the distance shouting as I spin on and on, never stopping through the void, further away from the one I love, further away from the one that saved me.*

DAY NINE

CHAPTER XXVIII

"TENOR! TENOR!" I FEEL MY BODY shaking terribly back and forth. Light beats the front of my eyelids, yet I cannot open them. I don't want to open them. Nightmares wait for me; they will carry me off into the night, beat me with glowing lanterns, and eviscerate my naked skin.

"Tenor! Come, man, wake up. You were screaming."

Slowly opening my eyes, I try to make sense of the words spoken to me as my pupils adjust to my surroundings. Brilliant light seeps through cracks of the ruined fortress tower, and suddenly, I remember where I am and how cold it is. Groping at my body for warmth, I realize I am not naked and that I am still fully dressed in my armor and leather coat with the brass buckles. Enivid is clutched tightly to my chest.

"Good God, man, you are frozen to the core. And to think with all of those clothes you should be nipped tight. I tried raising the fire as best I could, but the resources are limited, you know." Kronklich fusses around as I gaze bleary-eyed high above. The skeletons on the walls stare at me, still watching from the night before.

Those poor girls. Tortured and beaten, butchered from their navels to their necks. The evil of Stellamane and his undead servants burns through me. And my blessed D. She was here! It was her! She somehow saved me, and with a sword. But how? What sort of demonic happenings were taking place in the spirit world at this very moment?

"You have that look," says Kronklich, cooking up the last strips of dear meat for our breakfast.

I look at him confused. "What look?"

He pulls an apple from the bag and begins slicing it. "That faraway look. You saw her again, didn't you?"

Kronklich is reading my mind again.

"How do you know that?"

"Tenor, I think I know my best friend's reactions after all these years. How long has it been now?"

"I had the worst nightmare," I say, rubbing the temples of my forehead. "I saw him."

"Oh?" says Kronklich, raising his eyebrows in the process. "Egleaseon?"

"Stellamane. The one who used to inhabit this castle."

"Ah, yes, the vampire king banished by Egleaseon. Fascinating story you told yesterday, really."

"What if he is still—" I hate to entertain the thought. "What if he is still—here?"

"Nonsense. If the story you told was true, and his remains were cast down that blasted hole called the "Devil's Drain," then that is where he must be and that is where he'll stay. Not here within the ruined bombardments of a destroyed fortress."

Kronklich's words do little to ease my paranoia as we make ready to leave the tower. Surveying the bloody walls again, I shiver at the thought of this ruined castle being possessed. Putting this place behind me couldn't come quickly enough.

Avoiding looking at the hanging skeletons for the last time, I run my hands across my waist, ensuring my weapons are secure and accounted for. The caw of the ice crows echoes from the other side of the mortared walls, reminding me they are still here waiting for us. Of course. With the fire nearly smoldered to ash, we push our weight against the large wooden door, forcing it to groan into the wilderness.

Despite the dank gloom of the forest, it is still brighter out here than in the ruined tower. Already I feel my mood improving, breathing in the fresh crisp air of the outside rather than the smoky burn of wood inside. The cacophony of crows draws my attention to the canopy above us. There are more today than there were yesterday. Near the wall to the side of the tower, a carcass lies half buried in the snow, its frozen insides displayed for all to see. What looks like the remains of furry ears is the only clue as to what the creature was in life. The back torso is gone and its eyes have been pecked out. I recall the crow watching me last night.

Kronklich observes the same but never raises his crossbow and focuses more on his cane. He is moving slower today, and I have no doubt his condition is worsening. I watch him chew slowly on the ebon root, and he notices me staring and smiles. "Right, then, off we go. The day seems brighter. We should have no trouble finding Scepter's trail."

For hours, we travel through powdered mounds of snow and gnarled roots of trees, listening to the solitude of the Decameron Forest, searching for clues to Scepter's whereabouts. And within those hours, we find nothing, nothing to spark our interest, no leads of any kind. Watching a pair of atters chase each other through the trees, I begin to think Kronklich's optimism has run its course.

I want to scream my frustration in the forest. Scepter has my blood and the Carnalreesee have my son. The combination of the two uniting could be devastating. But no sooner do my hopes fade—and while the cold of the forest continues to weigh me down—does a light in the darkness show the way.

We come across a disturbance in the snow, an old cobblestone, one of many, which is part of a ruined and weathered road. With dry eyes, I look up and imagine the road snaking through the old forest of Stellamane's old territories. I'm excited by the find; however, there is still no evidence of tracks, no indentations of boots, and no traces of blood. We continue following hints of the road and eventually come to a scene of ghastly proportions, a stage set frozen in time. Rotted wooden caravan wagons and carriages driven by skeleton drivers escorting skeleton passengers. Memories of the caretakers come back to me, but I do not see glowing lanterns. Was it a trading caravan from one desolate town to the next? Or a failed escort transport of nobles? Their bony remains lie on their sides, still dressed in their traveling outfits, hats and scarves. Peering inside one of the carriages, I see an entire family of four, father, mother, daughter, and son, dressed in embroidered jackets and tailored dresses. Colors faded from time, they are locked in a frozen prison, bones and all, speckled with a sheen of frost that catches the light seeping through the trees.

"You're the doctor. How long do you suppose they've been like this?" I ask Kronklich as he comes to stand next to me, limping.

"I'd say a good couple hundred years, no doubt. The clothing is fine and their accessories are proper. I believe that's tobacco in his pocket. Nobility for sure."

Kronklich reaches into the carriage and grabs the top hat from the skeletal figure wearing the smoking jacket and gloves.

I stare at Kronklich intently.

"Well, he certainly doesn't need it."

We move on, scavenging the rest of the wagons and carriages for supplies, but come up empty-handed. Not a bit of rope or a bunch of tinder for fire. Everything is covered in sparkling white powder.

And ever am I reminded of the crows. Still following us— everywhere we go, every turn we make. As soon as it seems we lose them, a new group of birds wait in the trees ahead of us. It's as if they know our every move. Plotting and scheming.

The day presses on and I feel the cold seeping thicker and deeper into my bones. This is the second day of traveling through this cursed forest and I feel it taking its toll on me. Moving my legs is proving to be more difficult and Kronklich's health is declining. Even now, I hear him coughing behind me. Worry of alerting Scepter of our presence grows. I try my best to stifle my concerned looks toward Kronklich, but I can't completely hide how I feel for my friend. Poison from a black blade is lethal if untreated. Fortunately, the cold climate is slowing its progression.

Stopping at a shelter of circling branches, I make a small fire to warm us for a brief rest and share an apple with Kronklich and half a loaf of bread. He is getting along, but at what cost? Mouth stained black, I watch him reach in his secret pocket for another pinch of ebon root.

"Still no traces of blood," says Kronklich, chewing away on the black substance, "but I know he must have gone this way. I saw disturbed snow and broken icicles just a little ways back. I'm sure of it."

I want more than anything to believe Kronklich. "I'm sure your right," I say, trying to keep his hopes up. Mine have already diminished. The cold grows darker with every step we take deeper into the forest. I try not to say anything more as I watch him nod off.

I stand up and turn around to warm my backside, allowing the small reprieve to sink in. *Let him rest for now. He will need it.*

Surveying the trees beyond our small ring of protection, I watch an ice crow land in a tree nearby, the large blue and gray feathers of its underside stained red. *Too close for comfort.*

I find a rock and throw it.

Miss.

The rock hits a branch next to the crow and makes it jump to the next tree. I grab another one, following after it. "Damn bird, get out of here!" I shout, throwing the rock with anger, steam puffing from my face. This time the rock connects and the bird falls from its perch, landing in the snow below, cawing and flapping around. "Meat is meat," I say softly to myself as I move toward it, dagger drawn.

Stopping dead in my tracks, I reach for Enivid, forgetting about the squawking bird at my feet. All around me, faces glare at me, contorted in hideous ways. They are faces embedded within the bark of the trees. Some with long noses and others with jagged teeth, eyes hallowed out in dark shadows, they do not move as they stare, frozen in their positions of anguish. The scene is similar to that of a child's nightmare, however gruesome and macabre it appears. Yet this nightmare is my reality. Around and around I turn, sizing up the enemy, its long branches extending jagged arms toward me, its roots curling like claws to capture me. Breathing heavily, I calm myself after realizing they are not moving and slowly walk toward one of them, touching the bark and peeling it off like parchment. They are simply trees with faces, resilient to the cold like the rest of the trees in the forest. Nothing more.

Moving to examine the others, I see many more trees with faces, perhaps dozens. I walk from the clearing passing large flat rocks carved with yet even more faces. What is this place? It is like a forest of forgotten souls. Each entity bears the visage of sorrow or anger. I need to get Kronklich, show him what I found.

As I turn to leave, I nearly run straight into him. Torch blazing in hand, black mouth chewing furiously, he is awake and alert, burning a hole through me with his infernal gaze.

"How much ebon root did you take?" I ask him, looking into his wide, dilated eyes. "Are you ok?"

"Spectacular, sir. Good as rain," he says in excitement, brushing past me to examine one of the faces. "What do you make of it?" he asks, running his hand across the bark of the tree, inside the mouth and eyeholes. He is completely ignoring his condition. "Incredible. Part of the curse don't you think? Even the trees themselves detest the horrid power of Decameron Forest."

His word about the trees having feelings makes me think of Dora and his criticisms about the natural order—that those who hunt monsters upset the balance of things, but in actuality, it is the monster that jeopardizes the state of all things. Egleaseon. Stellamane. They are proof of it.

"What is that?" asks Kronklich from across the grove. I hear his voice trail off, and no sooner do I look than his form is far ahead of me, like a rabid dog searching for its next victim.

"Kronklich?" I rush ahead, following the glow of his torch through the gnarled branches of the trees. Entering an open clearing filled with nothing but wide expanse and snowdrifts, we come to an area of the forest where the sky, for the first time, is exposed. Significantly brighter, the overcast sky still bears down its dismal gray, adding to the dingy color reflected in the snow.

Kronklich comes to a halt, standing before a high precipice looming above. At its base, contorted among large boulders and shattered logs, a beast man, half wolf, half man, lies shattered and broken. The willdermen's blood paints the rocks, frozen solid from the exposure to the wind and sky. Teeth dislodged and scattered, its jaw lies agape, crooked at the wrong angle, exposing its neck. Bitten and drained of blood, chunks of skin are missing from its shoulder and back; its spine has been removed.

There is no doubt Scepter's passed this way.

Gazing up the height of the cliff, I experience vertigo momentarily and shut my eyes, shaking my head to rid the spinning clouds. Shading my eyes from the brightness, I look again. "That's a long climb. Think you can manage?"

Kronklich is off to the side checking the snow for tracks, and then looks back at the cliff, and then me. "Of course I can manage," he says in an airy voice. I sense a faint tinge of annoyance in his delivery.

Hopping from one boulder to the next, we clear the debris of rocks and wood and begin our slow ascension up the rock face. Despite my blistered hand underneath the glove, I do my best to grip the jagged edges of each ledge we come to. Looking straight up, the way is hardly simple. Trees have fallen off the mountain's side, catching into wedges on their way down, forming massive blockades of debris, making it harder for us to navigate. With Kronklich ahead of me, I feel better with his present state, even if it is drug induced.

We climb.

No rope, no security. We are determined to find Scepter, to find him before the day wanes again. Maybe he is somewhere at the top of this cliff, maybe not.

A gust of wind bursts from the north, sending flakes of snow stinging my face. On the side of the mountain, it is colder and the exposure is more intense. I am used to the cover of trees. The weather forces me to move faster and less carefully. I slip on a stone halfway up. Gasping, I hold on with one hand, the one that's blistered and burnt. The agony is unbearable with each swing of my body. Back and forth I sway, clenching my teeth, mustering what remaining energy I can. A strong grip grabs my forearm and pulls me to safety. Kronklich is beside me, grinning. Is he laughing?

"There'll be no tumbling off the side of the mountain today, my good man!" shouts Kronklich, slapping my shoulder.

"Right, then," I say, peering down the precipice.

We continue climbing.

It seems an eternity until we finally reach the top. The wind howls as we regain our strength, taking shelter within the hollow of a large tree. Here on top of the summit of the cliff, the branches sway with fury. The sun has nearly traveled its course for the day, and again, I am filled with dread we will run out of time.

Moving from the shelter of the hollow, we press forward, weapons at the ready. But our renewed vigor to find Scepter is cast aside at the vision before us. Shattered tree trunks, boulders split down the middle; we have entered a forest of death.

More willdermen lay dead everywhere.

Heads caved in, spines ripped from their backs. The carnage is the same as at the gypsy camp days ago. Monsters attacking monsters? What happened here? We walk slowly, examining the bodies one by one. Some are in wolf form, some in human. We find only one halfway through its transformation. All of their necks have been drained like the one tossed off the cliff.

Kneeling beside one of the male corpses, I brush away its long brown hair from its eyes. It is as I expected. They are gone.

Carrying on the wind, I hear the caws of the crows again. They are near and watching.

"This isn't good," says Kronklich surveying the mass carnage. "It's what we feared. He's getting stronger. With an endless food supply such as this, it won't be long till he's at full strength."

Standing back up, I survey the surroundings again, feeling as though I've missed something. But there is nothing, only more forest and an endless supply of trees. We were so close.

I turn to Kronklich. "Now what do we do?" I say breathlessly. "Dusk is here and the trail is cold." I listen to Kronklich's teeth grinding the ebon root.

For a moment, he says nothing, watching the ground with intense far-away eyes, and then he flicks them back at me. "Of course." Rushing away from me, he moves to the edge of the bloody massacre and stops before a set of footprints in the snow. "Blood."

It takes a moment to realize what he's getting at, and just as I notice the thin streaks of blood trailing away from the scene, he is already in motion, moving ahead of me, bum leg and all, shouting over his shoulder.

"Blood, Tenor! Always follow the blood!"

DAY TEN

CHAPTER
XXIX

IT'S BEEN THREE DAYS SINCE we entered this godforsaken forest and still no sign of Scepter. After discovering the massacre of willdermen last night, our hopes rose with the long blood trail leading us farther into Decameron Forest. There have been other leads: ancient ruins of evil, atters drained of blood, boot prints tracked through the snow, decaying spines. But they have all ended the same way. An empty road leading to an empty solution. Defeat has never been my friend. Being unable to find the one with my blood in the tiny vial is a horrible feeling. He could be leagues away from here by now with his vampire speed, far beyond the boundaries of this cursed forest, and I wouldn't know it. We are out of food. I can't feel my hands or feet. Sleep came quickly yet there were no dreams to consume me. No lasting memories of D to comfort me. Where had she gone? Fear besets me with the worst thoughts, that the demon spirit of Stellamane destroyed her. I shake my head, trying to banish the thought. What am I saying? What do I know of the dead realm? The cold is numbing my brain. I do not know what is real anymore.

Fortunately, we found the meekest of shelters—a grove filled with the contorted and twisted faces of the forest—yet the night was unforgiving. Wolves howled in the far beyond. Atters chattered in the branches. I awoke to glowing eyes floating in the dark more than once. At best, I would sleep for an hour then wake to the sound of a creature dying in some far-off place, at which point I would clutch Enivid tightly, hands cold and clammy with sweat. Kronklich, however, slept like a babe, the poison serving as a sleeping aid. I wonder what horrors he dreamt of last night or if dreams ever happen. He never tells me.

I shiver.

If we don't find warmth today, I am certain we will die. It is a struggle to press on, to find our footing, to find food. The cold cares not for the living. Not me. Not Kronklich.

Gazing over my shoulder, I watch him hanging on with determination. I can't imagine how hard it is for him. Every laborious step is a struggle for me, but the poison throbbing through his veins continues to weaken him even more. I can see it in his face. The sunken eyes. The discoloration of skin. Slowly and surely, he will die, and then shortly after, I will crawl into a little ball and close my eyes, letting my mind be taken by the black oblivion as it turns to frost.

Scepter is no fool. He knows the limitations of humans. He left us trails to throw us off, to waste our time and ensure our doom on this frozen mountain.

My desperation to find Kronklich help is paramount, but there is nothing here. I'm not even sure where *here* is. The snow-covered ground has banished the chances of finding ebon root, the only other thing that can slow the poison.

But of all the worrisome things considering this doom-forsaken day, is my concern about the growing darkness. The branches swell thicker with each step, twirling their way toward the living things. I've seen atters and birds ensnared within the foliage—the trees trapping and constricting them, sucking the blood from their carcasses like venomous spiders entrapping prey for later meals. The nodules blot out the day even more than before, and soon it will be eternal night. Then Scepter will have his way with us. Images of Malice glinting in the night and crushing my skull plague me.

I hear a soft thud in the snow behind me and fear the worst.

Turning around, I see Kronklich lying there in the snow, unable to move. Caws of excitement rise from the trees around us. Hundreds of them.

Quickly, I move to help Kronklich, scooping my arms under his shoulders to get him to stand. I grab him by his face and look into his eyes. "Can you walk?" His eyes are open, but there is no response. "Kronklich!" I try again over the rushing wind, rubbing his face to bring warmth. Maybe his lips are too numb to speak. "Kronklich," I say in desperation. "You need to keep moving. We will die if we don't keep moving." I can see it in his eyes, the look of defeat, the moment where nothing matters anymore. It would be so easy to lie down in the soft white snow and sleep forever. "Kronklich," I say again, shaking him firmly. Finally, he responds with a nod of his head. A "yes" barely escapes his trembling lips. "Good! That's very good!" I say.

Supporting his weight, I lead us on, one step at a time, disregarding the birds overhead, their disappointment screeching in the dark.

My energy is failing me. I'm not sure what time of day it is anymore. Dawn was many hours ago. Now darkness slowly ebbs its way over us like a cocoon. I adjust my hold on Kronklich and think to myself for the second time this day—we are going to die out here.

Walking soon turns to staggering, for the snow is very thick in some places. In time, the light eludes us completely. No more torches. No more kindle to keep us warm. I am bound to my other senses, of sound, feeling, and smell. More cold. More darkness. It consumes everything. My muscles begin to burn. The movement keeps me warm for a time, but soon it will fade too.

Up ahead, I see the faint glow of light wavering like a torch. Could there be someone out here, after all, surviving this eternal winter in Decameron Forest? Or was it a trap? Maybe Scepter lit the way to lure us to our doom. Regardless of the circumstances, I am left without options and press forward, nearly dragging Kronklich like a dead weight. "Come on, friend, don't give up now." Kronklich does not speak, but I can hear his breathing in my ear. "Good, that's very good," I say out loud, more to myself than him.

As we struggle through the increasing snowfall, the faint glow doesn't get any closer, almost as if it's moving with us. A moving light all on its own. Something within me wants to come out. Hope. If the light is moving, then the light could be her.

"D? Is that you?" I call out. I squint in the darkness, trying to catch a glimpse. It comes again. Hope. "We are coming, my love, we are coming."

Her voice wafts its way toward me; a whisper on the wind, swaying through the creaking branches, bending under sagging bows of birch. "Tenor, my love. Tenor. Come to me, my sweet love." Yes, it is her. She is safe after all. I had given up. I thought she was dead and the evil spirits had taken her. No. Of course not. She is strong. She is resolute.

Laboring to breathe the thin cold air, we come closer to the light somehow, and then the wavering white orb blends into another form, that of flickering flames. The fire casts images along the back of a hollowed-out crevice large enough to fit our bodies through. Yes. She is guiding us. To safety. To shelter. To warmth.

"Tenor," comes her voice again, and it is sweet. It makes my heart swell to hear that sound.

"Yes, my love. We are almost there."

A voice whispers in my ear. "Don't—Tenor."

"What?" I ask from the suddenness of Kronklich's voice. "Don't what?"

He says nothing in response, so I continue, entering into a hole in the side of the mountain. We pass through a threshold of warm air and howling wind; the snow on our coats melts and steams. The feeling is so desperately needed. I try to make sense of Kronklich's words moments ago. Leaning on a rock, I relieve some of his weight from me. "Don't what?" I ask again, trying to make sense of his gibberish.

"Th-there," he stutters. "Don't go in there." He barely lifts his arm, pointing.

I can see the poison is affecting him horribly, manipulating his sense of judgment. His pupils have shrunk to the size of a pin.

"Don't be absurd. We are going to die if we don't get warm," I say, glancing in the direction he indicates. A long windy tunnel waits for us ahead. Drafts of warm air berate my face. But I know it's more than that. I still hear D's voice calling to me. He doesn't understand. We need to keep going or I may lose this chance. Finally, after all this time, I openly admit it to Kronklich. "It's her, Kronklich. Diana. I thought she was lost to us but it's her. I hear her voice again, like before." I urge him to come with me, but his grip on my wrist is tight as he leans hard against the wall.

"No," he whispers. "It's not her."

I look at him startled. "What do you mean, it's not her? How are you—" Suddenly, I stop mid-sentence, realizing what I could not moments ago. I see it's quite possible some other entity could be impersonating Diana.

"You are not the only one hearing voices, Tenor."

A chill runs up my spine. Voices. I look back toward the hallway and hear multiple voices growing in volume. Echoing moans come from every shadow of the corridor. The comfort I felt moments ago dies. My stomach churns with pain. Any moment I feel that I will be sick. This place is damned. It's feeding off of my thoughts and body, manifesting from the very energy within my being.

"Go!" I shout, waving my hands in the direction we just came from, but Kronklich is slow to respond. I grab him by the hem of his coat and pull him toward the exit. "We need to get out of here before—"

I never have the chance to finish my words, as dark malevolent forces rise from the ground. Their anguished cries wreak sadness over me like never before.

Specters. Horrible wailing spirits from the dead realm. They block our escape and reach forward with their incorporeal arms. I can feel their blistering cold through my proofing, inches from my body.

"Come to me, my love," one of the specters says. A gurgling erupts from its delivery. Hovering not two feet off the ground, it glides toward us with ease, its transparent face hideous to look upon. Rotting flesh and brittle hair, it reminds me of a lecher wearing flowing garments of a coat and mantle.

I pull Kronklich back, moving into the cave of my original intent. It is a struggle to get Kronklich to cooperate. Tripping and stumbling, we pass through the long corridor, passing small openings along the way to either side of us. Forward is ever our destination. "Go! Go!" I shout, my voice echoing along the stone interior.

We enter a vast room filled with a mixture of yellow and green light. Its source seeps through a crevice deep in the earth, a large underground chasm, circular in nature, the main focal point of the room. It is so large, we have to navigate one way or another to get around it. Torches outline the edges, as if warning doom waits for those below. More wails and cries of the dead waft their way up through the chasm, lamenting sorrow and discontent. "*The Master. The Master,*" they say, summoning hatred deep from within me. They call to me like I belong here. "*The Master bids you stay.*" Black shadows rise from below like ants billowing from a nest.

Kronklich stumbles at my feet. "We have to keep moving!" I shout over the howling wind. I see him shaking his head. "Kronklich!"

I know this place and I won't go through it again. It's the Devil's Drain, the place in my dream where Stellemane tortured his prisoners. A skeletal hand rises from the pit as if something were trying to climb its way out. I keep pulling on Kronklich, forcing him to stand. He obliges finally and grabs a hold of me, and together we move as fast as Kronklich's weak body will let us. We exit from the pit of hell and enter into another daunting corridor. The smell of sulfur sends my mind into a dizzying madness.

Kronklich draws his cane sword. "Look out!"

Ahead of us, just before the exit of the hall, demonic spirits ascend from the floor, same as before, preventing us from leaving. Their moaning gasps join together as they rise, one by one. "*The Master. The Master beckons you!*" When we reach the first specters, Kronklich swipes at the closest one, but his blade passes through it as if it were never there. Pushing him to the side, I forget the sickening feeling in my gut and rip upward with Enivid, making contact with the demon ghost. White light explodes from it as it breaks apart into particles of fire and smoke.

It's as I expected. The properties of Enivid. The old man was a genius. Properties of the Bawaka and the Hand of God combined. Dora was able to create a weapon capable of destroying not only vampires, but those of the dead realm.

I see Kronklich pull up his crossbow, ready to fire, but I push his weapon down. "Don't waste your bolts. They're no use here."

With a look of defeat on his face, he sticks to watching my flank as we pair, side by side, lashing at the spirits as they come, bursting the air with more fiery smoke. There is a cold blast of wind against my face and I know we are closing in on our escape. Drifts of snow skim the ground as I slash through another dark shadow.

"Don't leave us!" The voices say. *"Don't leave us!"* The spirits taunt relentlessly. Then I hear Diana's voice again. *"Curse you, Tenor! Curse you forever for leaving me to this fate!"*

I can't take this torture! Why are they doing this to me? How do they know of her? Do they really have her imprisoned down there in that pit? "D!!!" I shout over the wailing souls.

"No, Tenor!" screams Kronklich as he slams into my body with a renewed energy. Is he possessed as well? His strength is resolute as he forces me forward, away from the heat and out into the freezing cold of the night.

The freezing snow stings my face as we collapse onto the ground, burying ourselves in the snow. The suddenness of it shocks me back to reality. I struggle, looking over my shoulder to see the glowing figures wavering in the firelight, lingering just before the exit, staring on with their hollow eyes. Their whispers linger on the wind. *"Come back to us."*

They cannot follow. They are bound to that place forever.

Depleted of energy, I struggle to stand, pulling at Kronklich's coat. "Come on! We need to move!" But there is no response. I shake him violently, but still there is no reaction. He is lying face down in the snow. "Dammit," I say, turning him over. Frustration sets in. We cannot linger here, not this close. We need to get far away from this place of death before—

All around us, the air is thick with movement. From the shadows of the trees emerges the cawing of crows. Dozens of them, maybe hundreds. My nerves stand on end at the sound of flapping wings.

"Come on!" I shout at Kronklich, banging on his chest, but still there is no response. I look back at the cave we passed through in hopes of a shelter. The spirits have gone, leaving only the flickering light lingering in the passageway. But I know we cannot go back there. The spirits will return.

We need to get out of this forest.

I pull on Kronklich's coat, but his weight is too much. I struggle, dragging him a few feet before collapsing in the snow out of breath. "Come on man, wake up!"

It's no use. The man is depleted of strength. Kronklich used the last of his energy to save me, to rescue me from that hole of the devil.

I can't give up. I know he wouldn't.

I move to rub his face, to restore the warmth that may have helped him earlier, and notice something I didn't see before. Black lines creeping from under the collar of his coat. Thick spidery veins spreading up the sides of his neck toward his jaw and ears. Pulling one of my daggers free, I remove the bandage from his leg and begin cutting back the cloth surrounding the wound. I fall back onto my elbows, shuddering at the sight of the black, festering mound. Worms crawl from the mangled skin, twisting and sliding across pus-covered scabs. It is what I feared. The wound has become exacerbated beyond hope. His entire leg is corrupted with the poison.

A cawing crow lands on the ground nearby.

"Get out of here!" I shout with frustration. Dagger in hand, I throw it at the bird, killing it on impact. The trees and darkness seem to come to life all around me from my actions. The birds react with sound. Just as the first crow came, two more land in the snow near us, hopping around on their tiny legs.

I stare at the wound on Kronklich's leg, wondering at the horrific pain he is enduring. I try to think of a solution, some other way to save his leg, but the same thought returns again and again. We are running out of time. If I don't do something now, we will become supper for the birds.

Holding Enivid before me, I look to the sky for guidance, as if someone was watching me or listening, but I know it is a waste of time. "I'm so sorry," I say under my breath as I raise the holy blade to sever Kronklich's leg. It's the only way to stop the poison. However, I pause, overwhelmed by the sheer number of crows landing on Kronklich's body. More and more of them land, pecking at his coat, trying to get to the tender meat underneath.

"No, damn you!" I shout at the birds, swinging Enivid wildly about. Their yellow eyes trace through the dark like floating spirits as they escape, their wings flapping about in a frenzy.

There are so many of them. The glow from the cave outlines their small frames in dark silhouettes. They resemble impish devils fluttering about and I start cutting them down, one by one, filling the frigid air with blood-stained feathers.

But they never stop.

Their numbers are relentless. They continue pecking Kronklich's body over and over, yet there is no response from Kronklich as if he were already dead. *Was he dead?* One of them flies away, a piece of flesh in its beak. There is no mercy here.

While I protect Kronklich, a crow lands on my back suddenly. Its claws scratch my skin and poke my ears. I reach to stop it, and clutch it within my hand while it pecks at me. I squeeze its tiny frame and hear the sickening crunch of its ribs collapse.

I do not let go.

I squeeze harder as anger floods through me. Blood seeps through my fingers as another lands on my shoulder and pecks at my neck. "Aaaaggghhhh!" I cry out as the surface of my skin breaks. Warm blood travels the length of my neck. More swarm me, blocking my vision as they engulf us like a death plague. I can no longer see Kronklich. I swipe back and forth, slicing apart crows with each blow, doing all that I can until my feet stumble over Kronklich's body. I am sent backward, landing supine in the snow with my arms out. I can no longer feel Enivid within my grasp as the white-feathered crows cover my body. Their red-stained beaks peck again and again. There are so many!

Suffocation overwhelms me. Empty-handed, I grab for anything I can find, digging my hands in the snow and the dirt underneath. But there is nothing. I feel the dull tapping of beaks against my proofing, but they cannot penetrate it. They resort to pecking my gloved hand and fingers. Anger and hatred corrupts me as I grab one of them by its wings and shove its head in my mouth. I bite down with determination, feeling the tendons and rubbery skin beneath, severing its head from its body. Blood fills my mouth as I cough and spit, trying to make room for air in my throat. For a moment, everything is red as one of the crows hops closer to my face, watching me, examining me suspiciously. Unable to move, I look at it as it looks at me. Its evil eye stares at me as it caws and blinks once, then twice, followed by a third time. Its beak jabs down into my eye socket, and there is a brilliant flash of light.

Stabbing pain explodes inside my head as I am left blinded from the attack. I cry out in torment as the bird takes flight with its prize. Red is my filter now as I look around with my one remaining eye. Paralyzed from shock and pain, I am unable to console the bloody hole in my face. Feeling has left me. The crows peck at other parts of my body. The world seems to slow down as I watch the bird with my eye, circle away, higher and higher, until its dim silhouette fades from my vision.

Something else comes. A dark figure cloaked in shadow. It moves forward with such speed, I can do nothing but accept its arrival. God is cruel. He has sent his dark servant to cleanse the earth of my filth. Within its grasp, a menacing weapon of wood and metal extends from its dark arms and cloaked face. A scythe of obsidian black. Blood drips from its edge as it raises its instrument of death.

The angel has come for me, I am certain, but I struggle to keep my eye open. My energy fades quickly. My mind wavers in and out of consciousness. Between the red world and the black, I think of yellow for some reason, the golden moths that come to visit me during the strangest of times. But now is not one of those times. My world is fading. Now, as I remain on the brink of death, my mind would like to choose one color, but there is only blackness.

CHAPTER
XXX

Walking.

Endless walking.

I feel it will never end. My hand slides along the smooth stone of the corridor. Wet and glistening, it sweats with condensation from the cold air outside meeting the hot air inside. Wind blows through the hallway but the candles never go out.

Walking.

Endless walking.

I come to fortified glass. A windowpane streaked from rain and dirt. I look out on the castle heights below. The moonlight reflects portions of the spires and turrets. Gargoyles. Sconces. Sharp jagged railings. How high am I?

The sound of ticking brings my attention back to the interior. It is a desolate echo among the stones of the never-ending corridor. There is no one here. At least, I think no one is. The last thing I remember is climbing the steps, one at a time. Bats flew by my face from a crevice in the roof. The crack is the source of the wind now.

Something is ticking consistently.

Agitation swells within me as I walk. To my right and left, beautiful mural paintings stretch from floor to ceiling. The watercolor images are breathtaking. Cold mountain forests. Pristine waterfalls. In one painting, a moon fills the entire sky. I stop to admire all of them, one by one, but dare not linger long. Horrible things happen to those who linger. I shouldn't dream such fantasies. I need to stay focused.

Again with the ticking.

Confounded hell! Relentless torment!

My pace quickens. The source of my agony lies just ahead.

Tick. Tick. Tick.

A clock stands before me, taunting my soul, leering at my form as I stare back. Immaculate framework, picture perfect interior. I can see the gears inside, the windup knobs, the intricate cog teeth, gold and gleaming. Its face consists of three moons. Not moons like the one in the painting, but circular impressions made from different-colored pearls, each having their own face. Blue of happiness. Yellow of sadness. Red of pain.

The faces are iridescent and shimmer in the candlelight. They look so alive. One set of brass hands point to the hour and minutes. They do not move, however. It is the same for the pendulum hanging motionless down the center column. At its base, three long levers project from the column, one for each face. Still though, the ticking persists, and it hurts the inside of my brain.

More ticking.

I search the hall for something to break the cursed thing with— to end my torment—and find a chair. Grasping it with both hands, I raise the piece of furniture over my head as if warning the clock of its imminent doom.

"I wouldn't do that if I were you."

The chair slips from my hand and clatters against the floor.

"Who said that?" I ask in disbelief, looking about the hall in every direction. The place is desolate just as before. Empty and cold. Devoid of life.

"We did," says a different voice. It seems to come from everywhere. Its tone is sorrowful, unlike the first bright cheerful voice.

Looking at the clock in wonder, I examine it from top to bottom, yet see no one hiding inside it or behind it.

"There's no use looking there," comes a third voice, raspy and tormented. "We are right here."

I look up at the faces of the clock. They stare back at me, never blinking. The one on the left, the one with the conniving grin and round eyes, parts its lips to speak again.

"Cheer up, man. Things could be worse. You could be dead."

The strange happy face seems smug with its words as it watches my every move.

"What is this?" I ask, realizing I'm speaking to a clock. "Is this some kind of joke?"

"No joke," says the middle face. Its frown smiles a little as it talks. "But the time has come for a decision."

"A decision? What are—"

"There is an echo," says the right face, cutting my speech off. "Yes, a decision." Its raspy delivery lingers in the air.

"What are you talking about? What's happening to me?"

"So many questions, yet so little time."

"I don't have time for this," I say, turning around to walk away.

"And where will you go?" asks the middle face.

"Yes, where will you go?" repeats the right face. The repetition of its question agitates me further.

"As far away from here as I can!" I shout at the clock. Talking clock or not, I have the urge to smash the damn thing into oblivion.

"Do as you must, but you will never be rid of us," says the left face. Its lofty tone permeates the room like a singing bird. "Time waits for no one."

I ignore the voices and keep walking, moving through the corridor as quickly as I can. I walk and walk for the longest time, never looking over my shoulder. Seems like hours. My mind churns in the vast emptiness, never resolving its thoughts. Like pieces of a great puzzle, I am misplaced and lost, never knowing my purpose or why I'm here to begin with.

Convinced they have vanished, I look back to ensure the clocks are gone.

I flinch.

They are no further than when I left.

"Now, you must choose," says the middle face with the frown. Its eyes blankly stare at me as the other two, happiness and pain, watch me the same.

I can't do this. I don't want to play their stupid little game. But I am trapped, apparently, bound to this hall forever, until... Taking a deep breath, I move back to stand before the three faces of the clock.

"Now, you see, we knew you'd come to your senses. That's a good lad," says the left face.

"What do you mean, we?" says the right face. "Your optimism makes me sick and poisons my thoughts." Its snake-like voice lingers on the last letter of the s.

Immediately, the middle face follows through with its sad voice. "Not again. The two of you, always bickering. Will it ever stop? You there!" says the middle face, glaring at me. "I'm telling you, stick with sadness, for it does not stray from its path. It will always be there to comfort you, even in the most desperate of times, happiness and pain will abandon you, for they will never be apart from each another." The middle face pauses as if waiting for a response from the other faces, but it never comes.

"I don't understand," I say, confused even more than before, "but if I must choose, I choose happiness. Too long I've dwelt in sadness and pain."

"A sound choice. A sound choice indeed!" says the left face exuberantly.

"What a shame."

"Imbecile!"

I stare at the left face of the clock waiting for something to happen but the silence lingers in the hallway. The faces say nothing more. But the ticking continues.

If the faces are going to do something, they better do it quick. Anger is returning to me. Even though I do not know my purpose, I sense so much time has been wasted. The feeling is worse than sadness and pain combined.

Suddenly, the left face speaks again. "Look alive and prepare yourself! Step up to me."

Complying, I step forward, and the ground responds to my first step. A tremor vibrates its way to the surface, just beneath my boot. "What's happening?" I ask, glancing at the three faces. They watch me with blank stares. "What's happening to me?" I ask again. "Answer me, goddamn you!"

The clock tones drown all other sounds from my ears. Loud and horrendous, it passes through me like a shock wave, forcing the joints in my elbows and knees to quiver. It happens again, and the faces smile at me. Happiness, sadness, pain. All of them, together.

A deafening roar bellows from the long corridor in both directions. The tremors return, rumbling and shaking, although this time, the ground begins to break apart, sending cracks from one wall to the next. I've seen this before, but where?

"Better hold on," says the smiling face on the left as a piece of the floor breaks away into the darkness below. I move toward the clock's left handle, but the rest of the ground drops into nothingness.

"Oh, dear me," says the second voice as I sidestep a falling stone. "What will you do now?"

The floor continues breaking away all around me and I leap, grabbing the edge of the newly formed chasm. My upper-body strength strains. There is no way to reach happiness now.

I glare at sadness, the middle face.

It manages a yellow smile, so I reach with my arm, attempting to reach the lever jutting from its front side. But the ground crumbles to dust. I slide down, catching myself on a stony protrusion, losing my chances at sadness. "Dammit. Nothing is ever easy."

Stone by stone, through quaking tremors, I navigate my way back up, straining the muscles in my arms. My fingers cramp from the intense exertion. Almost to the top, I see Pain's face just feet from my grasp. The clock is beginning to tip down into the fast-growing abyss.

It is now or never.

Hoisting myself over the edge, I run with everything I have left. I feel the ground leaving my feet, but I do not stop. Diving forward, I reach with both arms, latching on to the right lever below the red clock face. Feet braced against the ground, I push up on the heavy bar with all of my might. The joint locks into place with a click as the ground breaks away.

Down into abysmal darkness I fall like so many times before, forever reminding me of the infernal clock ticking inside my head.

DAY ELEVEN

CHAPTER
XXXI

The clock ticking.

It pounds at the back of my head with every throb of blood and every sway of the pendulum. Stabbing sensations explode across the side of my face as I blink once, then twice. Half the world is as it should be, while the other half is shrouded in darkness.

Why can I only see out of one eye?

Memories of crows cawing and claws pricking my face come back to me. I remember the beak plunging into my eye and half the world fading away. At the time, there was no pain, but now—now is different.

I move my hands to console the wound on my face, but they are sluggish and slow and miserably uncoordinated. Feeling for something, I can tell there are strips of cloth covering the gap where my eye used to be. Clumsily, my fingers brush the bandage and another surge of pain rips through my skull. The feeling is worse than the bogart's claw across my cheek.

Slowly, I open my remaining eye as the pain subsides, adjusting to a dimly lit room filled with many strange things.

Moving my head as little as possible, the spasms in my neck relent just enough to allow to me look around.

Where the hell am I? Everything spins from the rush of blood to my brain. A small clock on a table. Bottles stacked on each other. Vials spilt on the floor. A wall of daggers. A fireplace with a steaming black kettle. Cupboards filled with different-colored jars. I can hardly feel the bed I am lying in at the moment, for my entire body is filled with the sensation of a thousand pinpricks. There is a window next to the bed. From the corner of my eye, I make out frozen icicles hanging from a roof outside. There are trees covered in snow, and I see low-lying clouds passing by. Sensitive to the light, the overcast sky outside is enough to blind me.

Closing my eye, I lay my head back down and wince every time I try to open it again. Lying still, recovering from the slight effort, realization sets in, and I bolt upright in the bed.

"Kronklich!" I shout. The pain is too much and I feel myself fainting. More throbbing. At any second my head will explode.

"Settle down, friend," comes a deep voice from the other side of my bed. "If you continue moving around like that, you'll tear my handiwork and lose more blood." The calm voice floats around the bed as it speaks. "You won't get better if you're leaking." The voice chuckles.

I cannot see my captor, but I can see his weapon across the room, the dark scythe I saw when the angel of death came for me.

Immediately my thoughts turn for the worst. "Am I dead?"

There is another deep laugh, followed by "No. You wouldn't be talking to me right now if you were."

"Let me go, then! I need to find my son, Dorian!"

"You are not my prisoner, friend, and you are not bound. But if you leave, your friend is good as dead."

I freeze from his words. What was he going to do to Kronklich? "Stop calling me that. I'm not your friend," I say, trying my best to turn my head to see Kronklich. The pain is too much. *Kronklich. He is here. He's alive.*

"Not your friend? I saved your life. That's what friends do. I even saved your snoring Kronklich. I saved him from being eaten alive." The voice speaking pauses a moment, and then steps into the light. "Besides, we *were* friends once.»

A large mass of black robes and hood fills my vision, and I am taken aback at the man standing before me. Bushy black beard, dark stern eyes, it is Councilor, a member of the Black Blade assassins, a clan well known throughout the country of Ashton. I am astonished to see him, for I thought he died a long time ago.

"I could never forget your face, Tenor," says Councilor, grinning from underneath his hood. "Wolfgang, the famous vampire hunter. To think how different our lives have become. It's comical really."

Comical indeed. It is strange processing what I see before me, and I wonder if I am really alive or dead. Many years ago, we were acquaintances, having met at some insignificant banquet of some insignificant lord, only to end the night in an insignificant challenge against one another; a competition of throwing daggers. His reputation was known throughout the land as a blade slinger and I was made an example that evening. The aristocrats and the lovers that watched gawked at my failing abilities at hitting the target. To be in the presence of Councilor now, however, is a darkening thought all on its own, for rarely are Black Blades ever seen for what they truly are. There are only two instances in which they make their presence known. One, they were contracted to kill you, or two, they need something. Friend or not, it can only be the latter reason I still breathe.

"I saved your friend's life and your own," says Councilor, confirming my assumption. "That means a debt needs to be paid."

Regardless of my weakened state, I am suddenly very aware of meat cooking as my mouth begins to salivate. I turn my head to see a piece of meat roasting over an open spit.

"You will need this," says Councilor, drawing my attention back.

My hand fills with the sensation of pins and needles as he places something into my palm. Holding up the object, I look at the black root between my fingers, and then back at him. "No," I say flatly, attempting to give back the ebon root.

"No? You will need it for the task ahead of you," says Councilor confidently.

I sink back down into the softness of the bed. "I don't have time for this. I need to find my son."

"Your son isn't here, but your friend is. Do you have time to save him?" Councilor motions with his hooded head toward the other side of the large room. There in the corner, nestled under thick blankets of fur and animal skins, lies Kronklich. I can make out his wild hair around his ears, that same look of a mad scientist. "If you refuse, the poison will spread and claim your friend's life. But if you do as I ask, I will continue to stall the poison and he will recover in two days' time. You forget I am a Black Blade. I can kill the noblest of kings and cure the poorest of beggars; it matters not to me as long as I get what I desire in the end. It's your choice, although the choice is very clear to me."

It takes me a moment to process his words, but I persist, stammering out the words as quickly as I can. "You don't understand, the Carnalreesee have my son. They are taking him to Sunstone, and the vampire Scepter has my blood. I need to find them both or something terrible might—"

"Something terrible has already happened," snaps Councilor suddenly. There is agitation in his voice. "Your whining is tiring. Think for a moment, Tenor. Think rationally. Banish your son from your thoughts. If what you say is true, that the Carnalreesee have him, then it is too late for him."

My body is numbed by his words, and all the pain seems to leave me momentarily.

"Sunstone is far away from here," he continues. "Impossible and impassable. There is no traveling in or out of the mountains. The land has made sure of that. The wilderness is alive and the snow drifts higher than ever before. The winter solstice is upon us. The cold moon now breathes the night."

I watch as he points out the window at the gray clouds and falling snow.

It takes a moment to process his words. Images of Dorian flash across my mind. Young and old. Running in the cornfield. Training in the courtyard. We could have laughed many more times together if it weren't for my neglect. If I had been there at the manor when it happened, none of this would have come to pass. Guilt and grief overtake me, drowning me all at once.

Never have I felt despair like this. I try not to cry, but I feel as though my ship has sailed off the edge of the world and crashed on the rocks below. Failure has besieged me. A tear wells in my eye, blurring my vision. The place where my other eye used to be begins to sting horribly, causing me to tremble. My head aches and throbs with every sob.

I am not getting my son back. Oh, cruel world, how ruthless you are. I am left with nothing and feel lost.

I glance around the room at the clock, the jars, and the animal heads on the walls. I try to think of something else, anything to make it stop. *Please make it stop.*

I linger in my sorrow for what seems an eternity, not saying a word, smelling the aroma of cooking meat but never desiring its taste. So long, the time passes, me mentally exhausted in my stupor, not saying a word, never addressing Councilor, not acknowledging anything around me. What is there to live for, if not for the love of my son? His mother is dead. I killed her. Would he ever forgive me?

My eye falls on the crumpled-up form in the corner of the room under a pile of blankets.

Kronklich.

Now, there is a man worth a thousand lives, unlike me. A tragedy at such a young time in his life, his mother and father killed by vampires, a dowry of bronze and silver dauntess left behind. He alone put himself through school, the Five City Academy in the province of Sunstone, and became the physician, the mechanic, the connoisseur of etiquette. He is a real man's man. Yet who am I?

Kronklich gave up everything when the time came, dedicating his life to hunting the beasts that plagued his childhood. He lived a life of servitude and became a journeyman, seeking out the best houses there were to offer. And lo and behold, he found my family's name and my accursed soul.

For a moment, I examine myself.

There is nothing left to be done about the past. Yes, it is shattered and broken. Yes, my son is lost to me and my wife is dead, but let me gather the broken pieces. Put them in a jar. Focus on the now. There is someone I can still help and he needs me. The least I can do is give him my life.

Looking up, I see Councilor staring at me.

"So you've decided," he says in a satisfied tone.

I glare at him with hatred for making me feel this way, but remind myself I am alive because of him. "What is it that you want from me?"

Brilliant white teeth show beneath the hood. "I need you to kill someone for me." He says it plainly as if it were an everyday request.

"Kill someone? Me? I am no assassin. You are."

"It is not a man you are killing," Councilor says quickly. There is a certain anxiety about his speech. "It is a vampire. And you are the vampire hunter." He pauses, as if waiting for something to happen, but what? I can sense there is more.

From across the room, something stirs, like an unsettling presence, a noise in the static silence, but I cannot place it. It is a cold and empty feeling. I see Kronklich moving among his blankets, but there's nothing else.

Councilor pulls the hood down from around his face. It is the first time I really *see* him in the firelight. Scars burnt into his neck, scars running from his left temple to his jawline. There is no doubt the assassin has seen his share of hardships. For him to ask me such a task is a rare thing. Seldom does a Black Blade need help with killing things.

"The vampire Cresthaven killed my daughter," says Councilor.

There is intensity in his dark eyes. Is he crying?

"That filthy creature killed her, took my precious daughter from me, and now he must die."

Cresthaven.

Cresthaven.

The name turns over and over in my head. Where have I heard the name before? My mind is like mush trying to assimilate things, and I wonder if Black Blades are even capable of love. Losing a daughter to a vampire, well, I know how that feels. To lose your loved ones is the worst evil a human can experience. My thoughts dwell on Diana and Dorian for a moment, until the pain in my hollow eye socket brings me back to where I was moments ago.

"Cresthaven. I know that name," I say in a groggy voice, more to myself than to Councilor. Memory comes to me. "Cresthaven is a wealthy aristocrat from Westings, isn't he?"

Councilor stares absentmindedly out the window.

"He came to visit my house years ago," I continue, "on holiday searching for the perfect bride. He was a good man. Well prospered. He couldn't possibly be a vampire." My words fade from my lips as Councilor stands and moves to the meat spitting juices over the fire.

"But he is, make no mistake," says Councilor, turning the meat on its side.

"Why would he kill your daughter?" The question is reasonable, but Councilor says nothing more on the matter. If someone were able to kill the daughter of a Black Blade, then they were truly a capable and powerful entity. Since he is a trained assassin, I would think it impossible for such a thing to happen.

"If it is a vampire you want killed, then so be it. It's the least I can do for saving Kronklich."

Councilor nods. "Wise choice. Tonight you will eat and rest, and tomorrow you will go. That is when Cresthaven returns to his manor by carriage."

I watch him pull the steaming black kettle from the fire. He grabs two cups and sets them down on a wooden table. Taking two strains from a water bowl, he pinches a handful of dark herbs from a leather bag and places it in the cups, pouring the hot liquid into them shortly after. The aroma diffuses a dizzying haze over the room. Or perhaps it's my eye injury, which now causes vertigo.

Councilor hands me one of the cups. "Drink this."

I hesitate to obey and he looks at me quizzically.

"Bergamot blended with oats. It will restore you and give you rest."

Raising it to my lips, I savor the smell but remain ever weary of the room. I still feel the uneasiness about the cottage, as if eyes were watching my every move.

Taking a sip of the tea, I lay my head back down to ease the ever-present throbbing. Trying to focus on something besides the pain, my mind wanders on about the strangeness of these bizarre circumstances. Kronklich and I are alive, saved from ice crows by Councilor, who coincidently found us at the right moment. I wonder—how did he find us in the first place? I want to ask him, but I know he won't tell me. Black Blades never offer more information than necessary, and I know my petty question will go unanswered.

After a time, lying in the bed, dozing in and out of sleep, I notice the light dimming outside. Councilor moves about the cottage, lighting candles on mantles and on the tables. He never bothers with two sconces in particular. They are on the far wall, one on each side of a door. He skips over the candles as if they were never there. With the large room in order and at the correct level of light, he returns to the fire pit to remove the roasted meat. Dropping it on the table with a thud, he begins slicing tenderloins from the large bony center. I hear the carving knife break through the crispy parts of skin as the blade saws its way through the layers.

"I don't suppose you will join me?" asks Councilor. "There is a lot here and I'm sure you're starving."

Propping my head up, I turn to look at Kronklich's pathetic state in the corner, still crumpled up and non-responsive. The black lines spreading up his neck have progressed to his cheeks, but Councilor appears unconcerned with his condition.

"He is fine," says Councilor, taking a bite of the meat. "I assure you he has no appetite. The poison from a black blade is designed to debilitate the enemy, but not to outright kill them."

"He looks like he is in pain," I say, turning my head away in shame. "I cannot eat while he is suffering like that." Another wave of dizziness overtakes me and I nearly fall from the bed.

"You better eat something and regain your strength, or you won't have a chance killing any vampires, let alone Cresthaven."

"You speak as if you know him personally," I say, standing up for the first time. Blood rushes the length of my body, starting from my head and traveling all the way down to my tingling toes.

"I never actually knew him, but I knew he was a powerful man, that is, until I realized he was a vampire."

Still, I have a hard time putting things together. It's beyond me what sort of angle Councilor is getting at. I find it difficult to concentrate with the food before me. Roasted meat. Twisted peas. Golden potatoes. A massive feast for a massive man. Where did he acquire all of these provisions?

"Please," he says, "Eat as much as you can. You need to. Out here in the cold, if you don't eat, you die."

I waste no time obliging his words and carve my way into the savory meal of garlic and tellings. The taste of the telling herb reminds me of home when I was a child. A sort of strong basil and onion blended together. I made sure Diana raised our son on the same foods I used to eat, ensuring he would become a strong mighty hunter like his father. My chewing stops for a brief moment at the memory, but I continue eating as I force the thought from my head.

"You know, despite how different you and I are, living the lives we do, we are coincidently similar in certain ways," says Councilor through bits of chewing. "Both of us hunters, suffering the same fate of losing loved ones. You, your son, me, my daughter."

I take his words into consideration while we eat, but can't help remind myself that Dorian might actually still be alive.

"Her name was Winter, blessed by her mother's beauty." Councilor stops eating as he stares into one of the wavering candles. "Oh what a woman she was. Strong as a horse. Broad shoulders. It was a sad day when she moved on to another town." Councilor grunts, his mouth full of dripping meat juice. "It's what I get for trusting a damn gypsy."

With only a few short meaningless words shared thereafter by Councilor, the rest of the meal passes in silence. We eat and eat until every last piece of potato is devoured. Aside from the howling wind outside channeling its ways through the small cracks of the log cabin, I find it surprisingly warm in Councilor's sanctuary. The tea provided earlier seems to have worked like a miracle. The pain I felt hours ago significantly subsides, yet my demeanor becomes uncontrollably drowsy. Whether it was the meal or the tea, I'm unsure, but I notice my weapons and armor as I settle myself back down in the soft pillows of the bed. They rest on the floor next to the door with the unlit candles, awaiting their master to come claim them. But that won't be happening this night.

I watch Councilor whittling wood by the fire as my eyelid fights to stay open. He is an odd man no doubt. I need to stay awake, remain diligent, for what if this man turns out to be a madman? *Aren't we all madmen?* The thought is fleeting as I cherish the moments of comfort, lying in the bed of thick feathers. The last thing I remember is breathing in the aromatic fumes of the fire and candles lit about the room, but something strange occurs to me as my eyelid closes for the last time.

The scent of cloves and decaying leaves.

CHAPTER XXXII

I WAKE TO WHISPERS IN the night, not the kind that lull you to sleep through song, but those of a dark, twisted kind, the kind that startle you from the dead of slumber like skeletal hands reaching across the bed sheets to pull you to the floor. The beckoning words call to me now, but what are they saying? The words are slurred and distorted. Female in nature, the voice lingers, hovering around me like a spirit. It is similar to the cold air biting my face.

I sit up in my plush feather bed. The room is dimly lit. All the candles have gone out, yet the fireplace still burns with a glowing orangey yellow. Its embers crack and pop from the water dripping through the chimney. The familiar scent of cloves and burnt leaves returns to me. How long was I sleeping? It is evident I am still in Councilor's cottage.

Realizing this is not a dream, the whispers become more suspicious to me. Where are they coming from? Snoring mixes with the atmosphere from both ends of the room. Without thought, I find myself slipping from the bed with a blanket around me. The ground is freezing as my feet touch the wood planks of the cottage floor. The world spins as my hands reach for anything I can find to keep myself from falling over. I am still not one hundred percent. I move toward Kronklich's corner, where the snoring isn't quite so bad. The loud obnoxious breathing comes from across the room, where, undoubtedly, Councilor sleeps. His guttural breath reminds me of a bear sleeping in the winter.

Peaceful and serene, Kronklich has turned on his side, exposing his unshaven face and very straight nose. His pale complexion stands out above the brown and black furs, keeping him warm. The spider veins serve as a reminder of the task I need to complete tomorrow if I am to see him well again. I curse under my breath at the thought of knowing one of these vials or jars may have the antidote to heal Kronklich. We could escape out of this godforsaken place. But as the thought lingers, it fades away just as quick with the howling wind sweeping through the rafters. We wouldn't stand a chance out there right now.

The whispers continue.

Slowly, I tiptoe over to the other side of the cottage, maneuvering around the long table full of bottles and bones, over to the side of the fireplace mantle, where I remember Councilor whittling wooden stakes out of birch wood. Lined up against the wall, I count three short-length staves before my eye falls onto a massive form dressed in black, lying on its side. The outline of Councilor glows in the firelight as he sleeps near the door leading out. It is strange seeing him sleeping in the common room with the rest of us and not in the back room with the closed door. The position of his bed, pushed against the door, seems intentional. Did Councilor push it there to ensure Kronklich and I couldn't escape, or did he do it to prevent things from *coming in*? Resting within the crooks of his elbows, the massive scythe forged from obsidian black sleeps alongside him. Up close, I admire the metal in the wavering orange light. Its ore was probably found from the deepest and oldest mining tunnels ever dug, no doubt having come from the town of Delore.

Grabbing one of the wooden stakes, I finger its tip, feeling how sharp and pointed the edge is. He went through all this trouble for me. I look at the weapon, then back at Councilor's chest rising up and down. It would be so easy to end it here and now. But the thought of Kronklich stays my hand. Who would cure him? We could raid the cottage, take all the supplies, race off into the night, but the reality lingers at the back of my mind. Kronklich would die. Councilor knew what he was doing. I imagine him laughing in his sleep at me this very moment, mocking me from underneath all that hair.

The whispering comes again, and this time, I understand it. "*Is anyone there? Please help me. Please.*"

Quickly I move to the center of the cottage, stopping on the soft bear rug the size of a wagon. I hold my breath, listening, trying to pinpoint its location. "*I'm so hungry. I'm so cold.*" The voice sounds as if it is carrying a conversation with itself. Facing the door Councilor ignored earlier, I am positive it is the source of the voice.

Inching forward, my eye focuses on Enivid nestled amongst the leather coat and proofing on the floor.

The whispering seeps from under the door and through the keyhole. "*Why me?*" asks the voice again. "*Is someone there? Come close, sir. Please. I beg you, sir. Please save me.*"

What in the hell is going on? Could there really be a girl trapped on the other side of this door? My assumptions get the best of me, and I move even closer. Stranger still, the air grows colder as I draw nearer. Frost forms from my breath.

Wooden stake in hand, I lean close to the door, smelling its sanded-down finish. The scent of cloves is very strong. No light seeps through the cracks underneath and the whispers no longer come. I try pushing on the door, but it does not give. "Girl?" I ask through the wood, but there is no response. Kneeling down, I bring my eye level to the keyhole, straining to see what strangeness lies hidden beyond. But there is nothing. Only the endless darkness and the faint outline of crates and boxes.

Then the voice returns, a whispery hollow sound like before. "*I'm so lonely. Please help. Please.*"

Moving away from the door, I stare at it in disbelief, thinking of a way to pry it open. I contemplate smashing it down with my shoulder, but my hands fall around Enivid instead. I throw myself into the side of the door like a wedge, trying to force the blade into the crack. I look back to the corner of the room to see if Councilor is stirring, but his snoring continues. I shove and pull with the lame strength I have, but the door doesn't budge. Kneeling down, I search through the keyhole again. Maybe the child has come out from hiding. "Girl, if you can hear me, follow the sound of my voice."

Silence again. I strain my eye, desperately trying to see movement, but the room is utterly still. Suddenly, a menacing eye of purple veins moves into my line of vision, unblinking, unyielding. I jerk back with fright, landing on my backside, and scramble to get a hold of myself. Again, I press my face to the keyhole, hoping to see what it was. But whatever "it" was is gone. Only the shaded outlines of the crates remain.

"Damn," I say under my breath, listening for more signs of whispering. But nothing comes. My mind races with the memory of the past, remembering little Michael from the Danbury hovel, the little vampire boy I could not kill. It all comes rushing back to me, his older sister running to meet him at the window. The pleading look in his eye. The command I gave to Kronklich to burn the house.

I try to shake the horrible feeling surging through my mind, but it is a curse. I am afraid the haunting vision of sentencing Michael to death in front of his sisters and brothers will never leave me. I am a doomed man—this I know for sure—and as I back away from the locked door on hands and feet, I begin wondering about my sanity. Did I just imagine this? I look back at the looming door standing above me. Its dark frame and empty keyhole stare down at me like some judge.

Is someone really in there?

DAY TWELVE

CHAPTER XXXIII

THE SOUND OF WHIRLING BLADES FILLS the morning air as Enivid cuts through the chill wind.

Miss, again.

A sigh escapes my lips as Enivid returns to my gloved hand with a dull thud. Snow up to my knees, it is cold in the back of Councilor's cottage. Frozen flakes fall heavily, covering everything in a blanket of white. Lowering my arm to rest, I breathe heavier than moments ago. Three times I've tried hitting the target and three times I've failed. The thought of a fourth go-around compels me to stay my hand. Tired and deprived of real sleep, my full belly of warm oats and root sugar is the only thing keeping me going.

I can't stop thinking about last night, however. The girl's voice I heard from the other side of the door haunts me like a nightmare. I know I am awake now—the sheer cold burning against my skin is proof of that—but I can't stop thinking of *her*. Muscles aching, body shivering—the cold penetrates my bones. I can't think clearly. With teeth chattering, I glance at the only window at the backside of the cottage. It is filthy and frosted over and there is a plank of wood covering a small portion of its one side. I gaze every so often, waiting to see someone or *something* in the window, curtains drawn shut.

There is a loud slam from the other side of the cottage, and immediately, I resume calibrating my throw, focusing on the wood post across the field shaped like a cross. Enivid leaves my hand as Councilor appears under the icicles hanging from the awning surrounding the house. It spins faster than before as it catches the edge of the cross, skimming off of its surface and spinning with an ending *thunk* into a nearby tree.

Without saying a word, Councilor's massive form strolls toward the tree, plucks the holy blade from the bark and makes his way back to me. He juggles the weapon in his hands, passing it back and forth, nodding as if approving its construction.

"Nice weapon. And lighter than I expected." Councilor moves to stand before me, towering above my height by at least two feet. He holds Enivid up to the pale-clouded sky admiring it like a sparkling gem. "So this is the famous Bawaka blade. It is a beautiful contraption." He motions with it as if throwing it. "How many vampires has it killed?" He holds Enivid out to me, waiting for me to take it.

"I stopped counting long ago," I say, taking it back coldly, welcoming its warmth in my palm again. "All though it is no longer called the Bawaka."

Councilor steps back, smiling. His gaze watches me curiously as if waiting for something more.

Taking aim, I throw Enivid again, missing the target completely. I turn to face Councilor intently as the blade comes whirling back, landing in my hand with precision. "It has a new name. Enivid."

"Enivid? What a strange name. We hunters have such lonely lives. Makes sense to name our weapons. Gives us a sense of companionship in a world of desolation. I never got around to naming mine." As Councilor speaks, puffs of steam eject from the dark shadows of his face. Although the hood covers his features, I notice the black scythe across his back. It is massive like him. I wonder what sort of name he would give it.

Standing alongside me, shoulder to shoulder, he examines the field of distance before us. With thick arms folded over one another, the bulge in his biceps is obvious. The diameters of his arms are like great tree branches. "By now, you must have learned how hard and frustrating it is to see with only one eye." He waits for an answer, but I say nothing. "That is why you must forget all that you know and start anew. Any fool can throw with two eyes." Unfolding his arms from his body, one of his hands disappears into the folds of his cloak and emerges with succinct flicks of his wrist. Five flashes of steel draw my attention to the wooden cross thirty feet away. Loud cracks break the morning silence as the small daggers strike the target with deadly precision. Left, right, top, bottom. The fifth one hits the center, snapping the post from its foundation, sending it twirling into the gnarled brush.

There is the steady inhalation of breath followed by an exhalation as Councilor turns to face me. His teeth gleam white under his hood in the ashy color of the morning. "Pretty standard, you see?" He pulls back his hood exposing his massive mange of black hair. "Simply overrated. True throwing comes from feeling your surroundings, not from what you think you are throwing at." He raises his arms up motioning to everything around him. "The earth speaks to you all the time. You just have to listen."

I watch as he takes a deep breath and closes his eyes, seemingly focusing on something, but the cross has already fallen over. He reaches into his coat again. I cannot fathom him carrying more daggers, but my thoughts conclude with disbelief as a sixth emerges. Raising his arm to throw, he pauses a moment, holding his breath furthermore, then exhales as he sends the knife flying, twirling deep into the forest. A squeal emerges from the dark woods beyond, a sound I've heard before. The dying chirp of an atter.

"There. You see? A stroke never wasted, especially in the cold. You need to spare all the energy you can. Looks like squirrel for lunch."

The old days come rushing back to me as I remember when Councilor devastated me during the dagger-throwing contest. People laughing at me. Councilor in his glory. At the time, I was only a year older than Dorian's age now. I can't help feeling anger as I watch the back of Councilor's form retreat into the woods to recover the dead atter for our next meal.

Get a hold of yourself, Tenor.

I remind myself this man saved my best friend's life, let alone mine. Watching Councilor trek back through the snow, I know I need to change the subject before I lose my temperament. My eye falls on the window of the cottage again. I can't seem to wrap my head around its emptiness, its lifelessness.

"You never did tell me how old she was," I say to Councilor as he plucks his dagger from the atter with a *squish*.

His gaze meets mine suddenly and I realize my mistake before it's too late. He notices me staring at the window. From his visage of dark eyes and dark hair, I watch his lips part into a smirk. "You're right. I didn't."

I wait for him to bring the scythe down over my head, waiting for his retribution. But the moment never comes. Instead, I watch him stuff the squirrel into a pouch on his belt. He wipes the blood from his dagger on his trousers and comes to stand next to me again. "She died on her fourteenth birthday."

His voice falls into silence and the awkward moments following creep from the surrounding woods. The cold tone of his words causes me to tense with anticipation.

What have I done? I've crossed the line. I say no more on the matter but fear it may be too late as I notice his empty gaze. He stares off into the woods.

The awkward silence is broken by Councilor first. "We are wasting time here," he says through choked words. "Let us resume."

Hours pass as we practice throughout the day. Throw after throw, my aiming improves slightly, but still I miss the target on occasion. With my arm sore and burning from overuse, we take a small reprieve to go back inside the cottage and eat the atter and bread made earlier in the morning. The poppy-seed loaf is cold and hard from the weather and the atter tastes like meat cured three times over, an extremely gamey flavor. Regardless, I am thankful for the provisions and pass by Kronklich's corner of blankets once more before returning to the cold outside. Though I saw the veins creep up his neck yesterday, his condition seems stable and he looks more peaceful in the daylight than in the gray moonlight.

A large oversized hand clasps my shoulder, startling me from my thoughts. "Come. There is still much to be done."

We pass through the front door of the cottage and out into the cold where the sky is dismal gray and turning darker by the second.

"Won't be long now," says Councilor, parting the falling snow with his massive form. "Night fall will be here sooner than you think." He leads us around the side of the cottage, passing a shed nearly buried in the snow. I can hear the subtle neighing of Abel, Councilor's Clydesdale, and wonder if his horse is freezing or not. "We need to hurry."

We set up the targets once more, finding it difficult to navigate the thick snowy field. The closer dusk comes, the more it snows.

"Now, as you were," says Councilor, assuming his position next to me like before. With my smaller build next to his massive frame, I am like a mouse standing next to a bear. No longer thinking of food, I begin throwing Enivid with determination.

Again and again, I throw the spinning blade of death, losing more accuracy with each throw. I can feel Councilor watching me, criticizing me with his eyes. The cold is taking its toll. It is no surprise, considering how much blood I've lost within the last week. My face, my hand, my side, my eye, I have been mutilated more than any man I know.

"Pay attention," says Councilor with a deep voice. "You need to concentrate."

"I am concentrating," I say in frustration. He doesn't know what I've been through. "The cold has gone to my hands. I can barely feel them."

"You are thinking about your hands when you should be thinking of absolutely nothing. *Stop thinking*. Your mind should be devoid of thought. Focus on the outside, not the inside. Empty your soul."

I laugh to myself. *A little late for that.*

As I'm watching Councilor bend his knees, he pulls a dagger from the folds of his cloak, holds his breath and closes his eyes. A second later his blade finds its mark, hitting the dead center of the cross. Smiling and waving his hand, he turns to me. "Your turn."

With one eye on the target, I take a deep cold breath, and raise my arm to throw.

"Stop!"

My body freezes with tension. I gaze at Councilor with annoyance.

"Close your eye."

"I can't throw Enivid if I can't see what I'm throwing at."

"Close your goddamn eye," he says again, never wavering the tone of his voice. "Feel your surroundings. The air. The trees. They speak."

What the hell is this lunatic talking about? Ignoring his suggestion, I motion to throw Enivid once more, but he catches my arm mid-throw, sending the whirling blade straight down into the snow.

"What the hell are you doing? You could have killed us!" Anger rages inside me.

"I'm doing you a favor. Nightfall is nearly here and it is almost time for you to leave. Cresthaven will be arriving at his estate tonight by carriage. It is rare for him to stay in one place for too long." Councilor retrieves Enivid from the snow and places it in my hand. "Now. Again."

Pride has always gotten the best of me, and now is one of those times. I can't make sense of what he is saying. It is a struggle to convince myself otherwise, and after a few moments of trepidation, I concede to Councilor's whims, more so for the sake of Kronklich's condition and not for the thought of Councilor's gratification.

Lowering my arms, I finger the leathery grip of Enivid and stare down the snowy field to where the wooden cross awaits its demise. Following Councilor's direction, I close my eye, feeling the burn from its irritated dryness. Adjusting my feet firmly in the snow, I grind my boots into the earth below the ice. Inhaling deeply, I attempt to shut out my surroundings—the cold entering my lungs, the caws of the ice crows, the window with the curtain.

At first, there is nothing. I feel the worldly things around me and hear Councilor's voice close by, chanting to me, *concentrate, concentrate,* but all is the same. I try to clear my mind again, breathing in, then out, relaxing the tension in my muscles. My body sinks a little closer to the earth. Again, I do the same, and suddenly find myself floating on air. My ears burn as whispers float to me on tendrils of wind as if the very air were alive. The tree branches sway back and forth, the leaves bristle, and now I hear them speaking, guiding me to something. The dirt below my feet tremors and rushes forward, pulsating away from me in great rings. Everything speaks to me in unison, calling out my name like spirits left behind, and suddenly my heart is stilled. One voice stands out, unlike the rest. A voice pure of heart and full of beauty. The warming voice of my beloved Diana.

She is here. She is here with me. I know it. Her voice sings to me like the rustling of leaves and the tinkling of icicles. Warmth generates in the palm of my hand where Enivid rests.

Concentrate. Concentrate.

The words are no longer those of Councilor, but that of my precious D. Passion fills my void and I raise Enivid, arcing it around my waist, and then following through. I feel Enivid travel away from me even though I cannot see it, and know when it makes contact with the cross across the field. In moments, the spinning blade of death lands in my hand with ease and I am filled with the surge of power again. D is flowing through my veins. I can feel her strength welling inside me. I want to keep throwing Enivid. I never want to stop. Every time I use Enivid, I feel her presence. With every throw, she is alive.

My shoulders sink heavily and I open my eye.

"Well done, Tenor."

Councilor's giant hands grip me with praise, assuring me that everything is all right.

"You've done it. You're ready now."

But I don't really hear his words. It's not Councilor I want to speak to. I look around in wonder. Where is she? There is nothing but the snow and the cold. I look down the snowy field to see the cross, but it is no longer there.

"You knocked it clean from its foundation," says Councilor in an almost proud-father kind of way. "Did you feel it? Did you feel the earth speak to you?"

I look down at Enivid; I can still feel its power surging through my hand and up my arm. She is still with me. I know he wouldn't understand if I told him otherwise, so I nod my head yes instead. His bushy face fills with a toothy smile.

Gripping my other hand, he places something in it. "Now you're ready."

I look at the weapon in my hand and shiver at the sight of the extraction dagger, the same kind as the ones the Carnalreesee used on me. My thoughts flash back to Bronin and Scepter, the times they stabbed me. The pain they inflicted when they stole my precious blood.

"What—is this?" I say in horror, even though I know very well what it is.

"Standard practice. It is the way of the Black Blades. Before you kill Cresthaven, you must take his blood."

My head fills with questions as I look at the cursed dagger with a profound hatred. All of my troubles have stemmed from this damned thing. Constable had a black hook. Did Councilor know of Constable? Was he working with the Carnalreesee? The look of consternation on my face no doubt draws Councilor's attention.

"What's the matter? You look as if you seen a ghost."

Councilor's question seems sincere, yet I have my doubts about him. Ever since Bronin's betrayal, I have my reasons not to trust anyone. What is Councilor's motive?

"It's nothing. Everything is fine," I say, stowing Enivid under my leather coat.

"Good. Let's get you ready for tonight, then."

CHAPTER XXXIV

THE ROAD TO WESTINGS IS short along top Councilor's massive Clydesdale, Abel. The horse, muscular and obsidian black, traverses the piles of snow with effortless progression, constantly moving forward and never complaining. With his bag of oats at his side, the huge beast stands uncontested, content with his meals close by. I pat the side of his thick neck, wiping away snowflakes as we trudge through endless drifts of powdered snow.

Constantly observing the tree lines surrounding us, I can't shake my horrible suspicions about Councilor and where his allegiance lies. Mindlessly, my fingers trace the grooved extraction dagger at my waist. What motive did Councilor have working with the Carnalreesee? A trade of some sort? Money in exchange for human victims? Aside from the pathetic thought of him saving our lives, the other question still lingers at the back of my mind. The thing I saw last night locked up in the room—was it real or some delusionary vision?

I shake my head in confusion as if somehow the action will clear my head. I look up to the overcast sky and watch the twirling whisks of cloud churn in their cold winter state. Earlier, the color of the sky was consistently fading gray. But now, new colors splash across the sky, blending through the clouds in peach and red. Night grows quicker, and I wonder if I will make the rendezvous in time. Abel enters a steep ascension. As his powerful muscles haul us up the steep hill, I wonder who is really guiding whom.

I've never been to these parts of the mountains before, and the higher we climb the colder and thinner the air becomes. With the black cowl covering my forehead and dark fur draped over my shoulders, I am grateful for Councilor's gesture to keep me warm. His patronizing words still echo in the back of mind.

"Staying warm is an assassin's first and foremost concern in winter. A cold assassin is a slow assassin. And a slow assassin is a dead assassin. Things such as rest and sustenance are secondary. Forget sleep. Forget food. You'll sleep plenty when you're dead and you'll eat eventually when the work is done. What makes an assassin an assassin is simply this. Speed. If the enemy is faster, well, you'll never know what hit you."

Cresting the hill, we enter a sparse wintery wood full of evergreens, unlike the fir and birch trees of Decameron Forest. These trees are fuller and thicker, perfect for hiding in and concealing oneself. With a flick of my wrist, I encourage Abel on, having no idea where we are, for the road that once was is no longer visible. I am certain it is Abel that guides us now.

We descend into a deep valley and traverse the side of a steep gorge, traveling farther and farther down as if entering the hollow of some great tree. The more we go, the darker it becomes, and I fear we will not make it in time. Out here, lighting a fire for a torch would jeopardize the mission, and so in the debilitating darkness, I yield to the mercy of Abel's guidance. How does he know where to go? I remind myself this is Councilor's horse.

In the distance, I see tiny lights wavering through the tree canopy like ghost spirits. This must be the place.

The town of Westings.

The closer we get to civilization, the more prominent the clearings become. Long stretches of logged trees guide us to the perimeter, but we never enter. Instead, we circumnavigate, staying to the tree canopies and never coming in sight of people. Like black shadows we skulk through the woods. Assassins in an unknown territory.

I laugh softly to myself.

Does Councilor really think I have the makings of an assassin? I've never thought of myself as a Black Blade, but I guess there is always a time to start. If such is the case, then so be it. I will be the Black Blade that kills vampires.

I follow Councilor's instructions, finding the landmark of the old wall that once stood long ago surrounding the perimeter of the town like a broken rib cage, and track it to the ravine where a cobblestone bridge waits. Patiently, we watch within the cover of trees until there is no one on the bridge. We slip our way unseen into the town, passing over jagged rocks and frozen water. Staying within the shadowy confines of the wall, we make our way north. A steady wind blows from the bluff of the mountains. The snow is thick in the unused paths and I feel Abel struggling underneath me, stumbling over hidden rocks and roots. Up a sloped embankment, I spot a vantage point of thick patchy trees, which seems to be one of the highest points in Westings.

Cresthaven's manor waits in its aristocratic magnificence like a sleeping giant wearing a crown.

With high walls of cobblestone and roofs shingled with the finest brick, the estate is nothing less than extravagant. Large cathedral windows line the walls of the multilevel mansion. Unlike the rest of the town, the estate is hard to miss. A four-story tower erected in its center may have served as a lookout at one point long ago. Like a medieval castle from ancient days, the top is crowned with parapets and gargoyle statues. For now, it lies dormant in the menacing darkness, except for the tiniest windows near the third floor. As for the other areas, firelight glows from within the belly of the estate, casting wavering rectangles on the exterior snowy ground. A cobblestone drive encompasses the front of the mansion that trails along the side of the grounds to the back of the house. It is there I watch patiently, waiting for signs of Cresthaven's carriage.

Time ebbs slowly. It seems an eternity waiting in the sanctuary of trees on the hilltop. We saturate in the darkness until finally there is movement. Men in thick coats emerge from the mansion baring long shafts with flames at the ends. Dogs tethered to their wrists, the lamplighters walk the perimeter in haste, lighting tall metal posts encompassing the mansion grounds. Slowly, Cresthaven Manor comes to life like a brilliant monster awakening from its slumber. I shake my head in frustration. Sentinels were never mentioned. I begin weighing my options in deep consternation. Shouldn't be long now. Their master should be arriving soon.

I listen to the hooting of an owl somewhere off in the distance. Staying in one spot exposes my body to the creeping cold, and so I dismount and tether Abel to a tree. Feeding him more of the oats at his side, I am grateful for his company. "Thank you, my friend," I whisper, patting his neck.

The loud clopping of hooves on cobblestones draws my attention below. I watch in anticipation as the expected carriage comes into view with a pair of drivers finely dressed in linens of black and white, top hats and whips. Lanterns sway at each side of the windows making it impossible to see anything inside the carriage. Observing from a safe distance, I prepare myself for the task ahead, pulling at the straps along my chest and back, double-checking the numerous knives and stakes. My hand naturally skims over Enivid. "I'll be back sooner than you think," I say to Abel as if he understands as I turn to go, but before I make any progress, I stop suddenly and crouch to the snowy ground. Trailing behind the carriage comes another, large like the first one. Both carriages circle their way to the back of the manor.

Were they guests perhaps? Councilor mentioned the arrival of a single carriage, not two.

Running from my patch of snow, I descend the small hillock toward the estate. My eye darts in every direction as I approach, cautious of my surroundings, danger lingering around every corner. Crunching through layers of powder, I work my way to the perimeter wall as my eye focuses on the windows of the estate. It is a shadowy fortress of wood and stone growing larger and larger as I approach. Passing the perimeter wall, my body aches from the running. Each breath stings my lungs but I ignore the pain, thinking back on worse things. Entering the side of a garden, I pass tall pillars of intricate design possessing grooved-out stones carved from single slabs of rock. The architecture of this place must have cost a fortune.

A finely dressed figure in suit and ascot tie stands at the ready near a lamppost, arms extended and staff in hand. I watch as he refills the container and lights the wick. The ease of my approach tells me he is human. Pulling one of my knives from its sheath, I step behind the lamplighter and clasp his head, jamming the blade into the side of his neck. No cry or murmur escapes his lips as the lighting staff falls to the snow with a thud. Warm blood seeps over my hand as I softly lay his dead body in the snow.

Standing above the corpse, I look upon my gruesome work, wondering when the regret will settle in. But it never comes. Empathy has left me. Under normal circumstances, I wouldn't think of killing a human, but humanity is failing inside me. I am becoming an empty shell. With my wife dead and no way to reach my son, what more is there to feel? I have lost everything, except Kronklich, yet he too stands on the brink of destruction.

The concept of choice is a distant memory.

I drag the evidence out of sight and press on, following a thick hedge covered in snow. Reaching the nearest corner, I peer through the bushes to view the passengers, but I see nothing except the drivers I saw before now walking back in the direction of their carriages. Sinking deeper into the bushes, I close my eye and catch my breath. How am I going to get to Cresthaven unseen? And from where? From the side of the bushes, I scan the grounds in hopes of finding something, some advantage or angle I can work with. There are tall trees lining the property and stone walls galore, but they offer cover only.

I look up.

Far from the courtyard, a domed ceiling glows bright yellow. Massive in size, it encompasses the center of the estate, acting as a central location, easily accessible from all the other connecting buildings.

There.

I take off running as lightly as I can, creaking through the snow and ducking behind potted plants piled thick with powder. In the distance, dogs bark. I pause a moment, rubbing my hands together, when suddenly a lamplighter comes into view, struggling to keep his hound under control. I hear the dog's nostrils sniffing the ground as it advances, pulling its master along with a force. "What is it?" says the man as the large dog stops at one of the potted plants.

Taking a deep breath, I grip the side of a cobblestone wall and hoist myself up. Balancing on a foot-wide surface, I run along its top as best I can, concentrating on my breathing and jumping from the side of an archway to another. All is silent, windless. My boot catches a stone as I land and I hear it crumble.

Barking erupts behind me followed by shouting. "What was that?»

I never stop and never look back, knowing the slightest hesitation will jeopardize my operation. If the guard saw me, vampire or not, he will die if he follows.

Hands pressing firmly against stone, I look up at the glass-domed building looming upward. It is higher than I anticipated. Numerous uneven holes litter the way up, perfect for tucking my hands and feet in, but it is my strength I worry about. Have I recovered enough energy to scale a wall? Wind whips at my cloak as I climb. I try not to overextend my reach and find it harder than I thought, wedging my boots into the cracks.

Overcast sky. Icy wind. The elements are unforgiving.

I stop a moment to breathe, easing the pain in my side, my hand, and my face. With limited vision, I scan the grounds below and spot the dog and his master. They have convened with the other lamplighters and now begin frantically moving about the back gardens. Searching. Scanning. They won't find me up here.

Now that I have a better view of the situation, Cresthaven's arrival seems to be more than just any normal occasion. A party, perhaps? Something is amiss. Noble aristocrats were known for living brash lives. Why would it be any different for vampires?

Climbing the rest of the way up, I realize how extensive this place really is. The many roofs are in an array of different heights. My hopes dwindle at the prospect of spotting Cresthaven somewhere within his home. But nonetheless, I walk the circumference of the dome ceiling, looking down through hundreds of glass panes, and stop at the edge of a dining hall where chairs line one extremely long wooden table. Candelabras litter the table up and down its length, dripping their waxy residue onto wax-catching plates. I find myself holding my breath as I witness butlers and service maids moving about the chamber, tending not only to the man that could only be Cresthaven himself, but to three distinct others, a woman and two young children, a boy and a girl.

What is this? Councilor never said anything about a family. My world seems to shut down suddenly as I find myself stewing over Councilor's credibility.

Cresthaven had found himself a bride after all, and two children were the outcome of that union. I observe them through the glass panes; all of them are elegantly dressed. Cresthaven, wearing a fine black suit and velvet vest, casts his head back and forth with tremendous mirth, amused at the conversation at the table. His long brown hair is neatly tied down, and his back ripples in waves with every subtle movement. I find it hard to look away from the rest of his family as my eye wanders. The woman, voluptuous in curves and golden hair, smiles lovingly at her husband while she caresses the tips of his fingers. Dressed in a tight gown of gold and silver, she points across the table at her daughter, laughing uncontrollably. The girl with long dark hair tucked against her head in a tight braid bobs her head toward the little boy with the golden curly hair. Aside from their fine attire, there is nothing remotely vampiric about them. They are not vampires. They are humans. Was this another trick by Councilor? Had he sent me to do the dirty work of a Black Blade?

As I sit atop the roof of the grand estate in the middle of nowhere, brooding in the freezing cold, more and more thoughts churn inside my head. *What am I doing out here? I shouldn't be here right now.* I am transfixed by the Cresthaven family. Their laughter and talk seep through the glass like murmurs, and I regress into saddened thoughts of my family that once existed.

Deep down inside, somewhere far beyond any control I once possessed, I begin to cry. The tears flow faster than I can wipe them away. My body shutters with each sob and I turn from the torturous sight. Leaning my back against the shingled rooftop, I raise my face toward the cold moon glowing in the gray clouds. Snowflakes melt slowly on my burning face as I attempt to control myself.

There is a noise down below, and quickly, I wipe away my streaming face and run my hand across the foggy pane. Dinner is being served. Butlers enter the dining hall pushing carts stacked with covered plates. I watch in envy as the silver trays are placed in front of each family member, one by one. The boy fidgets around his dish, smelling the aromas seeping from underneath, eager to eat, but waits politely like the rest of them.

The boy was raised properly.

My stomach growls at the thought of food. I envision cooked venison and roasted mushrooms under those trays as I watch each butler move into position, resting their hands over the handles. One by one, the covers are lifted, and I am filled with dread.

Rabbits of the purest white squirm about the Cresthaven's plates, timidly, trying to escape from their inevitable doom. Pierced through their feet and bound to the plate with twine, they paw at the smoothly polished plates, unable to gain traction from the slippery surface. I watch in disbelief as Cresthaven's wife spastically claps her hands together with a joyful squeal at the sight of the sacrificial meal, her rabbit being particularly pinker in the fur than the others.

Unable to do a thing, my hands instinctively tighten around the stakes at my side as the Cresthavens delve into their devilish dinner. They lower their heads to the innocent rabbits, ripping into their fur and necks, spraying blood across the white linen tablecloth. Watching the little boy now sickens me, yet I cannot look away. It reminds me of Michael, the boy I left to die in the hovel, the vampire boy I could not kill. Shocked and in denial, I try to make sense of the carnage before me. Councilor *was* right. Cresthaven is a monster. His entire family is monstrous.

Through a set of double doors across the room, a servant bursts into the dining room. She runs to Cresthaven's side exuberantly and leans close to say something. I watch Cresthaven lend his ear to her, and then suddenly, he stops sucking the blood from his rabbit.

His gaze turns to me, and the hairs on my arms stand up. Eyes once cold and blue now burn red. All I can do is stare back as each of the Cresthavens' eyes fall upon me, Lord Wolfgang, the vampire hunter.

CHAPTER XXXV

ALL AT ONCE, I AM struck with feelings of anxiety, confusion, and fear as the Cresthaven family dashes from the dining hall like fanatic demons. One moment they are there bearing fangs with dead rabbits in their hands, the next they're gone. With the element of surprise lost, my heart races as I remember the lamplighter with the dog. *I should have killed him!*

There is a crash somewhere in the distance.

The Cresthavens are moving fast.

There is no time to linger. No time to think. I dash along the sloping rooftops of the estate, searching for some vantage point, some higher ground, but there is hardly anywhere I can go they cannot reach. In the next few seconds, they will be upon me like jackals for the kill. I wonder which of the four of them will reach me first. I know I cannot run away. I cannot leave, not until Cresthaven's blood is safe inside my vial and his head is effectively removed.

I come to a sliding halt at the edge of the second-story roof, sending bits of snow and icicles raining below. The gardens are alive with moving lights; the lamplighters and dogs search the shrubbery and oversize pots for the intruder. I hear the pattering of feet approaching fast behind me as I regain my balance, and turn to see a little girl and boy.

"Look, brother," says the girl in the red flowing dress. "Our guest doesn't want to stay for dinner. I believe he is trying to leave without saying goodbye." Her voice is old and disturbing, like a grown woman trapped inside a child's body.

"'Tis a shame, sister. I was looking forward to a little entertainment." The boy's words are mocking just the same and deeper in tone than I imagined.

"Shall we play a little game, then, Jackson?"

"Oh indeed, Victoria. Indeed!"

They come to stop just before me as I stand my ground, holding a wooden stake in each hand, waiting for them to make the first move. Unable to tell their true age, I'm not sure how fast they will be.

Victoria smiles. "Let's play who can throw the man off the roof *first*."

Pushing and shoving one another like quarreling siblings, they rush forward with immense speed, arms stretched out as if sweeping unwanted leaves from the rooftop.

Countering their move, I rush toward them, throwing myself to the ground, sliding across the ice, and passing underneath their arms. As they realize what is happening, I recover and jump back on my feet, running in the opposite direction, away from their confused looks.

"Where are you going?" teases Victoria.

Looking over my shoulder, I catch the young girl shoving her brother from the rooftop.

"Sister!" yells Jackson.

What the hell? They're quarreling over who gets to kill me first. I keep running, trying to think of a solution that won't end in death.

"Come back to me, my little mouse," chimes Victoria's voice behind me.

Running past the glass-domed ceiling, I enter a part of the roof where large rectangular pillars made of stone jut upward from the shingles. A forest of chimney stacks.

Catching my hands against one of them to slow my speed, I push off, changing direction to another pillar and overcompensate for my turn at the angle of the roof. My boots slip on a patch of ice and I crash onto my side and slide down the shingles to the edge, gripping for anything I can find. Catching the side of the roof with one hand, I strain the muscles in my shoulder. One wooden stake tumbles off the side of the estate as I stow the second one in my belt. I struggle to grip the ledge with both hands, noticing movement to my right. Jackson races toward me along the side of the wall at an impossible angle, hands and feet sticking to the surface like a spider. Blond curls bounce in the wind. He is determined to reach me before I can pull myself up. With a burning shoulder and painful stitch poking my side, I swing my body once, then twice, as Jackson lunges. I bring my leg up onto the roof causing him to miss and let out a deep growl.

His frustration echoes from somewhere below. "That wasn't nice."

Out of breath, I roll myself over and use one of my knives to jam a brace into the space between the shingles and the roof for support. I pull myself up to safety and move as far up the slope as possible. I need to hide before—something clings to my back suddenly, gripping the spaulders of my proofing. Reaching over my shoulders, I brace Jackson's head between my hands and use all of my strength to stop him from sinking his fangs into my neck. The air is too cold to feel his breath. With a twist and thrust, I send him spiraling away from me, and he lands on his feet like a cat. He smiles from the short distance between us and pulls a strange-looking weapon from his button-down dinner vest, a wicked-looking contraption resembling an oversized fork with two long prongs. He charges forward screaming, poised to stab.

I meet him with my own instruments of death, wood stake and dagger, parrying his wild strikes at my face and chest. He swipes overhead, jumping in the process, but I hold my ground. We clash, trading blow after blow. I bat at his forked weapon, trying to knock it from his hands but my attempts are useless. Enivid enters my mind, but I banish the thought instantly. I don't want to kill Jackson. I can't. Despite his tenacity and blood lust, he reminds me too much of Michael. I curse myself for being so weak. Why do these thoughts still hold sway over me?

"How are you so strong? Why won't you die?" growls Jackson. I can sense the agitation in his voice.

Over and over, Jackson brings down his deranged weapon, wearing away my stamina bit by bit. He strikes again and I trap his weapon between mine, crisscrossing the wood and steel with his fork. We stare into one another's faces, his expression malicious, while mine is troubled. He ducks below my arms and sweeps my legs out from under me forcing me onto my back, jumping onto my torso, pinning my shoulders down with his knees. With another growl, he drives the deadly fork into my chest, but fails, bending the metal with every blow thereafter. The prongs split in opposite directions, ruining his prize weapon.

"Graaahhhhh!" He shouts in frustration. "Bloody die! Why aren't you dying? What are you, a metal man?"

I nudge my arm forward. His knee slips from my shoulder, and I bring my own dagger straight into his face.

Blood bursts from his perfect skin as he roars in agony, clutching the side of his cheek. His body weight lightens. "Aagggghhh! That hurt!" he shrieks. The look on his face is disbelief. I raise the wooden stake to strike a second blow, but hesitate. Something arrests my wrist suddenly, strong and firm.

"You can't have all the fun, brother," says Victoria, speaking to her bleeding brother and twisting my arm. With an effortless flick, she sends me across the rooftop, light as a feather. "I want to bite the man too, Jackson."

Sliding through glistening snow, I collide into a chimneystack with a loud crack. Pieces of stone crumble over me as dust settles in my hair. Dazed, I force myself to stand, balancing on the snowy rooftop with vertigo. *This isn't good.*

The sibling vampires rush toward me, crisscrossing between each other in a dazzling blur of movement. In a desperate attempt to thwart them, I begin attacking the air all around me in the hopes of landing a blow by chance. But my efforts are useless. Their movements are in sync, their strategies synchronized. Unexpectedly, they grab my arms and swing me over their heads like a puppet. The force of hitting the rooftop knocks the wind from lungs and I feel my brain rattle inside my head. I hear them laughing as I scramble to get away from them. *They're toying with me.*

Finding a particularly wide chimneystack, I rest my back on the stone wall, knowing my situation is grim. It's not possible these children are so powerful. I look at my surroundings for some advantage I can use, but I find nothing except another ledge to my side and numerous chimney stacks all around. I look up and see the third and fourth floors of the mansion. My heart races at the thought of scaling them. The higher I go, the more distance there will be between the ground and me. My chances at living will dwindle.

So be it.

A shadowy figure passes on my right and I flinch, striking the empty air around me. It passes again and I lunge, chipping away a shingle. Something is here, but it moves quicker than I can react. I sense something above me, and there atop the chimney sits the vampire boy with his freakishly wild hair dashing about in the wind, his red eyes and fangs prominent over his facial features. Perched like a gargoyle, his face contorts into a smile as he observes me like prey he aims to catch.

I can't do it. Already I feel my hands trembling holding the wooden stake and dagger. It is profound that I am faced with this decision again. Flashes of Michael plague my mind as I back away, one step at a time.

"There is no escape for you now," says Jackson, slowly creeping down the side of the stone wall like a spider. "You have come here to kill us, yet it is you who will die. Father told us we would meet you one day, but I never thought it would be this soon."

The thought of a vampire family brooding within the confines of Westings disgusts me. Did the people not know? More words follow from somewhere behind me.

"Yes, you gave us all a bit of a shock."

A tall lanky man steps out from behind the shadow of the third-story wall. Dressed in a fine black suit, Cresthaven spreads his arms out before him, observing me with a look of admiration. The moonlight makes him look paler than the glow of the candlelight from before. "Victoria, Jackson, that will be all." He motions with his hand. "You've had your fun." To either side of me, Cresthaven's wife and Victoria approach slowly, the pair of them smiling the same. I can see they've grown weary of me, the look of danger all vampires give when facing me. Their eyes look to Cresthaven for affirmation every few moments, but Cresthaven is far more intrigued with me than they are. Despite all of their power put together, they know who I am and there is tension. I am the bringer of true death.

I look around at the four of them¾sick to my stomach¾before stopping on Cresthaven's gaze. "What have you done?"

Cresthaven returns a look of indignation. "What have I done?" His hands point to his chest innocently. "Let us remind ourselves of who showed up *uninvited*. We go back a long way, Tenor Wolfgang, but arriving at one's house, killing my servant, and lurking in the shadows is hardly the way of showing respect, which leads me to the assumption of your ill intent to begin with.

You aren't here by some strange chance, are you?" Cresthaven turns his head sidelong, eyeing me with his cold blue eyes, no longer brilliant red.

"You sick bastard."

Cresthaven looks at me appallingly.

"How could you do this to your own children?"

Cresthaven turns to the blonde woman who eyes me hungrily. "Kathryn, my dear, won't you take the children inside? My guest and I have some things to discuss."

There is immediate backlash from Victoria and Jackson, the ones who were having so much fun with me with their little game of cat and mouse amidst their massive playground. I wonder how many victims they've tortured in the same fashion before gorging themselves on their blood.

"Oh, Father, it's not fair!" retorts Victoria.

"We were just becoming aquatinted with our new friend," says Jackson, eyeing me with a playful grin.

"Yes, *yes*. You've had your fun. Now go. Kathryn, darling—"

My weapons never lower as Kathryn motions to her children to follow her. "Come, Victoria. Come, Jackson. Leave your father be. He has some *business* to attend to. I'm sure there is good reason in all this."

I watch as she eyes Cresthaven wantonly, then passes her judging gaze toward me. Her hips sway to and fro in her tight golden dress as she walks away.

"Beautiful woman, isn't she?" says Cresthaven, eyeing her bosom. He turns around to face me, allowing me to see him full on in the dim light of the overcast moon. "Now, where were we? Ah yes. Let us discuss this like gentlemen."

CHAPTER XXXVI

"So, you've come to slay me, is that it? Bring an end to the vampire menace?"

Cresthaven moves along the base of the third-story wall, gazing upward at the overcast sky. His eyes focus on the fading moon. His fingertips scrape along the frozen wall as he strolls away from me as if silently beckoning me to follow.

Walking after him, I tighten my grip on the wooden stake and dagger.

"I have to say, Tenor, there really is no end to the vampire menace. It is a foolish thought thinking that you and your family will eradicate every last vampire in the world. How absurd. It doesn't make sense."

My hand caresses the handle of the extraction dagger. "My family is dead."

"Oh," says Cresthaven. "I did not know." His cold tone insinuates anything but compassion for my loss. He stops at the edge of the second-story roof, precise and dexterous. "Look down there." He motions with a gaze. "Do you see those men searching the grounds for you? They do so because I will it so. It is power, you see? Does God offer you power such as this?"

I stop in my approach. "Don't talk to me about God, monster."

"Touchy, touchy. Sore subject?"

"You know nothing."

"Actually, I do. I know everything." He pauses. "Monster." He chuckles to himself. "You know, you are the first person to ever call me that. Not even the townsfolk refer to me as such." He lets out an airy sigh. "You have to ask yourself. Can a monster single-handedly restore a town from its poverty-ridden streets to a glorified market of trade and commerce, hmmm?"

It is sickening the way Cresthaven carries on like some advantageous noble of some high order. He is delusional. "You mean bringing a town under control by fear?" I counter.

"Oh please," says Cresthaven suddenly, spinning on the spot to face me. "You don't actually believe this town would survive without my guidance, do you?"

"I don't give a damn about this town. All this place is is a blood bank for you and your family to live off of."

"I am appalled by that comment," says Cresthaven immediately. "I am a civil lord, mind you. A practicing participant of profound elegance and philosophy. The true question here, however, lies within you. The real monster. Gallivanting about the countryside, destroying the natural order of things. Tell me, *sir*, what is the real reason you have come here?"

I unloosen the strap of my fur cloak, letting its restricting fabric slip to the floor. "Councilor sent me to collect your blood."

"Councilor? Collect my blood? Ha! The *fool*. The assassin sent the hunter to do his dirty work. How ironic. I suppose he is upset about his daughter, no doubt."

I watch Cresthaven's facial expressions contort into a series of smirks as he begins stringing one sentence to another.

"It is his own fault she is dead. He knew the terms. And to think, a Black Blade would dare ever conceiving children. Such a barbaric life. Such brutality. What could he have ever offered her anyway, a life of villainy? No, of course not." Cresthaven clicks his teeth together while shaking his head. "What does he plan to do with my blood anyway? Display it as one of his trophies? It is useless to him, as it is useless for you to be here."

Suddenly, Cresthaven's expression turns to a serious one. "Unless, perhaps—no, no. It's not possible."

"I have heard enough." I take a step toward Cresthaven and he eyes me with an amusing look.

"Quite a man, you are. Always ready to stop talking and kill the vampire. You know, it doesn't have to be this way between you and I. We were friends once. Why not rekindle that union once again. Why not share the wealth and restoration of this town? I'll continue bringing this town good fortune and prosperity and you'll keep—"

"My reputation?"

"Well, that too, I suppose. It coincides with keeping your life."

"Enough," I say angrily, raising my weapons to strike.

"Stop," says Cresthaven. Eyes glowing red, he holds his hand out before him, preventing me from moving closer. "You know, some humans say vampires are cursed, while some human scientists claim the blood of a vampire is diseased. Has it ever occurred to anyone, in that matter, what the vampires think?"

He lowers his hand and his eyes return to their cool-blue composure. The energy force against me falters.

"We vampires believe our state of being is a blessing."

"By who, Satan?"

"You don't believe me. Well, then, come. Come, if you dare."

He brushes past me and I am unable to raise my wooden stake against him. Not because of his power, but because I am compelled by his words. What the hell was he talking about?

I follow after him, watching him seemingly glide across the rooftop while I step through fresh powdered snow. We move around the base of the third-story building, around the corner he originally appeared from, and toward an entirely different side of the estate. Cautiously, I watch his back, ready for retaliation. We then stop in front of a small-sized door that is large enough to fit one person in at a time. With the snow falling lightly around us, he motions his hand at the door and it responds with a click, followed by a loud groaning creak.

"Come learn the truth, my friend," says Cresthaven with a smile before passing through the threshold. Looking over my shoulder, then at the door, I reluctantly follow, second-guessing my better judgment. This is dangerous. My father would turn over in his grave if he knew what I was doing. He would scold me till the sunset and all through the night.

I whisper under my breath, "Diana, give me strength."

CHAPTER XXXVII

THE LONG, WINDING STAIRCASE IS narrow and dark as I follow after Cresthaven, watching him ten steps ahead of me. A haunting wind whistles through the old mortar patchwork of the third- and fourth-floor wings of the estate, the old buildings constructed from stone and wood. Cresthaven, as if reading my thoughts, motions with his hand. A row of candles set in the hollows of the wall bursts to life.

"This way," he says in a low whispery voice.

Boots clicking along the treacherous steps, I wonder what sort of devilry he is leading me to. The heaviness in the air is like thick moisture hanging about the framework of the old castle. With the constant melting of snow during the summer months, no doubt mold infests this place. But then again, I second-guess myself; this high up in the Cordova Mountains, there could be no summer at all.

We reach what appears to be the end of the staircase. Cresthaven, with long fingers of dried skin and nails, motions at the door. There is a resounding click.

"Please, do try to keep quiet. I never know when there are new arrivals. The servants sometimes forget to inform me."

The door opens on its own and I follow Cresthaven inside, receiving answers to my quickly growing questions. We enter a rectangular room surrounded by dirty and seemingly abandoned glass-pane windows. Once within, I observe all sorts of furnished items of the kind one would find in a storage room. Old furniture covered in drags of white cobwebs, crates stacked to the ceiling, barrels against walls, lamplighting staffs sprawled across the floor, boxes filled with endless numbers of books, and a single desk scattered with pieces of parchment, inkwells, pens, and sealing wax. A door at the back of the chamber likely leads to another floor, and along the center of the room, eight boxes made of wood, long enough to hold a man, form two rows of four side by side.

I linger in the doorway, for I cannot muster the strength to enter. I can see inside two of the boxes, where, lying on the comforts of sheets and pillows, there are two young boys around the ages of twelve and seven. Their hair color varies between two different shades of brown; their eyes are closed within their pallet of milk-white faces.

"Some of them still sleep during the night," says Cresthaven. "It's hard to part from the old rituals. They'll come around in time." Cresthaven smiles at them with a look a loving father gives his own children.

A sickening feeling begins to rise within me. "What the hell is this?" I ask, barely able to speak. Cresthaven strolls over to one of them and pushes the young boy's hair from his face.

"This, Tenor, is the truth I spoke of." Cresthaven seems beside himself with pride. "To cure the sick, rid the world of disease, one child at a time." His gaze turns to me. "These children come from the local orphanage. Boys and girls, left to fend for themselves and contract diseases like wild dogs. What I am doing here is a noble thing."

My blood boils as I begin shaking. "You sick bastard."

"Shhhhhh, Tenor. Not in front of the children." Cresthaven looks away, scanning the remaining boxes lining the floor. He lets out a sigh of despair. "Oh no." He moves over to his intended box and stoops down to retrieve something inside. There, within his gangly hands, rests an infant not two months old. It doesn't cry and it doesn't move. A syringe and tube extend from its open mouth, dangling loosely about its limp body. Passing a saddened gaze over the infant, Cresthaven shakes his head. "This one was found at the steps of the orphanage as well, left to die, cold and hungry. Days later, we discovered it had a cough and would die very soon. I have never turned one so young before. Wasn't sure if it would even work. Poor soul. Kathryn would have loved him as her own." He drops the lifeless baby to the floor with a *thud*.

"No!" I blurt out, reaching for the baby. "What have you done?" I stammer through clenched teeth.

Cresthaven turns his gaze quickly on me. "You keep asking me that, but it doesn't change anything. This is the work of *your* God. At least I am trying to do something about it, something good."

"Good? You call this good?" I am in shock and disbelief. "This is barbarism! This is madness!"

"Madness, no, but genius—well, just look at them!" Cresthaven points at the two boys sheepishly. "They are healthy and alive."

"They are dead," I say in defeated breath. "How many more are there?" I ask, gripping the wooden stake in my shaking hand. The magnitude of this horror could be catastrophic if it were to spread.

"I beg your pardon?" replies Cresthaven; a faint smile lingers on his lips.

"How many?"

"I don't know. You lose track after a while."

At the moment, I feel another piece of my soul vanish from the world. Cruel man can be, but the vampire can be even crueler. Self-doubt plagues me further, more so than ever before. My weakness clings to me like a cold, dead chill. Children have always been my downfall. Their innocence. Their vulnerability. The memory of Michael from the Danbury hovel returns to me, burning away in the fire. Was Michael's death Cresthaven's doing from the beginning? Was Cresthaven's idea some sick demented version of a new utopia? All the children of the world, poor innocent children, trapped to wander the earth forever. I want nothing more than to rip Cresthaven's head from his body.

"Monster," I say through parted lips.

My hand tightens firmer around the stake, digging a splinter deep into the palm of my gloved hand. I say it again.

"Monster."

Cresthaven's face shows disgust. "I am no such thing."

"They are just children, you goddamn fiend."

"Tenor, stop," warns Cresthaven. "We were friends once. I am doing a good thing here. Haven't you been listening?"

"Yes, I've been listening. Listening to a psychotic undead maniac!"

The seal binding my anger inside bursts. I raise my wooden stake and bring it down into the chest of the younger of the two boys. "Evil prevails here!" The wedge drives deep, sliding against bone and fascia, past layers of skin, and out the back of his torso. The inside of the wooden box begins filling with blood.

"No!" screams Cresthaven. "What are you doing!" His anger flares as he grips me with invisible air—a force of hands around my neck, but with nothing there. I am thrown back as he whips his arm forward, his eyes glowing red, burning with hate and betrayal. "What have you done? What have you done!" His voice changes into something beyond this earth, like some being beyond the gates of hell.

Colliding with the wall, I draw in as much air as possible as I hit the ground, gripping at my throat where Cresthaven's devilish hands had been.

"Jordan! My poor Jordan! You will suffer a great deal for this, Wolfgang!"

It's as if Cresthaven no longer exists, but a new creature has taken his place. Staying low to the floor, I scramble about the debris of the room like an earthworm scavenging through dirt, trying to think beyond my blinding anger. My vision is a haze of red in the dull yellow of the chamber. I have to do the same to the other boy. Drive a stake through his heart. Save the poor child's sanctity with a human death in lieu of a cursed life.

Leaping to my feet, I half expect to see Cresthaven in the form of a demon, hook and horns protruding from his chest and arms. But instead, he approaches me in his elegant dinner jacket, eyes burning red.

"I gave you a chance to see. A chance to see that humans and vampires could exist together harmoniously," he begins. "But you couldn't see it. Your morality blinds you. Curse you and your bloodline, Wolfgang. I will see that it ends here and now!"

Cresthaven dashes forward with great speed. I dive over one of the empty boxes in the center of the floor as he rushes by, hands fanned out like knives. Again, he comes like a blurring wind, faster than before, and so I thrust down with the wooden stake, just as his hands come within inches of my face. His fangs putrid with the stench of death, he lets out a hiss in my face as he looks down at the object I've embedded in his leg.

Holding the weapon fast, I pull the shaft of wood from his femur as he swings at my head. I duck and roll backward into a counter stance, ready for the next assault. Energy surges from my hip. Enivid burns with passion. It wants to taste vampire blood. It aches to be free of its leather binding.

I find myself smiling suddenly amidst the danger and chaos. Diana is with me. I can feel her. I want to use her strength, but can't, not until I possess what I came for. I pull the extraction dagger from my belt.

"Quite the arrogant shit you are—thinking you can leave here with my blood," sneers Cresthaven. He rushes me, forcing me into a defensive posture. My boot braces against a barrel and I push off, knocking over crates and crashing into the desk. Ink and parchment scatter across the floor like splattered blood. Cresthaven tosses the desk aside to get closer to me.

Get to the boy, I think over and over to myself. *Get to the boy!*

Blow after blow, I parry Cresthaven's attacks. His hands are so fast—faster than I have ever seen. I do what I can to protect myself, but find myself losing very quickly. My boot kicks the side of one of the wooden boxes, the one with the boy I'm looking for.

It is now or never.

I raise my weapon to end his life and bring it down with force, striking soiled sheets and empty pillows. *Dammit. Where is he?* Turning to look up, I am struck suddenly in the shoulder with tremendous force. Half of my body goes numb and I collapse to the floor. Somehow, Cresthaven is stronger than the Carnalreesee.

Stunned from the assault, I open my one eye to see the young boy standing before Cresthaven.

"Father? Who is that man?" asks the boy, pointing at me inquisitively.

"'Tis no one, Dorian. Just a man. A simple pathetic waste of a man."

Dorian.

My blood runs cold at the mention of his name. I know he isn't my son, but I am sickened at the thought of Cresthaven naming his brood after him.

"Does that mean I get to eat him, then?" asks the boy innocently.

"You goddamn monster," I manage to say, drawing the attention of both vampires. "You're all monsters!" I scream. I watch Cresthaven coddle the boy, turning him around to face himself so he can speak to him directly.

"Yes, my boy, you can. Only after I have finished with him first, however."

I cannot see the boy's face, but his shoulders slump in response. Slowly and silently, I rise, clasping a firm grip over the bloodied wooden stake in my hand.

"What about Jordan? Why is he not moving?" asks Dorian, pointing with his hand at the box saturated in red.

Cresthaven turns his head and puts a hand on Dorian. "Do not worry about your brother, my son. He is just sleeping for now. He will be awake soon enough."

Dorian, seemingly content with his father's answer, turns to look up at him again. "Father, it is strange. I had the weirdest dream during the night. A nightmare of sorts—"

But before Dorian finishes his sentence, I thrust the wooden stake into his back, following through with all my strength. The point of the stake bursts through his chest, ejecting his heart from the cavity, and spraying Cresthaven's face and dinner jacket full of blood. The heart, still beating, pumps for the last time as horror melts over Cresthaven's face.

"*No!*" says Cresthaven with shaking breath. "*What have you done?*"

I raise the stake before me as part of my answer. "What I should have done the moment I saw you." I thrust downward and Cresthaven catches my wrist instantly. With the extraction dagger in my other hand, I jab at Cresthaven's side. But he stops this too, catching it just the same. With both of my arms trapped in his grasp, I feel his raw power growing with rage.

Cresthaven's red eyes glare into mine. "*You have no idea what you've done.*"

As I fight against his overpowering grasp, it feels like my arms will rip from their sockets. My body rises from the ground as he lifts me with ease—a simple plaything in his arms—and rushes forward, roaring and hissing with fangs exposed. We crash through a windowpane and descend into the freezing cold outside, landing on the third-story terrace under a grand assault of falling icicles.

CHAPTER
XXXVIII

My weapons dash from my hands as we collide with the stone floor just beyond the shattered glass of the window. They spin and skip away from me in opposite directions as a band of ice crows caw excitedly in the distance. I turn my head just in time to avoid Cresthaven's fist from crushing my brains into the cold hard terrace. His hand instead connects with stone, shattering the mortar and rock into rubble with one fell swoop. A burning power surges beneath my coat suddenly and a renewed energy sweeps through my body.

Enivid. It calls to me.

Cresthaven slams another fist into the floor. "You come to my home uninvited"—he strikes again—"disrupt my dinner"— chunks of stone fly—"prance around my roof"— he swings another fist, but this time I stop it with both hands—"catch up on old times, share in good conversation"—Cresthaven pauses and gazes at me quizzically—"only to gain my confidence, have me take you upstairs, and kill my children?"

Cresthaven's eyes burn with malice. The energy of Enivid rages at my hip. If only I could get to it.

"Farewell, vampire hunter." With mouth open and fangs exposed, Cresthaven lunges at my exposed neck, but I twist his arm just in time, borrowing the power of Enivid and throwing him to the side, escaping his grapple. Again, there is strength in Enivid. In Diana. In me.

With a look of surprise, Cresthaven rises to stand at the same time I do, hunter and hunted, facing off with one another in the fluttering snow. Enivid stands ready in my grasp, poised to throw.

"After I'm finished with you, I'm going to take that antique heirloom of yours and break it into a thousand pieces. I will melt it down into dinner plates so my family and their families after can feast on them in the centuries to come. Your blood will be the first to speckle the plates of history."

I throw Enivid with a flick of my wrist and the blade responds, whirling toward Cresthaven with lightning speed. He dodges, ducking underneath and sidestepping its return trip. I catch Enivid with one hand and recall Councilor's words as I watch Cresthaven in the distance watching me, planning his next move.

"That's a fancy weapon," shouts Cresthaven across the howling rooftop. "Does it do everything you tell it?" he asks, smiling, just before he charges forward with hands extended like a fan of blades.

Blocking out my surroundings, I close my eye and throw Enivid away from my body. I feel its channeling energy whirling away from me, but it never makes contact. Instead, I feel Cresthaven's presence before me and catch his hands in mine just as he strikes. I roll onto my back, thrust my leg into his gut, and toss him over me. Enivid comes back into my hand as Cresthaven lands on his feet like a cat. Again he approaches and I throw a second time. The blade flies low first, then high at the last moment, splitting open the vampire's shoulder and tearing his dinner jacket. Blood and fire spew from his body as he howls. The bright red in his eyes fades.

"What the hell is that thing?" he says, clasping his shoulder and backing off.

Enivid lands in the palm of my hand.

"Your doom."

Cresthaven stares at me a brief moment before turning and running from me, heading for the window we crashed through moments ago.

Dammit.

I dash to collect my weapons, grabbing the extraction dagger first and then the wooden stake tossed to the side.

I can't let him escape, but I know catching him on foot in his own element will be impossible. I run as fast as I can, but Cresthaven moves twice as fast as me. He reaches the area next to the broken window, and instead of climbing back inside where the dead vampire boys lie motionless, he clings to the exterior wall and begins scaling it like a nimble spider. Up and up he goes. Flawlessly. Effortlessly. Blocking out the view of the overcast moon. I am left at a disadvantage.

Reaching the base of the wall, I glance around and find nothing that will aid me in my pursuit. It will be impossible for me to catch him climbing two stories of straight solid stone.

Moving inside, I search for something that might help me stick to the wall. The barrels are full of empty sacks. The crates are full of empty bottles. I look over the upturned desk but find nothing. *Come on. There has to be something here. Anything.* My eye darts about frantically, and then, by sheer luck, I spot the outline of a rectangular frame within the shadowed confines of the room. A door blocked by crates. I remember seeing it when I first entered earlier, but I hadn't thought twice about it.

Shoving the boxes and barrels aside, I rush the door, throwing my full weight into its decayed state of rot and mold. The wood planks break apart like pieces of thin bark. Stumbling through the threshold, I am greeted with an old staircase, similar to the one Cresthaven guided me up. Dark and ominous, there are no candles to light my way. After securing Enivid to my hip, I navigate my way up as fast as I can, hands tracing the narrow walls. *Too much time. I'm taking too long.*

The long stairwell zigzags back and forth as I ascend. The wind blows harder, whistling through the many holes of the dying fortress. I imagine myself as one of the soldiers from long ago, running up the ramparts of the tower, peering from the arrow slits to spot the enemy, shouting up and down the multiple levels to my comrades. I think about the amount of blood that must have been spilt here. It reminds me of Stellamane and his castle walls coated in blood.

Fingers searching through the dark, I come to another door. Through scant light shining through the cracks, I see it is made of thick wood and bound in iron. Energy channels through me again, surging from my hip and traveling through my body. With determination, I ram the barrier, forcing it to rattle in defiance. Again, I try the door, and this time, I hear the cracking of ice. It is frozen shut on the other side. My third attempt ends with success and I stumble out onto the roof.

I am not alone.

My eye circumnavigates my surroundings. Gargoyles encompass every edge of the roof looking down like sentient beings watching over the eternal night of winter. Nothing for miles can escape their gaze. Catching my breath, I stand still amongst the eerie stillness of the statues and the vicious wind whipping around me. Without Councilor's cloak, I feel the cold creeping beyond the boundaries of my leather coat and proofing. Drawing Enivid and the extraction dagger, I begin wearily circling the rooftop.

"Cresthaven!" I shout over the wind but there is no response.

The gargoyles are shrouded in a thin mist from the low-lying clouds. Their gray skin glistens from the ice and looks real, as if any second they might come to life.

"There is nowhere for you to go. Not anymore," I say. "I know who you are. I know what you are. Your family. This town. You are a plague to this earth!"

I hear something shuffle close and I spin to face it. Nothing but the wind. Cresthaven is playing games with me.

Another sound in the distance and I react, sending Enivid on a death path, its blades whirling as it passes through the air. There is the sudden sound of steel on stone and a gargoyle's head in the distance slides from the base of its neck, shattering across the terrace floor. Laughter ensues from somewhere around me.

"You missed," echoes a voice.

My patience wears thin.

"No more games, Cresthaven. Come out and face me," I say to the audience of gargoyles. But only drawn-out silence is my returned answer. Meticulously, I maneuver around each statue, knowing any one of them could come to life any moment. The gargoyles, with their sharp teeth and gripping claws, cling to their stony perches with determination. I look for a sign through the obscuring mist, something that would lead me to believe it's Cresthaven. Then I notice a thing in the distance—is it a statue wearing a jacket perhaps? Or is it really him? Resisting the urge to throw Enivid, I make my way toward the possibility, approaching with caution. I need to get as close to him as possible, yet keep the element of surprise. Passing the statues, I make it a point to look at each one, slowly making my way toward Cresthaven so as not to let on my intent. With the combination of moonlight and twirling wisps of smoke, I position my backside to face Cresthaven, using myself as bait. Any second, he will pounce on me like a raging animal. My anxiety rises as I wait. Yet in the proceeding moments, nothing happens.

I cannot bear it any longer. I spin on the spot as fast as I can, bringing Enivid down on Cresthaven's neck. But the blade slices through stone, not flesh, cutting through the hard surface with a resounding scrape. I watch the gargoyle's head slip from its foundation in disbelief and notice the dinner jacket Cresthaven was wearing conspicuously placed over the haunches of the gargoyle's neck and torso.

Deception.

I turn on the spot. The sight of Cresthaven fills my vision as he throws his body at me, leaping from the pedestal I passed moments ago. He grips my shoulders and slams his knees into my chest. I struggle with him as if we were cat and mouse. Staggering backward, I pivot against his power. Cresthaven tries to pry Enivid from my hand as I attempt to penetrate his side with the extraction dagger.

We slam into a gargoyle, breaking off its wings, and then collide with another, bouncing off the statues. Cresthaven's teeth gleam in the moonlight as he pushes harder on my wrist, but I do not let up. The energy flowing through me is strong. I feel Diana with me, and her father, Dora, too. The power of Enivid is the turning point in my struggle and I can see it in Cresthaven's eyes, his amazement.

"What the hell is this? It's not possible!"

With Enivid gripped tightly, I overpower Cresthaven's attempt at disarming me, and in one motion, sever his hand from his wrist. The end of it erupts into liquid fire and smoke as his bony hand spins down into the darkness below. I feel Cresthaven attempting to scream as I grip his throat, but his air passage is blocked and he can barely make a sound. Lifting him off the ground, I extend his body over the edge of the fourth-floor terrace. His arms and legs dangle as he struggles to get out of my death hold but fails miserably. The glass dome of the dining hall below glows beneath Cresthaven like the flames of judgment.

With the extraction dagger in hand, I ram the serrated blade deep into his side as far as it will go. The vial at the base of the handle clicks and quickly begins filling with dark-ruby liquid, much darker than my own blood. Within moments, the tiny bottle is full and I stow it away on my belt, exchanging it for Enivid.

"I no longer require your services," I say into Cresthaven's terrified face. "Now I rid the world of one more vampire."

"NO! Wait!" Cresthaven manages to croak from under my crushing grip.

My hand stays as I feel my own eye burn, and see it as a feverish white light reflected in the gloss of Cresthaven's own eyes.

"Your son!" blurts Cresthaven. "He is alive! He is well!"

The power surging through me intensifies. I can hardly control my actions anymore. Enivid rises in my hand. "How do you know?"

"Rumor. I've heard rumor! The Carnalreesee. They went to Walters!"

"You lie!" I scream, clutching his throat tighter.

"It's no lie!" he croaks. "I swear it!"

I find myself remembering Blood Mountain Pass, the passage traveling the length of the mountain countryside during the spring, summer, and fall, the trade road connecting the upper villages in the mountains with the lower towns in the valley. But the floods always come in the winter; I saw the red water myself. I shake my head. It is not possible that Dorian is at Walters. The Carnalreesee would have already made their descent out of the mountains by the Great Carpella Road. They should be close to Sunstone. Unless the Carnalreesee were held up somehow and forced to take higher ground. The surge of the river might have caught them. Maybe they hadn't been quick enough. Then their route would have taken them to Walters for certain. All travelers pass through Walters to stock up on supplies before leaving the mountains. If the Carnalreesee and Dorian are there, they must be waiting for the snow to melt. Which means…

They can't leave.

Suddenly, I find myself in a daze, realizing I need to be somewhere else. Hope floods my heart and I find myself thinking only of Dorian. My son. My son! He is still in the mountains. I can think of nothing else. I have wasted so much time here.

Loosening my grip on Cresthaven, I decide to leave him to his cursed fate, to waste away in this cold desolate town of Westings with his demented family and his horrific science experiments. I will return one day, that is certain.

But before I utter a word of warning to Cresthaven with my decision, he suddenly breaks free of my grip and lunges for my neck, forcing me to drive Enivid into his corrupted heart. Cresthaven's eyes gleam red as he clutches a handful of my leather coat within his palm. His face turns even whiter as burning fire erupts from his chest. The weight of his body throws mine off balance and we slip from the rooftop.

Gripping Enivid tightly in my hands, I never let go as we plummet off the fourth-floor tower. Wind and snow sting my face as we descend like falling stars from the sky. Enivid's power surges through me as we smash through the domed ceiling, and then break our fall on the dining table where the Cresthavens feasted on rabbits. Sparkling pieces of glass shower down around us as the marble chamber is filled with an earth-shattering roar.

Shaken and distraught, I push myself off of Cresthaven, coughing and wheezing, attempting to get air back into my lungs. Pulling Enivid from Cresthaven's chest, his face cracks beyond recognition as his eyes regress into the hollows of his brow.

A scream echoes its way toward me from one of the marbled hallways leading out of the dining chamber. Yellow gown disheveled from running, Kathryn speeds toward me with black eyes and long freakish nails dancing. Red rivers drip from under lashes. "Jonathan!" she cries as she kneels beside her beloved, arms cradling his decaying head. Above me there is movement, but I dare not take my eye from Kathryn. I ready Enivid with the most vicious intent.

"How could you? How could you!" Kathryn screams as she places two fingers on her lips and presses them to Cresthaven's flaking forehead. With her neck stained, tears of vermillion race the length of her face. Pools of blood collect at her feet as she stands, her nails growing longer and wickeder by the second.

"He killed Father," says a calm and collected voice behind me. "Now can we bite the man?" Victoria approaches slowly from the shadows, flanking me, adjacent to her mother. Her dark hair spills over her solemn expression, leaving only her red eyes visible for me to see.

"I told you, you were going to die, sir." Jackson's voice hovers down from above like a ghost spirit speaking to me from every direction. He descends from the roof upside down, climbing, transitioning onto one of the pillars and jumping down to the floor. "I am master of this house now, and my first act as its head will be spilling your blood across this floor."

CHAPTER
XXXIX

THERE IS NO TIME FOR thought. No time for hesitation. The remaining Cresthavens surround me like wolves enclosing a fox, each of them snarling the insinuations of the pain they will bring me. But they do not know what I know. I lay claim over a terrible power. A power so cruel it can bring an entire empire down in one fell swoop. It is something they will never possess. Love.

I am the storm on the horizon. Nothing will stand between my son and me.

Absolutely nothing. I will find him. There is new hope. The purest love from Diana guides me. Even now, in her death, she is with me. I can feel the energy. I can feel her in Enivid.

But last of all, there are promises I must keep.

Jackson rushes me as Kathryn and Victoria flank me from opposite sides. They are fast, merely blurs, as they cross the marble floor, their shoes and heels clattering along the surface. Jackson reaches me first, producing a new-found weapon to replace his old bent fork. Did he muster it from a kitchen perhaps? It looks like a rusted knife for carving fruit. He cuts at me once, then twice, and I parry both with a twist of my wrist. I swipe forward, knowing Jackson will dodge, and I bring Enivid back over my head to greet Victoria behind me. At my downward slash, she leaps back, fangs exposed, fingers spread out before her with every intention to skewer me like a pig.

At the same moment, there is a presence behind me. Instantly, I crouch low as long black nails dash above my head. I twist my body around, spinning on heels, and slice with Enivid, slashing the empty air where Kathryn was. She maneuvers around my tactics like a tiger, dodging and curling. She is just as fast as the others, if not faster.

Damn the Cresthavens! Damn the lot of them! Knowing what I know now aggravates me. They are the one thing standing between my son and me and I am losing time.

Seeing an opening in their circle of death, I move to escape the trap, but Victoria appears briskly, filling the hole with her body and wicked smile. There is a dash of wind behind me and I step forward. Jackson's crude knife returns, glancing off my proofing with a scrape. There is nowhere for me to go as Victoria rushes me, her murderous nails poised to pierce my body like the poor helpless rabbits earlier.

Something strikes the back of my knees and I am sent sprawling to the floor, supine to the horrors before me. Victoria leaps on top of me, straddling my waist with her thighs, and squeezes, attempting to crush my ribs underneath the leather plate. At the same moment, I grab Jackson and pull him down on top of me, trying anything to distract Victoria's assault.

"Out of the way, you dolt!" she yells in a furious tone, scratching Jackson's shirt and neck, cutting his flesh without remorse. Trails of blood drip from his shoulders as he returns the favor, the two of them squabbling over me like some play toy. With them distracted, I bring Enivid around to pierce Jackson through his back, right where his heart would be, but stop, as I always do. I am still compelled by the haunting vision of Michael reminding me of Dorian. Jackson reminds me of both.

Ice-cold hands seize my wrists. Kathryn's scent of dead leaves and cloves lingers in my nostrils as she yells at her spawn. "Stop it, you two! Now is not the time!" Kathryn strikes my cheek, filling the inside of my mouth with blood. The pain numbs after a moment and I find myself staring into the porcelain face of pure hate.

"You've ruined everything!" She hits me again, catching one of her nails under my chin. Blood trails along my jaw and pools in the hollow of my ear. More pain follows. Victoria and Jackson beat on my armor like tribal drums. I feel the bile lurching into my throat with every hit, but this war is not over yet.

Ever present, Enivid's power channels through the palm of my hand. Its warmth speaks to me and I suddenly forget my surroundings. Momentarily, I fall into a dream state. Images flood my vision. Warmth. Fire. Diana descending the stairs. Kronklich steeping his tea. There is the back of Dorian's head. He turns and smiles at me.

With a mighty contraction, I pull the holy blade close to my chest, overpowering Kathryn's hold on me. Curling into a ball, the backside of my body is exposed as they continue to pummel me, kicking my body in every opening possible. They strike my head, my arms, my legs; but I am resilient.

"Stand up and fight!" says Victoria.

"You coward!" says Kathryn.

"I'm going to cave your skull in," says the wispy voice of Jackson.

I am a chrysalis. Absorbing. Enduring. Recalling. Their voices echo through my mind, back and forth. Words of hate. Their ashen faces haunt me. Soon, there is nothing I feel, and I wonder if the attack has stopped.

A spark ignites inside.

Like a great ball of erupting flame, the energy exhumes from my chest cavity, travels up my throat, and out of my mouth. I scream as if it were the last scream on earth, for there are no others to follow. The burning light sears, but I endure it regardless. Yes. Power drawing. Power increasing.

Whatever is near me, I cast it away from my body like brittle leaves. Kathryn. Victoria. Jackson. They are sent sprawling back in a great burst of exploding light. Opening my eye, I watch them collide into the stone pillars and walls of the dining room, breaking the architecture with their impact.

I am in shock as the vampires collect themselves. I look down at the glowing energy channeling through my hands, passing through my fingers like electricity. The sight is incredible and the feeling tingles. But just as soon as the power comes, it subsides and disappears into my palms, vanishing from sight. I am left standing bewildered.

"Get up!" screams Kathryn as she rises from cracked marble and crumbling stone.

Jackson rises from a pile of rubble, brushing the soot from his ripped silk shirt and shaking his head in disapproval while Victoria clambers onto her hands and knees like a cat.

"What was that?" asks Jackson in a long, drawn-out tone. He approaches me wearily. "You know what? I don't want to know." He smirks and backs onto one of the pillars, climbing up its surface with lightning speed.

"Jackson!" cries Kathryn. "Get back here now!"

But he is gone within the shadows of the ceiling before she is finished. Kathryn cries in frustration and rushes toward me with a horrible scream. Her long black nails scrape the ground, leaving deep gashes in the marble floor. Leaping into the air, she aims her fingers at me like tiny spears. I dodge to the side as she lands and pierces the floor with her hands. She whips her head back, sending her blond locks twirling around her face just in time to catch my descending blade within the grooves of her nails.

We jump back from one another at the same time.

Blood trails from her black eyes as she continues to wail harder and harder, saturating the floor with more blood. I watch her lips tremble and see through the wisps of her disheveled locks that she has more to say, but the words never come.

Victoria attempts to rush past Kathryn, but Kathryn raises a hand, stopping her in her tracks. "No, Victoria. No more time for playing. You will watch me destroy this human once and for all."

Fanning her hands and baring her fangs, she reveals a mouth full of sharp teeth. The thought of them sinking beneath my breastbone reminds me of the nightmare I had of Diana, the dream where she bit me.

"Leave me be," I say in a stern tone for the first time. "I will leave now and no one has to die. I swear it."

Snow flutters from the opening of the shattered dome high above us. For a moment, there is silence and hope. The possibility is there, lingering like a puff of smoke on the mountain. All I can think about is Dorian. He is in Walters. I need to get to him. He needs my help.

Expressionless, Kathryn's mouth suddenly closes, hiding away those horrible fangs as if retracting her intent. Her visage grows dark and her brow furrows like a doctor pondering a diagnosis. Kathryn's eyes fade from black to a glowing red, and already I know her answer before she utters a word. "You will never leave this place."

Thrusting her own daughter to the side, Kathryn charges at me. Stepping back and parrying her attack, my hand arcs back and forth with Enivid, spinning it within the palm of my hand, churning it like a deadly saw. Every time her nails come in to sting, a piece of them is chipped away. The attacks do not stop until there's nothing left but the tips of her fingers. A cry of displeasure escapes her lips as I back away, using one of the stone pillars to separate us.

With a furious roar, she glides across the floor and rams her entire arm through the pillar of stone like a mighty god, grabbing hold a hand full of my coat on the other side and pulling it back through, forcing my face into the cold hard stone. I am dazed and can do nothing as she grabs me with her other arm. She effortlessly pulls me through the pillar, breaking the rest of the stonework from its foundation, sending an avalanche of cobblestone and dust toppling down around us. With Enivid still clutched tightly in my hand, I drive one of the four blades up through her forearm, impaling the fancy gold sleeve of her dress. Shock riddles her face as liquid fire ejects from her arm. She staggers back, screaming as she tries to fan the flames burning across her roasting skin.

Now is my chance.

Tearing Enivid free of her arm, I rush forward with malice, envisioning my hands pushing the holy blade through her heart and out the backside of her spine. I gave her a chance. I gave them all a chance. Now there is no choice. She will end up like her husband. Dead and shrivelled. They will all meet their end.

I raise my arms to attack Kathryn and notice a shadowy figure pass above my head. I thrust downward with ill intent, but something blocks me from following through. A rusted knife stands between Kathryn and me.

Jackson.

He stares into my eye with seething hatred, forcing my weapon back with his own. "Trying to kill my mother?" he asks accusingly, shaking his head. "That is not acceptable."

Kathryn grips the sleeve of her son's coat. "Jackson, stop! Don't—"

"Let go of me, Mother!"

Jackson leaps at me, stabbing with the small knife.

Every jab I block with Enivid, never moving from the spot. Over and over, he flails at me with hatred in his eyes, yet I never retaliate. Again, I hear Michael screaming in the fire, his siblings running over to him, screaming for someone to save their brother. *What's wrong with me? Snap out of it, Tenor! Snap out of it!*

"What's the matter, hunter?" says Jackson in a frustrated tone. "Why aren't you fighting back?"

I struggle with my emotion to overcome the fear of slaying *this* child. *But he is not a child.* The vampire menace will never end unless I do this. *Do it now, or forever be damned.* Raising Enivid before Jackson, I look into his eyes one last time and thrust. But it is Kathryn I see at the last moment.

Sacrifice. There is no stronger bond than a mother's love for her child.

My blade passes straight through Kathryn's face, cutting deep between the bridge of her nose and the inside of her eye. Her cursed blood sprays my face. The sharp edge breaks through the back of her head with purpose, scattering bone fragments across the floor. Within seconds, her skin shrivels and I am left with Jackson screaming and crying over his dead mother, and Victoria yelling at him to shut up and get over it.

CHAPTER
XL

"Mother! Moooooother! What has he done to you?"

Hands held out before him, Jackson looks up at me in horror as I retract the weapon from his mother's destroyed face.

"You're an animal. You're a monster," he says, barely audible, his throat hoarse. "What have you done?!" he screams. "Raaaaaagghhhhh!"

Slowly, Victoria makes her way toward me bearing the same blank expression from before, unaffected by her brother's reaction. No feeling. No remorse. Her eyes glow red, yet there is no indication of emotion. "The Wolfgang killed her, you fool," she spits, answering Jackson mockingly.

"Moooooother!" cries Jackson again as he falls to his knees. Tears of blood stream down his face as he looks up at me for a second time. "You goddamn bastard! Look at her!" He lifts her head from the pile of folded and decayed skin.

I step back cautiously, watching his every move.

Jackson continues caressing Kathryn's shriveled head for a moment before laying it gently on the floor. Already, her skin breaks apart within his hands. Standing up, he looks at Victoria.

She is motionless and says nothing. He reaches for her hand, but she moves it away.

"I never liked you," says Victoria, addressing the corpse of her mother.

Jackson's eyes widen, a look of disbelief falls over his face.

"Oh shut up, Jackson," she says, turning to face him. "She treated us like little children. *Victoria, do this. Jackson, do that.*" She smiles wickedly at me. "You did us a favor, Wolfgang."

With her devilish eyes trained on me, a horrible feeling tells me what she says is sincere. *What is wrong with this family?*

"Now that *that* is over with,» says Victoria, folding her arms, «we can focus on the more important things. Shall we, Brother?"

Jackson looks at his sister, using the back of his hand to wipe away the tears.

"Let us reclaim our inheritance and purge this house of the Wolfgang," she says.

As they look at me with renewed interest, I know a new fire burns within them. They are fueled by the loss of their dead parents and what is now to be theirs.

Subconsciously, my hand glances over Cresthaven's vial of blood as I ready Enivid in my other hand. My eye scans for a way out. There are multiple halls leading from the room, but I do not know what leads where. It will be impossible to leave the estate. Not until they're all dead.

And so the dance begins.

They come for me, dashing quicker than before—their blurred, distorted images gone in a flash. There is movement behind me, and so I run as quickly as I can to the other side of the dining hall. My boots echo furiously across the marble floor as I survey the room. Leaping over the crushed dining table, I pass over the body of Cresthaven still lying in his miserable state of decay and continue running for one of the halls leading out of the chamber. As I reach the opening, however, Victoria appears before me, spinning what looks like a chain from a chandelier.

She casts one end of the chain to her side, whipping it across the passage way as if daring me to cross. "Look, Brother, the mouse is trying to leave."

Above her head, Jackson scrambles his way along the stonework and tapestries, before descending and landing on the floor next to his sister. "Oh, no. You can't leave. We're just getting started." Picking up the other end of the chain, he looks to Victoria for confirmation. "Ready, Sister?"

The chain rattles along the ground as they rush toward me. I see the determination in their eyes as I run straight for their little trap. I hold Enivid tightly in my hands while they pull the chain taut as they reach me and force it to snap up from the ground. I catch the chain in the handle of Enivid and let them run around me, interlocking the chain around my body like constricting snakes. Closer and closer they come as they encircle me, binding my arms to my proofing, the chain links grinding against the sharp edges of Enivid.

Laughter pours from Victoria and Jackson.

"That's it, Brother," says Victoria. "The little mouse can't escape now."

"Can you imagine?" replies Jackson. "His blood will be the first spilt inside *our* new home.»

Distracted by their narcissistic conversation, they continue running around me as I brace Enivid firmly against the chain. Soon, they will be out of chain, and then—

Round and round they go, Victoria in her red dress of silk ribbons, Jackson in his formal dinner jacket. They are thrilled at the thought of my capture, lost in their reverence of their little game.

Diana enters my mind. I whisper words to her thought, asking her again for guidance. "Give me strength, my love."

Victoria and Jackson stop inches from me, scrutinizing me with a look. The scent of clove and burnt leaves lingers in the air.

"Did you say something, little mouse?» asks Victoria in a cute voice. She holds the chain to her side, wrapped tightly around her arm like a snake.

Clenching my teeth and taking a deep breath, I push against the layers of chain, causing them to strain against one another.

The look on Victoria's face is that of disbelief. "What are you doing? Stop that!"

One by one the links pop, and the sudden loss of tension throws the two young vampires to the floor.

"Damn it, Jackson!" yells Victoria.

"What did I do?" screams Jackson.

They curse one another as the chains fall away from my body. With freedom to move again, I run for one of the halls exiting the chamber to make my escape, but suddenly jerk backward. Victoria managed to wrap the chain around my arm somehow.

"I don't think so, little mouse," she says in a playful tone. "We didn't say you could leave."

I smirk. Enivid's power is strong within me.

Pulling the chain hard, I flick it to the side and Victoria follows, stumbling across the floor, arms flailing. Using her momentum, I double back the chain like a whip and she hits the ground face first. The chain slips from her hand and strips the flesh from her arm as I yank it away. She stares at her mutilated body and screams.

At the same time, something collides with my torso, knocking the breath from me despite my armor protection. I stagger back into a stone pillar while Jackson stands near his sister protectively. Regaining control of my breathing, I close my eye, focusing on the vampire duo, and throw Enivid in retaliation. The blade spins straight and true, cutting through the air with great haste. But no sooner does it leave my hand than I realize I miss. It ricochets off the marble floor and comes back around like a boomerang.

They are so fast.

Opening my eye, I see Jackson has vanished and Victoria now barrels straight for me with hatred in her eyes. This time, I throw Enivid with my eye open and watch as Victoria dances around the blade. The chain I pulled from her arm now dangles from her other hand as she moves closer while whipping the air. She launches a sideways lash and I duck, rolling away as the chain rips pieces of stone from the pillar behind me.

Her laughter grows. She slashes everything around her in a feverish hail of strikes. I narrowly escape as the chain cracks the marble floor and explodes a statue bust. I throw Enivid again and she bends over backward, hands touching the floor as the whirling blade passes over her. On the return trip, she snaps back to position and launches the chain, forcing me to sidestep. It is here when I notice her shoulder is vulnerable when she strikes forward, and so I wait patiently for the next chance, dodging her relentless attacks.

Glancing around the room, Jackson is nowhere to be found. *Where the hell is he now?* With Victoria's fury of blows upon me, I cannot chance the distraction. Victoria raises her arm and lashes forward.

Now's my chance. Raising Enivid above my head, I motion to throw, but stop suddenly as growling comes from somewhere above me. Jackson descends from the shadows above, landing on my shoulders like a demon monkey from hell. Mouth open wide, he retracts his jaw beyond its limit, exposing his incisors. Biting down with a ferocious might, his mandible clamps my forearm like a fiendish insect, a parasite seeking lifeblood to sustain his own. His eyes burn red and his hair frays on its ends. I am shocked by the suddenness of the attack, yet all I feel is pressure. Underneath the sleeve of my black coat, the bracer infused with steel protects my arm. My proofing has saved my life countless times.

The burning light in Jackson's eyes fades as he realizes his horrible mistake. Before he can retract his hideous fangs back into his mouth, I strike his face with my free hand and hear the roots of his teeth tear from his mouth. Blood traces the air and drips across the floor as he hits the ground startled.

I can only imagine what he feels at the moment. One of the things separating himself from a human has been taken from him. Some say the fangs of a vampire are the roots in which the evil manifests. Other lore suggests they perish without them. But I know Jackson won't die. This is not the first time I've ripped the heritage from a vampire. They grow back eventually.

Jackson's shrill voice echoes through the chamber at an alarming pitch. With his hand over his mouth, blood streams after Jackson as he runs from the chamber, stampeding the wooden doors to exit the room. As the noise fades to other parts of the mansion, I slowly rise, shaking my head to remove its stunning effects.

"What have you done?" retorts Victoria as she casts the chain aside in a raging fit.

I say nothing at first while brushing the fangs from my arm like thorns from a rose. The teeth clatter against the marble floor and I know she is angry. I can see it in her face. "I have made the world a better place," I say, knowing it will enrage her even more. I need to push her over the edge. Make her sloppy.

My plan has the desired effect.

Victoria begins panting like a dog. Her mouth opens, sucking in air with great gusts. I see the fangs protrude from her small lips, the same as her brother. Each breath puffs a wisp of hair away from her face. Hands free of the chain, she extends them to the sides of her body and bends her fingers as if holding imaginary spheres. The sound from her mouth becomes louder. With each inhalation, the black nails from her fingers grow longer and longer—and longer still, until they reach the floor. With one of her long nails, she points at me.

"Tonight, you will understand pain. Just like my poor dear brother." She begins walking toward me and I begin moving back. "What you did to him—is inexcusable." She pauses, looks away, and then back at me. "I'm going to tear out your eye." She raises a second nail at me. "You will never see the light of day again."

My back touches a stone pillar, and quickly I move my head to the side as her nail shoots toward my face. The long black nail bursts through the stonework like brittle paper.

I hear frustration in her voice as I dash from the spot, dodging her dart-like attacks, her nails freakishly long and precise. One after another, I feel her nails miss me, passing through my hair and ripping through my coat. I never stop, running from one stone pillar to the next, avoiding her nails of death and the look of enjoyment on her face. Dust and rock explode from my surroundings. Panting, I attempt catching my breath while crouching low behind one of the pillars. Her voice is near.

"I never told you. After your eye is gone, I will fillet your skin and feed it to the hounds. Your blood, of course, I will drink."

The thought of her torture makes me shiver as I think of a way out of this situation. But my chances are grim. Victoria's nails are too long. I can't get close enough.

"Hello there," says Victoria peering around the edge of the column. Her nails come into view and my adrenaline flares. I take off running as fast I can for the next pillar, trying to think, trying to buy more time, but a nail graces my back, knocking me to the ground, forcing me into a roll.

Recovering from the fall, I run for the next pillar as Victoria chases after me like a wildcat in pursuit of an atter. My body collides with the column while my hands push flat against the stone. I dodge to the left, then to the right, just as her nails rush past my waist.

Using Enivid, I swipe down across her talons of death, shattering the nails' hard enamel into hundreds of pieces.

She lets out a cry of anger while striking with the other hand, but misses as I jump back. As she closes in, I ready myself and rush toward the stone column instead of Victoria. Using the momentum of my speed, I run my boots up the wall, lifting myself from the ground. Victoria passes under me as I flip over her head backward and, in one motion, sever her head and stab her through the heart.

No more cries of anguish. No more cynical laughter.

I stand over Victoria's motionless body, watching her head come to rest against the base of the pillar. Breathing heavily, I contemplate the reality of the situation. Three Cresthavens are dead. One is left.

I know what must be done, yet my mind races with anxiety. The laws of the Wolfgang house are paramount, always have been. Jackson still lingers somewhere in the estate. I hear his moans echoing through the old fortress. But can I bring myself to do it? Dorian enters my mind, and I realize I am wasting time lingering here. The town of Westings will have to endure the vampire's curse indefinitely. One day I shall return to set things right.

Damn this place. Damn them all.

My son is waiting for me.

Gathering my wits, I make way to leave this place, guessing which doors to pass, which halls to take, and eventually come to a foyer gleaming with brilliant candlelight. Through its front windows, lamplighters stand guard just beyond the door, ensuring no one passes in or out of the house. But it is not they who concern me. It is the bodies strewn about the foyer floor. Approaching cautiously, I recognize, through all the blood, the servants' attire. Senseless killings. Necks sliced open rather than bitten and drained. I kneel before the massacred people, trying to make sense of their deaths.

My eye falls on a servant girl, the one from earlier who came to warn Cresthaven of my arrival. Young. Beautiful. Face ridden with shock. A rusty knife protrudes from her belly, an eruption of congealed blood already amassed at the wound site. It is the same knife Jackson tried ramming through my armor numerous times before. I notice hundreds of tiny bite marks on her neck and along her arms, scars of the vampire's kiss. She was fed on frequently and kept a prisoner to this cursed family.

The horrors this poor child has seen. What had they done to her? Turmoil clouds my thoughts at the senseless killings. Why kill off his food supply? I remember the rabbits from before. Hadn't they sufficed? My thoughts concede to the inevitable conclusion.

Jackson has turned to madness.

My body shakes with anger as I rise from the mass of dead bodies, realizing my selfish intentions will have to wait. More innocent people will die. I cannot let Jackson continue to exist, not while the blood of Wolfgang flows through my veins.

CHAPTER
XLI

THE DOORS OF THE FOYER slam against the wall with a resounding crash.

I pass through the threshold, weapons drawn. Enivid glints in the glow of candlelight as I move forward into a long ominous hallway decorated with extravagant paintings and tapestries. My one eye darts back and forth, searching the numerous busts lining the walls. Unsure of their origin, I wonder if they are nobles to the Cresthavens long-dead past. They seem to watch my every move as I tread over thick embroidered carpets—I, the intruder in the midst of their family's home. I flinch from the picture frames as my reflection passes across the glass from one side to the other. Resisting the urge to break every piece of finery I see, I press on, keeping the dreadful task of slaying Jackson constantly at the forefront of my mind. It haunts me every step of the way.

I know what must be done.

I am coming for you, Jackson.

Making quick progression through the long extensive corridor, I pass through another set of doors, propped open by thick iron candelabras, and into a grand audience chamber. Checkered marble floor, similar to the dining room, covers the vast expanse of a ballroom. Plush carpets delineate where one should walk. Hundreds of chairs line the perimeter while a grand piano waits quietly at its center as if expecting the maestro to come through the curtains at the back of the chamber to play the ivory keys. Firelight leaps across the floor from the huge mantle at the far right of the room.

Unsure of which way to go, fully alert, waiting for someone or something to attack me from the shadows, I move to the center, toward the piano's cherry-wood frame.

I watch the reflecting firelight from candelabras as I stand waiting, perturbed by the silence. *Were there any servants left or did Jackson kill them all?*

Looking high above, fine chandeliers dressed in gold hang freely, burning brightly with purpose, watching the ballroom like forgotten sentinels. They are of new design in these modern times, cradling oil lamp basins to cut back on maintenance. The old traditional candleholders of old castles had to be replaced daily. These oil lamps could last a week if maintained properly.

The eerie quiet of diffusing oil and burning wicks gives me cause for caution as I move closer to the massive doors leading to the terrace outside. The large panes of glass make the outside look surreal. The torchlight from the lamplighters wavers in out of sight. They are still looking for me, the intruder on the Cresthaven estate.

A loud crash close by followed by shouting draws my attention immediately away from the windows and back into the flickering light of the ballroom. I catch the faintest light coming from one of the exterior halls. A rabbit hops into view, then disappears back the way it came. Quickly, I chase after it, traversing the chamber and keeping to the outer shadows so as not to draw attention to myself. A warm draft presses my face as I round the corner and come to another long corridor riddled with openings.

The hall is completely destroyed. Furniture upturned and smashed against the walls. There is no doubt Jackson passed this way. He is a hurricane wrecking everything in his path.

The rabbit scurries down the corridor where the base of the wall meets the floor. But it is the glow of kitchen that draws my attention. With weapon poised to strike, I charge forward, ready to receive whatever adversary awaits me.

I am greeted with rabbits hanging from long chains, pierced through their legs with large sharp hooks. Fluffy with white and gray fur, dozens of them sway about the room, squirming from their suspended prison. A man wearing a servant's uniform and a scarf over his head hacks away at one of them with a cleaver. His back is to me as he methodically splits its guts over the table. A series of large bins on wheels line the wall, filled to the brim with live rabbits. Other servants, standing along tables full of live rabbits and twisted tubes, turn abruptly toward me, their eyes wide from my sudden appearance. The tubes, used for blood extractions, drain into large glass pitchers underneath the tables for later use. A boy on his hands and knees scurries after escaped rabbits. There is a cart turned on its side, undoubtedly the loud crash I heard from before.

Blank eyes stare back at me.

"What the hell are you doing?" I say spastically, unable to think of anything else to say. "You need to get out of here now!"

A balding man with mutton chops steps forward. Bloodstains cover the apron around his waist as he wipes his hands. "Leave? What about the children, sir?"

Children? Do they not know who the Cresthavens are? Jackson, Victoria. They are anything but children. I try fathoming them as children, but shake my head in disgust.

I reach for one of the carts and push it over, startling the young boy. It crashes to the floor, sending rabbits scurrying across the dirty floor. I kick over a glass container filled with blood. Its content spreads across the floor in a wave of crimson.

"Are you people daft? Evil prevails this place! Leave at once!"

Their looks of sheer terror tell me they understand as they flee from the kitchen, leaving behind their instruments of butchery and torture.

Watching my footsteps so as not to crush the escaping rabbits, I leave the warm kitchen and re-enter the cool hallway. Looking down the long corridor of burning candles and shattered debris, I continue my search for Jackson, peering down other hallways as I advance. Movement in the distance catches my attention momentarily. I raise Enivid, ready to retaliate. But there is nothing, only the flapping of a curtain and the rustling of the tapestry. Through the darkness and wavering light, my debilitated vision plays tricks on me. *Was that a child I saw just now, crawling along the floor, stark naked?*

A rabbit hops by my feet and hides in the shadows of a huge stairwell before me. I pause. There is a body sprawled across the plush-carpeted steps. His neck, like the other victims, has been filleted open. Completely drained of blood, the lifeless corpse stares up at the ceiling with a final look of consternation, an undeniable look of betrayal.

As I begin my climb up the stairs, I am shoved aside as a servant woman descends past me. She doesn't stop and continues on as quickly as possible. Loud voices echo high above me. Someone shouts, "Out of the way fool!"

Jackson.

A horrid scream echoes from above as I bend my head over the railing to see its source. Quickly, I pull back just in time as a man falls through the center of the stairwell, breaking off pieces of railing with his arms and head. His life ends with a sickening crunch at the bottom of the stairs.

Two steps at a time, I ascend the stairs with haste, examining each platform as I reach it. Again, something moves just beyond the circles of light, and this time I am convinced it is a young boy.

Moving into the corridor of the third floor, I am overwhelmed by the excessive number of paintings and mirrors framed in gold. They shimmer in the eerie glow of the dying sconces. I strain to hear Jackson's voice again. The sound of a sigh passes my ears in the dead silence of the hallway.

I turn on the spot, glancing over my shoulder.

Nothing.

Damn the Cresthavens. Damn this house. And as I reconsider my options of leaving this place once and for all, I brace myself suddenly, bending at the knees and facing the dark, ominous doors waiting at the end of the hall. A small hand slips from view as the door closes quietly.

"Shit," I say under my breath, anxiety rising, knowing I must follow.

Cautiously, I traverse the hallway, passing images of myself in the mirrors. It is strange to me the Cresthavens have so many, for the vampire casts no reflection. The paintings, oil based and full of texture, depict images of buildings and architecture varying in degrees of ruin. They remind me of Egleaseon's ruins, the hall of lost paintings I accidentally found. I remember their twisted images and the damage they caused. Instinctively I rub my hand where it was burnt. I reach for the door handle, twist, and advance into a chamber of glowing yellow.

Straining my eye to make up for two, I see the room hosts a roaring fire burning brightly across an extravagant bedroom chamber. There is a four-poster bed lined with drapes and large plush couches embroidered with red and gold. An arsenal of weapons and shields line the walls like a museum. Old weapons from dark times. Studded maces. Halberds. Rounded shields with steel-fortified rims. The finery of crystal goblets and silver trays holding scrolls of parchment, ink, and pens are impressive.

It is the mantelpiece above the fireplace that captures my attention, however. Hanging above it is a hippogriff holster displaying two swords crossed against one another, yet one of the weapons is missing. Dorian suddenly comes into mind with the swords we used against each other when sparring in the courtyard, swords passed down generation upon generation clanging together, sparks flying, our footwork spattering in the mud. He was always the better one at sword fighting.

Movement to the left brings my attention to the figure staring out the open window. A cold draft blows through the room, sending flakes of snow past Jackson's face and hair. Arms tucked and folded neatly behind his back, he reminds me of how the nobles stand when addressing one another. The missing sword from the mantle rests in one of his hands.

As if watching the moon outside, his head never turns as he speaks. "You really wish to kill me?" A lisp hangs in the words he speaks, reminding me of the damage I caused to his mouth. "After what you've done? You've disgraced my family's name, killed them all. Truly, is that not enough?" Jackson turns to face me; his eyes glow red. "Of course it's not. You're just as bloodthirsty as we are. Your craving for war will never end." His words are patronizing and mature, yet very different from his presence earlier. Blood slowly drips down the front of his shirt from where his fangs used to be. Unfolding his arms, he turns to face me, raising the point of his sword.

"Disgraced your family's name?" My grip tightens around Enivid. "You don't know what you're talking about. You were never given a choice. That is how these things work. That is how your vampire lineage continues to exist." I take a step forward. "You can thank your dead father for that."

He takes the bait, coming at me with anger, full force, unrelenting, slashing away, throwing himself at my guard with a concentrated fury.

This is how I will win. I did it with Egleaseon's daughter Katrina and with Jackson's sister, Victoria. A vampire's pride is its worse enemy.

I parry and dodge, ducking under overhead swings and blocking the sword with Enivid. The air rings with metal, brightening the room with sparks. Jackson has had too much time to recover, his strength is returning. He slashes at my legs and I leap onto a table, knocking over the crystal goblets in the process. He swipes again, chopping the legs off of the expensive furniture, forcing me to slide from the surface on an angle as it crashes to the floor. Rolling across the ground, I recover, only to be met with Jackson's sword immediately. Over and over he strikes back and forth at my torso, meeting Enivid each time. An opening exposed, I take my chance to end Jackson once and for all, slashing at his chest, but he smacks Enivid with such a force the reverberation passes up my arm making it go numb.

Enivid drops from my hand.

Jackson shakes his head. "I'm quite shocked you've managed to kill my entire family, yet here you are weaponless against me." He bends down to collect the holy weapon from the floor and it burns his hand. "Aaaagghhh!" he screams, kicking the blade away into the dark recesses of the room. "So you're the only one who can use it. Great." He points his sword at me again and smiles. "What will you do now?"

He comes for me and I retreat to the fireplace, toward the mantle with the sword hanging on the wall. My hand finds the handle and draws the slender blade. Jackson steps into my line of sight and swings. We clash and my mind flashes back into the past. The memory hits me like a lightning bolt.

"*Watch your footwork, Dorian. Step back! Parry!*" *I force Dorian back with a shove, his blond hair swaying in the wind, covering his eyes.*

Rapidly blinking my eye, I try to focus on the fight with Jackson as he swings at me, but when our swords collide again, I am thrown back into the past.

"You always have to be two moves ahead, Dorian!" I shout over the wind in the courtyard.

"I'm trying, Father, I'm trying. You're much bigger than me."

"Size has nothing to do with it."

Dorian throws himself at me, lunging, but I sidestep his blade, parrying close to my waist, and ram him with my shoulder.

Jackson falls to the floor, sword clattering against the ground. As I stand over him, he scrambles to reclaim his sword, but a hard thrust with my boot traps his arm against the floor. Gripping my own sword with two hands, I ram the blade through his chest, listening to the sound of his voice strain under the weight of the steel. His body tenses and I hear liquid bubble into his throat.

"So, what were you planning to do after you killed me?" asks Jackson.

The smile on his face is startling to me, confusing even. Blood seeps from his mouth as he chuckles softly to himself. And although the sword has paralyzed him temporarily, he manages to raise an arm and point behind me.

Compelled to look, it's as if the world were cast in slow motion as I turn my head. There are children. Dozens of them. Staring at me. Their eyes glow red like the one who created them.

The realization is slow at first, but then it comes to me like a hot knife cutting through skin.

I miscalculated and misjudged.

There are more Cresthavens than I can count.

CHAPTER XLII

I was wrong. Dead wrong.

The Cresthavens are not just monsters. They are deranged lunatics, playing the role of God. Creating a new empire of bloodthirsty children. So many children. So many walks of life. Among the twenty or so orphans—finely dressed in tunics of woven threads, hair combed, and faces clean—crawl toddlers, not even old enough to walk, holding on to their older siblings with tiny hands. Fangs protrude from their mouths as if they were never taught to hide them before striking.

My worst nightmare has come true.

There is clapping behind me as I look upon the children. I can't stop staring.

"Ha ha ha! Look at them all," says Jackson, struggling with each word. "So many of my brothers and sisters. My father was a busy man. It's a shame you left them *fatherless*."

Stepping back from the madness, I can do nothing but watch the children approach, moving in to surround Jackson and me. One of the boys stares at me as he passes, never touches me, and positions himself behind Jackson. He places his unusually long fingers over Jackson's shoulders while one of the other children, a little girl holding a doll with hair braided and bowed, drops her toy and grips the sword sticking out of his chest. She pulls it free with ease, like plucking a feather from a chicken. Blood spurts from the wound as the sword clatters to the floor.

Slowly, Jackson rises, clutching his chest, hair in his face. My back already against the wall, I realize there is nowhere for me to go.

Jackson looks up at me, his grin bloodier than before. He shakes his head as if disappointed and motions to the girl who aided him. "Lily, come here, my sweet." The little girl collects her doll covered in blood and obliges his request. He places his hands on Lily's shoulders in a caressing way and kneels before her. "Thank you, Lily, for saving me. That man there—do you see him?"

She nods her head.

"He is the bad man. Do you remember what we do to the bad man?" His eyes stay focused on her despite his sneering grin.

"We eat the bad man," responds Lily innocently, her voice sincere and confident.

"That's right, Lily. We eat the bad man. Good girl." Jackson's eyes flick in my direction.

"You sick bastard," I say before the children swarm me— their arms and hands extended, fangs exposed, hissing with fetid breath. The little ones, holding on to their older counterparts, topple over and begin crawling their way toward me. Hands grope at my legs and torso, pulling on my leather coat. Despite their age, they possess the blood of the vampire and their undying strength is ever present. I kick one in the head and the boy shies away, hissing like a snake in the brush. I feel their teeth grinding on the armor covering my legs and one of them grabs my arm, opening its mouth to sink its teeth into my wrist. With a motion from my elbow, I send the little vampire sailing over the rest, but it lands on all fours like a cat. Another one clings to my back, a little girl with cold dead hands, scratching at my bare neck.

"You are going to die here," says Jackson amidst the chaos.

My hands grope at the fireplace mantle, searching for something to use as leverage. My fingers trace the outline of a brick and I tear it from its foundation, swinging it across my chest, striking the little vampire in the head. The stone breaks apart in my hand as the girl topples from my body, landing in a group of children, still hissing. They scatter, staring at her unmoving body; blood pours freely from her battered skull.

I need Enivid. It is there, lingering in the shadow beyond my grasp. There are so many children in the way. One by one, the Cresthaven children bombard me, using the weight of their bodies to bring me down, until finally, I am forced to the ground.

"Yes, brothers and sisters. Feed. Suck the life of the lord who killed your father. Suck every last drop of blood from him! The floors of our home are your feeding ground now..."

Nails find their way to my skin, scratching my elbows and scraping my knees. I push and pull to get them off me, but there are too many. Lily, the girl with the braids and ribbons in her hair, appears inches from my face, baring her teeth and opening her jaw, trying to sink her fangs into my neck. My hand stays her for the moment, but my strength is failing and hers is gaining. I see one of Enivid's blades protruding from the shadow. I reach for it, clawing the ground desperately as if commanding the weapon to come to me. The time I struggled outside Albestan Church comes back to me—when the bogarts clamored over my body and pinned me to the ground. As I thought then, I think again. My time of dying draws near. But no, I mustn't think such things.

Pushing against Lily's relentless desire for my blood, I feel her cold breath against my skin. The smell of cloves is strong in the air.

Goddammit. Come on. I strain the muscles in my shoulder and neck. Reaching. Groping.

My love. Give me strength. «Diana!» I shout in the face of my adversaries.

Enivid nudges toward me as if it has a will of its own, as if an invisible bond connects it to me. Yearning. Needing. Close to despairing. I try again. Slight movement. I fill with passion and it moves an inch closer.

Suddenly, Enivid slides across the floor with tremendous speed, connecting with the palm of my hand. A burst of energy surges through my body in an instant. With violent force, I drive the holy blade through the side of Lily's head.

There is no time for her to react. No time to change the expression on her face. A sighing breath escapes her mouth as she rolls off of my body, lifeless, crumpling to the floor. The others seem startled by her demise. A wave of sickness takes me and I want to vomit for having killed a child, but the feeling dissipates as quickly as it comes, filling me with the only thing that will save me.

Rage.

Rising from the collage of vampires, I slash and stab at the little monsters, killing as many as I can. But they are fast, scattering in every direction. Catching one by the neck, I sever its head with one slice of the blade. A little girl vampire, blonde curls bouncing and red eyes streaming, runs straight for me, hissing and flailing her hands. I drive my blade through her throat before she has a chance to make contact. Her scream is replaced with the gurgling of blood.

Jackson responds in a fit of rage. Collecting his swords from the ground, he runs toward me. "Stop him! Kill him!"

Whirling my body about, I slice all around me to keep the Cresthavens at bay. I cut at the empty air where shadows pass. One of the Cresthavens nearly tears my face off as I leap back, dodging with finesse. The vampire vanishes, moving more quickly than my one eye can see. Intuition tells me to step right and Jackson appears, blade missing my shoulder. He follows through with the next blade, attacking relentlessly, and I dodge each one. I block his overhead strike, catching his sword within the crook of Enivid. Another child lands on my back, groping at my neck. I spin away, breaking my bond with Jackson, and toss the child into the roaring flames of the fireplace. The effect is instant. Fire bursts from the mantle as the child scurries across the room, yelling for help, spreading the embers over everything. The plush carpets, the elegant furniture, even the flaking wallpaper. The child doesn't stop, crashing through the master bedroom doors and into the hall.

Everything catches fire. Great flames leap up the curtains. It won't be long before the entire house is consumed. Immediate departure is paramount.

Two of the Cresthaven children slam into my body, forcing me back. I trip over a toddler crawling along the ground and fall to meet face to face with yet another. Its beady eyes water blood. I shy away with anxiety, rapidly opening and closing my one eye, unable to kill the toddlers. Pushing them away with my boot, I stand, regaining my footing.

Dashing forward, I follow after the wake of the burning child, escaping the growing inferno. Passing the doorframe of smoldering flames, I traverse my way into the hallway, covering my mouth and nose with my coat. Staggering ahead, I see the Cresthaven that was on fire. Reduced to a smoldering pile of ash, an outline of a body wedged between the railing of the stairs.

The staircase catches fire, and as I descend, two balls of fire fly from the master bedchamber, screeching in terrifying fright. The Cresthavens head straight for me and I jump back just in time as they pass, bursting through the railing and tumbling down the stairwell with tremendous speed. As I gaze over the side, smoke and embers trail after them into the glowing darkness below.

A presence draws near me and I know I've lingered too long.

"We are not finished," says Jackson, appearing on the wall behind me, his arms and legs stuck at impossible angles like a spider's, and then springing his entirety at me. I lose my footing at the crest of the stairs and we both flail through the air, crashing through a portion of burning railing and landing one story below. Falling and tumbling the rest of the way down, we

474 | F.D. Gross

struggle against each other's power, hands on wrists, elbows in faces, subduing each other's strength.

Crashing to a stop at the bottom of the stairs, we land in the great hall connecting the kitchens and ballroom. Jackson's face is inches from mine as he tries to bite me with his open mouth. I see the holes where his fangs used to be.

"Pathetic hunter," he spits and laughs. "It's going to take more than that tiny blade of yours to stop the Cresthavens. Our name will live forever!"

Blood speckles my vision as he talks. Yes, forever in the Wolfgang history books.

"It's about damn time," says Jackson. "The cavalry has arrived."

He looks up and I follow his gaze. An entourage of lamplighters head straight for us, marching down the hall, lamp staffs bearing torch fire and swords drawn. The one in front calls out. "Sire! Are you all right?"

"Hurry up, you fools!" shouts Jackson. "Apprehend this intruder at once!"

The lamplighters advance, energized anew by his command, but suddenly they stop, bracing their weapons before them as if to blockade an approaching enemy. They seem to be shaking.

"What are you fools doing? Why are you stopping? Hurry up!"

Still locked in a death grip with Jackson, I hear the pattering of feet and the hissing and crying that can only be the Cresthaven children. They run past us, charging straight for the lamplighters with their eyes glowing and fangs ready to bite.

"Stop, you fools!" cries Jackson. "What are you doing? Not them!"

Within seconds, the Cresthaven children bombard the lamplighters, plummeting them to the ground and tearing their throats out.

"No!" screams Jackson, but the hall is filled with the lamentations of the dying. The sound echoes through the great hall like a wind tunnel. The fire about the stairwell has spread beyond the ceiling and tapestries, channeling down both directions of the corridor.

While he is distracted, I slam Jackson's wrist against the stone floor, bending it in half with a crack. Bones breaking through the skin, he cries out in agony as I lift myself from the ground and stagger into a run, limping my way down the hall.

I hear Jackson yelling from behind me, "Come back here!" but I never stop, bashing aside Cresthaven children and lamplighters alike. Every time one approaches, I jam Enivid's pointed tips up through the bottom of their chins, piercing their sinuses and brain cavities at the same time. For every man I kill, there is anger; for every child, there is nausea.

Reaching the ballroom, I see the fire hasn't spread this far yet. A lamplighter approaches to my right and thrusts his torch staff in my direction. I parry the attack, driving the shaft into the floor, splintering the wood, and slicing off his arm at the shoulder. He grips it in shock as he collapses to ground, staring and screaming at the blood spraying from his open body.

As I look across the room, slowly but surely my plan begins to unfold, as I remember the large wooden doors leading out to the foyer, propped open by the iron candelabras. There is no leaving yet. Quickly assimilating what must be done, my gaze passes over the chandeliers, the piano, the tapestries, the curtains, and then the carnage in the hall I just came from. Most of the lamplighters are dead, drained of blood by the Cresthavens.

Cautiously, the remaining children enter the ballroom one by one, with Jackson following last. His one hand dangles loosely at his side while the other holds one of his father's swords. It looks as though Jackson is going to speak, maybe to give some speech of how inferior I am to him, or perhaps to explain to his vampire siblings why most of their family is dead now. Looking up, I see the fire spreading; wavering blue and orange flames stretch along the farthest reaches of the high-vaulted ceiling. There is no doubt the hottest portions of the fire have compromised the integrity of the estate.

With the Cresthavens surrounding me in a circle, it is Jackson who walks to the forefront, the most prominent point. My back is to the grand piano and my thigh brushes its pristine keys. A bland chord of disharmony echoes through the chamber and then fades into silence.

None of the Cresthavens say a word, as if waiting for Jackson to make a command. But a command never comes. He enters the circle instead, eyeing his fellow brood with a serious look, and then focuses on me. He raises his sword, points the tip toward me, and then places the flat of the blade to his forehead, reminding me of the respect given before a duel. I feel like a captive in a gladiator pit, facing off with the notorious outlaw, attempting my chance at freedom.

So be it.

I move away from the piano, placing Enivid between Jackson and myself, and plant my feet, waiting.

In the silence of my surroundings, I close my eye, focusing on the small intricacies that others would not. The smell of burning wood. The heating of stone. The burning of candle wicks. The crackling of fire. The displacement of air. I feel it now—Jackson's approach.

I move forward, letting Enivid loose, smiling as I open my eye, knowing Jackson will evade. The whirling blade flies past him as he moves to the side. Jackson brings his sword to meet me, and just before we collide, I duck, sliding underneath his blade so keen on spilling my blood. The look on his face is one of surprise as I outstretch my hand for Enivid, summoning the blade to me. The energy collects in my palm and, with a terse motion, I flick Enivid, spinning the blade wildly, cutting through the air with speed and precision.

Enivid enters Jackson's chest, right where his heart would be, and bursts out his back. The same look I've seen so many times before, the look of terror and shock, freezes his face. Running up to him, I grip the handle, and in one motion, rip it from his body and sever his head. His body crumples to the floor, and I stand over Jackson as the champion. His death sets the Cresthaven children in motion, advancing on me with outstretched nails and hissing fangs.

Throwing Enivid high into the air, I guide its movement to cut each of the chains holding the chandeliers high above. There is a snap and a groan, and one by one they begin falling.

Leaping over the shortest of the children, I run for the doors, glancing back to see the chandeliers falling on the unsuspecting victims, the oil lamps bursting apart, the fiery wicks igniting the ballroom into a devastating inferno.

Slamming the doors shut, I seal off the exit by bracing the doors with the iron candelabras. My back against wood, I feel the intense heat radiating through the door. Hearing the screams of dying children on the other side, I feel their bodies slamming into the door one by one, trying to escape. But there is no escape. They will burn with their home.

The banging becomes harder, louder, and I scream while holding the door. They try breaking through the wood, but my constitution holds it fast. My mind shuts down and I find myself back in the Cordova Woods at the Danbury hovel. *Michael and his family. The screaming children. Kronklich holding them back.*

I shun the horrible memory but its vivid imagery lingers.

The ride away in the carriage. Smoke rising in the sky.

I shake my head with tears and pain.

Taking a deep breath, I can't help but cough from the smoke entering my lungs. Panting and exhausted, I feel my vision waver. I step away from the door and never look back as I exit the Cresthaven estate for the first and final time.

CHAPTER
XLIII

I FEEL NEITHER JOY NOR sadness as I race away from the Cresthaven estate atop Abel.

The night sky is full of burning fire and awakening townsfolk. Their heads pop from shuttered windows as I pass. It is only a matter of time before they realize what transpired this night, who the Cresthavens were and what their plans were for a new world.

The night is still young as the cold wind whips my face along the dark road back to Councilor's cottage. The thought of the mayhem I encountered, the killing of the children, lingers in my stomach like a heavy stone.

Victoria. Jackson. All those orphaned children, slain by my hands.

But they weren't children were they? I struggle with convincing myself what I did was right. *I did what I had to do. Chop off their heads. Pierce their hearts. Burn their home. I am Tenor Wolfgang, the vampire hunter, the vampire slayer. The bringer of death. I kill those who seek an immortal life. Those who live on a path of darkness. If I did not do it, who else would?*

But as I canter through the wood of whistling snow, lost in my solitude, I can't control my thoughts about Old Man

Dora's words. How destroying vampires disrupts the balance of the world. *They are natural to the world. Vampires were meant to exist.* Cresthaven's words seem to blend into Dora's. A *new line of hope for a better place. A world without disease and famine.* I remember the day when Michael burst from the closet in the hovel, pleading for me to help him and his mother. But there was no helping either of them. The vampire that bit Michael sowed their fate. Images of his tiny fangs sinking deep into his mother's throat plague my thoughts.

There is no control.

I recall Jackson and Victoria tearing into their helpless rabbits, ripping their throats open and drinking their blood. Their innocent faces smeared with the malice of the vampire. How many innocent people had they killed?

There is no control.

I shake my head, clearing my thoughts. What was I thinking?

With the smell of smoke lingering in the air and Westings behind me, I wonder what will become of the town in the years to come. If what Cresthaven said is true, the town will fall into despair and ruin without him.

So be it.

Mankind will find a way. It always does. I finger the small vial of vampire blood at my waist. The blood of Cresthaven. The blood of a father. God be damned, I have wasted so much time here.

Placing a piece of ebon root in my mouth, I wince at the bitter taste. I flick the reins and force Abel into a gallop. I feel his wide frame and strong muscles, somber with speed, moving beneath me, carrying me through desolation. With renewed awareness and dilated vision, my gaze never leaves the dark woods. Always scanning. Always searching.

Judging from the glow through the trees, it will be a while before the new day begins, when the sun breaks over the first peak of the Cordova Mountains, breaching the thick clouds covering this land. It is hard to believe so little time has passed since waiting in the patch of trees, watching for the Cresthavens to arrive.

Rushing through the damp woods of low branches and frozen icicles, my body becomes very aware of the missing fur Councilor gave me earlier. I am left with the cold and my chattering teeth keep me company now.

The remainder of the journey, I can think of nothing but Dorian. He is still alive, hidden somewhere in the town of Walters, out of sight, where no one will ask questions. If the goal of the Carnalreesee is to take him to Sunstone, then they would need him alive indefinitely. How much time do I really have? How much time does he have? The horrible memory of iron spikes driven through his hands flashes through my mind. His precious body, created from my stock, my blood, my bones, and my flesh. It is enough to make me vomit.

Bile rises in my throat.

Damn the Carnalreesee. Damn the Cresthavens. Damn them all to hell.

DAY THIRTEEN

CHAPTER XLIV

EARLY MORNING COMES AS I charge Abel down the snowy slope to Councilor's cottage. Light snow falls through the dense canopy as thick fog rolls along the embankment of the cottage. The mist saturates the rocks and brown grass, dulling what remaining light there is. Everything is the same as yesterday. Gray sky. Moldy wood. Tracks left in the snow days ago have vanished. Smoke rises from the red-brick chimney in great puffs, twirling, dissipating through the gnarled branches of the dark woods.

Guiding Abel to the stable for well-earned hay and water, I can't help staring at the boarded-up window as I pass, beyond which waits the voice I heard two nights before. There is a small glass pane at the bottom looking in, dirtied and stained yellow. *Is there a glow coming from the inside?* I remember the whispers and the eye that stared back at me.

I look away. There is no time to waste wondering.

I barge my way through the front door of Councilor's cottage. The interior is stuffy and warm and full of smoke. The smell of cooking sausage chokes the air with its sweet smell. Councilor, his massive form dressed in black, sits at the table slicing meat. He stops from my intrusion suddenly, sliding his chair across the floor with a groan and pointing his dagger at me. Eyes irritated from the smoke, he lowers his arm and summons a smile while sitting back down. He begins to speak, but I cut him off instantly, dropping the extraction dagger on the table with a bang. I slide the vial of blood across the surface as well and his hand slaps over the tiny glass container before it crashes to the floor.

"The Cresthavens are no more," I say with reserved irritation. "You failed to mention they were a family."

"You killed all of them?" he asks with an air of surprise.

"The medicine," I interrupt again, ignoring his question. "You said you would make him better. Do it." My eye passes over Kronklich's corner, and I can see the spidery veins running along his neck have been kept at bay. I turn around and return into the cold to fetch Abel, hoping the small reprieve of nourishment was enough time. I need to get to Walters as quick as possible.

"Wait," calls Councilor behind me. I hear his chair slide along the floor again but it doesn't prevent me from leaving. I slam the door, exiting. The cold rushes against my face.

"Where are you going?" shouts Councilor behind me, his voice trailing off.

"To find Dorian," I call over my shoulder.

"Dorian? I told you already. There is no way out of the mountains—"

"He's alive and in the town of Walters. I have to go. *Now.*"

"What? How do you know?"

I stop abruptly and face Councilor, wondering if he is truly on my side. "Cresthaven told me."

Councilor's eyes frantically search my one and his visage grows dark. "You shouldn't trust a vampire—"

"It makes sense. Everything he said makes sense," I say, becoming more irritated by the second. The longer Councilor detains me, the longer Dorian suffers at the hands of the Carnalreesee. "Besides," I continue, "vampires will do all they can to preserve their immortality, no matter what the cost. Cresthaven confessed to me moments before I destroyed him."

I pass into the warm interior of the stable and am overwhelmed with the smell of straw and horse. There is a neigh from some part of the barn as I run my hand along Abel's hairy mane. His massive hooves stomp the ground in appreciation as his head passes from trough to hay. *How many horses does Councilor own?*

"So you make to leave now, then?" asks Councilor from the barn's wide archway, his dark silhouette outlined in the morning light.

"I do."

"Walters is a two-day journey northwest of here. There are atters. Bogarts. Murderous ice crows. You will die before you get there. Without proper rest, you are doomed. This includes Abel." Councilor leans against the frame. "I cannot allow it."

My hand tightens on Abel's reins and bridle. I stroke the side of his face.

"Nothing will come between me and my son ever again," I say, grinding the Ebon root between my teeth, remembering the Cresthavens, and remembering Councilor's demand for his blood. I turn around to face the massive form of Councilor. He looks even more menacing than yesterday. "Not even you."

Instead of a stern look, a faint smile cracks under Councilor's bushy beard and his eyes brighten with ambition. "Well, since I can't persuade you not to go, the least I can do is offer you better accommodations." He moves past me toward the back of the stable, disappearing into the shadows where no lamp glows. "Here," he says, emerging from the shadows with tether in hand. "Take Jasmine. She will be your guide through the forest. Sleek and ridged, she is no stranger to speed. However, I must warn you to stay to the road. Do not veer from the path. Where she thrives in speed, she suffers in constitution. Unlike Abel, she is not attuned to the thick snow. We've made the run to Walters countless times. With her speed, it should take you a day and a half."

He hands me the reins, and Jasmine shakes her head and neighs. Muscular and slim, her jet-black coat shines in the light of the dismal morning. Nuzzling my hand, she nips one of my fingers, drawing blood.

"There, you see. You two are acquainted." Councilor turns and leaves, shouting over his shoulder. "See me before you set off."

Alone in the stable with Jasmine, I feel a sense of tension between us. Her dark eyes focus on me with an intensity I have not seen in a very long time. The look from my father, Bealeon. It's strange thinking of him at a time like this, his having died so many years ago right after Dorian turned the age of seven. He wanted to see him grow into a strong obedient grandson unlike his own son, one who would follow the unbending traditions of the Wolfgangs. What does it matter now? He's dead.

Fastening saddle and bags to Jasmine, I stroke her short-cropped mane, and she responds by trying to bite me again. *So much like my father.* She is impatient and ill-tempered, yet resolute and strong. Patting Abel's face one last time, I sigh, thanking him silently for all his help as I lead Jasmine from the stable and out into the snow.

"Food for the journey." Councilor tosses me a bundle of cloth. "Some sausages and bread. It's not much, but it will keep your insides warm."

I stuff the rations into the saddlebags next to the flint rocks and torches, accepting Councilor's gesture as a sign of good faith. With one foot in the stirrup, the leather groans as I mount Jasmine. She whinnies in protest, stomping the ground irritably. Stroking the back of her neck does nothing to ease her.

Councilor smiles, placing his hands over her ears. "Easy, girl. He doesn't bite. Not like me."

The morning is still early as the snow falls thicker and heavier. I brush a layer of snow from my shoulders as Councilor drones on about the treacherous countryside.

"Remember what I said. Stay to the path and you should be there more quickly than you know. We'll be right behind you."

I pause at these last words and stare at him in confusion.

He continues, "You shouldn't go alone. In two days' time, we will come to help. Besides, I'll be needing Jasmine back after you're done."

"What about Kronklich?" I ask, concerned for his recovery.

"Don't worry about your friend. He may be a doctor and hunter, but he's in better hands with me."

I'm not so sure about that.

I nod to him for now, conceding to his whims, for with every second that passes, the wind picks up. Already I envy their stay in the warm cottage as I think about what lies ahead. *I will have to trust Councilor for now. Kronklich's life depends on it.*

Councilor tosses another bundle of cloth at me, but this time it isn't food. «Try not to lose this one."

I unroll the thick black cloak made of cotton and leather. The inside is soft and the outside is sleek, perfect for repelling water and applying vitrol.

"Thanks," I say, bringing the horse around. Something doesn't feel right as I adjust to Jasmine's rigid back. For a moment, the same uneasiness falls over me, the feeling from before and the other night, that someone is watching me. Turning about, my gaze falls over the cottage one last time, its smoke whipping to and fro from the increasing wind. Red-brick chimney and decaying grout. Something moves in the small of the window below the planks of wood. It was a face, I'm sure of it this time. Before I can really focus on it, the image is gone, and the light that once emitted from within no longer burns.

"No time to waste, then. Off you go," says Councilor, slapping Jasmine's rear and sending her into a sudden gallop.

CHAPTER
XLV

HOURS PASS IN SILENCE AS we race along the frozen path along
the outskirts of the Decameron Forest. Riding close to its edge
is like passing through an ice cave, a fine line between light and
darkness. A forest—still as the dead, teeming with potential
energy. Ducking below bowing branches, I avoid sharp icicles
as best I can while still breaking some as my shoulders pass.
We stop seldom to rest, keeping the pace grueling, for, within
this desolate countryside of icy woods and jagged rocks, death
waits in the hills to take those who linger. Death follows me
everywhere now, watching me like the ice crows in trees.

The cold is biting. So cold in fact, it is enough to cut down
the strongest of soldiers of the strongest armies. It creeps through
all the vulnerable areas of my skin, chilling me further. I tighten
the black mask sown into the cloak over my face. Undoubtedly,
I am thankful for Councilor's support, his meager yet generous
offerings of aid.

Yet my thoughts stir about his intentions as we slow to a trot
along a patch of cobblestone. A pair of atters scamper up a frozen
tree. The request for Cresthaven's blood. What was he planning
to do with it? And why did he linger so far out in the countryside

away from civilization not having access to more comfortable means of living? What sort of thing was he harboring in that godforsaken cottage? A secret that no man can know.

Midday arrives as I start to feel the effects of the ebon root wearing off. My stomach growls in protest but I dare not stop. There is no time to think of hunger, for hunger is weakness. I sense Jasmine feels the same way. She is a good horse. Councilor was right. She is unbending and resolute. A force of strong will despite her constant effort to bite me. She knows these woods better than I do, so I let her lead as I did Abel.

While I grind another piece of ebon root between my teeth my senses burst to life as the juice seeps into my blood. It rushes through my body with the familiar tingling sensation, passing through my limbs, warming my fingers and toes. I recall the nightmare stories again of those who abuse the drug throughout their life, wondering if the same will happen to me. But the thought dissipates quickly as I think about Dorian.

Despite my heated fervor to arrive in Walters earlier than intended, we come to an arched bridge covered in white powder. Jasmine slows her pace as we approach, and I can only imagine she's passed this place hundreds of times. Icicles hang from its underbelly like the jagged teeth of a hideous dragon. Sauntering up to its sloped surface, Jasmine suddenly stops before setting a foot onto the iced-over cobblestones. She stamps her foot and snorts in protest, denying my urge to cross.

I guess here is good as any place to rest.

Boots slipping out of the stirrups, I land in the soft snow with a crunch. With the wind driving hard out of the northwest, my cloak snaps with each tumbling fold. I stare out along the horizon, surveying the dull gray sky before setting foot on the dilapidated bridge. Uneven stones connect to one another through mortar and pebble, forming an uneven ground. I admire its simple craftsmanship as I move to its center, tethering Jasmine behind me. My eye focuses on the tree line across the snowy plain, the place we will eventually continue through. In the distance, there is the howl of a wolf, but it doesn't faze me in the least. Taking a deep chilly breath, I look at the ground where my boots currently crush something into the snow. Examining it closer, I notice bits of broken ice scattered amongst the remnants of yellow moths. They are inanimate and layed about the bridge in some strange fashion. Wings and legs strategically placed. A sign of some sort? My mind races at the thought of Diana and my heart pounds. What is this? A disturbance in the nearby brush breaks my concentration as a blue fox emerges onto the path, its tongue slightly hanging out. I smile to myself as my hand instinctively passes over Enivid. She is always with me. Thank you, Diana.

There is the caw of a crow suddenly and I flinch, backing away from the side of the bridge. My hand rests over Enivid as I look for others. But there is only one ice crow. Feet tapping across the stone railing, the bird hops once, then twice, closer to me, moving its head side to side, watching me with its cruel blue eye. I raise Enivid to kill the blasted thing, but it drops off the side of the bridge without warning. No longer in sight, I hear its long drawn out caw droning below. I rush to the railing to follow through with my attack, but the crow is gone, vanished upstream into the woods. Damn it. My eye scans my surroundings. *How many more are there?* I notice something moving underneath the ice of the river and shiver from what I see. Faces staring up at the gray sky. Hallow and sunken. Their eyes have puffy complexions through the gray ice. Contorted faces of women and children and the elderly. Where were the men? Why were they in this river of death? Seeing the clothing of black furs and insulated coats, I recognize their attire as gypsies. Their dead bodies press against the ice as they slowly float upstream into the unknown of Decameron Forest. The evil of Cordova Mountains has claimed more lives. Nowhere is safe; that is for certain.

Standing quiet and alone on the bridge with Jasmine, I push back the hood of my cloak, raking my gloved hand through my hair. The cold soothes my burning scalp as I contemplate the ongoing atrocities. Evil will never be over. I shake my head, clicking with my tongue, "Come on, girl."

Our journey is far from over as the daylight eventually wanes. Westerly and north we move on, crossing dried-up ravines and dropping into short valleys. The path snakes and dips, rises and falls, and eventually, a blizzard stirs. It was a while ago I replaced the hood for my head and the mask for my face. I cannot pull them any tighter now. My stomach growls late in the day and I know nightfall isn't far. Rummaging through the saddlebags, I find the pouch full of ebon root and take another piece out. Again, I think of the consequences of using the drug, the addiction that can come later, the dependency that has wasted so many men and women in the past. But there is no choice. Eating is not an option at the moment. We have to go as far as we can before nightfall claims us. But as I place the ebon root to my lips, Jasmine staggers and the root falls from hand. Looking up, ready to scold her for the folly, I find we are engulfed in a blizzard of white snow. Harsh wind and pelting sleet bombard us. I feel Jasmine's muscles contracting beneath me, straining to keep her balance. I lean forward, hugging her neck, limiting the wind resistance for the both of us as I nudge her on, trying to keep sight of where the trees meet the sky. But they are gone.

The snowstorm engulfs us like a raging bear, slamming ice and rocks at our skin. I cover my brow, straining to see, but the white glare is everywhere.

"Dammit," I say through pursed lips, trying to keep as much warmth inside my body as possible. Jasmine neighs and snorts in disapproval as I press her forward, snapping the reins and kicking her sides. It is a struggle battling with the snow, the wind, and her. Ever present is her stubbornness; she staggers again, nearly knocking me from her back. I can tell she has lost the trail. I pull hard to the left, trying to help guide her through as if I knew where we were going, but it is a lost cause. Neither one of us knows where we are.

"Come on, girl! Hya!" Squeezing her sides, she bucks wildly, kicking her hind legs free of the thick snow, and then, as if realizing for the first time, she succumbs to my wishes by veering off to the left. We stagger out of the headwind on an angle and I feel my cloak flapping violently behind me. Not knowing where to go, we stay the course, for there is nothing we can do but move forward. If we stay in the storm and try to find the path again, we will be buried alive.

Dark-gray shadows appear overhead as we part a path through the snow, one hoof at a time. I nudge Jasmine on further, snapping the reins and yelling, but my voice is lost to the vortex of the wind. More shadows appear as the light begins to diminish at a rapid rate. I recognize the shadows as stony crags and realize we must be close to a hill or a mountainside. "Forward, girl, come on! Hya!"

The wind and snow suddenly dies out as we gallop into a vast opening in the side of the mountain. It is a gorge-like hole reaching to heights unknown. I slow Jasmine to a trot as we explore the newfound sanctuary full of bluish stalagmites and black ice. Twirling wisps of snow whip from the outside as I admire the massive cave. Whistling air blowing against my back, I dismount, brushing away the thick snow from Jasmine's mane, my attempt at restoring her warmth. She seems contented by my actions, but I feel her body tremble under my hand.

The inside of the cave is dark and dank, an improvement from moments ago. With hardly any light, I procure a torch and flint from the saddlebags and begin hammering away with a rock. As the torch springs to life, a new world unfolds before me. The cave is not just a cut out from the mountain, but a vast subterranean passage moving through the mountain. The distance is beyond the range of my fire. The yellow and orange light contrasts with the bluish hues of the thick icicles at the mouth of the cave. Waving the torch back and forth, I move about the chamber in search of hibernating animals, or worse, creatures of the night, but I find it desolate, devoid of any life. "So much for making time," I say to myself, misting the air with my breath. I stare out into the fading light of the blizzard, wondering how anyone could live out here, and then remember the dead gypsies floating under the ice. They didn't make it. I wonder what my chances are at finding the path again. The snow is already packing thick, up to my hips in some places. Councilor's words echo at the back of my mind, *whatever you do, don't veer from the path.* I run my hand over my face. "We'll sleep here tonight," I say to Jasmine as I turn to collect her and our things.

But as I move toward her, something catches my eye, something I didn't notice before. A reflection of light caused by the glare of my torch. A glint of steel.

Spreading some oats over a nearby rock, I leave Jasmine to eat as I investigate. I see the shimmer of light refracting more prominently as I quickly approach, shivering, dropping to my hands and knees, and lowering the torch to the hissing snow. Running my gloved hand over the white powder, I reveal raised metal bars running in long segments toward the deep dark unknown of the cave. Frantically, I pass my hand back and forth, uncovering more of the steel, until I stop in disbelief from what I discover.

Train tracks.

CHAPTER XLVI

The Iron Carriage.

The horrible memory of the train wreck comes rushing back to me in a terrible flash. The stress. The pain. The massive wall of ice the locomotive struck at high speed. The derailing and all the death and destruction that came with it.

I shiver, standing in the cold of the cave, wondering what sort of atrocities wait for me in the dark beyond. Should I follow the tracks? There was a reason why the train wasn't used during the winter portions of the year. The snowfalls, the avalanches, the glaciers. Despite these dangerous conditions and the path on the outside lost to the blizzard, I know there is no choice but to follow the tracks. And if these were indeed the tracks of the Iron Carriage, then they would lead me straight to the one place I needed to go, for the train ran through all the major towns in the Cordova Mountains. Of course, from Delore, the next stop would have been Walters, and the realization sinks in like a heavy weight.

Gathering Jasmine with renewed hope, I grab her reins and lead her into the darkness of the mountain. Maybe there was time to make up after all. Turning my back to the storm outside, I follow the tracks of the Iron Carriage on foot, leading Jasmine close behind me. As we go, traversing the massive corridor of howling wind is like standing in the presence of the train itself, a roaring steam engine passing by us, pumping its pistons and wailing its whistle. My torch flickers wildly from the breeze and I fear it will burn out before we reach the other side. Too much oxygen, too little fuel. To be lost in the deep dark without light is surely a death sentence. The memory of Egleaseon's ruins comes back to haunt me, when I fell from the clock corridor, down the dark pit of pitch black.

We must keep going.

At times, I lose sight of the steel rails, and find myself on hands and knees more often than not, heart pounding and stressed, wondering if the tracks are real. The determination to get to my son is all I care about. My mind could easily betray me, trick me into believing what is real or not, or perhaps, the evil mountain is to blame, influencing me the same as the Faust River. My head spins with uncertainty, and so I press harder, faster with the reins, pulling Jasmine in a demanding way. *I'm sorry, girl.*

The familiar aches of hunger return and I curse myself for being human. I know if we don't stop to eat, our energy levels will deplete and our body temperatures will drop. I look at Jasmine behind me and can hardly see her outline in the suffocating dark. *Just a little more, girl.*

The wind dies down as the tunnel bends to the right. With the torch returning to its steady burn, I am able to see more of the cavernous tunnel and nearly choke from my underestimation of how large it really is. Holding the flame as high as I can, shoulder aching and burning from muscle strain, the top of the cave is full of glistening pointed teeth. Long bulging stalactites riddle the ceiling like frozen hair follicles. With them overhead and my energy waning, I imagine myself inside a monster's belly. The screech of bats echoing in the distance adds to my anxiety. A loud sound might trigger them to frenzy. There might be hundreds of them, possibly thousands.

Time passes endlessly.

Walking has no end. I am not sure how much of the night has passed, but hunger pulls at my bones, and my feet ache. Coming to a rocky outcrop, it glows in the dark where the train tracks pass through a narrow portion of the tunnel. The source of the light is a luminescent fungus known as everglow, a rare lichen capable of emitting low-frequency light in the darkest of places. For such a phenomenon to grow here is extraordinary, but not surprising, for the mosses in these mountains are no doubt corrupted by the evils of Egleaseon's ruin.

Staring at the bluish light, I notice patches of eyestalks lining the cracks in the rock. There is a wall forming a sheer surface, perfect for leaning against and keeping our flanks protected. The brown mucous appendages sway in my direction as if triggered by my presence. I ignore their invasive stares, wondering how these abominations can live even in the harsh cold. I crush a few of them with my fist and toss their jelly residue onto to the spot intended for the fire. During our walk, I managed to collect old bits of cloth and pieces of wood discarded from the train during its previous transits. It is enough to make a substantial fire, and I am more than willing to take the risk.

The heat warms my bones and I feel Jasmine appreciates it the same. Placing a full sack of hay along the ground, I let her graze as I warm the sausages and break apart the bread. Easing myself to the ground, I stare into the fire as the sounds all around us seem to amplify while we rest, listening to the many noises— the squeaking of bats, the groans of ice, and at one point, an owl. Wrapping my cloak tighter around me, I ravage my meal with a hunger like never before. The cold depletes the body more so than any hunt or battle.

I doze for a bit, only to wake to the sounds of whispers. I get up, stretching my legs, and search the surrounding camp for hostility, but content myself with the idea the noises were nothing. The ice continues to creak and the occasional pebble falls somewhere in the distance. I sit back down, content with much-needed rest. I watch Jasmine as she chews away at her meal, and again, I am reminded of my father because of her, although I now realize she is nowhere near as stubborn, after what we've been through.

Bealeon. My father. What a fool he was. A fool like his father before him, Zander, my grandfather. I find myself thinking

502 | F.D. Gross

back on my heritage hundreds and hundreds of years ago, back from the days when the house of Wolfgang was more than just hunters of vampires. How time has led us astray. I remember the heirlooms in my home, the ones that burned away with the memories of my beloved wife, Diana. The trophies that once stood for something, a sense of purpose and accomplishment, now reduced to rubble and ash. Other creatures throughout the world were hunted in those times, each member of the house specializing in their monster. That of the minotaurs and the willdermen, the bogarts and the medusa. My ancestors hunted all sorts of monsters in those ancient times. But it wasn't until three hundred years ago the Wolfgang family ceased hunting these creatures altogether to refocus and hunt the vampire solely. For the time had come that vampires had grown out of control and their power exceeded beyond the balance.

Although Egleaseon had been around for centuries—no one really knows how long for sure—it wasn't until three hundred years ago he was recognized by his fellow brood as lord of the vampires, his position possibly imposed by his own accord, or through the sheer malice and power he demonstrated openly. His influence increased greatly and there was great woe over the land. The country of Ashton changed forever because of it, suffering at the hands of Egleaseon. Humans died while vampires rose. The way of life had changed, and fear was the only normality humans knew moving forward. The great change took place then, enough to influence the house of Wolfgang, and so all monster hunting ceased except for the one. That of the vampire. But during the time of transition and sworn oaths to destroy Egleaseon, none of my forefathers succeeded. Zander Bealeon Wolfgang. Bealeon Tenor Wolfgang. All of the ones before them. They all died trying to destroy Egleaseon.

I take a drink from my waterskin, giving my mind a break as I stare at the fire. The cool water trickles down my throat and into my stomach, soothing my innards of the digesting sausage and bread.

Thoughts of Egleaseon come swarming back to me. The battles we fought and the sacrifices I made still haunt me to this day. So many near misses. So many chances when he could have taken my life, yet here I am alive, having escaped each encounter, unlike the others before me. Was I special in some way? Or perhaps Egleaseon devised some other plan, sparing my life so that I could make more hunters like myself for him to hunt and continue the vicious cycle?

How indulgent. How evil and destructive such a thing was. And for it, I loathed Egleaseon. I made a pact with myself that I would do all in my power to destroy him and his cursed bloodline. So I looked to the church for guidance, inquiring about ways to gain advantage over the vampire horde in any way possible. It was the Archbishop Faeradon who knew of an artifact long lost through the ages, a relic highly sought after for the church, and that I could be the one to get it.

For years, accompanied by Bronin, we sought out the ancient relic that could destroy a vampire by the mere touch of it, the Hand of God, and eventually found it buried in a tomb below the catacombs of an ancient church long forgotten. Who had put it there, no one knew. With the weapon in our possession, vampires would cower in the night and fear the power of humans once again. After years of searching and discovering the wonder of the world, we returned home as honored and distinguished aristocrats. I was marked as a noble of high esteem, and Bronin was made a holy priest, next in line for bishop.

Word spread.

Rumors traveled over the land.

After a time, I received the red letter, the invitation signed in blood by Egleaseon himself, saying to come see him at his castle: "Bring the Hand of God to me so that I can commune with it and see firsthand its true power and glory." I was of course surprised by this request and so consulted Bronin about it. He expressed caution and vowed to travel with me to ensure my safety and sanctity with the audience of the most powerful vampire history has ever seen.

The screech of a bat startles me from my nostalgia.

Looking up, I see Jasmine stamping the ground with a slight neigh, shaking her mane and whipping her tail about. "Easy, girl," I say, never moving from my spot. My body is drowsy from the food and I ache all over. Clearly, the effects of the ebon root have worn off.

Still though, as my mind journeys in and out of consciousness, I wonder about Egleaseon and his brash decision to accept the Hand of God from me. His action was suicidal. Why sacrifice all those years of immortality for a few moments to be human?

As I finally disappear into the land of sleep, my lasting images of Egleaseon are that of his smiling face disintegrating into a pile of dust.

DAY FOURTEEN

CHAPTER
XLVII

LAST NIGHT WAS ENDLESS. A sleepless night full of sudden awakenings. Shadows danced about the circle of firelight, taunting me. Pebbles echoed in the distance. Bats rustled their wings.

Yet there is hope riding through the infinite blackness. A dismal light appears at the end of the tunnel.

I see it beyond the infinite darkness, beyond the stalagmites and stalactites, beyond the frozen icicles of death, beyond the eyestalks and crystal lichen glowing in the dark. Never did I think I would see the end of this everlasting night, riding ominously on, galloping across echoing stones forever.

My face burns from the wind as we ride faster, gaining more speed until we burst from the cavernous mouth like a cloud of billowing smoke. In the distance, I see the path of the train tracks, pronounced in the snow with their steel prongs cracking through the black ice.

Within seconds, we merge onto the path like black shadows with nowhere to hide from the day, racing along the forest's edge of murderous crows and deadly atters. In the distance, I hear their caws and chirps rising from the canopy as if waiting for us, knowing we would come this way. The animals of the forest give chase, emerging from their shadows of hiding, disturbing the snow caked on branches.

It is now a race for Walters.

Although it is day, the horizon is dark and bleak. Foreboding with all of its malice. It is a sign perhaps. A sign I may be out of time. Although the beasts of the forest chase me, it is Time that is my true enemy.

"Hya!" I shout over the swaying branches and leaves, cracking the reins and motioning Jasmine to leap over fallen trees. It's as if the entirety of Decameron Forest is after us. The crows swoop down on me and the atters nip at Jasmine. Is there no end to the madness? Egleaseon still holds sway over the land. How can it be, even though he is dead?

Standing in the stirrups, I ready Enivid in my free hand as the foul creatures dip closer and closer. *Come on, Jasmine, keep it up, girl. Get us to Walters and I will handle the rest.*

Jasmine whinnies loudly as she careens to the left, leaping over the exposed tracks in the snow, continuing her hellish pace. A pair of crows dive toward my head and I rake Enivid through the air, tearing one through its wing while the other spirals off, ducking back into the tree line. Plumes of glistening snow kick up behind as we run faster and faster. A pack of atters converge on the tracks ahead of us. They gather before our approach, thinning out their ranks to form a long line, a sort of barrier to prevent us from crossing.

Snapping black teeth and razor-sharp claws soar past my face as the atters leap into the air. A wave of black wrinkled skin, white eyes, and rancid stench look to unsaddle me from atop Jasmine. Startled by their actions, I adjust, lowering my torso and following through with slashes. I hack through the frigid air with disgust, remembering the atter's place of origin and filth, creatures from the unsanitary places of the world. I remember the peddler in Widow chopping up dead atters to sell in the market. The smell from acidic rain and pungent squirrel meat wafting through the town was enough to make even the hungriest of men choose death by starvation.

Over and over, I cut them down, splitting them in half, severing their heads, and spraying their blood across the snow. Some of the atters land on Jasmine's flank, digging their filthy claws into her backside, peeling up skin, and clamping down on her mane. I feel her muscles tense beneath as she shutters in protest. I do what I can to sweep them from her backside with my bracer, brushing them off like spurs from a grassy field.

Jasmine presses harder, galloping ferociously as another murder of ice crows descends on us from the clouds above. Like blue devils retreating from heaven, they swoop and dive, missing Jasmine's head, trying to gouge her eyes out like they did mine. They are smart and evil and they know it.

Jasmine whinnies again as some of the crows sink their talons into her neck. Pulling the reins hard to the right, I force her head to follow, guiding her back over the tracks in a zigzag motion. Mouth frothing and gums exposed, she reaches with her teeth, despite the bridle, and bites down on a crow in mid-flight. There is a loud *squawk* as blood spatters the snow.

I am startled by Jasmine's actions, yet she carries on as if cannibalizing another animal were normal. Moving back and forth over the rails, the tactic, although unorthodox, seems to work, for they stop giving chase instantaneously. Strange behavior on their part. It sets me to wonder whether our actions or the receding line of the forest have something to do with it. I cannot say, but I am grateful nonetheless.

How much time has passed? How much of the day were we in the tunnel?

The question lingers on the edge of my mind as we slow to a trot. The gray skyline bends into an infallible darkness on the horizon as the ground begins to curve down into a sharp descent. The decline is steep, yet Jasmine calms despite the wounds on her back. Within moments I understand why.

In the distance, dark spiraling rooftops sprout from the rising mist like fingers of a black knight's gauntlet.

The first signs of Walters.

It sits nestled at the bottom of a domed valley, lying quiet and desolate in the distance like a great open palm waiting to crush the life from those foolish enough to enter.

And so we enter.

Patting the side of Jasmine's neck, we descend along the center of the tracks, never crossing the rails on either side, as if passing the boundaries might summon the crows and the atters to us again.

"Thank you," I say softly in Jasmine's ear, flicking the reins lightly, encouraging her to press on a little faster.

Darkness comes quickly. Too quickly.

We gallop into the outskirts of Walters, solemn and gray, passing busy patrons roaming busy streets, and lamplighters reaching with their long staffs to light lampposts bedazzled with black iron crows at their crest. *How fitting.*

Dusk lingers like a poisonous cloud ready to consume all things. We charge forward, eventually breaking from the tracks that served as our guide, and into the long streets of town with charcoal three-story buildings rising on either side. Similar to the townsfolk in Delore, the people of Walters in their mono-color scheme of black carry on with their final chores of the day. The orange glow from the iron-crow lamps reflects off the patches of ice along the foundations of the buildings, illuminating them like great floating ships at the edge of a lake.

I wonder what the people think as we pass. Their heads turn to stare up at the stranger, disheveled and rugged, dressed in a black mask, cowl, cloak, and coat, riding atop a jet black mare, I sitting taller than any man in town. My weapons hidden, I ensure they stay that way to not draw more attention to myself. Already the strange looks are subtle yet obvious. We canter along the wide road, kicking up snow and splashing through muddied ruts.

Drawing Jasmine to a halt, I single out a middle-aged man wearing a short black cap and carrying a crate full of timber. The lumber looks excessive for his age, yet I pay no mind, addressing him in the most formal of ways. "Excuse me, sir, I am Lord—" I stop myself short just as the man looks up at me, squinting in the steady snowfall.

"Whas 'at?" says the man. "I'm a bit 'ard o' 'earing."

I have his full attention, yet realize something I should have thought of before. The Carnalreesee might be influencing this town. There is no way of knowing as of yet.

I stare down at the aged man from atop Jasmine. He looks feeble, innocent, and by the sound of his words, unaffiliated. "My apologies, sir. I was wondering if you've seen an adolescent boy. Blond hair, dark eyes, about this tall." I hold my hand out, demonstrating Dorian's height.

The man, with his salt-and-pepper beard, throws down the box and removes the cap from his head, scratching his receding hairline. He looks at me with a confused expression.

"Now thas a fancy word, ado-lee-sent," says the man, sounding the word out. "You men one of 'em sqwakin' boys? " The man leans on his hip and glares at me, then turns his attention down the street as if searching. "Can't say that I hev. Meh, I've been a' roaming the outskirts o' town, clearing them there land for Misses Tumlings to move in. She plans on building that house sooner than ya think."

It is clear the man doesn't know who I am but assumes I know the town's business. I push my luck. "Are you sure, friend? It is a pressing matter I find this boy before nightfall. His mother is worried sick and I promised to have him back by now." A memory comes back to me, when I saw Diana at the Rotunda in Egleaseon's ruins, how she urged me to look for our son and never give up, no matter the cost. I am doing just that. I feel the warmth of Enivid on my hip.

"What are ya, some sort of babysitter?" He pauses and looks at me keenly. "Nah. Yer one of 'em bounty hunter folks, coming to this 'er town like the others. Well, I say good luck. I ain't want no part."

The others? Bounty hunters? Did he mean the Carnalreesee? Or was he referring to my attire? There is no doubt I resemble a Black Blade.

"Your kind never lasts 'ere, 'em bounty hunter folks. Bah. I'd be gitten lost while ya still can," finishes the man as he bends down, lifts his crate of wood, and walks away.

Sitting atop Jasmine, I realize how much attention I'm drawing to myself. People are staring. I dismount, taking Jasmine's reins in my palm and leading her without direction through the streets of Walters. If I was marked as a bounty hunter, at least my true identity wasn't discovered.

We walk for a while as night besieges the town like death lowering its dark veil, snuffing out all life. Soon, the light of candles glows in doorways and windows as townsfolk close up their shops and shovel snow from their cobblestone steps. For now, more glaring stares are thrown our way. Windows fill with wrinkled faces and pursed lips. I pretend to mind my business as best I can, staring straight ahead, watching the flickering lamps glow on the street, but find it hard not to survey the town from the corner of my eye.

The streets of Walters are like a maze. We turn from one alley to another, passing under bridges, only to come about full circle. *I know we've been down this street already.* I stop. *Wait, have we?*

Shouting comes from a building directly across from where we've stopped, and so I stare from under my hood at its dingy yellow light wavering from the inside. The smell of sweet bread carries its way out onto the street, causing my taste buds to tingle. Looking up, I read the sign hanging outside the doorway: *Reyes' Baked Goods.*

There is a loud crash and the breaking of glass before I make out a coherent voice from within. "Goddamn it! How many times do I have to tell you not to use so much goddamn flour? This stuff doesn't come cheap! There's so much flour on the ground I slipped on it! You're trying to kill me!"

Licking my cracked lips, the inside looks warm and inviting. *Just a loaf of bread and I'll be on my way.*

I step into the shop, where the air is thick with heat and agitation. Row after row of bread loaves line the low-bearing shelves underneath a long wooden counter dividing the front of the shop from the rear. Immediately, my eye falls on the source of the screaming, and I wonder if this was a good idea. A short, stocky man with black flat-cropped hair stands in a doorway at the rear of the shop with his back to me. Gripping the doorframe with one hand, the man shakes a large meaty fist with the other to some unseen person beyond the dim light.

"Goddamn. Can't do anything right—" continues the heated man as he turns about, stopping in mid-sentence, startled by my appearance. If his hair is black, then his eyebrows are even darker. That, coupled with his stone-cold blue eyes contrasting with his tanned skin, the man's appearance is distracting and unnerving, and for a lack of better words—odd. He doesn't seem the least bit happy to see me standing in his shop.

"What the hell is this!" he says, pointing his hand at me in question. "A goddamn freak show. Can't anybody read signs around here?" The man points to the door beside me, and stares at it in disgust. "Ugghhh!" he grunts, wiping his sweaty face with his sausage-sized hand. "Hector, you ass, you didn't put the goddamn sign out!" The baker barking orders, who I assume is Reyes, shakes his head in defeat and looks back at me. "I guess it's your lucky day, freak show. What the hell do you want?"

My gaze never leaves him as I move about the shop, taking in the many fragrances I sampled from outside. My eye darts among the loaves of bread, admiring their textures and crusts. I notice him staring at my missing eye.

"Listen, freak show. I'm not running a sight-seeing charity tour here, nor is it a place to warm your ass. The shop's closed, remember? Hurry up and pick something."

"Don't call me that," I say, making my selection of a loaf covered in poppy seeds; I feel no warmth radiating from it and the consistency is stiff. I chance a look behind the counter, into the doorway, beyond which the mysterious Hector lingers somewhere, but I can see only an empty room. "And, the bread is hard as a stone," I finish, glancing back at the baker man, who is watching my every move.

"Listen here, freak show," says the baker man shaking a finger. "You're the one who came in here all dressed in black and with a mask. If you don't like it, then piss off."

Keeping my anger in check, I ignore his childish behavior and move to stand directly in front of him at the counter. I look down at his sweat-covered forehead—he stands about a foot shorter than me—and simply say, "This will do," dropping the cold loaf of bread on the counter. I enjoy bringing agitation to this man with every gesture I make. I cannot explain it. I just do. And as for the bread, it doesn't matter which loaf I choose. They are all stale and cold.

The counter rings with the sound of a copper dauntess as the baker's eyes suddenly flare to life. "It's two dauntess for a poppy-seed loaf!" he says, folding his arms and puffing his chest. My eye passes over him, searching for the mark of the Carnalreesee on his wrists and forearms, the X with the line down its center. But before I search all of his skin, he unfolds his arms and leans on the counter toward me.

"Hey, buddy. Are you deaf?"

Focusing on his face, I notice him staring at my missing eye again. The kind of look when someone stares straight at you and doesn't stop staring.

"I'm not paying two dauntess for this bread," I say, picking up the loaf and standing straight. "It's stale. Besides, your shop is closed and you will throw the rest of the bread in the alley before you leave tonight. Consider this your lucky day." As I turn to leave, I recognize the familiar deep-chested rumble that could only be laughter. Moving toward the door, the man calls after me.

"You're a crazy bastard, aren't you?" says the baker man behind me between fits of laughter. "No one's ever had the balls to talk to me like that before!"

Realizing I might have just made an acquaintance in this godforsaken town, I turn to face him and approach with renewed hope, smiling.

"You're a dark and scary bastard, aren't you? What goddamn rock did you climb out from under?"

"I'm looking for a boy," I say, considering the words I used before, remembering my encounter with the peddler. "A teenage boy, about this tall. Hair blond and eyes black like his mother's."

The baker man eyes me with a cold stare, furrowing his brow and scrunching his nose. "What are you, his babysitter?" He lets out a hearty laugh before controlling himself again. "Couldn't help it. You one of them bounty hunters or something?"

"What if I were?"

"Then I'd say you're a cracked loon. I hear there are certain folks in town that aren't taken to bounty hunters. Best watch your back, friend."

I consider his words. "I need to know about the boy."

"Easy, friend. I was just saying. But no, I haven't seen anyone with that description." He grabs a rag and begins wiping down the counter. "I don't get it. You're after a boy? What for?"

"His mother hired me to find him. She's worried sick."

"If he's a teenage boy, let him be. He probably left because he wanted to. No harm in searching out your own life."

"It's not that. His mother is worried about the monsters roaming these parts. She fears she'll never see him again."

The baker man slaps both hands on the counter and leans forward again. Spit nearly flies from his mouth. "Monsters! Bahh!" He waves his hand in an offensive gesture. "Always the monsters. Goblins. Ghosts. Vampires. Ghouls. I've heard them all! When will you people get it in your heads these things don't exist! Goddamn it."

I wonder if this man has ever left this town before as he continues ranting.

"Next thing you're going to tell me is that there are werewolves right?"

Obviously, he's never been to the south.

The baker man bursts into another fit of laughter as I realize I'm wasting my time. I turn to leave and hear him calling to the unseen worker in the back. "Hey, Hector. You hear that? We got ourselves a monster hunter."

Slamming the door behind me, I welcome back the frigid cold over the dingy stuffiness of Reyes' shop and his muffled poisonous laughter coming from within. Somewhat perturbed over the baker's ignorance, I ostracize myself for wasting time. Not only that, but now there was one more person who knew of my presence. One more person who knew too much. Tired and stomach growling, my mind wonders about the "certain folks that aren't taken to bounty hunters" as I stare down at the rock-hard bread in my hands.

A cold wind blows through the fork in the street, whistling through the iron lampposts and awnings, pushing my cloak aside. With hardly anyone walking the streets at night, I wonder whether my continued efforts searching for Dorian will be in vain. Raising the cold bread to lips, my vain thoughts become reality when I see two hooded figures moving rapidly across the road far off in the distance. One shorter than the other, they dart from the street as if one is chasing the other. A lock of golden hair trails from the hood of the shorter one as both figures disappear into the alley.

CHAPTER
XLVIII

THE LOAF OF BREAD DROPS from my hand like a stone. Running past Jasmine without a moment to spare, I do all I can to keep sight of the two cloaked figures disappearing into the alley.

A wisp of golden hair. Same height. Same shape. A cold shiver runs through my body. Someone is chasing Dorian. Some demon, or worse, a Carnalreesee.

Cold air rushes into my lungs as I charge down the center of the snow-covered street. Passing the iron-crow lampposts, they look down at me from their perches as if ready to attack. I chase after the ominous figure running after Dorian, and it is fast. Skidding to a halt at the edge of the alley, I peer down its lengthy narrowness, catching a glimpse of the figures disappearing down another passage. Looking back at Jasmine for a brief moment, I know she will be all right. She can take care of herself.

I turn, darting into the narrow darkness of stench and rats. I run full speed down the corridor, heart pounding in my chest. With the cobblestone buildings packed neatly together, I feel as if I'm in the train tunnel again, navigating the endless dark. The walls feel like they are closing in on me as I search every angle the alley has to offer. Yet I am afforded nothing. No clue, no trace. The yowl of a cat startles me as it sends a stack of crates plummeting to the ground. Pulse thumping in my ears, there is a scream up ahead.

Dorian.

I dart down the alleyway blinded by fear and determination. Coming around the corner, I witness the two figures struggling with one another, the taller one with one hand on Dorian, ready to strike with an open hand.

"No!" I shout, quickly running up and grabbing the hand before its strikes, casting the hooded figure aside with ease. The figure gives out a feeble cry, weak and pathetic, as I grasp Dorian by the shoulders and turn him to look me in the eye. "Dorian! Dorian!" I say frantically.

A girl gazes back at me, startled and confused. Blond curls, pockmarked skin. Her face is covered with a layer of dirt, and tears stream from her green eyes.

Out of breath and at a loss for words, I look over to see the hooded figure I tossed aside. With its hood pushed back and body splayed out on the snow, I see it is a woman with the same color hair. She slowly recovers from my aggressive display of force. "My—my apologies," I say, staggering back from the both of them. Fear is in their eyes, disbelief is in mine. "I'm so sorry," I say over and over as I back away.

The woman quickly grabs a hold of her child, shielding her with her own body. "Please, don't hurt us!"

Goddamn it. What was I doing? What am I doing here? Turning around, I flee from the alley without looking back.

The cold air pushes against my scarred face as I emerge back onto the desolate street. Not a soul in sight.

Backtracking to Jasmine, I see her patiently waiting for me tethered to the lamppost. They are all lit, yet the town seems to have retired for the night. Again, my stomach churns from hunger and I find myself staring at the rock-hard bread lying in the snow. "Come on, girl," I say, untying Jasmine, "We need to find you some shelter." Snow gathers quickly as I lead her up the street. Torchlight and the smell of cooking fires linger up ahead, wafting in the night air like some alluring demon.

I can do nothing but think of food as we stagger through the street, the cold having already numbed my appendages down to my toes and fingers. We pass more glowing windows traversing the barren streets of Walters. Each alleyway we pass, I chance a glance in hope of seeing Dorian. I know it is unlikely, but I am desperate and feel I am running out of time.

Jasmine nudges me and snorts into my back. I know she is cold. I begin to shiver and realize that if we don't get out of the cold soon, we might not live to see morning.

A low drawn out moan seeps from a nearby tavern, accompanied with laughter, and I decide that it will do. Moving onto a wooden porch riddled with misted windows, I pay a man tending the doorway to take Jasmine around back for hay and boarding for the night.

"Thank ye," says the man with broken teeth. He sneezes into his shirt and wipes it away with his sleeve. Passing a sign on the wall that reads *The Knotted Rope*, I step inside to a dimly lit common room smothered with candles, smoke, and the smell of onions. The room goes quiet as I enter, yet the low moaning sound from across the room never stops. After the awkward silence passes, the patrons of the tavern shift their focus back to the female hooded figure playing the cello at the far end of the chamber—the source of the moaning. A candle rests on a stand before her as if she were playing to the candle only, worshipping it in some strange way. Long dark wisps of hair flow from under her hood, accenting the pale complexion of her tiny nose. Vibrant red covers her lips. It is hard to discern whether they are red because of the cup she is drinking from or the heat generating from the room.

Slowly, I make my way across the back of the tavern toward the bar, noticing the rustic patrons dressed in black, some with their women close by, others still wearing their wide-brim hats from the day's work. The bar is nearly empty, save for two souls draining their mugs with the bottoms raised, and an angry-looking woman behind the counter. I take the seat closest to the wall, and immediately, the dark ebony woman locks her gaze on me. A long black braid streaked with a line of silver cascades down the front of her body, snaking between her breasts and ending at her waist. Arms folded high, she holds the visage of scrutiny. I can tell she has judged me the moment I entered this forsaken dirt hole. A large brown apron drapes the front of her black and red dress. Large ruffles jut out from the hem reaching to the floor. A fancy dress for a bar maiden to be wearing. The front of the apron is stained with multiple colors like a canvas of abstract art. In one swift motion, she moves forward, slamming her hands down on the bar top, and leans forward with her muscular arms, exposing a deep line of cleavage.

"I've never seen you before," she says perfectly, as if destined to say such a thing to all the strangers she meets. "There is to be no trouble here. Got it?"

My hands go up in silent defense as she stares at my bandaged eye and covered face.

"It will be difficult to drink my beer through that mask," she says, reaching for a mug under the bar and moving over to the kegs in the back.

I begin to protest the drink but another voice interrupts me.

"Well, well," says a slurred voice, "If it isn't freak show! Ha! Didn't think I'd see you in this part of town. Not in a million years!"

Without turning to look, I know who it is. Evidently, there is nowhere safe in this wretched town from Reyes the baker. I cringe at the thought of having to speak to him again and reluctantly turn to face him. Short hair askew, stains down the front of his mouth, he looks more disheveled now than a few hours ago when we met.

The barmaid returns, slamming down the mug of ale.

"And look, the monster hunter drinks!"

The woman immediately stares at me, eyes raised. "Your friend better not cause any trouble, Nicholas."

"There's no trouble here," I say to her, pulling down my facemask, revealing the scars beneath my remaining eye. I take a long pull from the thick brew.

"Don't mind Estoria," says Nicholas, nearly slipping from his stool. "She's harmless. She," he motions with a hand, "is the owner of this fine establishment." He slaps his hand hard on the counter. "Whoa! Look at you. Bloody near mauled to death with scars like that! Bet you got a story or two to tell."

It is clear Nicholas has had too many of the Knotted Rope's finest, with his eyes bloodshot and spit flying from his mouth. I muster what socially acceptable manner I can before he reveals to the entire tavern my state of business.

"As I said before," I begin, glancing at Estoria, "I am no monster hunter. I am simply here to collect a boy. His mother is worried sick. I need to earn my coin, and then I'll be on my way."

Estoria leans in, cocking her head slightly. "Well, you won't find any boys in here," she says with wide eyes.

A short, stubby man appears behind the counter carrying an iron plate of roasted chicken. Hands grimy and full of grease, he lifts up his arms as Estoria takes the plate, never saying a word to the dwarf-like man. She shoves the steaming, sizzling plate in front of me. "For all of this," she gestures with her hand, "one silver dauntess. It will be the best damn chicken you'll ever eat."

She walks away to tend to the tables while Nicholas gives me a sidelong look. "Told you she was harmless."

Estoria wasn't lying. The roasted chicken, crispy on the outside, tender on the inside, falls apart in my mouth as I bite into juices and spices. Grease drips from my unshaven chin and I wipe it away with my sleeve. I don't care at this point. Food has never tasted so good.

"So, you're still looking for that son of yours, eh? Am I right? I'm right, aren't I?"

I pause in mid-chew, completely caught off guard, and look around the tavern to see if anyone is listening.

"Don't worry, freak show, your secret is safe with me. These people can't hear you. They're too far gone and all soft-eyed over that woman singing to the candle for them to notice the mighty Lord Wolfgang present in their establishment."

Funny, how I didn't notice until now the woman has talent. Soothing music. Soothing voice. There is strangeness about it I cannot place, something familiar. I've heard that voice before, but where? As the candle wavers from her singing breath, the glowing light casts an outline over her sculpted features. Long dark hair pours from underneath her black hood like streaming waterfalls, and her lips are full and glistening in the accenting light. Where have I seen her before?

The room seems to spin for a second and I shake my head. Was the alcohol impairing my judgment or was it fatigue setting in?

"Easy there, freak show. You doing all right?" Nicholas has his hand on my shoulder to stabilize me.

"I'm fine," I say, turning away from the woman and directing my attention back to my food. "All this time you knew who I was and didn't say anything. I had taken you for a fool like all the rest."

"Listen here freak sh—er, Wolfgang. I am not a spring chicken!" His eyes land on my plate. "But I know how to play my cards. I like to feel out my customers, if you know what I mean. Like to see if they're going to be a one-time thing or a returning enterprise."

"How does anyone return to your shop? You sell old crusty bread." I nearly smile between chewing as Nicholas erupts into laughter.

The woman stops playing her cello for a moment, emphasizing her voice, singing louder a cappella across the room. She holds a high falsetto note, inhales, and returns to berating the strings with her bow. There is mild clapping as she continues playing.

"It's a bit of bad luck, if you ask me," says Nicholas, returning to his drink.

"What is?"

"Searching for your son when you're tired and hungry. Must be taxing on the mind. Probably can't think straight. Incredibly frustrating," he says, shaking his head. "No use searching when you're tired and hungry. Might as well be searching with your eyes closed—eh, sorry. I meant eye."

Later at night, lying in my bed of straw and feathers, it is impossible for me to sleep. Tossing and turning, back and forth from one side of the rickety bed to the other, my mind will not shut off. The horrible remembrance of the Cresthaven children returns to me. Victoria and Jackson. Their brothers and sisters chasing after me. Me—severing their heads and running their bodies through with Enivid. The actions repeat over and over in my head, tormenting me like residual spirits never parting from earth.

Eventually, I fall asleep, shunning the horrible nightmare from my thoughts, thinking only of D. My black abyss with her sea of ebony hair. Her endless cascades of showering kisses and, oh, those wonderful lips.

As I drift further into sleep, I cannot help but wonder about how the woman I saw downstairs reminded me so much of Diana. My Diana. Her mannerisms. Her hair. That wonderful sweet voice. I am amazed at the women I've encountered on this journey, the ones that seem to be Diana in some kind of afterlife, her voice, her encouragement, her seduction.

Somewhere beyond my subconscious, sometime between the twilight of late night and early morning, a subtle yet deep-rooted revelation washes over me. The woman performing last night was there by no arbitrary accident. The woman was meant to be there. She had a purpose, a calling, and that purpose, I am certain, had everything to do with me.

The woman was Belladonna.

DAY FIFTEEN

CHAPTER XLIX

I STARTLE AWAKE TO A shadow moving across the room.

Sitting upright in my bed, I think maybe it was my imagination playing tricks on me. Maybe not. I shiver from the cold of the room. The fireplace, once full of seasoned wood last night, has burned to ash. Looking about the small inn room, thoughts of last night's events flash before me. Nicholas the baker. Watching the mystery woman singing. Drinking the mugs of ale. How many had I consumed?

Head pounding, I realize dawn isn't far off as the first signs of light begin glowing through the window from the overcast sky. Turning over and reaching for the candle, I realize it has melted down to the table. With hardly any light to see by, I notice a small piece of parchment lying next to the dried pool of wax. Sitting up, I scrape the wax from the paper and read the elegant writing sprawled across its canvas in great spiraling loops:

Tenor,

If you can find it in your heart to forgive me, then do so, for I am merely a prisoner, a slave to the master. He uses me as he does you now. I never meant to hurt you. Never meant to betray you. I was doing what I had to. There was no choice for me. You understand, don't you? Although I cannot stay, I wanted you to know, that night in Delore was truly special. What we shared was real, no matter how brief or disillusioned it was. That was the true me then, before all things went south. You understand, don't you? You're a smart man. I know you know—and for me, that is enough.

Forever thinking of you,

B

Anger channels through me at the thought of Belladonna and her bold attitude. The night she betrayed me, handing me over to Scepter like a prized pig to be stuck for its blood. I could never forgive her for that. I remember how she looked so much like my Diana and I had fallen for it. It was the perfect cover-up, the perfect plan to use against an ignorant human. And that's exactly what I was. Weak. Ignorant. Vulnerable. Pathetic. Incapable of distinguishing fact from fiction. Scepter won that night. He stole my blood. Kronklich and I were barely able to follow after him. Then there was the train ride, and the rest is history.

Again, a shadow moves across the room from the corner of my eye, and the door to the chamber shuts with a click.

Goddamn vampires. It was her! She was just here!

Instantly, my senses kick in; I begin dressing as quickly as I can, realizing as every second passes, Belladonna is putting more distance between us.

I check my equipment and pull the mask over my nose. *How did she find me? What is she doing in Walters?* These thoughts plague me as I dash from the room, slamming the door open with a loud bang despite the early morning courtesy. *Did this mean Scepter was close? The Carnalreesee too? Goddamn it! Where are they hiding Dorian?*

Frantic guests emerge from their rooms as I reach the banister railing. Looking over the edge, I search for a sign, any sign of Belladonna's whereabouts, ignoring the slandering comments from the guests behind me. A great darkness suddenly passes over the interior of the inn like a huge shadow, swallowing the walls, floors, and windows. The inn guests cower from the phenomenon, retreating back to their rooms instantly. Chairs and tables fly through the air, parting from the center of the tavern floor, as if someone were hurling them, tossing them aside. Then, as quickly as it came, all at once, the unexplainable shadow dissipates from the tavern, leaving the chandelier above the entryway swaying. I run down the stairs, passing Estoria on the way out, never stopping to answer her questions of confusion, her protests of terror.

Feeling the freezing cold morning of Walters against my skin, I scan the street in every direction, searching for the slightest bit of movement in the dim light, the slightest bit of evidence to take a lead from. But there is nothing, only the soft breath of snow falling.

Grabbing a lantern from the doorway, I make my way onto the street thick with fog, searching for a sign, and notice tracks in the thick snow heading toward the center of town. I steal away into the purple dawn like a madman, parting the mist with the wave of my lantern back and forth. A patron, wearing a heavy worker's coat and top hat comes into view as I accidentally hit him with the lantern. He lets out a small cry from my assault but I have no time to apologize. A woman carrying a crying baby materializes in the mist as I continue. Never slowing, I glide past them as if they were ghosts. A silhouette catches my attention in the distance and I watch it move rapidly away from me, faster than any normal man or woman could possibly move.

Belladonna.

I see her, outlined in a fluttering cloak, holding what appears to be some sort of instrument in her hand. A cello and bowstring.

"Stop!" I shout through the early morning darkness.

Belladonna responds immediately, breaking into a run and knocking innocent people over in the process.

I do the same, shoving patrons aside, not caring in the slightest. I have found nothing up to this point, nothing at all, and now *this* was something.

I run with all my might, shouting at the top of my lungs. "Belladonna! Stop!" but the more I scream her name, the faster she seems to run. I continue running and my body warms from the exercise. Uncaring of the attention I draw or the people I run into, I push my way into a small square unfamiliar to me. It's been a long time since I've been to Walters; my memory fails me. Surrounded on four sides by tall buildings of dark stone and twisted canopies, the square's center hosts a black fountain in a state of rusting decay. No water pours from the flock of sculpted ravens covered in snow, and as I come to stand next to them, I survey my surroundings, watching the people watch me and the guards by the bank staring with great interest.

Not good. There are too many people. Where the hell is she?

Although dawn hasn't cracked the sky yet, many townsfolk walk the streets for such an early morning. Unable to see a thing, I climb the statue to gain a vantage point, straining my eye to see, covering my face from the icy wind blowing from the mountains. There is a commotion in the distance, a disturbance of bobbing heads and flailing arms. Cloaks and hoods move about frantically, and I know it must be her at the center of the commotion. Suddenly, I hear a loud bang, like the sound of wood breaking, followed by screaming.

"Hey, you! Get down from there!" shouts one of the guards across the road.

He begins moving toward me, but I know his intent is futile. I leap from the top of the fountain and land on the ground, running faster than he ever will, chasing after the shadow of Belladonna. Reaching the disturbance in the crowd, I see some of the townsfolk are on the ground bleeding, recovering from what looks like an attack. Had Belladonna assaulted them? Remnants of a cello lie scattered over the ground and a bowstring is left abandoned to the side, snapped in two. I grab a man by the collar and shake him hard. "What happened? Was it the witch?" My comment seems to strike fear into the crowd. "Which way did she go?" I realize I am shouting at the top of my lungs. The man feebly points to an alleyway nearby and I release him, following after Belladonna into the darkness of the narrow corridor.

Again, I find myself lingering through the dark alleyways of Walters, passing rat-infested piles of trash and spilt buckets of refuse. Soiled rags and the odor of rotting animal bones flood my nostrils as I navigate around broken fences and low archways. Finding myself in the alley reminds me of the woman and the girl from yesterday, and I hope a similar instance doesn't occur. My wish is answered as I see a shadow pass along a wall far in the distance, nimble and agile. Quickly I move after it, attempting to cut it off by leaping over a crumbled wall and meeting it head-on. Dropping down, I come face to face with a drunkard instead. I nearly sever his head with Enivid as I slam him against the wall, knocking the breath from his lungs, striking ungodly fear into his pathetic existence. He staggers around in the dark, gasping for air as I back away, disappearing into the shadows as if I had never been there. I watch him from the distance, reassessing my situation as he fumbles along the wall for support.

Damn. I breathe a sigh of disappointment. *How could I lose her?*

Tiny beads of sweat run down my face despite the cold. Catching my breath, I begin walking slowly back the way I came, the thought drumming over in my head—*Maybe it isn't Belladonna I'm chasing after.* Rounding the corner, I hear voices and turmoil coming from the street beyond and decide it might be better to go another way. The guards will not be happy at the sight of me.

I duck into another alley and walk quickly, losing myself in thought, dwelling over my discovery of Belladonna, and cursing myself twice for my lack of caution. The morning is lonely and cold. I watch two cats dash after one another over scraps of rib bones. It will still be some time before these back alleys see the rays of sunlight, for the height of the buildings loom high above me, making me feel less significant. Walking soon becomes therapeutic and my nerves calm.

Stepping into a large back-alley square, I listen to the wind whistling through the black cobblestone walls glistening with morning moisture. There are so many ways to go, so many ways to choose from, as I step out from the narrow corridor. Stopping near its center, I feel as though someone is watching me, and I pull the hood of my cloak tighter over my head. Whoever it is, whatever *it* is, won't stand a chance. My hand slips under the flap of my coat. Slightly bending my knees so as to be prepared to spring, I move my eye from one shadowed alley to the next until, finally, it comes to rest on the cloaked figure I've been looking for. Black eyes stare back at me from under a hood, yet the figure doesn't move an inch or respond in the slightest.

"There. You have me all alone now. It's what you wanted, isn't it?" I say, taking a step forward.

There is no reaction from the figure. The eyes continue to stare.

"It is you, Belladonna. Isn't it? You've come a long way to track me down. Why? What for?" I have so many questions, yet the figure never responds. The anger inside me festers. "Answer me, goddamn it!" I shout in frustration. I feel the heat radiating from my hip where Enivid is begging for use. "Where is Scepter? Where is Dorian being held?"

For a moment, it seems the shadow figure is going to speak, but the moment never comes. My temperance is nearly gone. This shadow is here for me, yet it will not speak. If it will not speak, then it will die.

"Why are you here?!" I shout, tossing my cloak and coat back, exposing Enivid at my side, its four straight blades glinting in the growing dawn.

The figure's eyes seem to respond with revelation, fixing its gaze on my hip. Fear perhaps? It could be sizing me up, preparing to attack.

Now is your time, love. Strike true.

I throw Enivid with precision, releasing all the hate and tension built up inside. Enivid slices through the early morning light, flying through the wind and cold with deadly intent. The figure simply steps to the side, allowing Enivid to pass, and waits while still watching me, leaping over the return trip of the blade. Landing on its feet with finesse, it finally speaks in a female tone. "Come, learn the truth about your son. It is the least I can do for you." The words echo through the alleyway, piercing my heart and soul as Belladonna retreats from the alleyway moving faster than before.

"No! Wait!" I scream as I run forward, catching Enivid as it whirls back into my gloved hand.

I chase after Belladonna like a madman.

Learn the truth about my son? She knows where he is! She is leading me to him! My stomach sickens at the thought of what I might find, and as I follow after her, I know there will be no mercy for Belladonna once I learn whatever horrible truth there is to be discovered.

CHAPTER
L

DORIAN IS THE ONLY THING that matters. He is all I can think about—even as I follow after Belladonna, traversing the stench-filled alleyways of Walters, emerging onto a wide street of bustling townspeople, and passing wagons full of carved meats and shouting vendors. My mind is blinded by the simple fact that Dorian waits for me and this hellish witch is the one who will show me how to reach him.

Far ahead, she keeps her distance, gliding through the growing crowds of people like water churning through stones in a river. I stay behind as she leads me, staying within the generous shadows the day still has yet to diminish. For a moment, I wonder what would happen to her if she were to step into the light, but the thought vanishes almost instantly as she passes into an inn just up the street.

So this is it. This is where they've been keeping Dorian all this time. Locked away in a tavern inn on the west side of town. Approaching from a distance with caution, I take in the building's features, seeing that it faces the main street and stands three stories high. Thoughts of ambush enter my mind as I pass horse-drawn carriages, but I quickly dismiss the thoughts.

Whatever is waiting for me inside won't have a chance. Dorian is in there and I will kill his captors, including Belladonna. It's as simple as that.

Crossing the cobblestone street, I approach the faded black building, realizing that it is far more upscale than I realized. Painted gold molding along each of the windows and doors. Ornate tarnished crows jutting from each of the building's corner awnings. There is an over-sized man, maybe twice the size of an ordinary man, dressed in a black suit eyeing me as I approach. How he found someone to tailor him such an outfit at such a large scale I cannot fathom. He nods his head, gesturing with his top hat for emphasis as I approach; his smile is wide and beaming, the whitest teeth I've ever seen.

"Good morning, sir," he says. "It's a fine day here at the Crossings West, fine day indeed."

His over-exuberance and enthusiasm is alarming and causes me to wonder. I pass by without uttering a word, climbing the many steps leading to the black- and gold-trimmed double doors of this extravagant inn.

The Crossings West. Where has this witch woman taken me?

Stepping inside, I am greeted with dim candlelight and the mixture of pipe smoke and incense. The smell is overwhelming and irritates my eye as I adjust my focus in the large expanse of the room. A thick fog hangs over smoking patrons and golden burning candles. The gray light seeping through the windows does nothing to improve the lighting. On the far wall, there is a massive staircase leading up to floors beyond, while to my right, a well-dressed host scribbles away behind a shiny counter adorned with a menacing black statue of a crow. The incense filling the room pours from its open beak as if the bird were breathing fire. A trail of lingering smoke twirls its way upward into the cathedral-like ceiling, well beyond the standard for an ordinary inn. Despite the smell of burning ash saturating this establishment, I can't help but think there is something odd about it, as if it were masking some other scent.

Looking about the room, I see no evidence of Belladonna. A voice to my right causes me to flinch.

"Name, please." The voice is overly proper and sophisticated.

I look with confusion at the man behind the counter and immediately think of Joachim. Dressed in a buttoned-up black jacket lined with golden studs and a crushed gold vest, an extravagant golden bow holds his hair back tightly. I can imagine how much grease is slicked through his hair to hold the escaping strands in place.

"Name, please," he says again. This time he enunciates each syllable with more vigor. His glassy eyes make contact with my one.

"Wolfgang," I reply, not knowing what else to say. I regret it the moment I say it.

The man returns to his ledger, not the least bit concerned, and glances over it with his monocle. "Wolfgang, you say?" His emphasis on my name sets me on edge, but I see no reaction from him or the people sitting at the tables. They are too busy enjoying their breakfast and tea. "Ah, yes, Lord Wolfgang. Here it is." The man takes something from the counter behind him and puts a cold brass key in my hand.

"What the hell is this—" I begin to say but he interrupts me without a second thought.

"Room sixteen," he says, glancing at the stairs. "Third floor, last room on the left." He quickly goes back to his ledger behind the counter as if I never existed.

Even more confused, I back away from the desk slowly, never taking my eye off the host. What the hell is going on here, I wonder, and where is Belladonna? Fingering the key in my hand, I contemplate whether I should say anything to him, but decide not to. It is clear there is a purpose for me being here. A room reserved for me. What was Belladonna's intent? Was this part of the truth she wanted me to know?

I turn around to face what I now realize is a full room of gentlemen, who appear to be aristocrats from all walks of life. Where had they all come from? Maybe they too are stuck here for the winter months until the snows pass and they can leave.

I circle the room, staying close to the walls and following the long black wooden bar, making my way to the stairs at the opposite side. I realize it is not just the high society of aristocracy that dwells in the room of swirling tobacco smoke and cheerful laughs. Some of these men are tethered to women loosely hanging from their card-playing hands. Dressed in elegant gowns of gold, silver, or black, there are just a few to sway most of their attention.

"Excuse me, chap," says a boisterous voice behind me, as a man descending the stairs pats me gently on the shoulder. He motions with his hand for me to step aside. A pale-skinned woman, her figure bound tightly in her dress, follows after him, smiling red lips plastered across her face. It is a wonder she doesn't fall down the steps in the high-heel boots strapped to her feet. What sort of establishment was this?

As I ascend the stairs, I feel like I am passing into another realm while the heat from below quickly dissipates. The second floor, darker than the first, is riddled with rows of candles. Freestanding candelabras burn at either end of the hall. No windows line the walls in this cluttered hallway where I count eight doors. I watch a man disappear into a room with a woman wearing a red dress—if one could call it a dress.

I keep going.

Each step creaks on my way to the third floor and the sounds of laughter and glasses clinking die out. I wonder if this place ever sleeps, but cast the thought away the moment I set foot on the landing.

There is no mistaking it now. The scent of death lingers in the air as in an abandoned cemetery. A dark, ominous hall waits for me as I stare ahead into the shadows of the third floor. Glancing down at the key in my hand, I take a faint breath and begin walking, swallowing back the bile in my throat. I watch the doors as I pass, my nerves on end, waiting for something to jump out at me. I banish the thought, thinking only of Dorian. He gives me strength. Diana gives me strength. My stomach hurts at the thought of seeing Dorian after all this time. His state of being is what worries me the most, and I start to feel sick. What if Belladonna has simply led me to his dead body? How long has it been?

Room fourteen.

Room fifteen. There are stains on the door of room fifteen, but due to the dark, it's difficult to tell if they are bloodstains.

I stop before the last door on the left, hesitating, reading the number above the doorframe. *Sixteen. This is it.*

Inserting the key into the lock, I gently push the door open, afraid and anxious as to what I'll find.

A room smothered in darkness. Hundreds of candles line the floor, desk, windowsill, and bed, and a chair in front of the shuttered window faces away from me. An empty birdcage sits next to the window and chair. Sitting cross-legged in the chair facing the closed window is a figure with its back to me. As I make out an elegantly dressed man with top hat and blond hair draping down his back, for a moment Dorian's image fills my thoughts. My son. Finally. Here in the flesh. But as the figure shifts in its chair to face me, I notice the long golden rod lying across its lap, the golden scepter used to cave in the heads of so many innocent people.

"Looking for something?" asks the vampire I thought I would never see again.

Scepter smiles from one pale ear to the other.

CHAPTER LI

"So good of you to join me, my friend," says Scepter as his long fingers tap the side of his knee. "But you're late. Oh, so very late."

Belladonna. The damn witch. I should have known. She led me straight to him.

Scepter's hair flows down his back from under his top hat in spectacular long locks of golden strands. Dressed in a crisp black suit with golden buckles and white ruffles, his face looks more immaculate than ever before. Ivory white as the clouds. Whiter than snow. No blemishes. No single part of him out of place. He is unscathed, to say the least. It is apparent he's had ample time to recover since the train wreck.

Beams of sunlight escape from the sealed window behind him, dangerously close to his flesh. He doesn't seem the least bit fazed as he stares long and hard at me.

Sitting in his chair patiently, he never stands to confront me, and instead points to the desk across the room covered in wax. There is a note with writing on it on the hardwood surface.

I hesitate, wary of a trap, but his demeanor is conniving and playful, looking as if he is enjoying every second of this un-accidental encounter.

"I assure you the worst that will befall you is a paper cut. Wouldn't want to waste all that precious blood." Scepter smiles and leans back into his chair.

Unsure of his intent, I snatch up the piece of parchment and read over its content. I try to make sense of the notations, but they are hard to read, as if written in an ancient language. I see the names Martyr, Vargus, and Archbishop Faeradon associated with another name, a location I am all too familiar with.

Sunstone. The land of endless seagrass. Meadows of green fields. They surround the great capital city, leading to its magnificent walls and towers of white.

Sunstone. The shining light to thwart the darkness. The city of a once-proud faith that I now know as fallen. And Cardinal Glass, was he too fallen like the rest? The last part of the note, I can read, and when I do, the note nearly slips from my hand:

The boy has arrived.

My blood runs cold.

I back away from the desk slowly, crumpling the note in my hand. The undeniable feeling of defeat settles over me with a wave of nausea.

I look at Scepter, clenching my teeth. "Where is Dorian? Where are you hiding him?"

"Hiding? Did you not read the note? Dorian *was* here," he says, pushing a lock of his hair back, "but was whisked away out of the Cordova Mountains." Scepter leans forward in his chair. "That was quite some time ago."

"No. You're lying," I say.

"Am I?"

"Cresthaven told me the truth."

Scepter laughs uncontrollably. "That moron? He did exactly what I knew he would do. Lead you straight to me."

Immediately Councilor's words of warning enter my thoughts. *You shouldn't trust a vampire.*

Scepter stands and moves to the birdcage, running his finger along the metal bars. "You are a capable hunter, no doubt, but a gullible one at that. When Councilor sent you to Westings, I knew you would destroy the Cresthavens, saving me the trouble, and the fool in turn would lead you straight to me."

"Councilor sent me? Why would he help you?"

"To exact revenge on the one who killed his daughter, of course."

Suddenly, I cannot feel my legs. I had my doubts about his loyalties, but—Kronklich enters my mind. What is Councilor going to do with Kronklich? All the trust built between us, saving Kronklich, training at the cottage, lending me his horses. All of it was a lie. "But why have Cresthaven killed? Why destroy your own kind?"

"Sacrifice for the greater good, of course." Scepter laughs at his own words, but I find nothing amusing about it. "There's no room in this world for vampires like Cresthaven. Visionaries. Liberals. Could you imagine? A vampire horde made of a thousand children?" *Rap!* He smacks his cane against the cage.

"Our food supplies would diminish within the decade." *Rap!* He strikes the metal bars again. "Even more vampires would be made." *Rap!* "Careless. Pointless." He raps on the cage two more times. "Vampires running rampant, unchecked, continuing the cycle. So on and so on it would go, until eventually every last drop of blood would be sucked from this world and the next."

I watch Scepter gripping his cane as if strangling a person, and then he points it at me. "I knew Cresthaven was going to tell you Dorian was here. He'd do anything to save his hide."

"Damn you," I say, shaking with anger. "What are you going to do with Dorian?"

Scepter turns to face me, smiling all the same. "Dorian Wolfgang, your son, will be the vessel of our salvation!" He raises his arms in the air.

"What!?" I shout, trying to keep a grip on reality. "He is innocent! There is no reason to take him! Take me instead! I will be your vessel."

Scepter chuckles to himself as he shakes his head. "That is not how it is done. You cannot offer what is not yours to give!" says Scepter, suddenly in a fit of rage. "We already have you!" His maniacal joy returns.

The vial of my blood. He still has it. I need to get it back.

"Yes! Now you see," says Scepter grinning. "I see it in your face. The perfect summation of an equation! But don't think I am a fool, my dear Wolfgang. Your blood is nowhere near here. I wouldn't be so foolish as that. No. Not again. Currently, it is traveling through the sky, being whisked away to Sunstone by crow," he makes a hand gesture of a bird flapping its wings, "bobbing up and down on the winds of snow." He taps on the empty cage again for emphasis. "I must admit, though, I was greedy on the train. I wanted more of your blood. More blood of the *father*. The blood that has killed so many *vampires*. So much potential. So much—power!"

What the hell is he talking about?

"Faeradon said, 'Don't destroy the hunter. We need him.' Martyr said, 'If you kill him, our lord will be most displeased.' Scepter swings his golden mace, striking the birdcage with such a force that it bends in half as it crashes to the floor. "To hell with them and their grand utopia of enlightenment! You, my friend, have killed my brothers and sisters, and for that, I will never forgive you."

Scepter begins walking toward me.

"Crimes must be paid for in blood. For every wrong you've committed, a correction will be made with *Malice*. A blow for a foe." He points Malice at me and smiles. "You will pay for what you did, Tenor Wolfgang, whether God watches or not. For, in the end, I get what I want."

CHAPTER
LII

SCEPTER EXPLODES INTO A FIT of rage.

He throws himself recklessly at me, swinging Malice with every intent of crushing my skull. His movement is fast and airy, as if he were floating above the ground, never even grazing it with his fancy shoes.

The whistling of the golden rod passes my ear as I tilt my head left and right, backing away in my defensive stance and circling about the tiny room. Dodging another blow, my heels dig into wood as I stumble across the desk. Papers spill from drawers as it topples over and smashes against the ground. Splinters of wood crack under my boots.

Enivid's burning heat radiates in the palm of my hand. I lash out in horizontal arcs hoping to connect Enivid with Scepter's flawless skin, but Malice intervenes. A loud ring reverberates through the air as the vibration travels the length of my arm. I move my wrist back and forth trying to break through his defense, but Scepter mimics my actions, moving his weapon the same, smiling still the same. He is toying with me, and my anger rises. He is trying to wear me down, but I break away from his locking embrace, lunging at his exposed neck. I slice through empty space as Scepter vanishes.

Stepping back, I glance around the room, looking for any sign of the vampire. Before I have a chance to react, he appears feet away from me as if nothing happened. He smiles and then blinks out of existence again, reappearing in front of me, slamming the head of Malice into my breastplate. I am sent sprawling backward, colliding against the wall with a debilitating force. The blow is devastating, but my armor preserves my organs. Air rushes back into my straining lungs as I stand up, wheezing.

Scepter doesn't stop. He comes again and again, smashing through the wall where my face was moments ago. I drop to my knees and roll to the side, kicking out Scepter's leg at the knee. He cries out, falling to the floor while I rise to the occasion. I thrust downward with Enivid.

But Scepter is not like the other vampires. He is quicker and more cunning, and he expects the unexpected. Enivid stops inches away from his face and I see him again smiling behind our locked weapons.

"Do you really think," he pauses blowing a lock of his hair from his face, "after all this time, you, of all people, can beat me?" He licks his teeth. "I am a Carnalreesee, a successor to the first bloodline of Egleaseon."

"I beat the others," I say, pitching my strength against his.

Scepter growls and pushes me away, moving about the room with lightning speed, knocking over candles and chairs.

I anticipate his move and spin, slicing the air about my body, and catch him in the shoulder. Blood sprays across the room as

Scepter jumps back screaming, clutching his arm. Eyes turning red, he exposes his fangs like the true vampire he is. I watch with bated breath as his anger grows, rapidly increasing, until finally, in a fit of rage, he rushes at me with a speed I cannot match.

His body rams mine, lifting me from the ground with brutal force. Hands clasping my coat, he charges forward, using me as a battering ram to break through the wall of the next room. Bone-jarring force radiates throughout my body. On and on we go, breaking through more walls, one at a time, until finally stopping in room thirteen. Pain riddles my body. My arms and legs tingle. I wonder if this is the end.

Wavering in and out of consciousness, I squirm on the floor in agony as Scepter backs away slowly, dusting off his suit. Dead faces fade in and out of my vision as I struggle to upright myself. A woman in a fancy gown sprawled on the floor, throat torn open. A man hanging off the edge of a bed, arms twisted in impossible angles. Maggots pour from their lifeless orifices while flies buzz around my head. The stench is unbearable. This place, the Crossings West, is a tomb of victims. The incense downstairs. The barren third floor. Windows sealed up with board and nail. This is how Scepter has been recuperating all this time.

"It is very rare that someone cuts me," says Scepter with the least bit of concern, "but when someone does, I am courteous enough to return the favor"—he spins Malice above his head— "tenfold!"

A shadow moves across the room as Malice comes down to split my skull. I see it only for a second, and then a red line suddenly traces the length of Scepter's throat, cutting his speech off and forcing him to miss. Blood gushes from the wound as he staggers back, dropping Malice and clutching his throat. He tries to speak but the blood gurgles from the gash, bubbling and dripping down the front of his finely pressed linens, golden buckles, and white ruffled shirt.

A cloaked figure appears between us, separating Scepter and me from one another. It is the same cloaked figure that led me to this foul place to begin with. It stands before Scepter in judgment with hand extended, black nails poised to slice a second time.

Belladonna.

She readies her next move to debilitate Scepter even further. Wrapped in a crimson dress with a black-buckled belt and stark shiny boots, her appearance has the same effect on me as the last time I saw her. She possesses the same stunning resemblance to my Diana. Her long dark hair now tightly pulled back into a high braid, her skin whiter and cleaner than ever before.

She lashes out with her hand but Scepter catches it, staining her skin red.

"You bitch." Blood drips from his mouth. "So quick to betray your master."

"I never wanted this! I never wanted—"

Scepter jams his hand into her side before she finishes, tearing through her skin as if it were paper. She cries out in agony at the backhand that sends her flailing and into shelves across the room, where she collapses in a motionless heap.

"I'll deal with you later," says Scepter, holding his throat and summoning Malice back to his hand. "Now, where were we?"

Still recovering from having been rammed through three walls, I watch Scepter reach behind his back to reveal a bloody skull with a spine attached to it. "I've been saving this one for you."

Scepter bends his head forward, biting into his wrist. It is enough time for me to act. With Enivid's channeling energy slowly giving me strength, I quickly release it with a snap of my wrist, sending it spinning, and severing the spine from the skull in Scepter's hand.

"Grrraaaaaah!" yells Scepter, batting away Enivid with Malice. Rushing at me with unprecedented speed, he swings Malice, striking me in the back of the leg, forcing me to my knees. Pain explodes up the left side of my body. He takes another swing, and I can do nothing to defend myself as Malice catches the side of my head.

Blackness fills my vision. As I come to a few seconds later, I feel my face lying against a hard surface. The feeling is short lived as I am lifted from the ground effortlessly with Scepter's menacing grip on both of my shoulders.

"Screw the ceremonies and rituals. I'll take all of your blood here and now and there won't be any left to pass on! The taste will be so sweet, so invigorating—to taste the blood of the hunter who's killed so many of my kind."

Head slumped to the side, I can do nothing to protect my neck as I hang loosely in Scepter's grasp. I watch as he leans in, his eyes blazing red, and wait for the sharp pain I've forever dreaded, that which has haunted my dreams and my entire life—

The vampire's kiss.

My eye closes and I feel myself giving into the darkness. Even Diana can't save me. Not this time, my love. Not this time.

As I brace myself for the worst, I hear the ripping sound of clothes tearing and a burst of liquid sprays my face. Instantly, I drop to the floor, delirious with my head spinning. I open my eye to see Scepter's confused face; a piece of splintered wood protrudes from his chest. Hands before him, frozen and unable to move, his body shakes and convulses as a pair of arms grip the underside of his shoulders. With one quick motion, Belladonna pulls Scepter to the ground. She holds on to him firmly like a snake constricting its prey as the momentary paralyzing effects begins to wear off.

"Hurry!" screams Belladonna. "I can't hold him for long!" She reaches over and places more of her body over Scepter, pushing the splintered wood farther into his heart.

At first, I don't understand what she is saying, but as the intensity unfolds and the aggression of Scepter's movement increases, my eye averts behind the two them struggling to just above Belladonna's head, where the sealed window of boards and nails waits.

"Graaaahhhhhh! It hurts, you bitch! You will suffer for this!" Slowly scepter begins worming his way out of Belladonna's grasp. His hateful gaze penetrates mine. "It's too late for your son. His fate is sealed. The snows have come and you'll never reach him in time! Not now! Not ever!" Scepter smiles despite his display of pain. "No one leaves the mountains in winter. Dorian—is—forfeited!"

Belladonna strangles Scepter, preventing him from talking further.

Without another moment's delay, I attempt to make it to the boarded-up window. My head spins from the last blow to the head, and as I clasp the windowpane, I look upon Belladonna's pain-ridden face once more and with sympathy. Without exchanging a single word, I know what she is saying. Her look is plaintive, begging. Death is better than being the thing she is. She never had a choice.

One by one, I rip the boards from their foundation until sunlight floods the room. I watch in empathy, not for Scepter, but for Belladonna, as she shields herself from the light, screaming. The light forces her fangs to extract. She cries in pain as her skin burns away, the same as Scepter. The sun paralyzes both of them. They are unable to do a thing as their bodies turn black. The light chisels away their skin, exposing the dermis below, then the white bone beneath.

It is over in a matter of seconds, the two of them reduced to flaking ash. While the room fills with floating particles of burnt skin, I stare at the golden rod glinting in the sunlight, wondering how many have suffered the fate of that ill-begotten weapon. So many families destroyed. So many lives claimed. So much blood tasted.

I'm not sure how long I've rested on the floor.

In and out of consciousness, it's impossible to know the passing of time. For what felt like an hour, the sun moved a fraction from where Scepter and Belladonna's ashes still lie.

Although the tyranny of Scepter is over, and where I should feel the smallest strain of hope, I am left with a worse feeling of despair. Everything Scepter said in the end was true. The crude note written in blood, no doubt my son's blood, proved it, signed and sealed by Martyr, one of the last two Carnalreesee. They still have my son, far, far away from here, in the city of Sunstone, the capital. With the full presence of the cold moon, there would be no quarter from the winter solstice this point forward. The snows are too great. Passage is impossible. There is no mistake. I will be here until the end of winter, and by then it will be too late.

Clutching my head, my vision still spins from the last blow Scepter gave me. A concussion, most likely. Surrounded by the fumes of death and decay, I try not to vomit. I struggle pulling myself up to the open window. The sunlight is welcoming as it bathes my skin; its warmth thaws the cold from my face. Such nourishing rays. It's been so long since the blue sky broke through the long gray clouds. Although the moment is brief, I welcome the cold fresh air over the smell of death, despite the back-alley stench of the Crossings West stables.

The sound of neighing horses draws my attention below. Numerous patrons come and go by way of horse-drawn carriages. I notice a particular carriage, an open-faced doublewide wagon, canvassed and loaded with crates and cargo, and pulled by two black horses. One is larger than the other, and suddenly, I am filled with a recollection I cannot explain. A knowing of horses. Large and stout, small and nimble. Abel and Jasmine stand about buckets of oats and troughs of water. My mind races at the thought that Councilor may be here, yet more so for Kronklich, who I thought I would not see at least for another day.

Before I can make sense of the possibilities, before I can make any preparation for what's to come, I hear shouting in the hallway. The hair on my arms stands up and a lump forms in my dry throat.

The familiar deep voice of Councilor calls my name.

CHAPTER
LIII

Councilor's shouting grows louder and louder until the door to room thirteen explodes into a hundred pieces of splintered wood. A massive black scythe passes through the doorway.

"Tenor!" cries Councilor as his massive figure fills the small room. Cloaked in his standard black, his scythe drops to his side as he surveys the scene. "You're all right," he says with an air of concern, his brow furrowed. "What in the hell happened here?" he asks, covering his nose with the hood of his cloak.

A broken voice responds from behind him. "Bloody devastation, that's what."

Kronklich.

Hearing his voice again after all this time invigorates me. I can't help but smile. Kronklich steps out from behind Councilor's massive frame, limping like a wounded soldier. No longer dressed in his usual gray suit, a dark vest and coat cover his torso, matching the color of Councilor's scythe. The poisonous veins that once spread across his neck are gone.

He hobbles into the room using the sheath of his cane sword as a crutch. With his thin sword drawn, there is no doubt he expected the worse.

"Tenor," he says, stopping to tilt his top hat. "Good God, man. The stench of this place is absolutely horrifying. Death himself has taken residency. Such a fine establishment gone to waste, if you ask me. And to think the front desk gave us such a hard time about allowing us ingress. Just look at this mess." He pokes around the ashes with his cane.

"It's good to see you too," I say, moving to embrace him.

He flinches from my advance, covering his leg with his hand. "Careful. It will be a time before she fully heals."

"Sorry," I say, backing off.

He manages a smile. "Well, you're not dead, so that's good. However, you've been gone less than two days and managed to destroy the entire place! Sounds about typical." He motions with his hand around the room full of dead bodies. His eyebrows raise at the large hole in the wall where I was thrown through. "Interesting."

"How did you find Jasmine?" I ask, still making sense of everything. "How did you find me?"

"It's not hard to find a man dressed all in black with a mask, riding a black horse." Councilor smiles. "You have to ask the right people. It helps when you know most of the town. I have my contacts."

I give Councilor a weary look, wondering about his contacts.

566 | F.D. Gross

"Turns out, you happened to run into one of my good friends, Reyes the baker. He and I go back a long time. We look out for one another."

I pry Enivid from the wooden floor and stare out the window. "Well, it doesn't matter. We have come in vain."

"What do you mean?" asks Kronklich.

"I failed. Dorian is gone." Already my thoughts of losing Dorian forever come to torment me again. I have failed him, and I have failed my promise to Diana. Even Enivid, with the handle resting in the palm of my hand, is cold to the touch. No warmth radiates from within. Its desire to kill seems lost.

"Impossible," says Councilor pacing the room. "Cresthaven said he was here."

"It was a lie. You said not to trust him and I didn't listen." I think about Scepter's words, wondering how much Councilor really knew.

Kronklich shakes his head. "The Carnalreesee are, without a doubt, cunning."

"Indeed," I say, kicking Malice and sending it spinning across the room into the wall. "They've taken Dorian to Sunstone, knowing we cannot follow. Passage out of the Cordova Mountains is impossible. Councilor said so himself." The realization sinks in deeper. I feel like collapsing as another wave of dizziness passes over me.

Councilor stops moving about the room, resting the head of his scythe on the wood floor. "That is not entirely accurate."

Silence falls over the room as Kronklich and I exchange glances.

"What do you mean?" asks Kronklich leaning on his cane.

"It is possible."

My list of questions grows as I recall the conversation I had with Councilor days ago when he swore otherwise.

"It's not possible," says Kronklich. He slides his sword back into its sheath. "The Iron Carriage is destroyed, and any and all travelers who have attempted the journey down the mountain during the winter have lost their lives. There are no stories, in fact, none. Not a single soul has made the journey and survived to tell the tale."

"But there *is* someone who can make the journey," says Councilor with a smirk. His dark eyes flicker with passionate intensity as he stares down the both of us, an intensity of caring I have not seen in him—until now.

Shouldering his scythe over his enormous back, he covers his head with his hood. "That someone is *me.*"

With the Crossings West behind us, and escaping the inevitable questioning that will follow by the local authorities, I try to make sense of Councilor's loyalties and where they lie as we load the wagon with supplies. Did Councilor really want me to kill Cresthaven for the sake of his daughter, or was it Scepter's idea from the start to simply lure me to him?

"Tenor—" Kronklich's voice startles me from my thoughts. "Can you hand me that satchel?" He sits atop the back of the wagon, collecting items as we hand them to him. "Can you believe it? After all we've been through, we still managed to find some tea."

One thought remains with me as I hand Kronklich the bag. Somehow, by some miracle, the three of us ended up in Walters together. Something tells me it's a good thing, despite our differences. And although my son is nowhere to be found in the dark, dismal town of Walters, I finally understand for certain where he is. I have only so much time to get to him before—I shun the thoughts from my mind. What sort of devious plan the Carnalreesee have conjured up, I do not know. But it does not matter. This journey, this *inquisition*, has gotten me this far, and I have no intention of stopping now. I will not stop until Dorian is safe by my side or I can claim his body for a proper burial. But I try not to think of the latter.

With a reassuring nod, Councilor climbs into the nest of the wagon to begin our journey into oblivion. There is a road, a secret road known by none except he and his Black Blade brotherhood, which will lead us down the treacherous paths of the Cordova Mountains. At this point in time, it is all I have to go on—putting my faith and trust in a man I cannot entirely trust.

The snap of the reins cracks the chilly wind of the afternoon, signaling me to get onto the back of the wagon as it shakes to life. Maybe there is yet a chance. With Abel and Jasmine pulling the wagon of reinforced wood, and Councilor serving as our guide, maybe success is attainable. I shiver at the thought of the frost-bitten journey ahead of us.

Settling down next to Kronklich, I pull my cloak tightly over my head to keep the cold out. I notice him staring at a large rectangular wooden box buried at the bottom of the wagon, underneath the crates and sacks full of provisions.

Kronklich leans close to my ear. "It's been there the whole time, ever since we left the cottage in the woods."

At first, I wonder if Kronklich has gone mad, possibly from the cold or the poison, and I try to make sense of his words. I stare at the box for a long moment and shake my head. "It's probably full of weapons. Black Blades are notorious for their weapons. They keep more than is needed. The journey will be long, treacherous, and cold, my friend. I suggest we get as much sleep as we can."

Holding Enivid close to my body, I feel the familiar power radiating from its center return to me, just enough to keep me warm. "Thank you, my love," I say softly to myself. "Thank you."

And as my thoughts become filled with Diana once again, I begin recapping all the events moving forward since the day I was forced to drive a stake through her heart. My mind slowly begins battling itself against the journey back into the realm of much-needed sleep. Eyelid blinking repeatedly, I can't help but stare at the box Kronklich pointed out, noting to myself, as my mind begins to shut down, how much the box resembles a coffin.

END OF BOOK TWO

The

Bawaka

Exhibit
A.

The

Hand of

God

Exhibit
B.

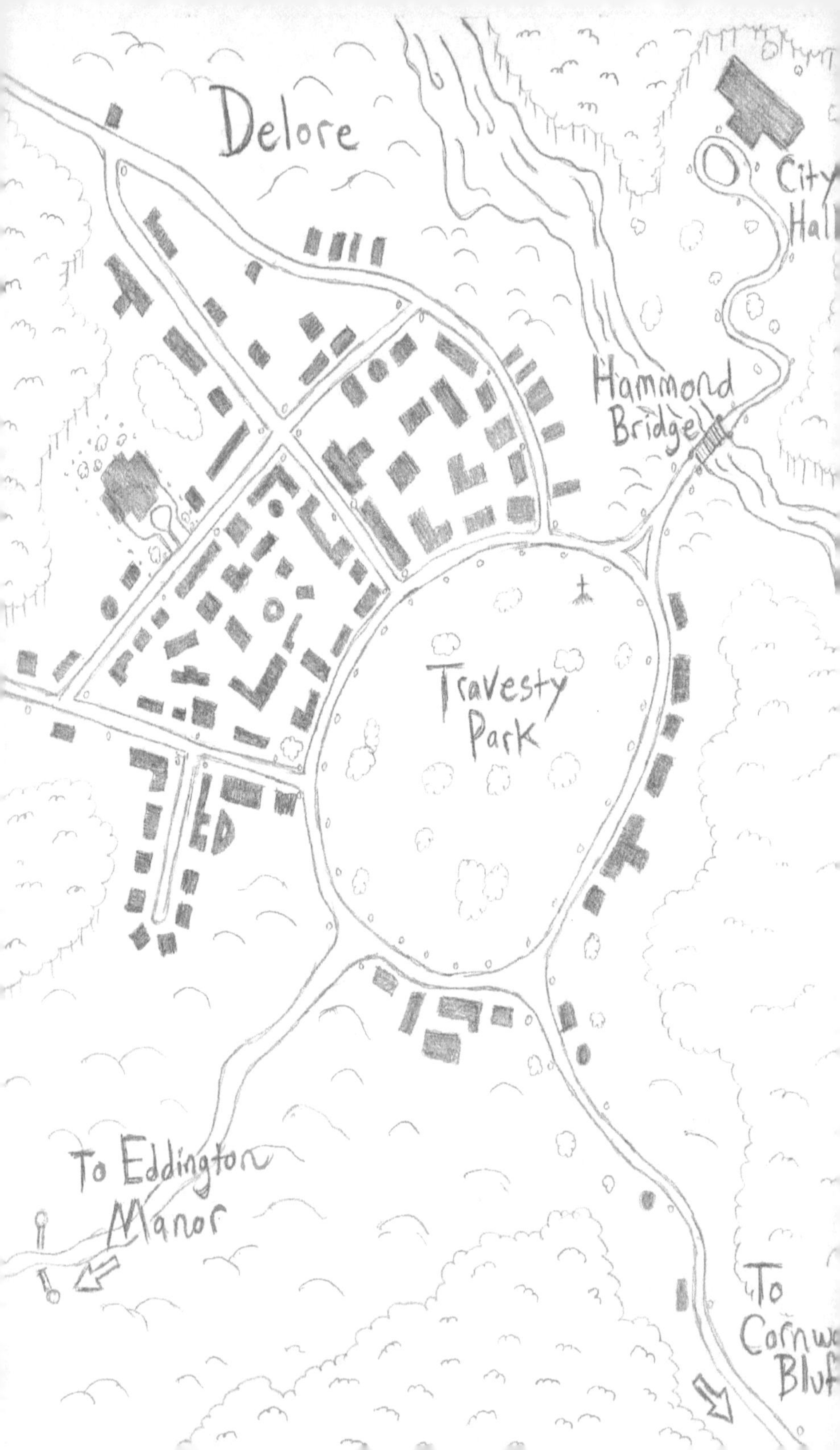
Delore
City Hall
Hammond Bridge
Travesty Park
To Eddington Manor
To Cornw
Bluf

The Cresthaven Estate

1st Floor

Stair well

Kitchen

Great Hall

Ballroom

Foyer

Terrace

Ante-Chamber

Dining Chamber

Garden

A Note to the Reader

YOU KNOW, I'VE BEEN WRITING for a long time but only recently within the last two years decided to start publishing my work. As a newly inaugurated author, you know and I know, it's what readers read and share and comment about that makes all the difference in the literary world. With that said, whether you enjoyed this tale immensely or hated it beyond all measure, I encourage you to leave a review. As flesh bound souls, we can say anything we want. It is one of the perks of being "us" and when that voice is shared by speaking to one another or written for others to see, believe me, it goes a very long way. "The response" is the very essence and guts of what writers like myself and others live for. I love to entertain. And like countless others, if you share your thoughts in the world today, there is something left to be said for the now, the future, and for all humankind.

Sincerely,
F. D. Gross

ACKNOWLEDGMENTS

THERE ARE SO MANY IMPORTANT people and things in my life that have helped and influenced my writing in some way or another. I would like to name them all here and now, but it is not possible, so if I don't mention you, please forgive me. In no particular order, I would like to thank: Deborah DeNicola for your wonderful skills in editing and wordsmithing, Janice Humpage for your belief in me and allowing me to entertain you, Nick Reyes for your undying dedication and commitment to Wolfgangs hell, Kady Young for supporting me always and in all ways, London Gross for carrying on the fantasy every day of our lives, David Peters for showing me what true magic is, Chrissy Moon for understanding my work, Kathy Booker for being superfan girl, Scott Hale for your continued support and answering my last minute questions (as always), Maxine Groves, Weston Kincade, Spencer Scott Holmes, Ryan Dunigan, Joe Compton, all of the crew at Bookfuel, especially Connie, Alyson, Lori, and Trent, My Dying Bride, Philip Glass, Johan Sebastian Bach, Bram Stoker, Dacre Stoker, Dracula, Castlevania, archways and moths that tap on the front door at night, Neil Gaiman, Cormac McCarthy, Vizcaya Museum and Gardens, long periods of haunting daydreams, Fern Forest, Orchid Park, friends, family, and finally, the one who understands me most, my best friend and companion, Diana. Thank you for dealing with me and putting up with my long nights lost behind the computer screen. You have the amazing ability to see what I see, and so I cherish you above and beyond all measure...

LOOK FOR THE CONCLUSION

TO THE WOLFGANG TRILOGY

IN

"COMMUNION"

BOOK THREE

In 2016, F. D. Gross published his debut novel, *Wolfgang*, the first of the Wolfgang Trilogy series. Since then, he's worked tirelessly to bring his latest creation, *Inquisition*, to life. He has worked on numerous short stories as well, one which has made an appearance in the recently published anthology called, Demonic Household (Demonic Anthology Collection Book 2). Frank resides in South Florida with his fiancée, daughter, and three cats, where he continues working on the third and final book of the Wolfgang Trilogy, titled *Communion*. When Frank is not writing, he is reading and playing music, and when he is not doing either of those, he is sleeping.

https://www.wolfgangchronicles.com/
https://www.wolfgangchronicles.com/books

https://www.goodreads.com/author/show/15919155.F_D_Gross

https://twitter.com/GrellDragon

https://www.facebook.com/Wolfgang.Chronicles/

https://www.youtube.com/channel/UCf-ODvSjFpN-21nxe8kVnRw

https://www.amazon.com/Wolfgang-Chronicles-1-F-D-Gross/dp/1622179951

https://www.amazon.com/F.D.-Gross/e/B01LXM86GO/ref=ntt_dp_epwbk_0

https://www.instagram.com/fd_gross/

ALSO BY F. D. GROSS

THE WOLFGANG TRILOGY:
Wolfgang

SHORT STORY APPEARNACE IN ANTHOLOGIES:
Demonic Household: See Owners Manual (A Dark Humor Short Story) by Valerie Willis

WOLFGANG

Book One of the Wolfgang Trilogy

The book that started it all...

On the search for his missing son, Tenor Wolfgang must explore the depths of a ruined medieval castle while battling against the forces of darkness.

See what reviewers are saying about *Wolfgang:*

"Such a great book about hunting the evil in the night. An amazing story, with great character development and all killer, no filler content." – *Spencer Scott Holmes*

"Great story! A book that after you read it, you feel compelled to read it again to make sure you didn't miss anything." – *Nick Reyes*

"Captivating and page turning!" – *MolleeB*

"If you read "Wolfgang" now you will be hooked!" – *Lucile Arnusch*

"This book had me from the start. It got right to the point and it's pretty much non-stop action till the end." - *Kelsey*

"Any fan of the paranormal and vampires will find this book an absolute treat to read." – *Laura Furuta*

"Very cleverly written. 5 stars." – *Susan Angela Wallace*

www.ingramcontent.com/pod-product-compliance
Lightning Source LLC
Chambersburg PA
CBHW050058120726
47904CB00004B/1134